THE MAN WHO NEVER WAS

A JOHN MILTON THRILLER

MARK DAWSON

PROLOGUE

The three Chevrolet Suburbans proceeded in formation, following the traffic through Avenida La Esperanza. The vehicles were painted black with privacy glass in the windows, and they carried a full protective detail from the Bureau of Diplomatic Security. There were three armed men in the lead and trail cars, all with extensive experience working in dangerous locales like this. Michael Cochrane had once been inside the Cadillac that carried the president in his motorcade; the Secret Service called that vehicle 'the Beast,' and this car was lacking by comparison. The glass in the Suburban wasn't five inches thick, for example, and there was no ceramic armour; but it was still a substantial ride, and he was well protected by his guys. He felt safe, even in Bogotá.

Cochrane had been given the title of ambassador for this mission, although he was not a normal Foreign Service officer. His previous role had been as the Assistant Secretary for International Narcotics and Legal Affairs, known within the diplomatic community as the Bureau of Drugs and Thugs. He had worked in the DEA previous to this posting and had spent all of his professional life trying to stem the flow of drugs into the United States. Cochrane's aide, Amanda Jones, was sitting next to him. She was buried in the briefing paper that had been delivered from Langley overnight.

The ambassador uncrossed his legs and leaned forward to speak to the driver. "You know where you're going?"

Harrison was driving them today. The two men had been working together for several weeks now, and they had an easy rapport. Harrison was a pro and, without taking his eyes off the road, gave a nod. "Come on, boss—I know where we're going. We're good."

"And the route is safe?"

Martinez was in the front, next to Harrison. "Yes, Mr. Ambassador. I went out in the pilot car and checked everything this morning. I'd still rather they were coming to us—"

"But you know that's not possible."

"I know, sir. I understand, and we've adapted. You're in good hands."

Cochrane slapped the back of the seat. "Never doubted it."

He plucked a piece of lint from the thigh of his slacks, examined it, then flicked it away. He reached over to his briefcase and pulled it onto his lap. He popped the clasps, opened the lid and took out the background file the DEA had prepared. The agency was involved in interdicting the supply of cocaine from Colombia into Mexico and then the United States. The State Department had stated that it was prepared to increase the help it was providing to the Colombians, but there were preconditions that needed to be met first. Cochrane was the point guy to make sure those requirements were satisfied. That had been the focus of his work in the embassy for the last three months. The Colombians were proud, and it had been like pulling teeth to get them to agree to gringo help. It had taken all his skill—a mixture of cajoling and threats—but he had made it stick.

The report had been stamped with the logos of both the DEA and the CIA and had been composed by senior intelligence staff at both agencies. Cochrane opened it and saw that it bore red pencil markings all the way across the first page. He recognised the handwriting—if that wasn't too generous a description of the scrawl—and laughed.

Jones looked over. "You okay, boss?"

Cochrane shook his head, his face breaking into a happy grin. "My six-year-old," he said, proffering the defaced report. "I left the report in my study for five minutes when I went to the bathroom. She must've got hold of it."

Jones read: "'Come home soon, Daddy.' Jeez. That's so sweet. What's her name?"

"Aimee."

"Too cute."

He should've been annoyed that she had defaced his report, but how could he be? Leaving Megan and Aimee was always the hardest part of a job that required extensive travel. He had been thinking for some time that he might look to take a more settled position once the accord between the Colombians, Mexicans and DEA was concluded. He had worked for the government for twenty years, and he was senior enough that he could exercise a little discretion in what might come next. Riding a desk in Washington didn't sound so bad, especially if that meant he could be more involved in his daughter's childhood. She was getting into Little League, and it killed him to watch the videos that Megan sent rather than being able to be there in person.

He glanced out the window at the streets of the city. The trip had been a long time coming, and he didn't want anything to go wrong. He had put too much time into the preparation, and he knew that the administration was counting on bringing this in. Winning the war on drugs was one of the key planks of the president's re-election campaign, and doing that started at the source. This—or rather, the jungles that made up the Amazonian rainforest—was where it all began.

State had promised the president that it would deliver the victory he had promised, and it was Cochrane's job to get the ball rolling.

DAVID FITZPATRICK WATCHED as the cars honked at one another outside the tinted windows of his SUV. Bogotá was full of the hustle and bustle of a modern metropolis. Fitzpatrick knew enough about Colombian history to know that it had transformed over the course of the last thirty years. The influence of the *narcotraficantes*—Pablo Escobar and the Gentlemen of Cali and all the others—had waned from their apogee in the eighties and nineties, and, although cartel tentacles still slithered up from the jungles and slums of Medellín, it was much less overt today. But, Fitzpatrick knew, it was still there.

That was why he was so nervous.

"Anything?" Frank Probert said from the back.

"Looks clear."

"You still shitting yourself?"

"You forget where we are? It's Bogotá, man."

Fitzpatrick would have preferred the meeting with the South Americans to have taken place behind the wire. He and Martinez had tried to persuade Cochrane that it needed to happen at the embassy, but the ambo had insisted that it had to be on Colombian turf. The optics were better with the Americans going to their hosts, he said, rather than insisting that the Colombians and Mexicans come to them. The accord had already been derided in the local press as evidence of revived gringo imperialism, and Cochrane had said that he didn't want to make that worse.

"He's stubborn," Fitzpatrick said.

"Who?" Probert said. "Cochrane?"

"You know I told him this was a stupid idea?"

"I know he got hot at you."

"You know what he said? 'I've been travelling around the city every day for the last three months and nothing has happened.' You believe that? I told him that the fact he had done a stupid thing with no consequences didn't mean that doing that stupid thing would always have no consequences."

"Maybe he was just lucky before."

Fitzpatrick nodded. "That's what I said."

"And?"

"You know what he's like. He just waved it off. I told him those times before were different. He wasn't on his way to sign an accord that was practically a declaration of war on the cartels then, not like he is now."

"And still no dice."

Fitzpatrick shook his head. "He told me his mind was made up, that there was no point in trying to change it, and that I should make the arrangements."

"Shut your mouth and know your role?"

"Words to that effect."

COCHRANE COULDN'T RECALL the last time he'd slept more than four hours in a single night. Putting together the coalition had been a Sisyphean task. It had required hours of hand-holding and backslapping and smiling until his face ached just to get all the parties on board. But he had done it. His patience and flexibility had paid dividends, and now he had everyone on the same page.

He leaned back in his seat and turned back to the start of the report. The diplomatic effort had been an urgent one; the Americans had needed to address quickly changing events. The Mexican cartel responsible for moving Colombian cocaine over the border was La Frontera. Three years ago, the head of the cartel—a man known as El Patrón—had been assassinated by an unknown shooter in the highlands of the Sierra Madre. La Frontera was itself an amalgamation of smaller cartels; El Patrón had brought them together and then held them in thrall with the fear of his retribution should they ever cross him. His death had changed things; chatter intercepted by the Mexican military suggested that the constituent parts would split away without him.

To the surprise of the analysts who had provided the briefings, that implosion had not taken place. There had been a flurry of murders as someone—the Mexicans didn't know who—had eliminated rivals and then consolidated power. And then La Frontera had outsmarted everyone by making common ground with El Centro, the most durable of the successors to the Escobar cartel in Medellín. The two organisations had cemented an accord to work together. The Colombians would be responsible for the production of the cocaine, meth and marijuana that the North American market consumed in such vast amounts. The Mexicans would be responsible for distribution and retail. The arrangement was mutually beneficial, with both cartels making outsized profits.

The arrangement was not a happy one for the United

States.

The merger ensured that the cartels could pool their resources. The leadership realised that the sheer volume they could now move meant that they could slash prices. Lower prices meant they could sell in greater volume, more than making up for the price cuts. Using La Frontera's long-established supply chains, they started moving vast amounts over, under and around the border.

Cochrane uncrossed his legs, then recrossed them. "How long?"

"Traffic's heavy," Harrison said. "Fifteen minutes. Twenty at the outside."

Cochrane looked back to the report. Influential journalists had raged at the epidemic of drug use flourishing across the country. New York, Washington, Chicago, Los Angeles, Miami. Huge shipments, larger than anything seen since the eighties, were intercepted, but everyone knew that the DEA and Customs only ever stopped a small fraction of the goods that were moved. For every ton that was detected at a border, they all knew that ten times more was getting through. Something had to be done.

Jones looked up. "They will definitely go for this?"

"They'd better," Cochrane said.

"I still can't believe they'll willingly have the US military down here."

"As advisors," Cochrane said, smiling at the euphemism.

The plan was simple and, he was confident, would be effective. The Mexicans would deploy their maritime Fuerzas Especiales to attack La Frontera's naval supply lines, and the Fuerza Especial de Reacción, a quick-strike unit, would hit the *traficantes* at their distribution points on the border with the US. The Colombians were readying the Agrupación de Fuerzas Especiales Antiterroristas Urbanas

—their elite counterterrorism group—to take out El Centro's kitchens deep in the jungle. The Americans would provide training, intel and logistical support, but try telling that to the DELTA soldiers at Fort Bragg, who were itching to get the green light to deploy. Those boys would raise holy hell once they were in theatre. Signing the accord would be the start. Teams from each country were already on standby. A list of targets had been drawn up: lieutenants who would be scooped up off the street, warehouses that would be hit. The police and intelligence outfits would flip the junior players, get them to squeal on the bosses, round them up, rinse and repeat until the whole sordid business had been wiped off the map. It would be the biggest escalation against the cartels since the start of the War on Drugs, and this time, the good guys would win.

The SUV eased to a stop, and Cochrane leaned forward to get a look out the windshield. They were at an intersection. A red light was suspended from a wire that reached across the street. He leaned back in the seat. The light above the car turned green. Cochrane watched the lead car move into the intersection. He turned around and checked that the trail car was still behind them.

Harrison must have noticed his wariness. "We're all good."

"This fucking place," Cochrane muttered.

"Ten minutes to Bolivar Square."

Cochrane nodded. They were fine.

"Hold up," Martinez said, and sighed.

The SUV carried them through the intersection, then slowed again.

Cochrane leaned forward. "What is it?"

"Traffic," Martinez said.

Cochrane looked through the windshield to see a line of

cars stacked up in front of them.

Harrison touched his earpiece. "Lead One, status?" He listened, then nodded. "Copy. We'll hold." He turned in the seat to report. "Accident ahead. They're going on foot to get eyes on it."

Cochrane nodded and watched as one passenger in the lead car got out and walked up ahead. He cleared five cars, then stopped. He raised a hand to his ear.

Harrison listened, then turned around. "Two cars tangled. Looks okay."

"We're fine, though?" Cochrane had heard the edge of concern in Harrison's voice. "Right?"

Harrison ignored him and touched his ear. "Lead One, copy. We'll wait for it to clear. Eyes out. Lead Three, copy?" He waited a moment, then nodded again and let his hand drop.

"Harrison?"

The soldier turned around. "It's okay, boss. We're good."

FITZPATRICK WAS NOT HAPPY. The lead car couldn't go forward, and the trail car couldn't go backward. The ambassador was stuck between them. They were penned in on all sides.

Sitting ducks.

Horns blared as drivers signalled their annoyance. Scooters weaved in and out of the gridlocked cars and trucks.

"This is bullshit," Fitzpatrick said. "Should've stayed in the embassy. Coming out here was asking for trouble."

Probert was about to speak, but paused. "You see that?"

Fitzpatrick watched as a woman on a dusty red scooter

snaked between cars, balancing a bag of groceries on her lap. A motorcyclist followed behind her, close on her rear wheel. Its rider was a woman, too, and she cut hard to her right in front of the old Volkswagen to the left of the ambassador's Suburban, then swung left again, drawing alongside the vehicle.

"What's she doing?"

Fitzpatrick saw the rider reach both hands into a satchel she was carrying on a strap around her neck and pull out a round metal object. It was olive green, and it looked as if it had a mechanism attached to one of the flat sides. She got off the bike and crouched down next to the Suburban, disappearing from view.

"What the fuck?"

The woman stood. Fitzpatrick saw that her hands were empty.

"Shit," he said. "Shit, shit, shit."

Fitzpatrick grabbed his 12-gauge Remington 870 from the seat next to him, exited the car, and rushed ahead.

"Stop!" he yelled.

The woman got back onto the bike, revved the engine and sped away.

Fitzpatrick levelled the shotgun, but didn't have a shot. He reached the Suburban and ducked down. He saw that the green object had been attached to the underside of the car, right below the fuel tank. He put his hand to his ear and activated his microphone.

"Get out of the car!" he yelled. "Get out now!"

COCHRANE JERKED AROUND at the hollow thud as something slapped against the underside of the Suburban. He saw the motorcyclist, her helmet visor down. The woman reached for the handlebars, cranked the throttle and sped away.

Harrison had his hand to his ear already. "Lead Three, what just happened?"

Cochrane turned around and saw Fitzpatrick hurrying toward them. He was carrying a shotgun.

"What's happening?" he said.

"Lead Three," Harrison said, "I need a status check now."

Cochrane saw Fitzpatrick's eyes go wide and, for the first time, panic turned in his gut.

"Get out of the car! Get out now!"

The mine detonated.

The car was tossed into the air and flipped over.

Cochrane, Jones, Harrison and Martinez were dead before it crashed back down on its roof.

HE HAD AN EXCELLENT VANTAGE POINT. Jeno's Pizza was just down the street from the location that had been chosen for the attack. He had bought a Hawaiian slice and had taken it to a table in the window from where he could look up and down the street. He had watched as the two cars had crashed into one another, carefully arranging the 'accident' so that the road was rendered impassable. He had listened silently over the radio as the team that had been put together for the operation reported on the progress of the convoy.

It had all been just as they had planned. They had worked on the attack with the information received from Langley. They had been supplied with the time of the meeting and the route that the ambassador would take to reach Bolivar Square. After that, they had relied upon the reports of the locals—the pedestrians and the drivers, the shopkeepers and customers—who worked for the cartel. The lookouts reported on the progress of the convoy through the city.

Cochrane had ignored the advice of his security detail and had insisted that the meeting to sign the accord should take place on Colombian soil. There had been so much pressure on him to conclude the agreement that he had ignored the target that his success in the negotiations had painted on his own back.

The man looked out at the consequences of the ambassador's chutzpah now: the burning wreck of the car, smoke billowing up into the pure blue sky. He took out his phone and tapped the screen to call the single number that had been stored in the memory.

"It's Number One," he said. "Tell her it's done."

He ended the call, opened the phone and took out the SIM. He left fifty thousand pesos on the table, stood and collected his things. He was a big man: six foot four and heavily built. His normally pale skin had grown tanned from working outside, and his sandy blond hair had been bleached by the sun so it was closer to platinum. There wasn't much he could do to disguise the fact that he was a foreigner.

He took out his cap and put it on his head and paused at the door, looking left and right. He was satisfied that it was safe to proceed. With another glance at the burning car, Björn Thorsson dropped the SIM into an open drain and tossed the phone into a garbage can.

He walked away from the crowd that was gathering near the flaming wreck, and disappeared.

PART I

TUESDAY

1

John Milton took the garment carrier from the wardrobe and unzipped it, removing the suit that he had selected for the evening's festivities: a plain navy two-button. The tailor who had served him in the boutique in Gelderlandplein had described it as the equivalent of the little black dress, a versatile choice that was still stylish. Milton had ignored his blandishments and had also ignored his advice on the measurement for the jacket, choosing one that was not quite perfect around his chest on the basis that he might want to pair it with a shoulder rig and a nine-millimetre at some point in the not-too-distant future.

He took off his jeans and T-shirt, taking a look at the scars that discoloured his skin from the top of his shoulders all the way down to his ankles. There was ink from the tattooist's gun, too: the angel wings on his back, the Roman numeral IX over his breast, and more besides. He could have read his history there, if he was so minded. He was not. He had business to attend to, and it would not wait.

It had been a frantic last few weeks. Milton had been

about to realise a long-cherished dream to drive an American muscle car from Oakland to the East Coast, but he had only made it as far as Las Vegas before fate had intervened. He had found himself helping a young woman who—or so he had thought—was in need of his assistance. Jessica Russo's father had been working an elaborate financial sting for a Mexican cartel and had made the foolish decision to rip them off. They had kidnapped the old man, and Jessica had tricked Milton into helping her to get him back. The cartel sent a *sicario* to locate their missing money, and the man had murdered Beau Baxter, one of Milton's only friends, a policewoman and three civilians. Milton had tracked the hitman to Tuscany and eliminated him, but that was not enough to satisfy his need for vengeance.

He wanted whoever it was who had given the orders to the *sicario*, and then the person who had given those orders, too.

Coming to Amsterdam was the first step on the ladder.

He took a fresh white shirt from its paper wrapping and put it on, adding a Foulard tie and securing it with a pin. He put on the suit and a pair of Gucci loafers and stood in front of the mirror again. He looked the part. No sophisticated dress would hide the hard edge that was evident on his face, accentuated by the scar that ran down to the side of his mouth, nor dull the startling ice-blue of his eyes, but Milton was not concerned about any of that. He wanted to make a particular kind of impression: rich enough to buy style, yet dangerous enough to be taken seriously by the man he intended to meet.

Milton was used to sliding through the world beneath the protective cloak of a legend, a pseudonym and manufactured identity within which he could submerge himself. John Smith. That was his preferred moniker, a structure upon which everything that was fake could be draped. He would be Smith tonight and for the next few weeks. He had something very important that he wanted to achieve, and a disguise would be a crucial part of meeting that objective.

MILTON STEPPED out of the bedroom and shut the door behind him. The penthouse in Houthaven was eye-wateringly expensive; that was deliberate, since they knew that Juan Pablo López would investigate John Smith thoroughly before trusting him, and extravagant taste was something that he would expect to find.

The others were gathered in the lounge. Milton looked at them: Ziggy Penn was sitting at the dining table, a laptop to his left and another to his right, with the remains of a McDonald's takeout scattered between the two machines; Alex Hicks was sitting on the sofa, his feet on the coffee table; Chase Baxter—Beau's son and the only one of the team who wasn't British—was pouring a coffee in the open-plan kitchen.

Hicks wolf-whistled as Milton came inside. "Look at *you.*"

Milton glanced down at the suit. He usually wore just jeans and a shirt.

"You look the part," Ziggy said.

"You're offering an opinion about fashion?" Hicks said. *"You?"*

"What?" Ziggy stood up and gestured down his body with both hands; he was wearing ripped jeans and the same Nine Inch Nails T-shirt that he had worn since picking it up at the store in Amsterdam Noord the day after he'd arrived.

"I'm just saying," Hicks said, "that no one's going to be coming to *you* for sartorial advice."

Ziggy coughed theatrically. "You're in a position to judge?"

He had a point. Hicks was dressed like a drifter. He had been surveilling López, and, because Milton's assessment had been that the Mexican was likely to be a careful man, they had decided that Hicks would need to blend into the background. To that end, he was wearing a blue woollen hat, a T-shirt that bore the stains of spilt beer and food, and jeans that were ripped at both knees. It was an authentic-looking ensemble.

"Are we ready?" Milton said.

Ziggy grinned. "Ready."

Hicks nodded. "Ready."

Chase put the coffee cup down. "Been ready since I got here. Feels like we've been arguing with a wooden Indian."

Ziggy frowned. "What?"

"Burning daylight," Chase said. "Kicking our heels."

"Oh," Ziggy said. "You mean we've been wasting time."

"Damn straight."

Chase Baxter had a colourful way of speaking, just like his father. The four of them had been together in Amsterdam for just a few days, and Milton could see that the American was already impatient, hungry to get started. Milton could easily understand his desire to get the show on the road, but, on the other hand, there was no profit in pushing on without being sure of the terrain ahead.

Milton stretched out his arm and checked the Rolex on his wrist. "I'm going to leave in fifteen minutes. We don't know how López will take the approach, so I'll be happier knowing that you're close at hand."

"In case they bundle you into a back room and kneecap you?"

"Thank you, Hicks. But, yes—I'd prefer to avoid that if we can."

"Don't worry," he said. "You won't even know I'm there."

Milton turned to Ziggy. "You've got what you need?"

He nodded and tapped his fingers against the lid of one of his laptops. "They've got Wi-Fi cameras everywhere, but they bought them cheap from China. All the data is stored in Shenzhen. Took me twenty minutes to get inside, and, once I'd done that, I could do this."

He turned the machine around so that Milton and the others could see what was on the screen. It had been quartered into equal-sized panes, and each pane showed the feed from a security camera. The footage gave them four distinct views of the interior of a club: the reception area, the bar, the corridor that led to the restrooms, and the VIP area.

"There are another six," Ziggy said. "I got them all. I'll be able to see you unless they take you into the back."

"Good," Milton said. "Well done."

"How long do you think this'll take?" Chase asked.

Milton looked over at him. His impatience was obvious and looked to be curdling into irritation. He stood and motioned outside.

"Come with me."

CHASE STOOD and followed Milton out the doors that led to the apartment's balcony. Milton closed the doors behind them.

"I know you want to get started. And I understand why. But

if we go into this without a very clear idea of what we want to do and how we're going to do it, we won't get anywhere. López works for a cartel. He's been doing that for years, and that kind of longevity, in that kind of business… It doesn't just *happen*. He's a careful and suspicious man. If we go out when we're not completely ready, he'll know. And we only get one shot at this."

"Fine. Grab him off the street, throw him into the back of a car and take him somewhere quiet. You give me ten minutes with him."

Milton stared at him. "And then what?"

"And…" He stumbled, unnerved by the ice in Milton's eyes. "And he'll give us everything we need to know about who killed my old man."

"He won't," Milton said. "He won't know. López is responsible for European business. He's our way in, but that's it. I work him carefully. I get him to trust me. I establish a business connection that might look like he's going to make a lot of money, for him and the cartel. I take advantage of his greed. And then I parlay all of that into an introduction to whoever it is who's up the chain from him. And then I do it again. I'm not just interested in whoever it was who gave the order to have your father killed, Chase. I want whoever gave the shooter the order and then whoever gave *that* person the order. I want them all, from top to bottom."

"That's too ambitious," Chase said, although Milton could see that his frustration was draining out of him.

"No," Milton said. "I don't think so. I've worked this kind of angle before. We can do it."

Chase nodded back toward the inside. "And them?"

"Who? Ziggy and Hicks?"

"They're good?"

"I wouldn't be able to do this without their help."

Chase sighed.

"And you," Milton added. "I need you, too."

Chase bit his lip and looked out over the docks below the apartment block. He sighed. "I'm sorry. This whole thing... it's been hard. What happened to my dad—it's..." He stopped and sighed again. "Shit, you know. He used to have a saying—"

"Your dad had a *lot* of sayings."

"He surely did. He said a man should keep his saddle oiled and his gun greased. He meant you needed to stand ready, and, when the moment comes, you go and you take care of business. I'm ready, John. And it feels like I been waiting a long while to get going."

"I know," Milton said. "It's hard. Harder for you."

"All I'm trying to say is... Well, shit, I don't want you to think that I'm ungrateful. I'm not. You didn't have to do this."

"We'll have to disagree about that," Milton said. "You ready?"

Chase nodded.

"Let's go saddle up, then."

2

Milton took an Uber to Rembrandtplein in Amsterdam's central district. He thought about the plan that he had worked out. He had considered starting with La Frontera's presence on the border of Mexico and the United States, but had decided that it made more sense to look for a way into the organisation away from the heat of what had just gone down in Nevada. He had been careful, as always, but he knew that there was a chance that his likeness would have been captured in Las Vegas and that the prospect of any connection being made in Amsterdam was much lower than if he had stayed in America. He had gathered up the team—Hicks for ops, Ziggy for intel and Chase because Milton couldn't deny him the chance to avenge his father—and had set up base here.

Ziggy had already begun his research into La Frontera's European operations and had suggested that Amsterdam was the hub through which all business was transacted. He had used an existing hack to get into the Police National Computer, pulling as much data as he could so that he could start to pencil in the lines that connected the United Kingdom's main distributor with his South American wholesalers. The man suspected of the dubious distinction of being the UK's largest importer of Colombian blow was a Liverpudlian who went by the name of Anthony Jackson. Ziggy had burrowed into his file and had discovered that the police had circumstantial evidence to connect him to Juan Pablo López, La Frontera's representative in the Netherlands.

Milton didn't always understand how Ziggy did what he did—and suspected that Ziggy quite liked to maintain an air of intrigue—but he had watched with admiration as he produced a dossier with extensive background notes. Ziggy discovered that López operated out of Amsterdam. He was in his late forties, built like an Olympic wrestler, with a taste for blonde women and expensive nightclubs, especially the three that he owned. He spent most evenings behind the velvet rope in the VIP section of a club that he had established several years previously. It was high end, catering to footballers and minor Dutch celebrities.

That had not been the extent of Ziggy's work. He had been busy building up the layers that would come together to form the fake identity that Milton was going to rely upon. He had travelled as John Smith for years, but the work that Ziggy had done meant that persona was now deeper and more convincing than it ever had been.

It would need to be.

Milton zoned back in and looked through the rain-smeared windshield of the Uber. Neon bled through the rain, swashes of turquoise and aquamarine and blood red, all spelling the name of the club—claire—where Milton hoped his prey would be found.

3

Milton stepped out of the Uber and took a moment to scope out the neighbourhood. He had visited it earlier that afternoon, but it was nighttime now and that meant that the atmosphere had changed. The building facing him was four storeys high and looked as if it might have served an industrial purpose before being put to its present use. The name of the club was spelled out in lowercase letters that were lit from the back. The place had been a gay club and, according to its website, in previous incarnations it had welcomed David Bowie, Elton John and Jean Paul Gaultier. It had been a student club after that, before López had gutted it and turned it into a higher-end destination. The clientele tonight looked like a mix of gay and straight; the impatient revellers pressed themselves against the wall in an attempt to shelter from the drizzle. Milton could hear the thud of bass from somewhere inside, a subterranean throb that he could feel through the soles of his shoes.

Milton glanced over to the green square opposite the club and saw Hicks, dressed in his dirty clothes, sitting on a bench. He had an excellent view of the club. They had confirmed that there was no rear exit, so anyone who sought to leave would not be able to do so unobserved. Hicks was armed and would be able to move quickly to intercept should that prove to be necessary. Hicks acknowledged Milton with the slightest tilt of his head.

Milton made his way to the door. A woman in a cocktail dress stood behind a lectern. She was evidently in charge of the guest list, stifling the protests from the couple at the front of the queue with a hatchet face and gimlet eye. Chase was six places from the front of the queue. He had charmed a group of three slightly drunken women and was engaged in conversation with them.

A doorman noticed Milton's approach and turned to face him, blocking the way ahead. The man raised a meaty paw and said something in Dutch that Milton didn't understand.

"Good evening," Milton said. "I'm afraid I don't speak Dutch."

The man switched to accented English. "Back of the line, please."

Milton shook his head and smiled. "I'm on the list. Could I speak to your friend, please? I'm sure she'll be able to find me."

The man cocked a disdainful eyebrow at Milton. There was only so much that an expensive haircut and high-end clothing could do; Milton still had the scar on his cheek, the cold eyes, and the look of a man with whom it would be unwise to argue. He held his ground and the man's eye, giving him a neutral smile and waiting the two seconds it took for him to capitulate, standing aside so that Milton could approach the lectern.

The woman turned to look at Milton. "Your name?"

"John Smith."

The woman ran her finger down the screen of an iPad that rested on the lectern. Milton wasn't concerned and waited patiently until she found him. Milton exchanged a quick glance with Chase, then looked back to the lectern without expression as the woman completed her search.

"Thank you for waiting, Mr. Smith. I have you."

Milton nodded with equanimity, as if the news was exactly what he had been expecting. In truth, it was; Ziggy had hacked the club's servers that afternoon and had found a way into their reservations software. It had been a simple thing for him to amend the records and add him.

She unclipped the velvet rope that prevented entry to the club and led the way down a flight of stairs. Milton followed, leaving Chase and Hicks behind him. The thud of the bass became a little louder and a little less muffled.

"Have you been here before?" she said.

"I haven't."

"The club is on three floors. The VIP area is on the top floor. Shall I take you there now?"

"It's fine," he said. "I'm happy to wander."

"Of course."

She opened a wide pair of double doors; the music flooded over them and the bass throbbed through him. Lasers burned overhead, lancing over the heads of the crowd, splitting and pirouetting in time with the beat.

The woman turned and left him to make his way inside. Ziggy had pulled fire department plans of the club and they had reviewed them together. There were three floors, each with multiple bars. Milton looked for the restrooms and identified the best way to reach them and the emergency exits beyond. The space was full of revellers. People were pressed together, straining their necks so that they could see the DJ on the stage at the front of the floor. He had two old-style decks set up, and he ministered between them, his headphones pressed to one ear as he adjusted the vinyl with his free hand. Milton worked his way around the edge of the crowd, stopping at the bar briefly to pay and overtip for an orange juice that he might be able to pass off as a screwdriver, if he were asked.

He found the stairs and climbed to the second floor and a new room with a different DJ. A projection on the wall behind the DJ revealed his *nom de plume*: KELTEK. Milton grabbed a flyer from the bar. It was for the night's festivities, and, in Dutch and English, the DJs were announced: KELTEK was joined by Headhunterz and Run-D. The type of music was described as 'hardstyle.' Milton hadn't heard of it before, but, to his ear, the rapid BPM was close to being uncomfortable. The club nights that he remembered—as much as he could remember anything from those booze-soaked army days—had been more... well, *melodic.*

He caught himself: that was the kind of thing his father would have said.

Getting old, John. Getting old and out of touch.

Milton pushed through the crowd until he could look up through the open ceiling to the third floor. A wide balcony ran around the walls so that the people seated at the tables on it could look down onto the dance floor. Milton moved to the stairs and climbed up, sipping the orange juice as he moved around the balcony. Half of the circumference was given over to the VIP area, with velvet ropes strung across from the balustrade to the wall. That half-moon of balcony could have accommodated fifty or sixty people with its plush velour booths and leather banquettes, but tonight it was empty save for one man and his guests.

Milton recognised him. It was the owner of the club: Juan Pablo López.

4

López was entertaining a pair of women.

Milton drew nearer. Large men had been positioned behind each rope to restrict onward access. Milton walked right up to the nearest one. He saw him, turned so that he was facing Milton dead on, and straightened up.

"Hello," Milton said.

The man stared at him. "No entry."

"I want to talk to López."

The man frowned. "Who?"

Milton smiled at him. "The man behind you. Your boss. I want to talk to him."

The man's face hardened. "Go away."

"No," Milton said. "I want to talk to him and he's going to want to talk to me."

"I'm not going to tell you again."

"Fine. How about this—go and tell him that I want to talk about a deal that will make him a lot of money." Milton watched the man's face and saw it: a flicker of surprise. "Come on. Do we have to drag this out? Go tell him. I'm not going to wait all night, so it'll be you who'll have to tell your boss how there was a man here who was interested in making him a lot of money and you let him walk."

The man pursed his lips, took a step back and a quarter turn away. He cupped his hand over his mouth and spoke into his throat mic. Milton watched as the man on the opposite side of the balcony turned and walked toward López. He leaned down so that he could make himself heard over the clamour of the music. Milton saw the annoyance on López's face as he received the message; then he leaned all the way out so that he could get a proper look at Milton.

Milton held up his glass.

López watched him impassively for a moment, then said something to his man. The bouncer spoke into his microphone.

The man blocking Milton's way gave a nod. "You can see him."

Milton smiled. "Thank you."

The rope was unhooked and the man stepped up to him. "Arms out."

Milton did as he was told, as if being frisked inside a nightclub was the most natural thing imaginable. The man worked quickly and efficiently: right arm, left arm, right torso, left torso, right leg, left leg.

"This way."

THE MAN LED Milton to López. The two blondes made their way out of the booth, casting reproachful looks over their shoulders in Milton's direction.

"Five minutes," the man said.

Milton slid into the booth. López had moved so that he

was deeper inside, shielded by the curve of the high-backed bench. Milton sat down opposite him. Ziggy had found several photographs of López, and Milton could see that it was the same man, with the same hard eyes and slender nose. He wore a beard, and Milton detected the hand of a cosmetic surgeon in the absence of the fine lines that had creased his forehead in some of the photographs. He was dressed well, and his wrist—laid with ostentatious ease on the table—bore a thick gold Rolex.

"I appreciate you seeing me," Milton said.

López watched him with a look of amusement on his face. "Do I know you?"

Milton shook his head. "You don't." He extended his hand. "Not yet, anyway. John Smith."

López made no move to take it. "And what are you doing here, Mr. Smith?"

"A little business, I hope."

"Are you in the nightclub business?"

"No. I'm in your *other* business."

López feigned innocence. "What other business might that be?"

"Come on," Milton said. "Are we going to waste our time?"

"Well, I don't intend to waste mine. Goodnight, Mr. Smith."

Milton smiled, unfazed. "We have a friend in common."

"Do we?"

"Anthony Jackson."

López shrugged. "Who's that?"

Milton smiled at him. "From Liverpool. He gets his product from you."

López leaned forward and plucked the half-full champagne flute from the table between them. "Be careful how you go from here, Mr. Smith. You should think about how much you want to have this conversation."

"I want to have it," Milton said. "I travelled here just so I could speak to you."

López shrugged.

"I've worked with him," Milton said. "I've done time for him, too."

"Is that so?"

"Eighteen months in Wormwood Scrubs. I got out last month and, to be honest with you, I'm not interested in working for him again."

"Why is that?"

"How long have you got?"

"Not long."

"Because he's sloppy. Because he's been using the product a little too much—getting high on his own supply. It's making him make mistakes. So, there's that—and the fact that I wouldn't trust him as far as I could throw him."

López cocked an eyebrow. "Why not?"

"Jackson had a little trouble of his own. Two years ago. The police were investigating him—did you know?"

López shrugged, but Milton could see that he had piqued his interest.

"They had a man inside the operation. Low-level, but he knew enough to do damage. Jackson did a deal with the police—that's the only conclusion I could come to. He's got officers on the payroll, and he knew that he had to give them something. So he gave them me."

López swirled the champagne in his glass. "So, what? You're here for revenge? I'm not in the revenge business, Mr. Smith. It's not profitable."

Milton leaned back and crossed his legs. "I don't need

you for that. If I wanted revenge, I'd take care of that myself."

"Then why are you wasting my time?"

"Because it's my turn. I want to make some money of my own." He leaned closer. "Look—I know his business inside and out. I know he distributes your product. I know the mistakes he makes. The vulnerabilities he has, and how close he's been to making a mistake that would cause *you* trouble. He's going to slip up eventually, and when he does, he's the kind of man who will sell you out if he thinks it'll help him."

López stared at him for a moment, then chuckled. "I doubt that very much."

"Do you?" Milton waved a hand around the club. "How do you think I found you here? He's always running his mouth. He said you owned the club."

López sat up straight, put both elbows on the table, and stared at Milton. He was an imposing man, and Milton could see how he might be frightening. Milton, though, was not scared. He knew that he was getting closer to getting what he wanted.

"I would never be indiscreet or sell you out," Milton said. "I did eighteen months for Jackson and I never said a word."

"Even when you say he betrayed you."

"Even then." Milton nodded. "Where I come from, you don't talk to the coppers. Never. No excuses. I'm sure it's the same where you come from, too. Right?" Milton stopped now and held his tongue.

López raised his empty glass, and, on cue, a waitress came over with a fresh bottle and refilled his flute. López did not suggest that a glass be poured for Milton, and the bottle was deposited in an ice bucket.

"Go on," López said. "I'm listening."

5

"The way Jackson runs his business is shoddy," Milton said. "I can do it better. He cuts your coke until there's no quality left. I'd step on it, but not as much. I'd sell a better product so that customers would come back more often than they do with him. And I'd sell it at a higher price. That's more product shipped and more money for you."

The music thumped, the bass rattling the champagne flute. Milton glanced down onto the dance floor and saw Chase making his way through the crowd to the bar. He finished his orange juice and put the glass down.

"Is that why you are here? To make me an offer?"

"It is. I know you have the best product, the best network, the best distribution. I'm not interested in working with second-rate players. I'm ambitious. I only want to work with the best."

"And I'm not interested in flattery."

"I have a lot of money to invest."

"Is that right?"

"I'd like to start with half a million dollars."

López raised an eyebrow. "Half a million to start? That's quite an offer."

"Like I said—I'm ambitious."

"And naïve. Let us say, just for the sake of argument, that I do work with Jackson. A relationship like that—forged over many years, with mutual trust and respect on both sides—cannot be ignored. A relationship like that would have an understanding that would prevent one party taking advantage of the other. The purchaser, for example, might insist that he is only prepared to pay a certain amount on the condition that the distributor does not sell significant amounts into his market via any third party. The amount that you are offering, with all this uncertainty—I don't *know* you, Mr. Smith—would certainly be beyond what a reasonable business partner would tolerate. And so, while this has been an interesting meeting, I am afraid that I must bring it to a close."

He raised his hand, and the man from the rope stepped closer.

"You said significant amounts," Milton said, thinking quickly.

"I did."

"What about an insignificant amount?"

"What would be the point? You already told me that you were only interested in a larger deal."

"One key. Let me buy that, and I'll show you how professional I am. Give me the chance to demonstrate that I can dispose of a modest amount like that, and that my money is just as good as his."

"A test, then?"

"Exactly. A test. In the meantime, you can take a look at what I've said about Jackson. When you agree with me about him, you won't have to spend weeks—months, maybe

—finding someone who can take his place. I'll be right there. Ready and waiting to step up."

López stared at him, running his finger around the rim of the flute. He leaned back, pursed his lips, and smiled, as if surprised at himself for the decision that he had made.

"A kilogram?" he said.

Milton nodded. "How much?"

"Twenty-five thousand dollars."

"That wouldn't be a problem."

"Just like that? No haggling?"

"You have the better bargaining position. I'm happy to pay a premium."

"I'll need proof that you have money."

"I'll pay it tonight."

"Without a guarantee that we will be able to work together?"

Milton nodded. "I understand that."

There was a napkin dispenser on the table. López pulled a napkin out, took a pen from his pocket, and then wrote on it. He finished and slid the napkin across the table. Milton looked down and saw the details of a bank account.

"Thank you," Milton said. "I'll see that the payment is made this evening."

"How can I contact you?"

Milton took a second napkin and López's pen and wrote down the telephone number that John Smith was using. The number was brand new, allocated to the SIM that Ziggy had purchased at the branch of T-Mobile in Beethovenstraat the day before. Milton had been concerned that López would be able to find out that it was a virgin number and, if he did, that it would arouse his suspicion. Ziggy had taken measures to make it look a little more authentic and had reassured Milton that if López *did* have the means to check, he would not find the registration was recent. Instead, he would find that the number had been registered to a Mr. John Smith two days after his release from Wormwood Scrubs.

López took the napkin, folded it neatly down the middle, and slipped it into the inside pocket of his jacket. "Thank you, Mr. Smith. Transfer the money and then give me a day or two. I'll be in touch."

6

Milton left the club and set off on foot. He hadn't given López any notice that he was going to try to meet him that night and, on that basis, it would have been impressive if surveillance could have been arranged in the time that elapsed between Milton leaving the table and exiting the club. It wasn't impossible, though, and Milton had not managed to stay alive in a profession as dangerous as his for so long without treating all possibilities —no matter how unlikely—with the respect that they deserved.

Milton came to a stop in the centre of a bridge over one of the city's canals and looked back: nothing. He looked at his watch and saw that it was coming up to half past eleven. He felt the cool night air on his face.

He had sown a seed of doubt in López's mind as to whether the relationship with Jackson was stable, and, although Milton knew that his story would not stand up to a significant investigation, Ziggy had scattered enough misinformation to maintain those doubts long enough for Milton to push through to the second stage of his plan.

That was his focus now.

He took out his phone and called for an Uber.

~

MILTON GOT out at the foot of the apartment block and took the lift to the penthouse. He opened the door and stepped inside, finally allowing the tension of the evening's activities to melt away. He stood on the landing and looked out of the long window onto the sparkling lights of the city below. He knew that he had taken a risk with López, and, although the danger was only going to escalate from now on, at least he had respite for a few hours.

He took off his jacket, unlocked the door and went inside. The others had already returned. Hicks was taking off his dirty jacket and Chase was fixing a drink. Ziggy, who had been monitoring proceedings from the apartment, got up and stretched out the kinks in his shoulders.

"How did it go?" Ziggy asked.

"I think it went well."

"He bought it?"

"Maybe. He'll research me—it's on you now."

"You don't need to worry," Ziggy said. "The legend is secure."

"Good, because if it isn't..." Milton sliced his finger across his throat.

"It's solid. Trust me. And," he added, with a wink, "I own all his devices. His internet security is practically non-existent. If he sends an email or makes a call, I'll know about it."

Hicks took a beer from the fridge, popped the lid and came over. "You weren't followed on the way out."

"You're sure?"

"Definitely. I tailed you until you got the Uber. You didn't see me?"

"Of course I saw you," Milton said.

"Probably *smelled* you," Ziggy suggested.

Hicks raised his middle finger. "What was he like?"

"López? Suspicious."

"Is he going to take the bait?"

"Don't know. He's not interested in the bigger deal—doesn't want to step on Jackson's toes."

"We knew that."

"We did."

"The smaller one, though?"

"That's possible."

"Possible?" Chase said.

"I think he'll go for it. We need to make him a payment. I said I'd do that to prove that I'm serious." He turned to Ziggy. "You need to do that now."

"How much?"

"Twenty-five."

"Got the account?"

He took the folded napkin from his pocket and handed it to Ziggy. Milton had confiscated the five million dollars that Richard Russo had extorted from the cartel in Las Vegas, and intended to use that to fund this operation. It had secured the rent on this property and the clothes that he had bought to maintain the illusion that he was a man of substance; now it would pay for the cocaine that López would ship. There was a pleasing symmetry in the arrangement that was not lost on Milton: use the cartel's money to buy the cartel's product and, eventually, bring the cartel down. He liked that.

"Will you be able to get into his account?"

"Probably. Anything you'd like to know?"

Milton shrugged. "Money in, money out. Who's he paying? Who's paying him?"

"Leave it with me," Ziggy said.

Hicks took off his battered and holed sneakers, stretched out his legs and rested his feet on the table. "You think he'll call Jackson?"

"I doubt it," Milton said. "What's he going to say? As far as López knows, an old friend of his business partner just turned up out of nowhere and said he was unreliable. It's more likely that he'll start looking into *that*."

"But if he does call?"

"I'll intercept the call and handle it," Ziggy said. "Get your feet off the table. You stink."

Hicks winked at him.

Milton turned back to Ziggy. "Where's Jackson now?"

"Manchester. His days are all pretty much the same: get up late, go to the warehouse, go to the club."

"Keep an eye on him," Milton said. "We'll have to move quickly if López takes the bait."

"What's next?"

Milton started to the kitchen. He was hungry.

"We wait."

PART II
WEDNESDAY

7

Milton was in the Alps. He was in the woods, crouched on a hill. He could almost smell the trees —the tall pines and spruce and fir—grouped closely enough to provide shade against the sun. The road was an aged asphalt ribbon, flecked with potholes and cracks, grass and moss at the edges.

He heard the car and readied himself. He aimed the rifle and waited as the BMW turned into a lay-by for a rendezvous that was never going to happen.

Milton remembered it all.

The squeezes of the trigger.

The shattering of the windshield and then the window to the side.

The blood across the glass.

The gendarme—another shot and the man lying in a pool of his own blood.

The walk back to the first vehicle, the warning chime noting that the driver's door was ajar. The child in the back seat, terrified. A boy, perhaps seven years old, dark hair and his parents' features, a smear of blood across his forehead, a final gift from his father. Deep brown eyes, wide and terrified.

⁓

HE SAT BOLT UPRIGHT, his torso bathed in sweat and his muscles cramping hard. It took him a split second to readjust, to realise he was in the bedroom of the penthouse in Amsterdam. He took deep breaths, in and out, afraid to close his eyes again.

He pulled back the covers and swung his legs out of bed. He sat there, his face in his hands, for a few moments as he tried to recall what he had remembered.

He remembered the child and what he had almost done.

He had suffered from nightmares for years. He had found peace in the rooms, and, eventually, they had stopped. But now that he had temporarily put the support of the Fellowship to one side, the dreams had returned with an intensity that left him hollowed out and drenched in sweat every night. He knew the cause: it was his guilt. Lying in bed had become an exercise in waiting for the inevitable. The recollections, as real as if he were living through them all again, one after another after another. There was a lot of material for his unconscious to draw upon.

He laid a palm on the damp sheets and then reached for his watch. It was five in the morning. He knew that he wouldn't be able to sleep again, so he got up and took out his trainers and running gear. He dressed, pulled on his shoes, and crept out of the apartment, careful not to wake the others.

⁓

Milton ran. He headed south along the docks until he found Westerpark and then started the first of three circuits around it. He considered a fourth and decided against it, heading south again and following the road to Anne Frank Huis and then the Van Gogh Museum and Vondelpark. He decided that he needed to lose himself completely, to hide the churn of his thoughts beneath the metronomic beat of his feet and the regular in and out of his breath.

His music was interrupted by an incoming phone call. He stopped, reached up to his AirPods and squeezed the stalk to stop the music. He took out his phone and checked the screen; he didn't recognise the number.

His breath was still a little ragged as he accepted the call. "Hello?"

"Mr. Smith?"

"Yes," Milton said. "Who's this?"

"I work with Señor López. He would like to see you again."

"When?"

"Eleven o'clock tonight. He will be at the club. The same place. He will be expecting you."

Milton was about to respond, but the line went dead.

He drew breath as he stood staring at the blank screen. Had López swallowed the bait, or had he seen through the subterfuge that they had put together? There was no way of knowing without accepting the invitation.

8

Milton told the others about the call and what they would be doing that evening. Chase and Ziggy each had questions as to what they might expect, and Milton answered them as best he could. There was little to say, other than that there could only really be one of two reasons for the requested meeting: either López was prepared to do business, or he had seen through the charade. Ziggy had protested that the latter was impossible, that his work was watertight, and Milton had agreed that, on balance, the former was the more likely of the two reasons. But he couldn't dismiss the possibility that they had made a mistake, that López was more perceptive than they had given him credit for, and that meant that he couldn't dismiss the possibility that returning to the club would be walking into a trap.

They had no other option.

He would do it anyway.

~

THERE WASN'T any preparation to be done prior to the meeting, and, rather than stay in the apartment and find an excuse to fret, Milton decided to go for a walk. He walked for miles, and without really being aware of where he was headed, he found himself outside the social club that had hosted his one and only AA meeting since he had arrived in the city. The little sign—the interlinked A's on blue cardboard—was fixed to the door, and it fluttered in the wind. Another meeting was in progress.

Milton stopped and stared at the sign. He had not found the sense of peace that he usually found when he had attended the meeting. He hadn't *wanted* peace. He had sat in the back row and, rather than maintain his usual silence, he had raised his hand to share. He had admitted to the roomful of drunks what it had taken him years to discover: his drinking had been to drown the side of his personality that had allowed him to work for the Group for so long. Alcoholism was his sickness and his cure, or, at least, the only way that he was able to forget. Finding the meetings had given him another way to deal with the burden of guilt that he had to carry.

Beau's murder meant that the solutions that he had found to his problems—the bottle and then the Fellowship—now seemed counterproductive. He wasn't going to drink the guilt away, and neither was he going to mediate it through the things he learned in meetings. He didn't want to forget that darker part of himself.

The killer.

The assassin.

The *murderer*.

Not now. He no longer wanted to drown that side of his personality.

He *needed* it.

He knew that what he had elected to do was likely to get him killed, and he was happy with that. He deserved it, and always had. But, if he was preparing to go out, he was going out on his terms, and he would be bringing those responsible for Beau's death with him.

And, to do that, he needed to be Number One again.

He needed the old Milton.

9

Milton returned to the apartment and changed into a new suit, pairing it with a fresh shirt and a box-fresh pair of loafers. He took a moment in his room to compose himself again. The fact that he was unarmed was a problem, but it could not be avoided. He would be frisked again before he could see López. And, despite his distaste for the Mexican, killing him was not Milton's objective. Milton had a plan to deliver the punishment that López deserved, but it was one that would bring ruin upon him rather than death. López was a rung on the ladder to a more deserving target; no more, no less.

He did up two buttons of the jacket and went out into the living space. Hicks, Chase and Ziggy were waiting. They were going to run the same operation as before, but with a slight variation. Milton did not want to run the risk—albeit small—that Chase might be identified as a repeat visitor to the club on the same night that Milton made his second visit. Instead, Hicks would take his place. He had gone out that afternoon to buy suitable clothes, and Ziggy had enjoyed himself with a series of comments about how he was more presentable, and better smelling, than he had been for weeks. Chase had dutifully dressed himself in Hicks's discarded jacket and trousers and had defused any potential ribbing by declaring that he smelt as if he wanted to be left alone.

"Ready?" Milton said.

Ziggy laced his fingers and cracked his knuckles. "I'm up," he said. "I have eyes inside and outside the club."

"Where's López?"

"He's there."

"Anything that I need to know?"

"No," he said. "Nothing else on email about you. And just that one phone call."

Ziggy had been monitoring López's devices since the first meeting and had reported that the Mexican had placed a call to a contact in the Korps Nationale Politie, the Dutch national police. The man was senior—a *Hoofdcommissaris, or* chief commissioner—and had reported back that a check with his contacts in the Metropolitan Police had confirmed that a John Smith had been convicted of supplying drugs and had recently been released from prison.

"Good," Milton said. "If anything changes while I'm in there, tell Hicks."

"I know the drill," Ziggy said.

Milton straightened out his jacket. "All right, then," he said. "Let's get it done."

~

Milton took a cab to the club and found that his name was on the guest list, and, this time, it was legitimate. He thanked the woman at the lectern, made his way inside and climbed up to the VIP area. The security guard was expecting him, but, despite the familiarity, the same routine was observed. Milton was frisked, quickly and professionally, and waited behind the rope until López waved to signal that he should be let through.

The Mexican watched Milton with an amused cast to his face as he took the same seat in the booth as before.

"Señor López," Milton said, "thank you for seeing me again."

"Señor Smith, thank you for coming back. You like tequila?"

"I don't drink," Milton said.

"Not at all?"

Milton shook his head. "I had a problem with it, so I stopped."

"Pity," he said. He raised his hand and a waitress brought over a silver platter that bore six shot glasses. Two had been filled with white tequila, two with shots of lime juice, and two with shots of Bloody Mary mix.

"*La Bandera*," he explained, gesturing to the shot glasses. "Red, white and green, like the Mexican flag. You're sure I can't tempt you?"

"I am. But thanks."

López shrugged, put a dab of salt on his tongue and then took a sip from each glass, swirling the liquids in his mouth before swallowing.

Milton waited for him to empty his mouth.

"Thank you for the money," López said.

"All received safe and sound?"

"Yes. And very promptly."

"It's like I said—I'd like to get off on the right foot with you. I see this as a long and fruitful relationship."

López sipped the tequila again. "I also looked into your background."

"I wouldn't have expected anything less."

"And it seems you are what you say you are. The conviction. The prison time. Everything just as you told me."

"I'm not going to do something as stupid as lie to you."

"Military, too?"

"That's right," Milton said. "I was a paratrooper."

"Before you were discharged."

"You *have* done your homework."

López smiled.

Milton feigned discomfort. "I had a disagreement with my commanding officer," he said. "I'd rather we left it at that."

López shook his head. "I'd like to know."

"Sounds like you already do."

The Mexican gave a little shrug. "You want to work with us. It's important that I understand you."

"I went out one night and was stupid enough to do a line of coke. They got me with a random test the next day. What can I say? I was young and stupid."

"And you don't make mistakes like that anymore?"

"No," Milton said. "I don't."

López laid his glass down. "I think we should speak frankly with one another. You worked for Jackson. You know that a man does not rise to a position where he dominates the supply of a product like ours into his country without a certain ruthlessness. He is dangerous. There have been others who have tried to take his place. We don't hear from those men now. You would be wise to tread carefully."

"You don't need to worry about me."

"I'm not worrying. I don't care what happens to you. It is my relationship with Jackson that I am talking about. You have promised me that you will confine your activities to areas that do not interest him. Provided that you do that, I see no grounds for him to complain." He sipped more tequila, holding it in his mouth and then swallowing it.

"But *you're* not afraid of him, surely."

López laughed. "Don't be ridiculous. He knows it would be foolish to threaten us. Señor Jackson is dangerous, but he knows his place. He might be ruthless, but the people *I* work with? They are something else entirely. Do you understand?"

"Of course. That goes without saying."

"The consequences for displeasing us are significant. I'd rather make sure that we are on the same page."

"We are."

"And this is still something that you want to do."

"It is."

"Very good. We agreed upon a key. It is ready for you now. We just need to agree on delivery."

Milton had anticipated that. "I'm ready whenever you are." He looked at his watch. "It's just after midnight. How about three o'clock?"

"Tonight?"

"Why wait?"

López waved his hand dismissively. "Of course. There's a small village outside the city. Zaanse Schans. Do you know it?"

Milton remembered it from his guidebook. "The windmill village?"

"Yes. There is a car park near the Albert Heijn Museum. Be there in three hours."

López slid out of the booth and stood, signalling that the interview was at an end. Milton got up, too, and offered his hand. López took it. His skin was soft, as smooth as a baby's.

"Thank you," Milton said.

"Good luck, Señor Smith."

"Maybe we can do it again?"

López smiled. "Let's see, shall we? Three hours. Don't be late."

López finished the tequila, left the glasses on the platter, and left the table. His protection left, too, one of them in front and the other one behind. Milton got up and went to the balcony, watching as the Mexican led his retinue to the stairs and then down to the club below. The crowd parted for them and, in a moment, they were gone.

Milton found that he was gripping the rail. He took out his phone, woke the screen and composed a quick text.

We're good. Make the preparations.

10

Milton looked out of the windshield of the Ford Mondeo and into the darkness that lay on either side of the Julianabrug bridge. The windmills of the Zaanse Schans were illuminated, and a red warning beacon marked the top of a tall chimney that poked up from an industrial park to the right, but, those points of light apart, it was dark. A thick bank of cloud was blocking the moon and the stars, and, at this hour, there was nothing else on the road.

Ziggy and Hicks had purchased the Mondeo earlier that day in the anticipation that they would need transport to bring the cocaine across the border and back into the United Kingdom. It was a legitimate transaction; they had found a dealership in Amsterdam, selected a suitable vehicle and then transferred the ten thousand euros that the vendor requested. Milton had made a few small changes to it since then, but nothing that would be visible from the outside.

"Milton—this is Hicks. Copy?"

Milton's phone was on the dash with the speakerphone activated and an open line conferencing Hicks and Chase.

"I'm here."

"They just pulled in," Hicks hissed. *"Range Rover Sport. Two in the front."*

"Chase?"

"They've got privacy glass in the back. Can't say if there's anyone else."

Hicks was hiding in the vegetation near to the car park that López had proposed for the swap. Chase was over the road behind a hedge that fringed a warehouse complex. Neither man was armed, but that wasn't why they were there. Milton didn't think that López would double-cross him. They were there to follow his men back into the city. Milton had plans for the Mexican's business once he had dealt with those who delivered him his orders.

"Where are you?" Chase said.

"On the bridge," Milton said. "Hold position."

Earlier, Ziggy had asked whether Milton thought that Chase was capable of handling what would be required of him. Milton said that he was confident that he would be. Beau Baxter's son had been a Marine, and Milton knew that another person who could handle himself would be useful.

There was also the matter of his very personal motivation.

Milton didn't add that he still felt guilty for what had happened to Chase's father. The old man had been murdered by the *sicario* who had been sent to clean up the mess that had been caused by the Russos. Beau would not have been put into a vulnerable position if Milton had not asked for his help. Milton knew that he was asking Hicks and Ziggy for their help, too, but both men had worked with him before and were able to make calculated decisions on the level of exposure that they were prepared to countenance. Hicks could look after himself, and Milton would make sure that the impetuous Ziggy—always keen to impress—didn't do anything that might put him in the firing line. And, more to the point, Milton had offered them a quarter of a million each from the Russos' haul to help. Chase was different. Milton didn't know him, and, while he would do his best to keep him safe, the American was his own man and he was capable of making his own decisions. Milton was not about to patronise him.

Milton reached the other end of the bridge, approached the exit for the museum and flicked the indicator to turn off to the left.

"Ready?" he said.

"Ready," Hicks reported. *"I'll need them distracted for ten seconds."*

"I can do that. Just be careful."

"I've done this before," Hicks hissed.

Milton saw the Range Rover. It was parked with its front facing out, the running lights casting a wash of white into the empty space. He decided not to park directly alongside and instead chose a space fifty feet away. He slowed the car and brought it to a halt.

He opened the door and stepped out into the cold, damp night.

11

The Range Rover reversed and made a quarter turn so that it was facing down the car park at Milton. The running lights were still on, and, as Milton held his ground, the driver switched on the high beams. Milton wasn't quite quick enough to look away and had to blink, annoyed with himself, his night vision temporarily compromised.

He heard the sound of a door opening, and then another, and saw the silhouettes of two figures—male, and on the large side—on either side of the vehicle.

"Hands," one of the men barked out. He spoke English, but his voice bore a heavy Dutch accent. "Let me see your hands."

Milton slowly put both hands above his head. "Take it easy," he called out. "We're all friends here."

There was no reply, but the shafts of the high beams were interrupted as the first and then the second man stepped through them. They closed the distance to Milton, their shadows thrown forward a hundred feet, elongated shapes that cast their darkness over the Mondeo.

Milton brought one hand down to shield his eyes from the glare.

"Above your head!" one of the men called angrily.

Milton did as he was told. He saw a flicker of movement from behind the Range Rover. At least both men were out of the car and had their attention on him; Hicks would have his chance to do what he needed to do.

"Come on," Milton called out. "Is this necessary?"

The two of them were close now, and, despite the silhouettes cast by the headlamps, Milton recognised them: it was López's muscle from the club. They drew together and approached. Milton saw that they were both carrying items. The man on the left had a pistol held down against the side of his leg, and the man on the right was carrying a medium-sized bag.

The man with the gun stayed back, shuffling over so that he could cover Milton as his colleague drew nearer. The man with the bag came up to Milton and held it out. Milton took it, but the man did not release his grip on the handle.

"Coming unannounced to the club like that? Not clever, friend. Don't do it again."

The headlamps silhouetted the man almost completely. Behind him, Milton now saw another shadow crouched down by the side of the car: Hicks.

Milton needed to hold them for a moment longer. "Don't threaten me."

"You do as you're told, *kutwijf*."

Milton's Dutch was non-existent, but he knew that he had just been insulted. Hicks was still at the side of the Range Rover. The man with the pistol took a step in Milton's direction.

"I'm doing a deal with your boss, boys—all right? You keep this up and you're going to have to tell him why the customer who was ready to invest a ton of money in his business just walked away. Your choice."

Milton saw the shadow disengage from the Range Rover and melt back into the vegetation at the side of the road.

"*Mierenneuker*," the man spat derisively.

"Give me the bag, please," Milton said.

The man held onto the strap for a beat longer—his childish point made—and then let go. He turned and went back to the car. The other man waited until his colleague was inside and then followed suit. Milton stayed where he was. He heard the Range Rover's powerful engine turn over, and then watched as it lurched ahead. It bounced over a speed bump, rejoined the road and sped toward the bridge and the city.

Milton went back to the Mondeo and got in. He put the bag on his lap and unzipped it. There was a small oblong parcel, wrapped in brown paper and then wrapped again in cellophane. He took it out and held it up. He had paid for a kilogram, and the weight felt about right. He peeled back the corner of the cellophane and then the brown paper. There was a solid brick of a white substance inside.

"The magnet wouldn't stick," Hicks said over the phone.

"But you got it on?"

"Think so."

"Ziggy?"

"I got it," he said. *"Signal received loud and clear. They're heading back to the city."*

"Good. Chase?"

The American responded, *"Just tell me where to go."*

Ziggy had provided Hicks with a small tracking device. It was simple: a GPS receiver attached to a battery that was secured to the target vehicle by way of a magnetic plate. Hicks had pressed the plate against the chassis, most likely at the top of the wheel arch so that it was hidden from view. Ziggy was able to monitor the device from the apartment, and Chase was standing by to follow it back to wherever it was the two goons were headed. The odds were good that they would go to wherever it was they stashed the cocaine; Milton wanted to find out where that was. It would be useful for later.

"The package?" Hicks said.

Milton folded the brown paper back around the brick and then replaced the cellophane wrapping.

"Looks good," he said.

Milton opened the glovebox and took out the screwdrivers that Ziggy had purchased from a home improvement store when he was making the arrangements for crossing the border into the UK. He swivelled in his seat so that he could get to the console that sat between him and the passenger seat, and then loosened the screws that secured the cupholder. The unit came out as one, revealing an empty space below. Milton lowered the brick into the empty space, replaced the cupholder and then tightened the screws.

He started the engine and pulled out.

"I'll call you when I get to the ferry," he said.

12

Milton drove south. Ziggy called after thirty minutes to say that the two men who had delivered the cocaine had proceeded to a warehouse in the Westport district of the city. Chase was on his way there now and would conduct a careful reconnaissance of the site.

Milton was pleased. The plan had worked as well as he could have hoped. He had established a relationship with López, had collected a sample of the cartel's product, and had most likely found where the European operation kept its stash. None of that had been easy, or without risk, and he knew that every next step along the way would be even more difficult and dangerous. They had made an excellent start, but there was a long way to go.

He followed the A4 to The Hague and then, after turning onto the A13, to Rotterdam. He had purchased a ticket on the 0658 ferry to Hull, and he arrived with an hour to spare. He found the dock and joined the queue to board the ferry. A member of staff arrived to check him in and gave him a coloured card to hang from his rear-view mirror to confirm that he was cleared to travel.

Milton leaned back in his seat and waited. Crossing the border with the cocaine held risk, and there was no reason why that risk should be faced by more than one of them. Since all that was required was to drive the car onto and off the ferry, Milton had decided that he would do it alone and had instructed the others to fly. Hicks would arrive first and would find a place to set up. Ziggy would be next. The two of them would locate Anthony Jackson and put him under surveillance. Chase would be the third to arrive, and Milton, facing eight hours on the crossing and then a long drive at the other end, would be last.

A man in a high-visibility jacket waved the queue onto the ferry. Milton followed the line to the edge of the dock and bumped up and over the ramp and into the cavernous deck beyond. He was guided to an empty space and noted the red staircase that was closest to him.

He switched off the car alarm so that it wasn't triggered by the movement of the ferry, then stepped out and went up to the café.

13

Ellie Flowers was sat toward the back of the Avianca A330 that was flying them from Washington to Bogotá. It was a quiet flight, and the rows behind and ahead of her were vacant. Ellie had her tablet on her lap and was reviewing the new intelligence from the DEA team that was running the operation in Medellín. The DEA was reporting that the walk-in who had offered information on the cartel in exchange for immunity and the five-million-dollar reward looked as if he might be legitimate. The man —they had given him the cryptonym of CHILD—had suggested that he could provide the coordinates of a jungle camp where El Centro's decision makers could be found. It was that information that had sent Ellie to the airport. There had only been time to make a quick call to her brother to let him know that she would likely be out of contact for the next few weeks.

Five million bucks. It was one of the largest bounties the US had offered, but the stakes were high for anyone who was prepared to lay a claim to it. Fingering the cartel leadership responsible for the hit on Michael Cochrane would be a dangerous thing to do. The cartel had a long reach and a longer memory; anyone ratting to the gringos was accepting a life where he or she would always be looking over a shoulder. There had to be serious compensation for a risk as big as that.

Ellie had gone for a walk up and down the aisle on the pretext of stretching her legs, although the real reason was to try to identify the others who had been assigned to this operation with her. Men from two JSOC operational sabre squadrons—Blue and Black squadrons—had been deployed. Blue squadron was responsible for direct action and Black squadron for recon and surveillance. The latter were already in theatre while the former were travelling on a number of flights to avoid tipping off the Colombians that something was afoot. Ellie had seen a handful of potential suspects on her own flight: male, early to mid-thirties, relaxed, often grabbing sleep now in the anticipation that it would be harder to find later on. Others would be taking other flights.

The captain's voice came over the PA, announcing that they would be landing in twenty minutes. Ellie closed down her tablet and slipped it back into the Faraday bag that protected it from external interference. Her previous visits to Colombia suggested that this operation would present interesting challenges. The country was founded upon a precarious relationship between legitimacy and criminality that meant that the functions of the state and the underworld often blurred together. El Centro was the pivot upon which the edifice was balanced; there was a risk that removing its leadership would be destabilising, and that the whole structure would come crashing down.

But those assessments were for others to consider.

Ellie had been given her orders. She was excited to start.

14

Ellie had once again been booked into the Four Seasons in Casa Medina. Early check-in had been arranged, and she went through the formalities before following the clerk's directions to her room on the fifth floor. She went to the minibar and took out a bottle of Diet Coke. She popped the top and went to drink it at the window.

Good morning, Bogotá. She gazed out over the city and found herself wondering what her father would have said if he could see her now. Her career had taken a crooked path to bring her to this point. She had never doubted that she would one day end up working for the government. She had spent a year at college convinced that she was going to join the Secret Service, but her old man had been in the bureau, and she had eventually decided there was no point in fighting it; she was going to end up there, too. Her career there had been decent, and then she had found herself in the woods up in Michigan and dealing with a local militia that was planning on blowing up a trailer full of fertiliser during the vice president's visit to Minneapolis.

She had played a central part in bringing them to justice, and, for a while at least, it looked as if she could have her pick of assignments. That might have been the case, except for the fact that she had made a bad decision with her boss and had then been forced to try to disengage her personal life from her professional one. Orville wasn't a bad guy, at least that was what she had thought, but he had taken the end of their relationship badly and had started making life difficult for her. She had hoped that the situation would quiet down after Michigan, but that had not been the case at all. Orville had stayed clear of her for a month or two, but, once the press had moved on and the investigation into the militia had been handed over to other agents to conclude, he had tried to force his way back into her professional life. It was like her father said: a man like him was like a bad smell; you could never really wash it all the way off. Ellie had given some thought to making an official complaint. Her stock had been high after she had helped close out the case against the militia, but she had known that it wouldn't last forever. Orville was a consummate agency player, and, more to the point, he was male. He would have been back at some point. She could have filed her complaint and gone toe-to-toe with him, but there would have been no guarantee of success and it would have been a bitch of a thing to handle.

She'd decided against it.

Instead, she had parlayed the fact that her star was in the ascendant and engineered a transfer to the FBI's counterterrorism division. She had found a home in one of the two sections in CT: International Terrorism Operations Section II. It was responsible for the Middle East and other regional groups. The CIA was involved in the section, with an agency officer serving as deputy chief.

Ellie had worked all around the world ever since. She had been in Libya and Iraq and had worked against ISIS in Syria. She had contributed to the ongoing investigation into the assault on the US embassy in Benghazi. The attack had been back in 2012, but the case was still being processed all these years later. She'd made her name as a diligent and hard-working agent with a series of successful operations under her belt. She had no personal life to speak of, and that lack of attachment to home had meant that she had often volunteered for some of the more onerous assignments that others had shied away from. That, and her first-class closure rate, had seen her make a rapid ascent through the ranks.

Despite all that, she had started to wonder whether now was the time to leave the bureau and strike out on her own. Her brother's private investigation business was doing well; he had been on her case for years to come and work with him. They had just scheduled an exploratory meeting when Cochrane had been blown up in Colombia, and Ellie had been dropped into the FBI team that had been established to find out what had happened.

∼

ELLIE REFRESHED herself with a session in the hotel's gym. She ran for half an hour and then lifted weights, finishing with twenty laps of the pool and then a sauna. She went back to her room and showered, then picked out a pair of jeans and a white shirt together with a pair of boots. She checked her reflection in the mirror. She was five eight and knew that she was pretty when she could be bothered to try. She had a delicate face—smooth, pale skin with freckles that she had hated at school—thick hair that she had to work on all the time, and spirited grey eyes.

She checked for any messages that might have been delivered while she was in the air. There was some fluff, plus one missive that was more important: the walk-in who had contacted the DEA in Medellín had given a preliminary briefing, and the intel that had been provided was being checked. If it held up, half of the money would be advanced and a full debrief would be undertaken. CHILD was now promising that he could name the men and women responsible for the murder of the ambassador, together with the cartel higher-ups who had green-lit the assassination. CHILD had stipulated that, in addition to the money, he would require an extraction plan for both him and his family. The DEA and State were liaising to draw that up.

Ellie mused on the message for a moment. She had expected that the investigation would be protracted, and, indeed, she had told her brother that she didn't expect to be back in the States for weeks. This new lead promised a significant abbreviation of the time that would be necessary in prosecuting this investigation.

The meeting was at ten. She had time for breakfast. The hotel catered to Western visitors, and there was a smattering of businessmen and women at the tables. Ellie ordered *arepas de huevo*—corn cakes filled with egg—and a strong coffee.

"Excuse me?"

Ellie turned and looked up. Colonel Jaime Valencia was standing behind her.

"Colonel," she said, starting to stand.

"Please, Ellie. Sit."

Ellie did as she was told and waited as the soldier pulled back the seat opposite her and lowered himself into it. Valencia was in his late middle age, although he could have passed for someone ten years younger. He was of medium height and build, with a wiry compactness that suggested that he spent time in the gym. His skin was tanned, and his black hair was perfectly coiffed, slicked back with product that made it glisten in the light. His uniform was immaculate, as ever; the olive-green jacket and trousers were beautifully pressed, the shirt was as white as ice, and the tie—in a nod, perhaps, to his education in England—was worn in a Windsor knot. He had been made available by the Colombians as their primary military contact. Ellie had reviewed his file before their first meeting last week. He was the national director of the Colombian drug enforcement unit and had made his name with a number of impressive coups against the cartels.

She could have asked him how he knew that she was in town, but it was unnecessary. She knew that she would have been picked up as soon as she disembarked from the plane. The Colombians had operatives at the airport, and she had never made any secret of her identity and whom she worked for. A phone call would have been placed, hotel records checked, and *voila*—as if by magic, here he was.

Valencia took off his cap and laid it on the table so that the brocade faced toward her. "You didn't tell me that you were coming."

"It was a last-minute call," she said. At least that was true; she suspected that everything else she would say would be a lie.

"Can I ask why?"

"We're bringing more agents down," she said.

"Really?"

"The president wants a result. He doesn't think we're making progress fast enough."

Valencia shrugged. "Then he expects a miracle. An operation against El Centro will take months, if it is possible at all. If it was easy, it would have been done by now."

"Politicians," she said. "I know you have to deal with the same expectations."

Ellie wondered whether he could see through her obfuscation. She knew that she couldn't tell him about CHILD and the intelligence that had been promised.

He nodded in assent. "Do you need anything while you are here?"

"I'm good," she said. "But thanks."

"And you will tell me if you are able to develop anything?"

She clenched her fist under the tablecloth. "Of course," she said. "Likewise?"

He gave a deep nod. She knew he was as full of it as she was, but it was part of the dance that they each had to play.

"Excellent," he said. "It is good to see you again, Ellie. If you need anything—anything at all—then, please, you only need to ask."

"Thank you, Colonel. I will."

"I'll leave you to your breakfast." He gave her a nod in farewell, stood, and made his way back to the entrance of the restaurant.

Ellie exhaled. She had never been a comfortable liar and always found duplicity stressful. She was relieved that it was over, at least for now. She finished her corn cakes, drank the rest of her lukewarm coffee, and signed the check. She refreshed herself in the bathroom and then asked the concierge to call her a taxi.

15

The US embassy was equipped with a secure briefing room, but they knew that El Centro would have people watching the building on Carrera 45, and the last thing they wanted was to tip them off that something big was being planned. Instead, the DEA had provided premises where they could meet in private. There was a business park next to Avenida El Dorado that accommodated the South American headquarters of several prominent companies. Online businesses, including Google and Amazon, had based their operations there, and a steady flow of gringo visitors was expected. A few more would not raise any alarms.

The taxi delivered her to the drop-off zone outside a building that accommodated an oil and gas exploration company. Ellie paid the driver and got out, collected her bag and made her way inside. The bureau had done a deal with the company, and a large conference room had been reserved for them. Tech staff had attended the previous day to ensure that their discussions would not be eavesdropped on.

The Man Who Never Was 73

Ellie was the second person to arrive. Her boss, Patrick Baker, was the first.

"Ellie," he said, "all good?"

"All good," she said.

"Good flight?"

"Long. I got plenty done."

"Hotel?"

"It's fine. I had a visitor, though. Valencia came to see me at breakfast."

"What did he want?"

"He's suspicious. Wanted to know what I was doing in town without telling him."

"So we put his nose out of joint. Whatever."

"I know," she said. "I'd rather have him on our side, though, if we can."

"We won't need him after this. You see the email?"

She sat down on the edge of the table. "I did. We know who this guy is?"

"CHILD? No—won't give up his name. Says he needs to be sure he's going to be safe."

"Can't blame him," she said.

"You can't. It's a big risk. Not sure I'd do it."

There was a flask of coffee and a platter of Danishes on a table to the side. Ellie filled a mug and snagged a pastry. "Five million makes it a little easier to take."

"That it does."

∼

As she munched her Danish, Ellie began to prepare for the meeting. She took out her tablet and connected it to the projector that she was going to use during her presentation. She flicked through her notes as the others began to arrive.

There were senior staff from the DEA, the FBI and the Joint Special Operations Command, and she was a little nervous. She had given presentations before, but she had never really reached a stage where she was comfortable with doing it. Her old man had been the same. They both much preferred being in the field.

The others gathered their refreshments and took their places around the table. Baker tapped his pen against his empty glass. "Let's get started," he said. "There's a lot to discuss." The room came to order. "Let's go around the table and introduce ourselves. I'm Special Agent-in-Charge Patrick Baker, FBI. Ellie?"

"Ellie Flowers," she said. "Also FBI. Lead investigator on this case."

"Gerhard Schmidt," said the man to her right. "CIA. To my right are my colleagues Fiona Jules and Luke McKibbin."

"Nicholas York," said the tanned man with the impressive moustache that looked as if it belonged in the nineteen-eighties. "DEA."

"Commander William McSweeney," said the man with the short black hair and the narrow face. "JSOC."

"Elizabeth Flynn, also JSOC. I'm here as the commander's intelligence chief."

Ellie glanced around the table at them all. Five men and three women. They were keeping the list of attendees as compact as possible. They suspected that the ambassador had been sold out by a rat in the embassy, and there was nothing to suggest that the traitor had been found. The rat hunt was underway, but hadn't turned up anything yet.

"Thank you," Baker said. "Ellie has point on this investigation. I'm going to hand things over to her."

She got up and collected a clicker that had been left on top of the projector. Baker dimmed the lights and Ellie pressed the button to wake the machine. She waited a moment until the FBI seal filled the screen. She looked at the motto—"Fidelity, Bravery, Integrity"—and knew that they were going to need plenty of all three if they were going to bring this case home.

"As you know," she began, "Michael Cochrane was murdered in Bogotá ten days ago."

She pressed the clicker and a photograph of the ambassador's bombed-out car was displayed.

"He was on his way to sign an accord that would have presented a serious threat to the cartels, both here and in Mexico. The Colombian, Mexican and United States governments had agreed to work together in a significant pushback against the cocaine and methamphetamine that is flooding over the border. The cartels were aware of what we had planned, and they decided to let us know that it's not something they're prepared to take lying down. Besides Cochrane and his aide, three members of his security detail were killed."

She pressed the clicker and cycled through the images of the dead: Cochrane, Harrison, Fitzpatrick, Martinez, Jones.

"We've had plenty of business down here before. Escobar and the Cali Cartel both took up a lot of time and energy in the eighties and nineties. The difference between the Escobar way of doing things and El Centro is discretion —they're quiet, they don't make a fuss, they stay in the shadows. Escobar made it impossible for the government to ignore him. El Centro just wants to get on with business."

"Until they take out a serving US ambassador," Schmidt said.

"Until then," Ellie said. "Agreed. It's out of character, but you can understand why they might have done it. The accord is an existential threat."

"And taking out the ambassador isn't?" Schmidt spread his hands incredulously. "I mean—*seriously?*"

It was hard to disagree with his assessment.

"Go on, Ellie," Baker said.

"Yes, sir." She gestured to York. "I was going to ask Nicholas to speak about La Bruja."

The DEA representative stood and took the clicker from Ellie.

"All right, then," he said. He pressed the clicker, and an image of a woman was projected against the screen. "Say hello to La Bruja, otherwise known as the Witch. I'll get to the reason for that in a minute. She's been hard to pin down. You all know how little we have on her—trying to get more has been like trying to pin smoke against a wall. She's a ghost. This is the only picture we've ever been able to find."

Ellie looked at a picture that had become all too familiar to her over the course of the last week. It was a grainy, long-distance shot that had been zoomed in until the pixels were visible. The picture showed a slender woman, medium height, early middle age, with long brown hair. Not much more was discernible beyond that. She was standing next to a wooden shack surrounded by jungle. There was a Jeep behind her, and men with rifles were milling around it.

"She started out with the *Ejército Popular de Liberación*—the EPL, fighting for a socialist revolution in rural areas with the long-term aim of taking over the country. Men and women, all ages. She marked herself out as a particularly ruthless fighter. Lots of stories about what she did. The EPL was fighting the Popular Liberation Army, and one story was that she was personally responsible for the execution of twenty-five PLA soldiers. The story is that she killed them, then drank their blood."

"Apocryphal?" Ellie said.

"I sure as shit hope so," York said. "But some of it is true. She keeps a low profile, but she's never been afraid of not correcting mistakes or exaggerations if it helps her legend to grow, and there's more than enough out there to confirm that she's dangerous. The EPL was demobilised and she joined a rival paramilitary group: the *Autodefensas Campesinas de Córdoba y Urabá*. Again, her time in the ACCU was marked by more stories of what we might consider atrocities, but what the locals down there see as acts of great heroism. Robin Hood shit—you know what it's like. The ACCU was absorbed into the *Autodefensas Unidas de Colombia* and she was sent to join the AUC's *Centauros bloc*. Seems like she got her first taste of the criminal life under the group's finance chief, a particularly slippery customer by the name of Don Lucas. He was in charge of laundering funds and collecting extortion payments. The AUC was demobilised in the early 2000s, but La Bruja wasn't ready to hand over her guns. She and Don Lucas got together to form El Centro. We nabbed Lucas three years ago and then—as far as we can make out—she took over."

"Did Lucas talk?"

"Not a word, even when he was looking at spending the rest of his life in a supermax. He said he was too scared of her."

He clicked again and a map of Colombia appeared on the screen.

"So, she's moved decisively over the last few years. Under her leadership, El Centro expanded across the country. They started in Rionegro, but moved west and east until they were in control of a band of jungle that was two hundred miles deep, stretching from Puerto Berrío in the east to Antado and Nabuga in the west. She's always been strategic in how she gets things done. She can cut deals or go in hard. But however she's done it, it's worked. They've either absorbed their rivals or taken them out. El Centro is now the most expansive and successful cartel in Colombia since Escobar."

"And the Mexicans?"

"That might have been her masterstroke," York said.

He clicked again and an image of a dead man filled the screen.

"This is—or was—Felipe González, otherwise known as El Patrón. He was the head of La Frontera, a key narco-cartel responsible for Chihuahua, including the key narco crossing point at Juárez. González was killed three years ago, taken out by—we think—one of the rival cartels that was looking to take over his routes. The cartel was in a mess after his death, and La Bruja made them an offer they couldn't refuse. They would merge their operations—El Centro would handle production and La Frontera would handle distribution. But it was just a temporary arrangement, at least as far as she was concerned. She found out everything she needed to know, and then she proposed a change—she would be in charge of everything, from the farmers growing the plants to the preparation to the smuggling networks the Mexicans had been running for years. She made the same offer that Escobar made thirty years ago: *plata o plomo*. Silver or lead. She told La Frontera she'd make them more money if they went along with what she was proposing, and it turns out she was right about that. The enlightened beaners have done very well. And those who didn't drink the Kool-Aid? They got the *plomo*. The whole thing has been masterful from start to finish. That's why they call her La Bruja. She does things other people can't do. Like magic. They say she can do miracles."

Ellie stood up again and took over. "The Colombians have agreed to put everything into finding her. We have been talking about a joint operation in Medellín, using their soldiers and our intel to shake the trees so we can see what falls out."

"'We *have* been?'" Flynn said. "Past tense? Something's changed?"

"The DEA had a walk-in last week. A man. We haven't been able to confirm his story yet, but he says that he's reasonably senior and that he has intelligence on where we can find La Bruja. It has been decided that we don't need the Colombians for this. More than that—we don't trust them. If the intel holds up, we go in hard and nail her and anyone else with her. We take her out before anyone knows what's happened."

McKibbin tapped his finger against the table. "We know what an operation might look like?"

"We do," Ellie said. "Commander?"

McSweeney nodded. "I have a Special Mission Unit transiting to Medellín now. Thirty SEALs. They'll be in Medellín by this evening. We have an advance team looking at a safe house and fixing up the transport we'll need to get into the jungle. Once we have that arranged, they'll be ready to move on an hour's notice."

"We're definitely not telling the Colombians?" Schmidt said.

Baker snorted. "Their government is a shitshow from top to bottom. El Centro's bought it—lock, stock and barrel. There's no way of knowing who's on the payroll and who isn't. Situation like that, better to assume they *all* are."

"Understood."

"The bottom line is straightforward, ladies and gentlemen," Baker said. "You don't get to blow up the US ambassador without serious consequences. We go in and we go in hard—and we wipe those bastards off the face of the earth."

16

Milton had been able to catch a little sleep during the crossing, finding an empty bench and stretching out across it. He had always been able to sleep on demand; it was a skill that he shared with plenty of the soldiers with whom he had served. The ability to drop off quickly was invaluable, especially when working in hostile territory meant that the chances for sleep were not always predictable.

He had woken after three hours, a little stiff but mildly refreshed, and had bought a cup of strong black coffee from the café. He took it out onto the deck, pulled out his phone and opened the file that Ziggy had emailed to him. It was a dossier on Anthony Jackson: the man's operation, the addresses and vehicles that he used, the associates he worked with. Ziggy had produced detailed research that included photographs of the smuggler, together with the habits that they could use against him.

He put the phone away and looked out as the lights of Hull appeared through the gloom of a dank and dreary afternoon.

"We'll be coming into dock in fifteen minutes," a voice announced over the PA. "Would all drivers please return to their cars."

Milton finished the coffee, dumped the cup in the trash, and made his way down to the car deck.

⁓

Milton drove the car out of the back of the ferry, bumping over the ramp and then merging into the queue that led to the large building that was used as the customs area. Immigration formalities had been taken care of before boarding in Holland, and now Milton's onward progress would be determined by whether he was selected for a check. The queue edged forward enough for Milton to see into the building to his right. Three cars were being searched, with another three waiting behind them. Sniffer dogs were leading their handlers around the vehicles and, when they failed to sit, the handlers gave the all-clear and the cars were allowed to drive away. Four officials in yellow hi-vis tabards were walking along the queue of parked cars that had just left the ferry; the two men and two women were speaking to the drivers of the cars and, based on what they heard, deciding whether or not each car needed the more detailed check that the canines could provide.

Milton picked up his phone and placed a call.

"Ziggy?"

"I'm here. Where are you?"

"Waiting for customs. Now would be good."

"Okay." Milton heard the sound of Ziggy's fingers tapping on a keyboard. *"Here we go. Now."*

Nothing obvious happened, and Milton wondered whether what Ziggy had planned had had any effect whatsoever. If it did not, Milton was concerned that he would find himself in a spot of bother that might be difficult to remove himself from.

"Nothing's happening," he said into the phone.

The official came up to the car in front of Milton and indicated that the driver should wind down her window. There followed a quick conversation, and then the official skirted the car, looking into the windows as he made his way around it.

"Ziggy..."

The official completed his circuit and indicated that a detailed search would be unnecessary and that the driver could go about her journey.

"Got to be now."

"Wait." Ziggy's voice was a little tense. *"It's been received. It's decompressing."*

The official gestured that Milton should drive forward. Milton put the call on mute and did as he was told. The official gestured that he should wind down the window.

"Afternoon," Milton said.

"Hello, sir," the man said. "How are you?"

"I'm very good, thank you."

"Passport, please."

Milton handed the fake document to the man.

"What's the purpose of your trip?"

"Pleasure," Milton said. "I'm visiting friends."

"Where will you be staying?"

"Manchester."

"Do you have anything to declare?"

"I don't believe so."

"You don't *believe* so? Yes or no, sir. Anything to declare?"

Milton shook his head and smiled in apology. "No. Nothing."

"Wait there, please."

The man started a circuit of the car. Milton watched his progress in the mirrors as he unmuted the phone. "Ziggy?"

"It hasn't done anything?"

"Nothing," Milton said quietly.

The official returned to the window. "I'm going to ask you to drive the car over there, sir," he said, pointing to the shed.

"Is that necessary?"

"Just a check. Won't take long."

Milton was about to remonstrate when he saw the man glance down at his tablet. He frowned, tapped the screen once and then twice, and turned to a female colleague who was administering the queue of traffic to Milton's left. The woman was also struggling with her tablet.

"It's gone down," she called over.

The man stabbed his finger against the screen. "Me too."

Milton didn't understand exactly what it was that Ziggy had done. He had described it as a 'zip bomb'—an email containing what looked like a small file that, when checked by standard virus scanning software, opened and decompressed several petabytes of data, freezing the system and disabling other software running on the same server. Most modern antivirus software was able to detect malicious files, and Ziggy had ruled out deploying the technique at an airport on the basis that those systems were generally kept up to date. The defences at small ports like this one were archaic by comparison, and Ziggy had stated—with a *reasonable* degree of confidence—that the exploit would work. Milton had allowed Ziggy's uncharacteristic lack of bombast to sow doubt in his mind, but, as he looked around the dock now, he chided himself: he should have known better.

The car behind Milton sounded its horn, and the driver waiting in the queue to the left got out and remonstrated with the customs official who was still trying to wake up her device. Another horn sounded, and then another. The two officials conferred, with one taking out a phone and placing a call, and then, after another minute of being serenaded by the frustrated drivers who were waiting to drive into the UK, they stepped out of the way and waved the cars through.

"All good?" Ziggy said.

"Good as gold," he said. "Never doubted you for a minute."

With the cocaine undetected in the void beneath the centre console, Milton gently accelerated away.

17

Anthony Jackson had a stinking hangover when he finally awoke. He looked over to the clock on the bedside table, saw that it was coming up to one, and wondered whether he could sneak in another hour of kip. He was warming up to the idea when he remembered: he was expecting a delivery at the warehouse, and the load was supposed to have been taken off the boat at Liverpool at midday.

He blinked bleary eyes and reached down onto the floor for the jeans that he had discarded as he stumbled into bed earlier that morning. He checked his messages. He had received a text from Frankie McMahon confirming that he had received the green light from the customs official they had on the payroll. The container had come off the MV *Discovery* at eleven fifty, had been loaded onto the back of the lorry, and was now being cleared through customs. No issues were anticipated and, everything being well, the driver—Christopher Jacobs—was expected to arrive at the warehouse with the load just after four that afternoon.

He showered and changed, fumbled in his pocket for the unfinished wrap of coke that he had been enjoying last night, and emptied it out on the back of the cistern. He had a twenty in his other pocket; he rolled it into a tube, pushed the end up his nose and sucked up one line, then switched nostrils and did the other. The coke was from his personal stash, as pure as it had been when he had received it in the last load, not stepped on with the powdered milk and laxatives that they used to bulk up the weight before they sent it out to the dealers to be shifted.

He dropped the wrap in the toilet and flushed it away. He pulled on his shoes, swiped his car keys from the table and headed downstairs.

Vanessa, his wife, was in the kitchen.

"About time!" she complained.

"Shut your mouth," he said. "I had a late one."

"I know you did. You know what else I know?"

"What?"

"I know you were out with those two sluts again. You know how I know that?"

"Piss off, Vanessa," he said, starting for the door.

"I know, you stupid prick, because you took pictures on your phone and forgot that they upload to the Cloud. They were on the iPad this morning. It's a miracle the kids didn't see them when they were watching their cartoons."

Jackson groaned inwardly. Linzi and Becca were call girls who liked to consider themselves "high end." They were a pair of slappers, of course, but that didn't mean that they weren't both fit, or that he wasn't open to the prospect of rolling around with them both every now and again. He had ended up in one of the bedrooms above the club last night and tried to remember if he had taken pictures. Probably. What a dick.

"I've had enough," Vanessa was saying. "I can't keep on living this way."

"There's the door, then," he said. "Don't let it hit you on the arse on the way out."

"You piece of shit."

"You know why I did it? Because I can't stand the sight of you. I come back here and the place is a dump. I wanted a beer last night, but we're out. And you know what's worse than that? I'll tell you—look at you. Look at the way you've let yourself go."

She reached down for the vase on the sideboard and launched it at him. He ducked out of the way. The vase smashed against the wall behind him, and, as she came in with her fist raised, ready to hit him, he reacted faster and planted a straight right jab in the middle of her face. Jackson was a big man, and he caught her flush on the point of her nose. She went down, blood already running freely from her nostrils.

"Clean that shit up," he said, pointing to the glass that had fallen across the floor. "If this house isn't spotless by the time I get back, you can fucking do one. And get me some beer, you lazy bitch."

He snagged his coat and left.

18

Jackson drove up to the gate at the side of his warehouse and waited for McMahon to notice that he was there and buzz him in. He looked around the cabin of his Bentley Continental and allowed himself a flush of pride that he was able to afford a set of wheels like this. He had picked it up from the dealership two weeks ago, and it had quickly become his daily drive to and from the office; he kept his Ferrari in the garage at home and used it at weekends for a change. He had a vintage Jaguar in the space next to the Ferrari, and the new Porsche Taycan—the top-of-the-range Turbo S, of course—that he had on order would fill out his collection, at least until he felt like changing one of them. He had the better part of a million pounds invested in those cars, and that was ignoring everything else that he had been able to amass over the course of the last three years. The house on the Wirral was worth five million, bought from a Liverpool footballer after the greedy Scouse tit had been transferred to Barcelona. Even his business—Northwest Lead—was worth several million, and that was only considering its *legitimate* activities. The company was a front, and, when the business that it shielded was taken into account... Well, Jackson thought with a self-satisfied smile, it was hard to put a value on what it was *really* worth.

Money bought him more than just fancy cars and a big house, of course. It bought him influence and respect. He had been at the golf course yesterday and had enjoyed lunch with three of the local businessmen with whom he often played a round, at once pleased by the fact that they saw him as a legitimate businessman and smug with the knowledge that his criminal enterprise generated more than all of their companies combined. He liked to feel part of the local community and had made a name for himself as something of a philanthropist. A primary school near his house had burned down six months ago, and Jackson had agreed to provide a sizeable proportion of the funding needed to rebuild it. There had been stories in the local newspaper and a profile of him on the local BBC news. He wanted people to like him, and this kind of attention was something that he cherished. He had been in the game long enough to know that his operation, and the real source of his wealth, was safely hidden. He was confident that there was no prospect of the police being able to delve into his real business, and even if there was, he had several high-ranking officers looking out for him. Some of them had been bought, and the cooperation of others had been secured by the fact that Jackson held incriminating information over them that would end their careers if it ever saw the light of day.

The gate was still shut. He laid his hand on the horn, letting it blare until McMahon realised that he was waiting and hit the button to open the gates. They slid back on their runners and Jackson drove the Bentley inside. He parked in his usual space and stepped outside, locking the door and making his way into the warehouse.

19

McMahon met him inside. "How's your head?"
"I've been better," Jackson said.
"It was a good night."
"From what I can remember of it."
"You remember the girls?"
Jackson frowned. "Did I take pictures of them?"
"You told them you were going to make them famous."
He chuckled at his stupidity. "Posted them to the Cloud, didn't I?"
"And Vanessa found them?"
He grinned. "Won't make a difference. She ain't going anywhere, is she? Knows what side her bread's buttered."
The two of them walked onto the main floor of the warehouse. It was a large space, kitted out with the equipment that they needed to at least make it look like the business was running as a going concern. They had a big automatic ingot casting and stacking machine along one wall. It was used to cast liquid lead into moulds, to cool it so that it could be condensed into standard ingots, and then to stack those ingots layer by layer. Another machine turned the

liquid lead into balls, and a third used high-pressure water to slice the metal into workable chunks. The machinery had cost several hundred thousand pounds to buy and install, and had been a sizeable investment for what was a fig leaf to disguise what really went on behind the tall roller doors: the extraction, processing and distribution of millions of pounds worth of high-grade Colombian blow.

"You heard anything from Jacobs?"

"He cleared customs," McMahon said.

"I know that," Jackson said. "He's supposed to be here at four, though, right? It's ten past."

They both heard the sound of the horn from outside before McMahon could answer. Jackson looked at the monitor and saw the truck that had turned off the road.

"Speak of the devil," he said.

McMahon jogged across the warehouse and pressed the button to raise the roller doors. Jackson watched as the truck with the Northwest Lead livery reversed into the warehouse. McMahon waited until it was all the way inside and then lowered the door again. Jackson strolled over as the driver's door opened, and Christopher Jacobs climbed out and dropped down to the floor. He was grinning.

"Everything go okay?"

"Like clockwork," Jacobs said. "It was waiting for me on the dock. We got it onto the back and that was that."

"Customs?"

"Already handled."

Jackson grinned too, bumping fists with Jacobs. There had been checks of the lead before, but the cartel's deliveries were so sophisticated that the only way they could have found themselves in trouble was if someone had tipped off the authorities. None of his men would do something as stupid as that; Jackson had worked with all of them for years, and they all knew exactly what would happen to them and their families if they were ever tempted to rat him out.

"Let's have a look," Jackson said.

They went around to the back of the truck and lowered the mechanical tailgate. The cargo space accommodated three wooden pallets upon which rested more than a hundred individual wooden boxes. McMahon used a pallet truck to manoeuvre the nearest pallet onto the tailgate and then lowered it down to floor level. Jackson took a crowbar and wedged the end into one of the corner seams of the crate. He put both hands onto the bar and yanked it backward. The wood cracked and snapped, a small gap opening between the two sides. He pulled hard again and the gap widened until there was enough clearance to get inside. He opened the crate all the way, dropping the dislodged lid onto the floor. He looked inside: there were smaller wooden crates, each the size of fruit boxes. He lifted one out—it was heavy—and put it on the floor.

"Get it open," he said.

McMahon used a small jemmy to prise off the lid. All three of them looked inside. There were two dozen small rectangular bars packed neatly into the crate. Jackson lifted one out and examined it, turning it over in his hands. He found himself admiring the workmanship once more. The cartel used robust steel containers, ingeniously concealed within the lead ingots. The ingots appeared entirely unremarkable, each meticulously crafted to match Jackson's exacting standards and impervious to x-ray. Jackson's inside man at the customs office added an extra layer of security by providing details about the drill bits customs officers used during inspections. It enabled the cartel to put a sufficient layer of lead around the containers; the drill bits weren't long enough to discover anything that might compromise the operation.

McMahon took one of the ingots to a workbench and sliced off the end with a saw. He tossed the end into a box, ready to be smelted, and carefully withdrew the steel container inside. He opened it and pulled out the first of the long, wrapped blocks. McMahon used a knife to slice open one end, peeled back the inner wrapping, and turned the block around so that Jackson and Jacobs could see the bright white cocaine inside.

Jacobs whooped.

McMahon used the edge of his blade to scrape out a little of the cocaine. It was hard, but he used the side of the blade to break it down into a powder. He scooped up a little on the edge of the blade, put it to his nostril and inhaled once and then twice.

"Well?"

"Give me five minutes and I'll let you know."

"But?"

"Looks good to me."

Jacobs went over, took out a credit card from his pocket and scooped out a bump for himself. "Three hundred keys. Holy shit."

Jackson knew his basic cartel economics. Buying directly from the cartel had been the difference between doing well and doing *really* well. He had started out buying from a wholesaler who had themselves bought from another wholesaler. Those two men had both wanted to make their margin, and it had added to the cost that Jackson had to pay. Buying from the manufacturer stripped those additional layers out, with the caveat being that they would only deal in large quantities. Jackson had been able to find the million he needed for his first shipment, and had reinvested the profits from that and subsequent shipments until he could afford these kinds of big loads. There was another factor to bear in mind, however, when working with the Mexicans: they were not the sort of partners that you would want to piss off. Jackson kept that in mind at all times. He was respectful when he dealt with them, discreet in the way he ran his operation, and he paid promptly, making them a lot of money.

"How much will we make?" Jacobs asked.

"Profit?" Jackson shrugged, trying to be nonchalant but unable to keep the grin from his face. "We'll clear ten million, easy."

Jacobs whooped again.

Jackson pointed to McMahon and then to the truck. "Get this unloaded."

20

Milton drove the Mondeo west, taking the M62 all the way to Manchester. It was early afternoon and the traffic was flowing without issue. He made good time, arriving in the city two hours after he set off. Ziggy had sent him a message, confirming that—in line with Milton's instructions—he had found them two flats in the city. The address was for Union Street in Manchester's Northern Quarter, two serviced apartments in a block that came with underground parking.

Milton followed the navigation on his phone until he arrived at the building, turning off the street and rolling carefully down the ramp into the garage. He found the spaces that came with the apartments, reversed into one of them and switched off the engine. He opened the door and got out, stretching his arms and rolling the kinks out of his shoulders. It had already been a long day.

He looked around, satisfying himself that the garage was empty, and then took out the screwdrivers from the glovebox and used one of them to unfasten the centre console. He lifted out the cupholder, reached into the void beneath and took out the packet of cocaine. He dropped it into his rucksack, put the console back together and locked the car.

He made his way to the lifts. They had work to do.

~

Ziggy had rented two Airbnbs in the block, one next to the other. Each featured a single bedroom, a living area with a sofa-bed, and a kitchen. Milton knocked on the door of flat 212 and waited until he heard the sound of approaching footsteps.

Ziggy opened the door. "All okay?"

"All fine," Milton said.

Ziggy stepped back and Milton made his way inside. The apartment wasn't nearly as luxurious as the place in Amsterdam, but he was fine with that. These units were nothing more than places to sleep, plan, and house their gear.

Ziggy led the way into the sitting room. Hicks and Chase were there, too.

"All right?" Hicks said.

"It went well," Milton said. "I wasn't stopped."

"You just drove straight through?" Chase said.

"I must have a trustworthy face," Milton said.

Ziggy cleared his throat. "Excuse me?"

Milton smiled. "Ziggy worked a little of his magic."

"'A little of his magic,'" Ziggy grumbled. "That was a work of art. They're still down now."

Milton ignored his customary plea for recognition and sat down at the small dining table. "Update me."

The four of them ran through the preparations that had been made. Hicks had been allocated the task of rounding up transportation. He had purchased a second-hand Ford Galaxy from a lot in the north of the city, paying in cash and using fake ID to ensure that the vehicle could not be traced back to them. Chase had collected the things that Milton thought they might need. Ziggy had continued his research into Anthony Jackson.

"What have you got?" Milton asked him.

"I already had a lot," he said. "Did you read the dossier?"

"I did. It was good. What else?"

"His phone," he said. "I used a backdoor into Facebook to get his date of birth and his mother's maiden name. We own it now. He went out last night to his usual club. Looks like he had an interlude with a couple of women after hours. I have photos and videos. Very salacious."

"What else?"

"He drives a Bentley Continental that comes with a Vodafone tracking contract. I've been in their database for months. Took me five minutes to find the car and spoof the data to me. We'll know where the car is at all times."

"Where is it now?"

"At his warehouse. I've looked through the last week's data. He follows a routine most days: leaves the house at midday, plays golf, drives to the warehouse, stays there for an hour or two, then heads into Manchester to eat. He sometimes goes home after that, sometimes goes to a club."

"Excellent. Good work."

"What do we do now?" Chase said.

"Scout the warehouse and the route he takes to the city. You want to come with me?"

Chase stood up. "Sure."

Hicks looked up. "When are we going to make our move?"

"You see any reason to wait?"

"None at all."

"We'll aim for tomorrow," Milton said.

21

Milton, Chase and Ziggy made their way down to the street where the Ford Galaxy had been left. It was old and battered, with a dent on the rear end and duct tape securing the wing mirror to the side. It was perfect. Ziggy opened the back door and pulled himself inside. Milton and Chase got in the front. The interior was tired and tatty, but Milton had no problem with that. It was inconspicuous, which was the main quality that it needed to have. He put the key in the ignition and turned it; the engine grumbled to life and, after a moment of spluttering, it settled into a steady thrum.

"We good?" Chase said.

"Think so."

He turned around and looked back into the rear of the vehicle. There were two rows of seats in a similar condition to the ones up front. The windows were tinted, offering only minimal visibility from the outside. That was good. Ziggy had taken a spot at the back and had already opened his rucksack to take out two of his laptops.

"Will this be okay for you?" Milton asked him.

"Should be fine."

"Good. Let's get going."

Milton put the vehicle into first gear and pulled out.

"This guy, then," Chase said. "Jackson. What do we know?"

Milton glanced in the rear-view. "Ziggy?"

He recited it from memory. "Anthony William Jackson, born on the sixth of July 1970 in Ormskirk. Long list of previous convictions as a teenager—robbery, assault, all the usual highlights—but he's been more careful the older he's become. He has properties in the Wirral, a villa in Tuscany and a beachfront condominium in Miami. Previously included on the *Sunday Times* Rich List, although they referred to his front business—the buying and selling of lead—rather than the real source of his wealth."

"Which is?"

"The buying and selling of cocaine."

"The police don't know about him?"

"They do. There's a file as long as your arm on what they think he's been getting up to. But *knowing* what he's doing and *proving* it are two very different things. I pulled everything I could find from the Police National Computer. Much of what I've found out is speculative, but it looks like he went to Mexico to meet senior representatives of La Frontera. He set up an arrangement with them to take regular shipments of Colombian coke, using the Mexicans' expertise to get it across the border. He's the biggest importer in the north, probably in the whole country."

"Dangerous?"

"Suspected for multiple murders, although none have been proved. So is he dangerous? Yes. I'd say he's *very* dangerous."

22

Jackson's front business was in an industrial park in Worsley that comprised a grid of roads offering access to similar properties. There were warehouses and offices, all with small parking areas that separated them from the pavement and the road. Milton drove slowly, checking both sides of the road as they rolled down it. There was a packaging business, a business that produced fabric for workwear, a showroom featuring sheds and playhouses that was open to both the trade and the public. Jackson's property was a medium-sized building built from brick and corrugated iron. There was a row of windows on the ground floor and then metal facing that protected the rest of the elevation all the way up to a pitched roof. There was a parking area for five cars and, to the left, a gate that looked as if it offered access to the rear. The sign that was fixed to the wall announced the building as belonging to Northwest Lead.

Milton drove past the warehouse, made a U-turn when they were well past the entrance, then moved the Galaxy to the kerb. They had a good view of the building from there.

Ziggy took a camera from his rucksack, attached a lens to the body and started to take pictures. Milton kept an eye on the road to make sure that they were not attracting undue attention.

"What does he drive?" Chase said.

"A Bentley Continental GT," Ziggy said. "One hundred and fifty thousand pounds of pure ostentatious bling."

"Don't see anything like that. You sure he's here?"

"He wouldn't leave it out the front," Milton said. "Too expensive."

"There's a car park around the back," Ziggy said. "Behind the gate. Transponder looks like it's in there."

"What about security?" Milton asked. "Cameras?"

"Two out front, and looks like one on the side of the building," Chase reported.

Milton squinted into the deepening gloom. "Ziggy—can you get at them?"

"Probably. But I'd need to see the make of camera to know for sure."

"I can do that," Chase said. "Give me a minute."

The American opened the door and got out, pausing behind the Galaxy as a delivery truck pulled up outside the factory that was opposite the warehouse. Chase waited until the truck disappeared into the building before ambling away, crossing the road and heading for the warehouse.

Ziggy and Milton watched.

"How much do you know about him?" Ziggy said.

"Enough. He's competent."

"'Competent'? That's hardly a ringing endorsement."

"He was a Marine," Milton said. "Got a medical discharge."

"That's the limp?"

"Shot in the leg."

Chase was approaching the warehouse, slowing his pace.

"You're sure he's up to this? I mean… Hicks, I know. I've seen him working before. He's full of it, but he can back it up. Right? But this guy?"

"I knew his father," Milton said. "He died because of me. Chase wants revenge and I'm going to help him get it. And that's all quite apart from the fact that we're going to need all the help we can get. This"—Milton gestured out of the window—"is the easy part. Jackson's dangerous, but we can handle him. It's when we start working our way up the ladder that things are going to get more difficult."

Chase reached the warehouse and changed direction, crossing the parking area at the front so that he passed directly under the camera that had been fixed to the side of the building. He had his phone in his hand and aimed it upwards, then continued along the line of the wall to the second camera that had been positioned above the door that offered access to the interior. He angled his phone upwards for a second time, walked right beneath the camera, and then continued on. He walked on for another few paces until he was out of sight, then crossed the road and came back on the other side. He made his way back to the MPV and got back into the front.

"See anyone?" Milton asked.

"I looked through the door. It's a reception area. There was a man behind a desk." He took out his phone. "Got some footage of the cameras they're using. Here."

He handed the phone to Ziggy, who chuckled as he scrubbed through the footage.

"This is going to be easy," he said.

"You can get into them?" Chase asked.

Ziggy took one of the laptops from the seat and put it on

his lap. "It's funny," he said. "People are worried about security on their networks, but they don't think about the things that *connect* to the network. Take your phone, for example. If you get the password wrong enough times, it'll lock. The cheaper peripherals don't always do that, like the cheap Chinese cameras they're using."

His fingers flew across the keyboard.

"What are you doing?" Chase asked.

"I'm connected to the camera over the office door," Ziggy explained. "And now I'm running a program that'll fire thousands of possible passwords at it every second."

"You'll be able to guess it?"

The laptop pinged. "It's not guessing," Ziggy said. "It's a brute force attack. And... and I have it—SuperSafe132. Hilarious."

He typed in the password, hit return, and then turned the laptop around so that Milton and Chase could see the screen: they were looking down from the camera's vantage point onto the area next to the door that Chase had passed through just minutes earlier. Ziggy had hijacked the stream from the camera.

"Well done," Milton said. "Get the others, too."

"Already on it. Looks like there are cameras inside, too. I'll get them all."

They waited as Ziggy worked his magic on the other cameras, adding them to his screen one at a time.

Chase nodded to the warehouse. "You think that business is legit?"

"Very likely," Milton said. "But it won't be how he makes most of his money."

"You think he's keeping drugs in there?"

"I'd say there's a good chance. I've seen something similar in Vegas."

Chase gazed out at the warehouse. "Getting inside's not going to be easy."

"We don't need to get inside."

"No?"

"I have a much better idea."

Ziggy put the laptop down. "Ten cameras. Three inside, seven outside. Got them all."

"Good."

Milton put the MPV into reverse, turned around, and headed out of the estate.

"What now?"

"We need to find a spot to take Jackson out."

23

Worsley was to the west of Manchester. Milton drove south, through the industrial estate, until they reached the junction for the A580. It was a dual carriageway with industrial units to the north and residential properties to the south.

"He comes this way?" Milton asked Ziggy.

"He has done the last couple of nights. He goes into Manchester. The A580 through Pendlebury is the best way to get there from here."

Milton merged onto the A-road and followed it toward the city. He drove for five minutes until they reached a busy four-way junction: roads fed into it from the left and right, the flow of traffic governed by a set of traffic lights. He flicked the indicator and turned off to the left. The road led into another business estate; Milton found a spot where he could park and pulled off to the side.

"What do you think?" he asked Ziggy.

"I think it could work. I'll need to go and look at the control box. When are you thinking? Still tomorrow?"

"That long enough for you?"

"Should be easy. I'll go when it's quiet tonight."

They heard a beep from one of Ziggy's laptops. He tended to it and chuckled.

"What is it?" Chase asked him.

"Want to see Jackson? He's headed this way now."

∽

JACKSON LEFT the warehouse and slid into the Bentley's leather driver's seat. He started the engine and enjoyed the powerful rumble for a moment, then switched over to CarPlay and played the old Sasha mixtape that he had been listening to on the way into the warehouse. He reversed out of his space, waited for McMahon to open the gate, and then drove away.

He knew that he could leave McMahon and Jacobs to supervise the unloading of the product. They would get it down off the back of the truck, transfer the pallets to the space against the wall and then, one by one, and with great care, they would slice open the ingots and extract the contents that had been hidden inside. Both men were trustworthy and good at their jobs. They both had incentives to do good work, too: they would each score half a million from this delivery alone.

He started to think about the stages after the product had been unpacked. He would contact his usual network and warm them up. He operated a professional wholesale business; his dealers were the retailers who delivered the product to the punters in Liverpool and Leeds and Manchester whose addictions had, ultimately, paid for Jackson to live this kind of life. They bought their fifty-quid wraps for their Friday and Saturday nights, then did it all again next week and the week after that. He had one dealer, a dubious Northern Irishman who lived in Stockport, who had made a very good living for himself supplying the bands who played the arenas in Liverpool and Manchester. Some of Jackson's favourite musicians went on stage with his product buzzing in their veins; it was a trip, and one that gave Jackson a sense of enormous satisfaction.

Jackson saw a Ford Galaxy parked at the side of road, wheels half on and half off the kerb. He slowed, flicked the indicator, and went around it, glaring at the driver as he did. The man behind the wheel held his eye and, for a moment —and without any idea why—Jackson felt a little tremble of discomfort. He cleared the obstruction, put his foot down again and accelerated away.

He was looking forward to getting to the restaurant and then, after dinner, the club. He had a lot to celebrate.

PART III

THURSDAY

24

Anthony Jackson was woken by the ringing of his phone. He tried to ignore it and, after another half dozen rings, it fell silent as the call diverted to voicemail. He closed his eyes and sank back into his pillow again. It had been another late night, fuelled by the blow that had been delivered yesterday, and it had taken him longer than he would have liked to get to sleep. In the end, he had taken two zopiclone to try to counteract the buzz of the coke, and, when that had not worked, he had added a Valium from a bottle that had Vanessa's name on it. But he still felt hollowed out.

The phone rang again. He reached for it and took the call. "What?" he said, putting the phone on speaker and holding it in the rough vicinity of his mouth.

"It's me, boss," McMahon said.

"It's early, Frankie," he groaned.

"I'm sorry. It's important."

"What is it?"

"On the phone, boss? You said not to do that."

He gritted his teeth with frustration even as he knew

McMahon was right. "No details, then, Frankie. Just say yes or no. Something's wrong with the delivery?"

"No. That's all just like it ought to be."

Jackson felt relief and then, without the sickening fear that something bad had happened, the irritation at being awoken so early returned. "So what is it?"

"It's Dessie O'Sullivan," he said. "He needs to speak to you. I know what he wants and it has to be in person. Can't be like this. I'm sorry."

Jackson rolled over, scrubbed one big paw across his face, and grunted with the exertion of sitting up. "Fine. I'll be there as soon as I can. And, Frankie?"

"Yes, boss."

"I'm telling you, this had better be good."

25

Milton got up and went for a run. He followed North Western Street along the line of the railway, noting the businesses that had been established in the arches. He saw the Mancunian Boxing Club and thought of Elijah Warriner. Milton hadn't been back in the United Kingdom since he had travelled to Vegas for JaJa's first fight overseas. He had been looking forward to watching it at the casino, but events had conspired to make that impossible. He had caught up with the bout on YouTube in Amsterdam instead and had watched proudly as the young Londoner had stopped his opponent in the sixth round. The boxing commentariat were suggesting that Elijah would be fighting for a world title within three years; Milton knew the boy and, aware of how driven he was, he would have abbreviated that a little. He thought about that as he pounded the pavement and it gave him pleasure. He'd done bad things in his life, and now he was trying to balance those out by doing good. Elijah had been one of his successes.

He continued southeast and made his way through Ardwick and Belle Vue and then into Longsight and Levenshulme, allowing his concerns about the day ahead to float away as he concentrated on his breathing and the slap of his feet on the pavement.

∼

MILTON RETURNED TO THE AIRBNB, where he showered and changed into the clothes he had been wearing yesterday. Ziggy was staying in this flat, too, and, when Milton emerged, he saw that he had set himself up with his equipment. All three laptops were arranged on the kitchen table.

"Jackson's on the move," Ziggy said. "Left his house fifteen minutes ago."

"Early for him."

"Yes," Ziggy said. "Very."

Milton looked over Ziggy's shoulder at the laptop that showed the location of the transponder on Jackson's car. He was just passing through Partington. "The warehouse?"

"I think so."

They watched as the flashing dot merged onto the M60.

"Why go early?" Milton said.

"He just got a phone call," Ziggy said. "The number is registered to a Francis McMahon. His name came up when I was digging into Jackson's business—I think he's part of his crew."

"Play it back."

Milton listened to the conversation between Jackson and McMahon. "Who's O'Sullivan?"

"Don't know. The name's never come up before."

"Keep watching him."

Milton went out into the corridor and banged on the door of the adjacent apartment. Hicks opened the door.

"Jackson's on the move," Milton said.

"You want to go now?"

"Maybe. Get ready—get Chase, too."

"Give me five," Hicks said. He closed the door.

Milton went back to stand behind Ziggy. The red dot had just turned into the industrial estate.

"Can we look at the cameras?"

Ziggy reached across and tapped a finger on the second laptop. The screen awoke, revealing that it had been quartered with the feeds of four of the warehouse's external security cameras. They waited until they saw the Bentley approaching, and then Ziggy switched from a camera that was angled down the road to a second that looked down from above the security gate. The car turned left and rolled up to the gate. The angle was too steep to look into the car. They watched as the gate rolled back; the Bentley drove through and the gate closed behind it.

"Inside?"

Ziggy tapped out a command and the feed from the four external cameras was replaced by three new feeds. These were inside, with two showing the main space of the warehouse and a third looking into the reception area. There were three wooden pallets on the floor and a number of oblong boxes stacked atop them. Two men were ministering to a large machine that was equipped with what Milton thought was a cutting tool. The end of an oblong was sliced off and fell to the floor. One of the men used a pair of long-handled tongs to reach into the box and withdrew a metal case. The case was placed onto a trestle table and opened up. A brick wrapped in brown paper was carefully extracted.

"You have to give them credit," Milton said admiringly. "It's neat."

The brick was taken to another table and arranged next to three or four dozen similar bricks.

"How much do you think that's worth?" Ziggy asked.

"A lot."

One of the doors at the rear of the building opened and a man came inside.

"Zoom in."

Ziggy selected the feed and enlarged it, then zoomed in as the man stopped to speak to a second who was already inside.

"Audio?" Milton asked.

"Afraid not."

Milton recognised Anthony Jackson from the surveillance photographs that Ziggy had extracted from the Police National Computer. He was a large man with an earring in his right ear. He was wearing a dark suit jacket and jeans, with a pair of chunky boots on his feet. He reached up to scratch his scalp, and the sleeve of the jacket fell back to reveal what looked like a substantial watch on his wrist.

They watched as Jackson finished his conversation with the second man and made his way across the warehouse floor to a door on the other side of the room. Ziggy had downloaded the plans for the property and had identified the door as leading into an office space; there was no camera there, not that it would make any difference.

Milton looked at his watch. "Nine fifty," he said. "What do you think?"

"He's off his schedule," Ziggy said. "No idea how long he'll be there."

Milton drummed his fingers against the edge of the table. "I don't see any point in waiting."

"You want to do this now?"

"Are you ready?"

Ziggy closed two of the laptops. "I am."

Milton got up, grabbed his jacket and put it on.

"Let's go," he said.

26

Jackson pulled up against the gate and laid his hand on the horn. The gate rolled back and he drove inside, slotting the Bentley into its usual spot. He got out, slamming the door behind him, and went to the work area. The pallets had been unloaded and, from the looks of things, a good number of the ingots had been cut open and the cocaine bricks withdrawn. A course of them had been built on one of the trestle tables that had been set up for the purpose of receiving the goods. The sight of all that cocaine—and the money that it represented—put Jackson into a slightly better mood, and, as Frankie McMahon came over to him, he managed not to snap at him.

"Did I *really* have to come in for this?"

"I'm sorry, boss," McMahon said. "You said not to use the phone."

"What is it?"

"It's Burselm. Dessie went to see him last night to talk about how much weight he wanted. It didn't go well."

"Meaning?"

"Burselm is trying to screw you on the price."

"Where's Dessie now?" Jackson said.

"In the office."

Jackson went into the room that he used as his office. Dessie O'Sullivan was sitting on the sofa in the corner. He was a wiry man, tough and nasty, but he looked as if he had gone ten rounds with Tyson Fury. Both sides of his face were bruised, and there was a downward crescent of dried blood from the middle of his forehead to his temple.

"I'm sorry, Tony," he said.

"No, no, no. You got me out of bed. It's Mr. Jackson today." Jackson went around the desk and sat down. "What happened to your face? Burselm did that?"

O'Sullivan nodded. "I went to see him last night, like you said. I told him we had product to move and asked him how much he thought he could handle. He said he wants five keys, but that he's only going to pay ten per key."

"And you told him he could fuck off."

"I did. I said the price was the price and that you don't negotiate. But he said that he wouldn't discuss it with me. And then he..." He stopped and gestured up at his cuts and bruises.

"You let him do that?"

"I wasn't looking," O'Sullivan protested. "He blindsided me."

"You're pathetic."

Jackson sighed. Burselm was a mid-level dealer who worked north Manchester. He had a little network of dealers beneath him, and he had been causing trouble for the last few months. He had somehow fostered the idea that he was in a position to barter on the price that he paid for Jackson's coke. Jackson didn't barter—never had and never would—

and now it looked as if Burselm was going to need a reminder of how things were.

"You need me to do anything?" O'Sullivan asked.

"No, *Desmond*," he said, using the man's given name because he knew that he hated it. "Just piss off."

O'Sullivan got up, the pain on his face suggesting that Burselm had worked him over pretty good, and left the room. Jackson opened the safe that he kept under the desk. He had a CZ-75 semi-automatic 9mm pistol that he had bought from a contact in the Czech Republic. He wrapped his hand around the black pistol, popped out the magazine and checked that it was loaded. He pushed it back into the port and slid the weapon into the waistband of his trousers. Burselm was an irritating little blowhard with ideas above his station, and Jackson was going to make an example of him. He knew how the business worked: you gave an inch; they took a mile. That wasn't about to happen to him. He closed and locked the safe and went back out into the main room.

"Where you going?" McMahon said.

"Burselm." He turned to O'Sullivan. "Where does he live?"

"He's got a place in the city."

"Where?"

"The Leftbank building in Spinningfields. He rents the penthouse."

"Of *course* he does," Jackson said.

27

Milton, Chase and Hicks left the apartments and got into the vehicles that they planned to use for the job: Milton and Hicks were in the Ford Galaxy, and Chase was in the Mondeo.

Milton heard Ziggy's voice in his ear. *"This is Ziggy,"* he said. *"Comms check. Over."*

Chase had purchased four pay-as-you-go phones yesterday evening and they each had one, all of them patched together on a conference call. Milton pressed his finger into his ear until the earpiece was tight and brought the microphone around so that it hung just below his chin.

"This is Milton. Copy that. Over."

"This is Hicks. Roger. Over."

"Baxter. Over."

"This is Ziggy. Comms check all good. Over."

"Update on Jackson?" Milton asked.

"Still at the warehouse. Having a vigorous exchange of views with the two other men there. No sign that he's leaving yet."

"Keep us posted."

"Copy that. Traffic is clear to your destination. You'll be on site in ten minutes."

They passed the stadium for the Salford City Roosters Rugby League club and kept going, continuing beneath the interchange where the M60 met the M602. Ziggy's report was accurate; the morning rush hour had died down and traffic was flowing easily. They reached Worsley, and Milton navigated onto the eastbound A580. They reached the junction that Milton had selected during yesterday's scouting and turned off the road. He drove on until he reached a small business estate with a car park between two rows of industrial buildings. He slotted the Galaxy into an empty space and waited until Chase parked up alongside.

He opened the door and hopped down.

"Good luck," Hicks said.

"And you. See you after."

Milton went over to the Mondeo and got into the front next to Chase.

"Ready?"

"Ready."

"Just follow the plan. I'll be there if you need me."

"I can handle myself."

"I know you can. But we don't know how he's going to react when his day goes bad. He has form for violence."

"Relax. I got this."

Milton nodded and clapped Chase on the shoulder. He opened the door again and got out.

The earpiece crackled. *"This is Ziggy. Target is on the move."*

"This is Milton," he said into the microphone. "Confirmed. I'm on foot, heading back to the junction. Over."

Chase and Hicks reversed out of the parking spaces,

turned the vehicles around and drove south again, retracing their route.

Milton set off, walking briskly.

∽

ZIGGY POPPED the top on a tube of Pringles and stuffed a handful into his mouth. His visit to the junction at midnight last night had yielded dividends. First of all, he had hijacked the live feed from the traffic camera on the pedestrian bridge that was just a little distance from the crossroads. He had that feed on one of three screens, watching as traffic rushed beneath it. His second screen included two command lines: the first would communicate with the override that he had installed in the control box that oversaw the traffic lights at the junction, and the second allowed him to interfere with Jackson's Bentley. His third screen included a muted police scanner tuned to the frequency used by the Manchester police, and a map with four moving dots: three showed the locations of the phones being used by Chase, Milton and Hicks, and a fourth represented the position of the anti-theft beacon in Jackson's car.

Hicks and Chase were stationary, near to the junction with the main road.

Milton was walking along the side of the A580.

Jackson was approaching from the west.

He took out another handful of Pringles and slotted them into his mouth.

"This is Ziggy," he said as he munched the crisps. "Target will be in the box in three minutes."

∽

Hicks pulled out in the Galaxy, turned left and puttered down the road. Chase was in front of him in the Mondeo, with no one else between them. Hicks glanced into the mirror and saw three cars behind him, with the lights of another further down the road.

"*Check in,*" Milton said over the conference line.

"*This is Baxter. I'm in position.*"

"This is Hicks. Same."

Ziggy's voice came on the line. "*Target is thirty seconds away.*"

⁓

Milton ambled slowly up to the traffic lights that controlled the flow at the junction between the A580 and Moorside Road. He reached the junction and looked to the left. He could see the Ford there now, ready to turn right but held up by the red light.

Traffic was flowing from right to left. Milton tried to spot Anthony Jackson's Bentley. He couldn't.

"Ziggy?" Milton said.

"*Fifteen seconds. Get ready.*"

Milton walked up to the junction. He reached for his rucksack and took it off his back, unzipping it and reaching inside until his fingers brushed against the edge of the sealed packet of cocaine.

⁓

Chase was held at the junction by a red light. The road ahead was wide by British standards, with three lanes in each direction and a pedestrian bridge immediately to his left. There was a decent flow of traffic in both directions, with the lights that he could see showing green.

He looked into his mirror and saw the Galaxy three cars behind him. That was just as they had planned it; Hicks was there for backup and, if that was not required, would provide Milton with a means to quickly leave the scene.

He heard an angry honk of the horn from the car behind him. Chase raised both arms in a gesture of helplessness that he hoped would be visible to the driver.

What could he do? It wasn't his fault the light wasn't changing.

∼

ZIGGY WATCHED the blinking blue dot that represented the Bentley, then changed his attention to the traffic camera on the pedestrian walkway.

The Bentley came into view.

"Switching lights now."

He pressed a button on the keyboard and activated the command that he had prepared in advance.

The traffic lights were wirelessly connected to the wider Manchester network. The components were simple: each light had a sensor that detected oncoming cars and was connected to traffic controllers that read the sensor's inputs and controlled the colour of the lights. The controllers for this junction were located in a metal cabinet next to the footbridge, and they communicated with themselves and the central server by way of radio. Ziggy had opened the box and found a debug port that had been left open for testing purposes. He had plugged in a small homemade radio receiver. Now, as the controllers received his message, they switched over to the script that he had prepared: the lights on the east and westbound A580 went red.

Ziggy looked over at the feed from the camera on the bridge and zoomed in once until he could make out the distinctive shape of the Bentley Continental. He was about to radio the information to the others, but Milton got there first.

"This is Milton. Jackson is the third car in line. Repeat: the Bentley is the third car."

"This is Ziggy. Confirming that. Ready, Chase?"

"This is Chase. Do it."

Ziggy moused down to the second open command box and hit return.

"Switching lights to green."

28

Milton waited at the pedestrian crossing. He could see Chase inside the Mondeo: he was watching the lights.

All of the lights that governed the junction were red; then, all at once, they changed.

Red and orange.

Green.

The first car to cross the junction was a VW Golf.

Chase held his position.

The second was a Range Rover Sport.

The third car, just behind the Range Rover, was a Bentley Continental.

The Golf rolled out.

The Range Rover followed.

Chase pressed down on the accelerator and the Mondeo lurched ahead. The impact looked unavoidable. The Mondeo struck the offside-front wheel of the Bentley with a hefty impact, causing the front of Jackson's car to slide out into the middle of the road. The rear end skidded into the traffic island, slicing through the yellow plastic warning bollard and coming to rest against the raised kerb.

Milton kept walking.

The rear of the Bentley was alongside the dotted lines where pedestrians were encouraged to cross and, as Milton approached, he could see that he would be able to reach over without even breaking stride. He couldn't have asked for more.

The driver's side of the vehicle was facing Milton and, as he approached, the door opened and Anthony Jackson stepped out into the road. He was a big man, with rounded shoulders that looked powerful and arms that were bunched with muscle. His waist was tapered and his legs were solid. He went around the front of the car so that he could inspect the damage.

The front of the Mondeo had tangled with the Bentley, with the result that the two cars had been locked together during their slide across the road. The Ford had continued onward so that it was now facing down the road in the wrong direction.

Chase got out, stared at the damage, then turned to Jackson. "What are you doing, man?"

Jackson turned. "What am *I* doing? You ran the light, you dick!"

"I was on green. *You* ran the light. Look."

He pointed across the road to where Ziggy had switched the light back to red.

Jackson was distracted. It was now or never.

Milton closed in.

"This is Ziggy. The doors are unlocked."

THE CRASH HAD BLOCKED the road in all directions, and traffic was snarling up on both the main road and the road from which Chase had emerged. An older woman was getting out of a Fiat Punto and, behind her, two men in a white panel van were watching proceedings with obvious interest.

"My light was green," Chase protested.

"*Mine* was green," Jackson said.

Chase shook his head. "You must have run the red."

Jackson got a little closer. "What are you?"

Chase looked back down the road and saw Milton. He was walking toward the stricken Bentley.

"What do you mean?"

"Your accent. What are you—American?"

"What does it have to do with anything?"

"What does it have to *do* with anything? You drive on the other side of the road. Maybe you think you can drive through a red light."

"It's the same," he said. "And, anyway, it was *green*."

The old woman behind him stepped forward. "It *was* green."

"Mind your business," Jackson snapped.

"I think maybe the police would like to know what happened," she said, standing her ground.

"No one asked you," Jackson spat. "Go back to your car and drive away."

Milton was at the car now. Chase didn't need to hold Jackson for much longer.

The old woman took out a phone from her purse and tapped the screen.

"What are you doing?" Jackson said.

"Calling the police. You could've killed him."

"Put it away," Jackson said.

He took a step toward her and reached out with his left hand, grabbing her by the wrist and yanking the phone away from her ear.

Chase reached over and took Jackson's wrist, forcing it down and away from the woman. He left himself open to what he suspected might come next, knowing that a moment of pain would be worth it to seal his unfortunate antagonist's fate. Chase left his chin undefended, inviting Jackson to strike him, and he did just that, a right-handed jab that landed on the side of his jaw.

His vision sparked with little detonations of light as he stumbled back. He went down on one knee.

Chase heard sirens from somewhere close at hand.

The woman screamed.

～

MILTON REACHED the back of the Bentley. He opened the rear door, took out the brick of cocaine and tossed it onto the back seat. He had used a knife to slice open one end of the plastic that sheathed the brick. The cocaine inside spilled out, a splash of white against the dark leather upholstery.

Without breaking stride, he continued on his way.

～

CHASE GOT UP. He saw the flashing blue light of a police patrol car as it raced in from the east, cutting across the junction and coming to a stop next to the two crashed cars. Two officers got out and hurried over to where Anthony Jackson was arguing with the old woman.

"He stole my phone," she said. "He ran a red light and hit

that man; then he punched him in the face. It's road rage, that's what it is. Assault. You need to arrest him."

One of the officers came over to where Chase was standing. He made a show of being unsteady on his feet.

"You okay, sir?"

"He hit me," he mumbled.

"Do you want to sit down?"

The other officer made her way over to the Bentley and looked in through the rear window. Chase watched, saw her eyes widen and then her jaw drop. She put her hand to her radio and spoke into the microphone. Chase guessed that she was calling for backup.

Jackson noticed her, too. "What are you doing?"

"Stay where you are, please, sir," the male officer said to him.

"What is she looking at?"

Jackson turned his back to the male officer as he swivelled to face the car. Hicks saw the weapon in his waistband at the same time as the policeman did.

"Gun!" the officer yelled. "He's got a gun!"

The policeman reached for his belt and took out the yellow Taser that he wore in a holster. He aimed and fired; the two electrodes snaked out and hit Jackson in the shoulder and arm. The Taser clicked and chuckled as it sent fifty thousand volts along the wires that tethered the prongs to the unit; Jackson went stiff and then collapsed, his muscles contracting all at once.

"Taser, Taser, Taser," the officer called out. "Stay calm, sir. You've been Tasered."

29

Ellie sat in the back of the car as they drove north. There were three hundred and fifty miles between Bogotá and Medellín. The Autopista was in excellent condition and not particularly busy. The satnav had predicted a journey time of eight and a half hours, and it looked as if the prediction would be accurate. They had left Bogotá at six that morning, and the satnav suggested that they would reach their destination around half-two, in ninety minutes.

She was with Luis Miguel and David Fuentes, the two DEA agents who had been on La Bruja's tail for the last six months. Miguel was driving and Fuentes was in the passenger seat.

"I never asked," Fuentes said, looking at her in the mirror. "You been to Colombia before?"

"First time," she said.

"And? What do you think?"

"Not exactly what I expected."

"You expected it to be like it was? Escobar? Gold-plated revolvers?"

"I don't know," she said. "I read the file. I know it's different now. Even so, it doesn't match what you see on TV."

"Medellín is pleasant now. It's a tourist destination. There are parts you wouldn't want to get lost in, same as anywhere, but Poblado is nice. The botanical gardens. Guatapé. You get the chance, you should check it out."

"This isn't a vacation," she said, and then, because she realised she sounded catty, she added, "Sorry. I know what you mean. How long have you two been down here?"

"Years," Miguel said with a rueful smile.

"Two years," Fuentes added. "They sent us down after we got reports that El Centro and La Frontera were looking to work together. We were here when La Bruja made her move."

"The locals got a kick out of it," Miguel said. "There's always been a romantic side to the narcos. They saw Pablo as Robin Hood, despite the fact that they knew he was a mass-murdering scumbag. There's an element of taking it to the man about it, that kind of thing, and she's got the same thing in spades."

"It's almost a source of national pride," Fuentes said. "Their soccer team might suck, but their narcos are the best in the world. I mean, obviously totally fucked up, but in a place like this, where there hasn't been much to be proud of for years, you can kind of see why they might think that way."

"It's also the main reason why we're going to have to tread really fucking carefully when we get down there," Miguel said. "It's better than it was, but the *Paisas* still won't like the idea of us taking her out. They'll see it as a slap in the face."

Ellie felt the usual irritation at having basic intelligence recited to her by male colleagues, as if the two of them thought that she hadn't spent hours in the file as she prepared for the operation. She was used to it, though. Orville had been the same, and there had been male colleagues all the way back to the Academy who had taken it upon themselves to help her out when help was the last thing that she needed. She remembered the early days and the frustration that she had felt at their condescension. Taking it personally hadn't gotten her anywhere, however; on the contrary, it had started to give her an unjustified reputation as prickly and difficult to work with.

So she had made a decision, years ago, that, instead of allowing it to get under her skin, she would demonstrate to her colleagues in terms that they would understand that she didn't need their help. That meant that she would be a better shot on the range at Quantico. That she would train until she was fitter than they were. And that, most of all, she would bring in the kind of scalps that no one could ignore. It was the inspiration that she had relied upon to bring down Morten Lundquist in Michigan, and it would be the same for La Bruja in Medellín.

30

Sergeant Benjamin Weaver looked out of the window of the car at the wide-open spaces in front of them. They had chosen the same spot as before for the meet, a track in the middle of nowhere, surrounded by banana plantations on all sides. It took them an hour to drive here from Urabá, a large town that was buried deep in Colombia's Caribbean jungle. It was a long and uncomfortable drive on poor roads, and that was before they turned off and had to negotiate the potholed tracks that eventually led here. It was hot, too, and the air-con in the four-wheel drive had only worked intermittently, perhaps in complaint at the amount of work that it was being asked to do. But the inconveniences, while irritating, were necessary. Discretion was essential. It would not do for a senior member of the Firm to be seen meeting the leader of the biggest cocaine cartel in the world.

Weaver was in the back of the car. Number Eight was driving and Number Six was in the back with him. Eight had only been recruited to the Group a year earlier, and this was to be his first operational posting. Six was more seasoned. She had been one of the first recruits brought into the Group after it had been reconstituted. Seniority was a relative concept when none of the new agents had the tenure of the men and women whom they had replaced, but, of course, that would be something that came with time. Control had been pleased with the restocking of the roster, and the early results as the agents had gone into the field had been encouraging.

"Just up here," Weaver said as they approached the tumbledown shack that he remembered from before.

"I can't see anything," Eight said.

"She'll be here," Weaver said.

Eight had been in 22 SAS, B Squadron, until Control had plucked him out and offered him the chance of a career with far more excitement than even the Regiment could offer. Weaver had reviewed his file and had noted that the headshrinkers in the basement had observed an occasional impatience in his character. It was a small blemish on an otherwise spotless report. Eight's physical prowess was exemplary, as one would have expected from a member of the SAS. More to the point, he had shown nothing in his psych evaluation that would have disqualified him from membership in the Group. The screening process included a variation of the Milgram experiment, with possible recruits measured for their willingness to obey an authority figure when asked to perform acts that conflicted with their consciences. The files that Control would hand down for action often contained instructions that could be said to be —at best—ethically questionable. Eight's results had indicated a degree of psychopathy in his makeup; far from striking his name and pulling him from the process, Control had instructed Weaver to fast-track him.

"What time were they supposed to be here?"

"Fourteen hundred hours," Weaver said. "We're early. They'll be here."

Weaver had been in Colombia for three months, handling the pointy end of an operation that had required a very specific kind of diplomacy. He had served in Colombia before, all the way back in the nineties when the country had been ruled first by Escobar and then by the Gentlemen of Cali, with the government locked in battle with the cartels and the communist guerrillas who terrorised the south of the country. The CIA and MI6 had nudged and prodded the Colombian government so that it did not stray from the path the West had chosen for it. The communists had become a serious problem, and it had been decided that the country could not fall; it was a bulwark against communism, and, if *it* went, then all of South America might easily go with it. Weaver had operated in the grey spaces behind official British policy, working with—and often against—the Drug Enforcement Agency's efforts to destroy the cartels in an attempt to enforce the War on Drugs started by George H. W. Bush and then continued by Bill Clinton.

The cartels were important to the functioning of the state. They owned the government, with ministers and even the president bought and sold like chattels at the market. If the cartels went down, the government would go down, too; a void would be created and chaos would ensue. Weaver had helped to hold back that chaos, and he was still holding it back now. Twenty years later and nothing had changed.

"Eyes front," Six said.

Weaver looked out of the windshield, squinting into the bright sun as a Jeep rolled to a stop on the other side of the road.

"They're here," he said.

31

Weaver got out of the car and made his way across the rough stretch of land that led to the shack. The banana plants had been cleared away here, and the building was used as a store by the farmer who worked the fields. There was a wide overhang that offered a respite from the sun, and Weaver waited there for La Bruja to join him. Eight and Six came, too, taking up position a little way off so as not to crowd the meeting.

La Bruja stepped out of the vehicle. Weaver didn't know very much about her other than her *nom de guerre* and a little of her history, although how much of that had been polluted by the legend that had attached to her was difficult to make out. The Antioquians had always invested their criminals with outlaw status; it had been that way with Escobar, and it was the same with her. Her nickname was a reference to her ability to do things that could only seemingly be explained by recourse to the supernatural. No photographs of her had ever been published. She had the ability to disappear into the jungle. And her reach extended across all of Central and South America and even into the

United States itself. Songs had been written about her and the things that she had done. Weaver had listened to a *norteño* track on YouTube that eulogised La Bruja's role in the death of the United States ambassador.

A big man got out of the vehicle and led the way across the road and up to the shack. Björn Thorsson—Number One—was broad shouldered and had the blond hair that marked him out as a Scandinavian. He was six foot four and built like a truck. He had been recruited to the Group by Michael Pope and had been the only agent to survive the cull that had been instigated following Pope's disappearance. Thorsson was an Icelander, although he had lived in the United Kingdom for years. He had served in the SAS with distinction, and he had carried that excellent track record into the more clandestine world of the Group. He had risen to the pinnacle of the Group on merit as much as by the fact of his survival, and had been an obvious choice for this particular operation.

La Bruja and Thorsson reached the shack.

"Good afternoon," Weaver said to La Bruja.

"Señor. It is good to see you. I hope the journey was not too difficult?"

"A little hot."

"Summer in Colombia," she said with a shrug. "It is what it is."

Weaver turned to Thorsson and nodded in acknowledgement. "Number One."

"Sir."

La Bruja did not know Number One's details, not even his name. She referred to him as Eidur, a name that the big Icelander had suggested as his legend in a nod to Eiður Smári Guðjohnsen, the country's most famous footballing export.

La Bruja gestured to Eight and Six. "Who are your friends?"

"They work with me," he said. "Like Eidur."

"And you have need of them here?"

"I don't," he said. "But you do. Shall we go inside?"

32

They opened the shack and went in. The planks of wood that made up the walls were rotting in some places and did not fit together neatly in others. Shafts of sunlight arrowed their way inside, lancing through the gloom and highlighting the motes of dust that had been disturbed by their arrival.

Weaver took off his dark glasses. "It went well?"

"Simple enough. Cochrane was an arrogant man—a typical gringo. They think, because they are Americans, that they can treat Colombia as they wish. They think that they can seek to dictate its future without fear of consequence. He learned the error of his ways."

"It won't be the end of the matter," Weaver said. "The accord might not have been signed, but the DEA is sending more agents. And the president will be making a speech tomorrow, in which he will make it clear that putting an end to the cartels is now a declared aim of his administration."

"We have heard that many times before from many different presidents."

"I know you have," he said. "But the assassination of a

sitting ambassador demands a very public response. The Colombian government has no option but to cooperate."

"None of this is unexpected. We discussed it."

"We did. But our friends in the CIA wanted you to know that there is going to be a lot of additional heat down here. The advice I have been asked to pass on by our friends in Langley is that it would be wise to keep a low profile for a while."

She smiled. "Do I look like Don Pablo, señor? I do not have a ranch. I do not have a dozen *fincas* or mansions in Bogotá. I live here." She waved her hand to encompass the dense trees outside the shack. "In the plantations. In the jungle. I can only be found by those who *I* wish to find me."

"Don't underestimate the attention that you're going to get. They will be putting drones in the air."

"And we will shoot them down."

"These drones fly at sixty thousand feet and stay in the air for days at a time. You wouldn't see them even if you knew where to look, and you won't. You might even warrant a satellite."

"What do you advise?"

"Don't use a cellphone. And no one should mention you by name if *they* use a cellphone. Be sure of the loyalty of everyone in your inner circle. *Everyone*. The bounty on your head will be significant—fifteen million was the number I heard."

She snorted. "Loyalty? You are funny. No one would be so foolish as to betray me. Money is useless when you are dead."

Weaver had met La Bruja several times over the course of his time in the country. The security services of the US and UK had kept tabs on the swirling vortex of smaller cartels that had sprung up after the demolition of the global organisations that had dominated the narcotics industry at the start of the millennium. They had watched as she had consolidated her power, wiping out those collectives who were at her level and swallowing up their soldiers and resources. She had grown quickly, moving on to larger targets and wiping *them* out, too. She was impressive and ruthless. The West had been looking for a proxy, and La Bruja had been shortlisted.

Weaver had been sent to vet the elusive woman at the cartel's head and had been impressed. Indeed, he had been so impressed with the scale of La Bruja's ambition that he had reported that she might be open to the more audacious ploy that had been on the drawing board ever since the assassination of El Patrón in Mexico. His death in the Sierra Madre had left La Frontera vulnerable to a hostile takeover, and there existed an opportunity to merge both production and distribution of cocaine into one body. The kind of influence that an enterprise of that magnitude could wield in South America had been the West's wet dream for years, and the spooks at Langley and Vauxhall Cross had leapt at the chance.

Official US policy was that the war on drugs had to be won, but an influential clique within the CIA was happy to let the flow continue if that meant it could use the cartel to wield its influence. Lincoln, Navarro and their cronies were wary of going into overt opposition to the DEA and State Department, so the Firm had been tasked with heading up the operation. Weaver had returned to Antioquia and had made her the offer. The Western security services would help her to build a Pan-American cartel, more powerful than any that had gone before, in return for her assistance in buying influence in local and national government.

And she had said yes.

Weaver looked out of the open door. The heat rose from the baked ground in heady waves, and, high above, a hawk called out as it drifted on the thermals.

"I expect you would like an update on the matter you mentioned the last time we met?" she said.

"I would."

"We have made contact with Diego Pastrana and Alberto Serpa. They were both open to the idea of receiving our money to assist them with their re-election campaigns."

That was good. Pastrana and Serpa were jostling for the leadership of the Liberal Party. If La Bruja could buy them both, it would guarantee political influence that could translate into real power if the Liberals formed the government after the next election.

"The president?"

"Rubiano makes a virtue of his purity. We do not believe that there is a realistic prospect of arranging his cooperation."

"So we just make sure that he loses."

La Bruja smiled. "That might not be necessary. We have found some suggestion that his virtue does not extend to his marriage. He has been having an affair with a member of parliament."

"Go on."

"The member of parliament is male. My country has many qualities, señor, but tolerance is not one of them. If it were to become known that the president is cheating on his wife with a man..." She let the sentence drift away before adding, "It could precipitate the general election that you are so keen to see."

"That's very interesting. Let me take instructions. Don't use it yet."

"We will wait."

Weaver mopped his brow again. If anything, it was getting hotter.

"There's one other favour that I need," she said.

"Go on."

"An associate of ours has been arrested in your country."

"'An associate'? What do you mean—a drug dealer?"

"One of our partners. He is responsible for imports into the United Kingdom."

"What happened to him?"

"He was arrested."

Weaver spread his hands. "So hire a lawyer and get him out."

"It won't be as easy as that. He was arrested with a firearm and a kilo of our product in the back of his car. The best lawyer in the world wouldn't be able to help him and, speaking frankly, we are worried that he might try to do a deal. He tells the police what he knows about us, they let him go."

"And you don't want that to happen."

"No," she said. "We do not."

"What's his name?"

"Anthony Jackson. Can I leave that with you?"

"You can," he said.

"Thank you."

Weaver walked out onto the porch and La Bruja followed him.

"I think we're done," he said. "Be careful. Don't underestimate the government response to what happened. I'll provide you with intelligence when I receive it through the usual channel."

"I understand," she said. "Thank you."

"There's one more thing—we need to make sure that you are well protected."

She nodded over to Number One. "I am."

"We think that you might need more."

"So that is why you have brought your two friends?"

"It is. I'd like them to go with you."

"And if I say that I don't need them?"

"I would say that was unwise."

"Or if I told you that I don't want them? If I said that one gringo is enough, that three would make me look weak, like I needed to beg for help."

"Then I am afraid that I would have to insist," he said. "And I would remind you that the success that you have achieved over the last few months is almost entirely due to the help and support that we have been able to provide. I would ask you to cast your mind back to the favours that were done for you when you said that you were ambitious. Do I need to remind you what those favours included?"

He was ready to list them: the drive-by shooting of Felix Rivera, the head of the Colombian Ministry of National Defense; the bombing of the meeting between the capos of the Medellín cartel when the question of how to deal with El Centro was discussed; the eliminations—six killings, all within an hour of one another—of the recalcitrant old-timers who had been holding up the merger of El Centro and La Frontera. Group Fifteen had been busy on her behalf. Indeed, Six had been responsible for several of those deaths.

She looked as if she might argue, but she was nothing if not shrewd. She knew that it would do her no favours to make enemies of her friends. The intelligence that was being supplied by Lincoln—tip-offs on Colombian army action, satellite imagery, the location of rivals and the relative strengths and weaknesses at the Mexican border—was all invaluable. On top of that could be added the benefit of having a soldier with Number One's pedigree as the notional head of her security. The flip side, which Weaver knew she was also smart enough to grasp, was that it could all be very easily turned against her.

She nodded to Six and Eight. "What are their names?"

Weaver indicated that the two agents should come over to join them.

"This is Rebecca," he said, pointing to Six.

La Bruja squinted into the sunlight as she looked at her; then she turned to Eight. "And you?"

"Justin."

"Rebecca and Justin. Not your real names, I suppose?"

Six shook her head. "No. But they'll do for now."

"Very well," she said. "Welcome to Colombia."

Weaver turned to Björn. "A word, please."

33

Weaver led Thorsson a little way from the shack. He found the big Icelander a daunting presence. He was huge, with a physicality that was impossible to miss, but there was a calm confidence about him that was just as impressive. He had been recruited to the Group by Michael Pope after he had observed how Thorsson had gone about seeking revenge on the man who had killed his sister. He had assaulted a castle in Scotland and taken out an American financier and his colleague, the men responsible for sending a hired gun to murder the girl. Pope had provided Thorsson with the killer's location at the same time he offered him a place in the Group.

Thorsson had killed the assassin and accepted the offer.

He had more blood on his hands since then.

Much more.

"Sir?" he said once they were out of earshot.

"Tell me about the hit," Weaver said.

"It was simple enough. The intelligence was accurate. Six came alongside, deployed the mine and drove off. It took seconds."

"And we're completely deniable?"

"I believe so."

"Good. Because discretion can't be understated here."

"I know, sir. You can relax."

"It's Control who needs reassuring, not me. She hasn't been in post long. She needs to get a result with this, but if your involvement came out? That would not be good."

Group Fifteen's reinvigoration had not been without its challenges. The murder of Vivian Bloom hadn't helped. The old man had held the disparate parts of the Firm together, but his death had removed some of the lubrication that had made things work. The new Control had been fighting hard to make the case for the old way of doing things. Weaver knew that there were people in the Firm—newer brooms, spooks with big ideas and no experience—who would have preferred that the Group be disbanded forever, and its functions taken over by nameless drone operators who would bomb the enemies of the state from Portakabins a thousand miles away from the target. Control had argued that they would always need to have agents on the ground, men and women able to gather intelligence and then take nuanced decisions based upon what they had found. She had won the debate for now, but she knew that she would need to demonstrate the continued utility of the Group until the case was unarguable.

Number One sensed Weaver's disquiet. He nodded to the car where La Bruja was waiting for him. "She doesn't come out of the shadows often," he said. "There's no reason why anyone would know who I really am, beyond her and Hector del Pozo and a couple of others. And if I get the impression that I've been compromised"—he shrugged—"well, I'll make sure I leave everything nice and clean. My orders on that are clear."

"Good." They walked on a little. "Just make sure she knows how serious the blowback on this is going to be. The State Department has no idea that Langley—more precisely, a small subsection of bitter old spooks at Langley—effectively sanctioned the assassination of an American diplomat. The reports that we're getting out of Washington are that they are very, very angry and very, very serious about demonstrating the consequences for those kinds of actions. American hegemony won't survive for long if the bad guys get the idea that you can knock off their diplomats without getting even a slap on the wrist for it."

"How big is this slap likely to be?"

"Very big. La Bruja needs to take it seriously."

"She's no fool," he said. "But I'll make sure."

"You have backup, too. You know Six."

"I do," Thorsson said. "She's good."

"And so is Eight."

"I don't doubt it. We'll keep her out of the way until this blows over."

"Good man. Stay in touch."

"Yes, sir," Thorsson said.

34

Milton sat back in the window seat and gazed out of the porthole window as they started their descent. He had spent the morning shutting down the Manchester operation—cleaning out the Airbnbs and disposing of the Galaxy. Chase had been taken to the police station, where he had been interviewed by officers about what had happened with Anthony Jackson. His account of the crash—that the lights had been green—had been corroborated by the elderly woman who had witnessed it from behind. She had gone on to confirm what had happened between Chase and Jackson in the immediate aftermath, corroborating his account that Jackson had been the aggressor. The police had asked Chase to remain in Manchester until they had taken a full statement, which, they suggested, might take a day or two.

Milton, Hicks and Ziggy had travelled separately once again, and the time alone had allowed Milton the opportunity to reflect on what they had achieved and what remained to be done. The operation to remove the obstruction that Jackson had represented was a success, but it was just the first step of many. Jackson was an impediment to Milton's ultimate objective, simply an obstacle that he had needed to remove. That, now, was done. The road ahead was clear, at least until the next obstacle.

He realised, as he gazed down through the clouds at the Netherlands below, that if he was to be successful, he would be following the supply line that delivered cocaine backwards. He would start with its final destination and trace the chain all the way back to its source. Anthony Jackson was the penultimate stage of that supply line. He took deliveries from the cartel and divided them up, remitting consignments to partners around the country. Those men and women would divide their shares again, providing stock to the dealers who would then be responsible for the retail side of the operation. Milton had had experience of that grubby final transaction before; it didn't take much to recall the time that he had spent on the streets of East London in the aftermath of his attempted resignation from Group Fifteen. If he achieved nothing else beyond this, at least he would have choked the flow of cocaine on its way into the country. He wasn't naïve; business would adjust and someone would appear to take advantage of the gap in the market that had been created—but that would take a little time.

The next person up the chain was López, and then, through him, Milton would try to follow the drugs to the source.

"We'll be on the ground in ten minutes' time," the captain announced over the intercom. "Crew to prepare the cabin for landing, please."

Milton knew that his tactics would have to change now that he had more seasoned operators in his sights. Anthony Jackson didn't know it now—and never would—but he had been fortunate. Milton had given some thought to the option of simply taking him out. It would have been simple enough to break into his house and put a bullet into his head, and he could have achieved that without needing help from Hicks, Chase or Ziggy. But he had decided against it. He knew that eventually he was going to have to embrace the side of his personality that he had tried to smother for so long, to welcome back the pitiless violence that had been his stock-in-trade for the better part of a decade, but he had decided that that could wait.

There were ways to sideline Jackson without murdering him.

The murdering would come later.

35

Milton took an Uber to the apartment in Houthaven. Hicks and Ziggy were waiting for him. Hicks was cooking an omelette in the kitchen and Ziggy, not surprisingly, was busy at work on his laptops.

"Hey," Hicks said.

Milton took off his jacket and tossed it over the back of the sofa. "When did you get in?"

"An hour ago," Hicks said.

Ziggy took off his headphones, music audible from them until he moused over to his Spotify window and pressed pause. "Evening."

"All okay?"

He nodded that it was. "I've got something for you both," he said. "Here."

Hicks slid the omelette out of the pan and onto a plate and brought it over to the desk. Milton followed. Ziggy turned one of the laptops around so that they could both see the screen.

"I just downloaded this from the police," he said. "Watch."

He pressed play. It was a video recording. The camera was up high, looking down on a table with four people sat around it. Anthony Jackson was in shot with a middle-aged woman sat alongside him. Two men Milton hadn't seen before faced them. The room was bland and spare, with no furniture visible apart from the table and chairs. A caption at the bottom-left of the shot read MANCHESTER CONSTABULARY, and to the right was the date—this afternoon—and a running clock.

One of the men facing Jackson spoke first.

"Mr. Jackson, my name is Detective Inspector Richard Wright. I work for Manchester CID."

"I know who you are," Jackson said.

"I'd like to talk to you about what we found in the back of your car."

"Mr. Jackson is not prepared to discuss that," the woman —evidently Jackson's solicitor—said.

"I think he'll want to answer the allegations that we're going to make against him," the detective said. "In particular, I'd like him to explain why there was a kilogram of cocaine in his car."

The solicitor started to reply, but Jackson spoke over her. "I've never seen that before," he said. "I swear on my kid's life, I have no idea how that got in there."

Ziggy pressed pause. "Look at his face," he said. "Just look at it. He knows he's fucked."

Milton gestured for him to be quiet and pressed play again.

"I'm sorry, Anthony," the detective said. "'I've never seen that before' isn't going to be good enough here. You're going to have to do much better than that."

"It was a fit-up," Jackson spat. "Isn't it obvious? The whole thing was staged. The crash. The bloke who got out of the car—fuck, the old woman, too. Why not? It was all to distract me while someone else planted that shit."

"He's no fool," Hicks opined.

"Sounds very elaborate," the detective went on. "Sounds like the sort of thing that would require a lot of planning."

"So?"

"Who would do something like that, Anthony?"

Jackson started to speak, then stopped.

"What about the gun you were carrying?"

"I got no comment on that."

"You know what you're looking at just for the gun, right?"

"No comment."

Ziggy pressed stop.

"Minimum sentence is five years," Ziggy said. "You've seen his file. He's been a target for customs and the police for years, but he's been too shrewd to give them anything. Not now. They've got him with a gun *and* a kilo of coke in the back of his car. Game over."

"What do you think?" Hicks said. "Ten years?"

"The gun and the coke, plus his history? At least."

"It doesn't matter," Milton said. "López is going to need another partner."

"You got any ideas who that might be?"

"One or two," he said with a thin smile.

36

Milton went out for a haircut and a wet shave and settled back into character as the ambitious John Smith, the upwardly mobile drug dealer who was looking to establish himself as a serious player in the British market.

He returned at seven in the evening.

"Anything from Chase?"

"Just called," Ziggy said. "He's flying out in the morning."

"Jackson?"

"They've charged him. Possession of a prohibited firearm and possession of a class A drug with intent to supply. He won't get bail for that. He's out of commission."

Milton nodded with satisfaction. He took out his phone and the napkin on which he had written the number that he had used to contact Juan Pablo López. He typed out a message, requesting a second meeting.

"Here goes," Milton said.

He pressed send.

"What next?" Ziggy said.

"We wait."

They didn't have to wait for very long.

Milton's phone buzzed. He picked it up and read the message.

"What did he say?" Ziggy said.

"He wants to meet. The club, same as before. Tonight."

~

Milton changed into a pair of two-hundred-euro Edwin jeans and a black turtleneck. He pulled on a pair of brogues and went into the living room.

Ziggy pointed down at his shoes. "Take them off."

"What?"

"Your shoes. Take them off." He held up a pair of boots. "These ones tonight, please."

Milton recognised the boots. They were black leather, with nine metal eyelets on either side and a fashionably distressed look. Milton had bought them in Diesel while they were waiting to approach López for the first time.

"Those are mine," he said. "Right?"

"They are. I've made some changes. Here—look."

Ziggy handed him the boots. Milton took them and realised that one—the right one—felt just a little heavier than the other.

"What have you done?"

"Look at the sole," Ziggy said.

Milton turned the right boot in his hands and looked down at the thick sole. He ran his finger along it and, when he reached the heel, he felt a little indentation that ran in a straight line just below the join between the heel and the midsole. He looked at it more closely and saw the line. It would have been impossible to see if he hadn't known to look for it.

"I've made a little adaptation," Ziggy said, holding up a scalpel and a tube of Gorilla Glue. "There's a GPS receiver and a battery inside. Quad band and operates over 2G, so it should work pretty much anywhere you might end up. The battery ought to last for four, maybe five days."

Milton wondered how safe it would be to wear the boots, and how easy it would be to detect the addition that Ziggy had made. He doubted that he would get through airport security if they x-rayed the boots separately, but that wasn't standard these days. He could put them into hold luggage, too, he decided. The risks, if there were any, were that the device would be discovered by López or whoever came after him. Milton thought the risk was low, and, he had to admit, knowing that his position could be tracked was reassuring. He had no idea where he might end up, and whether he would need backup.

He unlaced the brogues and slipped them off. He put on the boots and laced them up.

"Thank you," he said.

37

Milton called an Uber and sat quietly in the back as the driver made his way through the streets to the club. He was a little nervous, but did his best to put it aside. López would be expecting the same confidence as before, and presenting anything else—especially given what had changed in the interim between the last meeting and now—might be taken as a sign of guilt.

That might be dangerous.

Ziggy was staying back in the apartment to provide operational assistance, and Hicks would be nearby in the event that Milton needed backup on the ground. It was difficult to know how López would react to seeing him again. There was nothing to link Milton to Jackson's difficulties; by the same token, it would have been impossible for López to miss the fact that his business partner had been arrested within a day of the man who was pitching for his business learning that the existing relationship was a problem.

On the other hand, a vacancy had opened up. Milton would offer López a way to fill it, but he was not naïve enough to think that the cartel would not react badly if it suspected that it had been played.

~

THERE WAS no need to speak to the woman at the lectern to get into the club this evening. One of the men who had delivered the cocaine to Milton was waiting there, and as Milton approached, he indicated that he should follow him inside. They went up to the third floor, but, rather than going to the VIP area, they continued to a short corridor with a secure metal door at the end. The man tapped out a code on a keypad that was set into the wall and waited until the lock was released. He pulled the door back and indicated that Milton should go through.

The door opened into a suite of rooms that looked as if they were used to administer the business of the club. There was a plain room with boxes of spirits stacked along two of the walls, and another that had been equipped with a wooden desk that held a PC and several screens displaying the feeds from the club's security cameras. Milton looked at the screens as he passed through and felt vulnerable; Ziggy would be able to access that footage, but there were no cameras in here and, even if there were, Hicks would be unable to get to him if he needed backup.

He was alone. It probably wouldn't be the last time.

"Through here," the man said, opening a door and gesturing that Milton should go through.

He did, and passed into an office. There was a desk with chairs on either side, a sofa opposite that and prints on the walls. It was functional, not lavish, and Milton suspected that it would more usually accommodate the manager of the business rather than the owner. López was sitting on the other side of the desk and, at Milton's approach, the Mexican indicated that he should take the seat opposite.

"Señor Smith," he said, "how are you?"

"Very good. Thank you for seeing me again."

López smiled indulgently. "How can I help you?"

"I wanted to say thanks."

"I heard the delivery was smooth."

"It was. Your men are very professional."

"I pay them well." He glanced over Milton's shoulder to where the man who had brought him inside was standing. Milton couldn't see him, and his presence there was disconcerting; Milton knew that the man's placement in his blind spot was intentional. "And the product? How was it?"

"Just as advertised."

López regarded him shrewdly. "Where is it now?"

"In the process of being sold."

"London?"

"That's where we agreed."

"Very good."

Milton held his eye. "I'd like to place another order."

López clucked his tongue against his teeth. "I don't know."

"Not for the same amount," Milton said, ignoring López's stage-managed hesitation. "I know what we said before, but I want more."

He shook his head. "You know that isn't possible."

"Because of Jackson?"

López was still watching him; surely he knew what had happened in Manchester?

"It's as I said," López said. "We have an existing arrangement."

"I was hoping you might be persuaded to reconsider. I won't step on his toes. He won't even know that I'm there."

"And if he *did* know? How do you think he would react to that?"

"I'm a big boy," Milton said. "I can look after myself."

López exhaled. "I really think that might be more trouble than it is worth."

"How can you say that?"

"I'm sorry?"

"I haven't told you *what* it might be worth."

López smiled. "True. I suppose not." He flicked his fingers. "Fine, go on—indulge me."

"A million dollars. Twenty-five per key, for forty keys."

"Forty? Really?"

Milton held his eye. "Surely that's not more than you can handle?"

López snorted disdainfully. "The weight is not a problem." He leaned back against the upholstered back of the seat and crossed his arms.

"So?" Milton pressed. "What is?"

"You know the problem, señor."

Milton leaned back. "That's for you to consider. The offer is there. My money is as good as his."

López paused, then gave a nod. "Let me think about it."

"Fine," Milton said. "I can live with that." He knew not to outstay his welcome, and stood. "Thank you."

López remained seated. He smiled again and pointed a finger in Milton's direction. "You are tenacious, Señor Smith. I hope you understand how seriously my employees and I take our business. I would counsel strongly against wasting my time."

"Was there anything wrong with my money?"

López shook his head.

"I paid quickly."

"You did."

"And I didn't negotiate."

"That's not necessarily a reason for pride. Perhaps it suggests that you are a bad businessman."

Milton shook his head. "I didn't want to show you any disrespect. You didn't know me. You still don't. And I appreciate the fact that you said yes."

"Saying yes to our first transaction was a lot easier than saying yes to what you are proposing now."

"I know that. And I know you have to check me out. It's fine. I'm not offended—I'd do the same. But I'm not wasting your time."

"So you say." López dismissed him with a wave of his hand. "We will contact you."

"When?"

"Soon. Stay in Amsterdam. Goodbye, Señor Smith."

∼

MILTON LEFT THE CLUB. He paused outside, looking first at the long line of impatient revellers before pretending to flick through his phone, using the opportunity to glance out into the darkness of the park that was opposite the building. There was a dirty-looking tramp on the park bench opposite the club, laid out flat and seemingly asleep. Milton ignored him and walked away, calling an Uber.

The car was nearby and arrived within minutes. Milton got inside and looked in the mirrors as the driver pulled away; the lights of a car that had been waiting outside the club had flicked on, and now it had pulled out and was trailing along behind them.

Milton took out his phone and called Hicks.

"You saw it?"

"The Audi A5? Two guys inside."

"Thanks," Milton said. "I'll see you when you get back."

He ended the call and put the phone back into his pocket. He wasn't remotely surprised to have his suspicions confirmed. He had expected more attention this time and, on balance, concluded that it was a good sign. López wouldn't have gone to the trouble of checking him out unless he was entertaining the idea of doing more business with him.

On the other hand, there was an alternative explanation: López knew about his involvement in putting Jackson out of commission and had invited him to the club so that he could flush him out. On that reading, the goons in the car had been told to follow him so that they could extract the truth.

There was no way of knowing, save to hold his nerve and wait.

PART IV

FRIDAY

38

Milton allowed himself the luxury of a lie-in and awoke at seven the following morning. He got up, showered and then went to his window and looked down onto the street far below. The Audi that had followed him from the club was still parked on the side of the road.

Chase and Hicks were both up, drinking coffee.

Hicks raised his mug as Milton closed his door. "Want one?"

"Please."

"Morning," Chase said as Milton sat down.

"When did you get in?"

"Early this morning."

"All okay?"

He nodded. "All fine. The police wanted to speak to me again yesterday evening, but that's done now. I told them what happened, and they told me that I might need to come back for the trial, or maybe I could give evidence remotely. I said I was happy to help however I could. They said I was good to go."

"Well done," Milton said. "You did good."

Hicks poured out a mug of coffee and brought it over.

"You see outside?"

"I did," Hicks said. "You think they've been there all night."

"Looks like it. You get anything?"

"I got their registration. Ziggy looked it up."

"The guy who owns it is Dutch," Ziggy said, "name of Vincent de Jong. He's got form for assault. Nice guy."

"They'll be trying to find out which apartment I'm in," Milton said.

"That's not a problem, though?" Chase asked.

Ziggy shook his head. "The transaction's in the name of John Smith. Everything looks like we want it to look. They won't see anything suspicious."

"What's next?"

Milton sipped his coffee. He was about to answer when he felt his phone vibrate in his pocket. He fished it out, put his finger to his lips to ask for quiet, and answered it.

"Hello?"

"Mr. Smith?"

"Yes?"

"I have a message for you from Señor López."

"I'm listening."

"He says that he would like to get to know you a little better."

"Okay," Milton said. "That's fine. Where and when?"

"He would like you to travel to Colombia."

Milton paused. "What?"

"Specifically, to Medellín."

"Can I ask why?"

"He would like to show you some hospitality."

Milton was elated—an invitation was what he wanted most of all—but he knew that they would expect him to protest. "That really isn't necessary. Why? What for? He doesn't trust me?"

"He would like you to meet some of his colleagues."

"I don't know," Milton said.

"It is non-negotiable if you would like to work with him."

"When?"

"Señor López has business there tomorrow. He suggests you should leave today so that you can meet him then. Call this number when you reach Medellín."

The line went dead. Milton put the phone down on the table and stared at it, aware that the others were looking at him.

"Well?" Hicks said.

Milton leaned back in the chair and folded his arms. "López wants to meet."

"Where? The club?"

"No," Milton said. "Not the club. Medellín."

"You made an impression," Hicks said.

"It looks that way."

"This is good, right?" Chase said. "They wouldn't want you out there if they weren't serious."

"No," Milton said. "Probably not."

"On the other hand," Hicks said, "it'll be easier to get rid of you there than it would be here."

"That's also true," Milton said.

Chase looked as if he was about to speak but, instead, he bit his lip.

"Ziggy," Milton said, "could you book me a ticket on the first flight out?"

39

Milton would not ordinarily have chosen to fly business, but he knew that there was a very good chance that he would be observed while he was in transit, so he made a concession to appearances and turned left when he boarded the KLM 737 from Schiphol to Medellín, via Barcelona and Bogotá. He was taken to his seat and offered a glass of champagne, which he politely declined in favour of an orange juice and a bowl of warmed nuts.

He sat down, clipped the belt around his waist and took out his phone. He dialled, and after a moment, Hicks answered.

"You were followed," he said.

"Go on," he said quietly.

"Leather jacket. He tried very hard to be discreet, but it was obvious."

Milton had seen the man, too. He had been loitering outside the terminal's entrance in a position that offered a good view of the taxi drop-off zone. Milton had made him as a potential tail at once, his suspicions confirmed when he looked back in the reflection of a window and saw that the man had discarded a cigarette that he had only just lit and had followed behind him. Milton was entirely comfortable with that; indeed, it was reassuring that López and the cartel were continuing to take him seriously. He knew that they would have men waiting at the airport when he landed, and that he would be followed back to whichever hotel he chose, and that there would be employees there who would be taking the cartel's shilling to report back on him. He would be watched whenever he left the hotel and, most likely, when he was inside it, too. He would operate on the assumption that his room was bugged.

"Where are you now?" Milton asked.

"At the gate for my flight."

"Chase and Ziggy?"

"They're just closing down the apartment. They're on the ten fifty-five—they transit in Frankfurt."

They had bought tickets that enabled Hicks to take a later flight than Milton so that he could watch him leave Schiphol yet still arrive first to begin the counter-surveillance at the other end. He was also flying KLM, but his flight took off an hour later. The time was made up by the fact that Milton had to change twice and Hicks just the once. Milton arrived at 22.23; Hicks arrived two and a half hours before that.

Milton gazed out of the rain-smeared windows as the final pieces of luggage were deposited into the hold and the cart was driven away. He was idly watching a jet coming in to land when he saw a reflection in the glass and turned to see the man in the leather jacket making his way to the front of the cabin.

"Milton?" Hicks said. *"You still there?"*

"I have to go."

Milton ended the call, put the phone into flight safe mode and plugged it in to charge. He got up, opened the overhead locker and took down his carry-on luggage. He took the opportunity to look over the two seats in front of him to where the man in the leather jacket had sat down. He was not paying Milton much attention—at least not in any obvious way—but Milton knew that he had bought a ticket from the KLM desk so that he could keep an eye on him during the flight. That was fine. Milton would play his part as well as he could, and his tail could report back to López and his bosses.

The steward came by to collect Milton's empty glass.

"Thank you," Milton said.

"You'll need to put your luggage back in the locker, sir. We'll be leaving on time."

"Sorry," Milton said. "Of course."

He opened the bag, took out his copy of *One Hundred Years of Solitude* and his AirPods, and sat back down. The man in the leather jacket put his head around the back of his seat and glanced down the aisle as Milton sat back down again. Milton ignored him and intended to maintain his apparent obliviousness for the duration of the flight. As far as López knew, John Smith was an ambitious criminal, making up in determination and ruthlessness what he lacked in sophistication. Smith was not the sort of man who would have made a potential tail before the tail had even noticed him getting out of a cab.

By the time López knew that, of course, it would already be too late. Milton would delay that revelation until later. John Smith still had plenty of work to do.

40

Milton had a short two-hour hop to Barcelona before a two-and-a-half-hour layover. The guy in the leather jacket ambled behind him into the terminal. Milton took a seat at the bar and watched the replay of El Clásico from the night before. There was a mirrored wall behind the shelves of bottles, and Milton could see the man's reflection passing between the gins and vodkas and whiskeys as he found his own seat and made as if he were reading a newspaper. The barman gave the bar an exultant slap as Messi rolled in a penalty, and when Milton looked up, he saw that the man was on his phone, his eyes on Milton, no doubt reporting back to whoever had given him the assignment.

Milton ignored him.

∽

THE SECOND LEG, from Barcelona to Bogotá, was eleven and a half hours. Milton asked for his bed to be made up and managed a little sleep. They landed at two thirty local time and had another ninety-minute layover. He went through into the lounge and grabbed a plate of *chilaquiles* from a counter service restaurant, more to flush out any fresh tails than because he was particularly hungry. He ate the tortilla chips and watched for repeats—faces that he saw for a second time—or for people who were lurking where they weren't supposed to lurk. It was a large airport, and busy, but Milton was good. He identified two potential suspects: a woman in her late thirties who followed him into the terminal and then ordered *huevos rancheros* from the counter, and an older man, late forties with salt-and-pepper hair, who sat down to have his shoes shined at a spot that afforded a good view of Milton's table.

It was impressive: the cartel had people airside who could be deployed to watch new arrivals. Milton was in their territory now. They were changing things up, trying to ensure that he didn't make the people they had deployed to watch him. He finished the tortillas, leaving a slick of red sauce and egg smeared on the plate, and set off for the gate for the final leg of the journey.

The woman finished her eggs and left money on the table. The man, as Milton passed his chair, reached down to pay the shoeshine boy and followed behind the woman. Milton made no attempt to shake them. They followed him all the way to the gate, where, to Milton's complete lack of surprise, the man in the leather jacket was sitting. They kept going, handing the surveillance over.

Milton sat down and finished his book.

∼

THE AVIANCA A321 landed after a short one-hour up-and-down flight, and Milton joined the short queue of business-class travellers who were disembarking first. He wheeled his carry-on through the terminal. He switched on his phone, waited for it to connect to the local network, and saw that Hicks had left him a message telling him that he had arrived. There was a second email from Ziggy with the details of the hotel that he had booked for him.

The man in the leather jacket followed him into the arrivals hall, but then dropped back. Milton quickly made his replacement: a younger man in a Hawaiian shirt and electric blue shorts who was reading a copy of the local newspaper.

It was eleven in the evening when Milton made it outside to the taxi stand. The air was hot and humid, despite the hour, and short-tempered cabbies shouted and leant on their horns as they jostled into place to pick up their fares. Milton climbed into the first cab on the row.

"The InterContinental, please," Milton said.

He looked out of the window as the taxi pulled away. The man in the blue shorts walked quickly across the sidewalk to a waiting Nissan, and, as the cab nestled into a queue of slow-moving traffic, the Nissan did the same.

The driver made no attempt to engage in conversation, and Milton enjoyed the flamenco music that was playing on the car's stereo. He looked out of the window. Medellín was a beautiful city, described as the City of Eternal Spring on account of the consistently temperate weather. It was hot and stuffy today.

Milton took out his phone and texted Hicks, telling him that he had arrived and suggesting that they meet. The reply was swift; Hicks said that they had taken a second room on the fifth floor of the same hotel and that he should come up when he arrived.

The hotel was in El Poblado and, with minimal traffic,

he arrived in twenty minutes. The district was bright and airy, with greenery everywhere and many of the walls decorated with vibrant street art. A huge red and yellow parrot had been painted on the side of a brewery and, as Milton looked up at a high-rise, he saw an enormous mural of a gorilla looking down at him. The area was evidently something of a nocturnal destination, and they passed bars where music thumped out into the street, and restaurants with diners eating al fresco on busy patios.

"We are here," the driver said as he swung into the forecourt of the hotel.

He parked up by the entrance and charged a fare that he had obviously inflated in the hope that the gringo wouldn't realise. Milton did notice, but wasn't inclined to quibble. He paid him and stepped outside. A bellboy offered to take his carry-on, but Milton politely declined, instead asking him where he could check in.

He glanced back and saw that the Nissan had pulled up behind the cab.

The cartel knew where he was.

Milton was fine with that.

41

Milton unlocked the door and went into the hotel room. It was pleasant: two queen beds, a functional bathroom, a bureau and a television. It was clean and tidy, and the air conditioning was effective. It would suit him very well.

He put his case on the bed and started to unpack when the telephone next to the bed started to ring.

Milton sat down and picked it up. "Hello?"

"Señor Smith?"

"Yes. Who is this?"

"A car will come to pick you up tomorrow morning. Be outside the hotel at eight o'clock."

"Where am I going?"

There was no response.

"Hello? Are you there?"

There was a click as the call disconnected, and then the steady hum of the dialling tone.

MILTON LEFT HIS ROOM, checking that the corridor was unoccupied, and, once he was certain that he was not being observed, he made his way to the elevators. At the last moment, he decided to take the stairs and climbed to the fifth floor.

He went to room 505 and knocked. Ziggy opened the door and stood aside so that Milton could come in. The room was the same as the one that Milton had been given, although the view from the window was more impressive. Hicks's suitcase was on the bed, and Ziggy had one of his laptops set up on the desk. Chase was sitting with his back against the headboard of the second bed.

"You're a popular man," Hicks said.

"You see the guy with the Hawaiian shirt?"

"He's downstairs in the lobby with a friend," Hicks said. "You see the man in the baseball cap?"

"I didn't."

"Checked in next to you. The two of them had a chat when you went up to your room."

"They're not very discreet," Chase offered.

"They don't need to be," Milton said. "They won't expect me to be particularly observant, and, even if I was, what difference would it make? They want me to be on edge. It's in their best interests."

There was a Keurig coffee machine on the bureau. Ziggy went over to it and switched it on. "Who wants one?"

They all said that they did. Milton went over to the chair and sat down.

"I had a call," Milton said. "López is sending someone to pick me up tomorrow morning."

"Any idea where you're going to be going?"

"None," Milton said.

Ziggy brought two mugs of coffee over and gave one to

Milton and one to Hicks. "That's not particularly auspicious."

"But not surprising," Milton said. He crossed his right leg over his left and tapped a finger against the sole of his shoe. "You'll still be able to track me?"

"Should be fine," Ziggy said. "It's working now."

"How long will the battery last?"

"You've got eighty per cent left," he said.

"And it'll work if I'm away from the city?"

"Depends if you have a 2G signal. If you do, it'll be fine."

Milton sipped the coffee; he decided he didn't want the caffeine after all and put the mug down on the desk.

"What do you want us to do?" Hicks said.

"You're going to need to be equipped," he said.

"Any ideas on that?"

"Actually, yes. There should be an arms cache in the city."

"What?" Chase said.

"The organisation I used to work for," Milton said. "It often had reason to send people around the world on short notice. It wasn't always possible to have them take their gear with them, so they hid arms dumps in plenty of the major cities. I'm not sure, but I suspect there's one here. Ziggy?"

"I'll find out," he said.

"Apart from that," Milton said, "there's not too much that you *can* do. Keep an eye on where they take me."

"How will we know if you need us?" Chase asked.

"It depends if they let me keep my phone."

"Will they?"

"Probably not."

"So?"

Milton got up. "I'll just have to be adaptable," he said. He checked his watch. "It's midnight. I'm going to get some sleep. Hard to say what tomorrow might look like."

"If we don't see you?" Ziggy said.

"Do your best," Milton said. "Thanks for all you've done so far. I appreciate it. It's going to get more difficult now, though. We're on their territory and it'll be harder to stay in touch. Follow me if you can."

"And if we can't?" Chase said.

"Then it'll be up to me," he said. "I'm not worried. I've done this before. I'll be fine."

Milton said good night and left the room. What he had said was true, at least for the most part. He had done this kind of thing before, although then—when he had been on operations with the Group—he had had the benefit of the best logistical and intelligence backup that the state could provide. Now, though? He was on his own. And, although he was experienced, he was still anxious.

Tomorrow had the makings of a very difficult day indeed.

42

The safe house was an old DEA property that they had been running for years. It was a working business—a garage with a car wash alongside it—and Fuentes was confident that it had never been compromised, and that the cartel did not know that it was there. They needed a large space for the number of men who were engaged on the operation, and the garage offered that. It was wide enough for three cars to fit side by side, with two pits dug into the floor so that the mechanics could work on the undersides of the vehicles that they were servicing. There was a separate booth with a smeared glass window from where the business was run, and equipment stacked around the walls. The floor was damp with puddles from where the rain had fallen in through the holes in the roof, and light from the caged bulbs that dangled from long wires overhead glistened colourfully against spilt fuel and oil.

Long wooden trestle tables had been erected along the walls, and a wide array of weapons, ammunition and other equipment had been arranged neatly across them. Ellie went over to the nearest table and walked alongside it, looking down at the variety of automatic rifles, submachine guns and sidearms.

DEVGRU was split into squadrons. The SEALs who were taking part in the assault were from Blue Squadron. The men in the squadron were divided into three troops, and eighteen men from B Troop had been deployed to the safe house. There was a second floor above the garage that had been turned into a temporary dormitory. The SEALs had set up there, with bedrolls and sleeping bags arranged in two neat lines. They were staying inside to avoid any possibility that they might be observed out and about. A troop from Black Squadron—specialising in intelligence, reconnaissance and surveillance—was already in the jungle.

Three senior commissioned officers were gathered around a table across which a map had been spread. They were discussing something while looking down at the map, occasionally reaching down to make points with their fingers. The men concluded their discussion and broke up. One of them—the grizzled Lieutenant Commander Dan McCoy—saw Ellie and came over to her.

"Special Agent Flowers," he said.

McCoy was in command of B Troop. Ellie had been introduced to him upon her arrival and had been taken with his calm sense of confidence. He had an impressive résumé and was just as impressive in the flesh.

"Commander," she said, "you all good to go?"

"Just running through the finer points of the operation before we brief the men."

"Still looking like tomorrow for go-time?"

"Tomorrow or the next day, ma'am," he said. "WITCH is due into camp, but we don't know exactly when. We're just waiting for CHILD to give us the update."

Ellie nodded. WITCH was the cryptonym that they were using for La Bruja, and CHILD was their source.

"How long do we think she'll stay there?"

"Don't know that for sure, but more than long enough for us to go get her. We'll keep an eye on her, confirm she's in the camp, and then we'll move. We can be on site in four hours. She's not going anywhere."

The plan called for a full deployment of the troop. It would be challenging on several levels: first, they would need to move the men without arousing the suspicion of the local authorities; second, they would have to trek through the jungle while ensuring that the cartel did not notice them; and, third, they would have to take La Bruja. Ellie had insisted that she be part of the operation, and, perhaps sensing the almighty row that would follow if she were denied, McSweeney had agreed.

"You mind if I ask…" McCoy said. "You done anything like this before?"

Ellie thought back to the adventure that she had had in Michigan. "Not *quite* like this," she said. "But if you're asking if I've seen action before? Sure, I've seen action."

McCoy nodded. "The thing with the militia?"

"You been reading up on me?"

"You're coming into a hot zone with me," he said. "I'd check up on anyone I was going to be responsible for in a place like that."

"You don't need to worry about me," she said. "I can look after myself."

He grinned. "Not doubting that for a minute."

PART V

SATURDAY

43

It was five in the morning and the drive out into the countryside had been quiet, with not much traffic on the roads. Chase was driving, with Ziggy in the passenger seat beside him. They had reached a large stretch of farmland, and Ziggy had directed them to a chapel. It was derelict and looked as if it might have been for years.

Ziggy looked at the screen in his hand. "Pull over there," he said, pointing.

Chase took his foot off the gas, and the car coasted to a stop next to a path that led up to the chapel. "In there?"

"That's what it says."

They both got out of the car. Ziggy checked the screen again. He had logged into the Group's servers last night and had confirmed the information that he needed. He looked around at the chapel and then at the deserted landscape that surrounded it. This was definitely the location.

Chase led the way up the path. "So," he said, "let me get this straight. The people you and John used to work for—they have places like this all around the world?"

"They do," Ziggy said.

"And they just leave them in place?"

"It's not original. The Soviets did it during the Cold War. They're still finding those now. There was one near where I used to live back home."

"But this one hasn't been found?"

"I don't think so. The records were updated a month ago."

The building was at the top of a hill that was reached by way of a gentle trail. The door was secured with a chain and padlock. Chase found a rock at the side of the path and crashed it down against the hasp, breaking it on the fifth strike. He removed the chain and opened the doors. Ziggy took out his flashlight and shone it into the dark space. The chapel would have been beautiful when it was still in use. It was compact, with four rows of wooden pews facing an altar at the other end of the space. The windows were high up on the walls, most of them without their glass. The plaster was peeling from the walls; loose bricks and debris were scattered around, and nature was starting to reclaim the building, grass shoving through gaps in the tiled floor and creepers reaching in from the outside. Dawn was slowly breaking, and a few lazy golden rays shone through the empty portals. One beam shone on the wooden cross that still hung from the wall above the altar.

Chase took out his own flashlight and went inside. "Where is it?"

"There's a loose flagstone behind the altar," Ziggy said.

They made their way between the pews. Ziggy knelt down and shone his flashlight on the ground. One of the flagstones was obviously loose; one edge was very slightly raised.

"That's been moved recently," Chase said.

Ziggy ran his finger along the raised lip. The other stones had been covered with a fine layer of debris that must have fallen down from the ceiling at some point in the past. The dirt that would have laid atop the joins between this stone and those adjacent to it had been disturbed.

"Step back," Chase said.

He opened the socket and screwdriver set that he had brought in from the back of the car and selected a flat-bladed screwdriver. He shoved the tip into the gap between the loose stone and a neighbour and pushed down on the handle, prising the edge of the loose stone up. Ziggy reached down, forced his fingers into the gap and heaved the stone all the way up. The stone was heavy, and the two of them muscled it out of the way.

The freshly opened gap revealed a dark void beneath the floor. Ziggy shone his light down into the space. It was deep and had been excavated so that it was wide enough to accommodate two metal Peli cases.

"Give me a hand," Ziggy said. "They'll be heavy."

They rested their flashlights on the ground and both grabbed the handle of the nearest case.

"On three," Chase said. "One, two, three, *pull*."

The case came up out of the hole a lot more easily than Ziggy had expected. It was weighty, but he had anticipated it being even more cumbersome given what he was likely to find inside. The case was around a metre and a half long, seventy centimetres wide and sixty centimetres deep. They laid it down on the floor and Ziggy undid the clasps that held the lid closed. The hard shell was waterproof, and the contents were protected by a foam insert and silica gel packets.

Chase shone the flashlight down.

"That's it?"

Ziggy stared down at the contents in puzzlement: there were two Sig Sauer P226 handguns, a lever-action rifle and a selection of ammunition in various calibres.

"Someone's been here already," Chase said. "Look."

He pointed to the foam insert. There were spaces for additional hardware, but they were empty.

Chase took out the rifle. It was chambered for big-bore .45-70 rounds. "Haven't seen one of these for a while," he said. "Tough to get ammo for it. Might be why it was left."

"Let's check the other one."

They hauled out the second case and found that the situation was worse. This one had been completely emptied.

Chase reached into the first case and took out one of the handguns. "Who else would've known that the cases were here?"

"No one," Ziggy said.

"Apart from the people you used to work for."

"Yes," he said. "Obviously."

"So they've been here."

"There was no sign of that."

The stash had been marked as green, meaning that it had recently been restocked by the local quartermaster. The only way that this made any sense was if Group Fifteen agents were in theatre and had visited the chapel to arm themselves.

But what would Group Fifteen agents be doing in Medellín?

"Come on," he said, turning to the first case. "We'll take what's left."

They transferred the pistols, the rifle and the ammunition into a canvas bag that they had brought with them and then slid the case back into its hiding spot. They dragged the flagstone back into place and started for the car. Ziggy thought about the people who might have been here before them, and found that the nerves in his stomach—already bad enough—had just got much worse.

44

Milton found it difficult to sleep. His thoughts raced with what the morning might bring, and he eventually resorted to reading his Márquez for thirty minutes in an attempt to quiet his mind. He fell asleep with the book splayed open on the pillow next to him, and when he awoke five hours later, he felt groggy. He got up and stood under a cold shower for five minutes, not getting out of the cubicle until his skin was tingling. He dried himself off, dressed in a pair of jeans and a T-shirt, and pulled on his boots, thinking of the tracker hidden in the sole.

Milton went to the window and looked down onto Medellín. Suspicion and paranoia had been inculcated in the cartels as a result of their decades-long battle with the state and with each other, and, as far as Milton was concerned, they knew nothing about him. That was the purpose of this visit: they would try to provide themselves with the confidence that he was someone with whom they could do business. If they didn't think that he was, they would put a bullet in his head and dump him by the side of the road. There would be no question about that and no hesitation. There would be very little that Milton could do about it, either.

His only hope was that Ziggy had done his work properly. The legend that he had spent so much time putting together—its resistance to investigation and Milton's ability to play the part—would be the difference between life and death. Milton had to persuade them that he was John Smith. It was the only way that he would walk out of today's meeting in one piece.

He inhaled deeply, closing his eyes and finding a point of balance. He would have no control over what came next, and that—helplessness—was one of the triggers of his alcoholism. There was a minibar beneath the bureau, but Milton had resisted the temptation to open it up until now, and he found—to his relief—that the urge to go and take a drink was not strong. He needed his wits about him.

He grabbed his phone from the bedside table, dropped it into the pocket of his jacket and made his way to the elevators. He summoned one and rode it down to the lobby.

∽

THE LOBBY WAS QUIET, with just a single guest checking out. Milton looked at his watch.

Five minutes past eight.

He wandered over to the comfortable chairs that were set out opposite the check-in desks, but did not get the chance to sit. A man wearing a linen jacket, a white shirt and dark slacks pushed through the double doors and made his way into the hotel. He saw Milton and diverted across to him.

"Señor Smith," he said. It was a statement, not a question.

"Yes," Milton said.

"Come with me, please."

The man put a hand on Milton's elbow and guided him out of the double doors and onto the street. It was already hot, the sudden warmth washing over Milton after the relative cool of the air conditioning.

"Where are we going?" Milton asked.

"We have a short drive," the man said.

"Where to?"

"Please. No questions."

A black Escalade that had been parked on the other side of the turning circle pulled out and looped around, stopping next to them. The man opened the rear door and held it for Milton to get in.

Milton paused; not because *he* was particularly frightened, but because John Smith would have reason to be perturbed by the mystery, and because he needed these men to see him behave as they would expect.

"What is it?" the man said.

"I'd like to know where we're going."

"Get in, please."

"Where are we going?"

"I take you to a meeting," the man said with an irritated shrug. "You come or you don't come. Is up to you. But if you don't come, my boss—he won't be happy. You understand what I am saying?"

"Where is the meeting?"

"Outside the city. It will take two hours and then we will be there." He indicated the open door. "You come? Yes or no?"

"All right," Milton said. "I'll come."

He climbed into the back of the Escalade. There were two men in the front—the driver and a passenger—and the man in the white shirt got into the back next to Milton. His jacket fell open as he sat back, and Milton saw the metallic glint of the pistol that he was wearing in a shoulder rig.

"What do I call you?" Milton asked.

"Francisco," the man said with a gruff finality that was obviously designed to forestall the possibility of small talk. "Now—give me your phone."

"Sorry?"

"Your telephone, Señor Smith. Give it to me."

Milton knew there was no point in arguing. He reached into his pocket, took out his phone and handed it to Francisco. The man held down the button until the phone powered down, and then gave it to the man in the front passenger seat, who put it into the glovebox.

"Thank you," Francisco said.

Milton clasped his hands together in his lap and looked out of the window as the Escalade moved away from the hotel and bulled its way into the traffic. He crossed his legs and ran his finger over the sole of his right shoe. He wondered whether the tracker could really work quite as well as Ziggy had suggested. Milton wasn't armed, and the people he hoped to meet would be dangerous. He did not plan on needing assistance, nor could he say that it definitely would not be required. He was proposing to make an unscheduled meet with people who would be suspicious and, given the audacity of the approach, possibly hostile. It was hard to predict how something like that might go.

45

"There they are," Hicks said.

Chase leaned forward. "Where?"

They were parked half a block down from the hotel. Hicks had been in place since five in the morning, and Chase had joined him when he had returned from the arms dump. Hicks had chosen a spot that offered a good vantage point of the hotel while not being so close as to attract attention. Chase had dozed off. Hicks slouched down in the seat, but he never closed his eyes.

"First car at the canopy," Hicks said. "Black Escalade. There's a trail car, too. At the kerb. It didn't pull in, but they came together. Silver Mercedes GLC."

"Got them," Chase said. "They've sent a team."

Hicks nodded. "Yeah." He grabbed the binoculars from the middle console and trained them on the Mercedes. "Two men, no passengers in the back." He rotated the binoculars to his left. "Two men in the Escalade, plus the one who went inside."

Hicks saw Milton coming outside with the man from the Escalade.

"There he is," Chase said.

Hicks watched as Milton nodded at the man holding the rear passenger door open for him. There was a conversation—Milton looked reluctant—and then he got into the vehicle. The man slid in next to him and closed the door. The Mercedes was still idling on the street, waiting.

The Escalade pulled away from the hotel and the Mercedes glided in behind it.

"Go," Chase said.

Hicks waited several seconds then pulled away from the kerb, made a U-turn, and got in behind them. They stayed well behind the two cars as the Escalade led them through the Túnel de Ote and then southeast out of the city and onto the main highway that headed east.

Chase dragged his finger on the satnav, looking ahead. "This goes to the airport," he said. "You think they'll fly him somewhere?"

"Maybe."

It was simple enough for Hicks to stay back in traffic and track them. The Escalade was big and easy to see up ahead. The Mercedes maintained a position to the Escalade's rear left, usually with a car or two in between them.

The turn-off for the airport came and went, and the convoy swung right and continued towards Candilejas and then La Victoria. It was an easy tail until they turned off the highway on the approach to El Cebadero. Hicks knew immediately that he was going to have to make a decision.

"What do we have off this exit?" he asked.

Chase looked at the satnav. "It runs due north," he said. "There's a village and then nothing much."

Hicks let the car slow as the Escalade and the Mercedes angled off the highway to the off-ramp.

"Too exposed?"

"Not worth the risk," Hicks said. "We follow them off, that Mercedes is going to wonder what we're still doing behind them. Maybe not right away, but eventually they're going to figure us out." He shook his head. "We have to call it off."

"Shit," Chase said.

He put his foot back on the pedal and drove past the off-ramp. He looked across at the junction. The road that the convoy had taken was narrow, with barely enough room for two cars to pass. He had made the right call.

"Get Ziggy."

Chase placed the call.

"Where are you?"

"In the sticks," Hicks said. "Coming up to La Victoria. You still got him?"

"No. Lost the signal five miles outside the city."

Hicks looked to the right, into the foothills and then the mountains beyond.

Shit was right.

Milton was on his own.

46

They drove north. Milton watched through the windows as they climbed up into the mountains.

"Where are we going?"

It was the third time that Milton had asked, and the third time that he did not receive a reply. He decided not to press. The man in the passenger seat was big, with blond hair and fair skin that suggested that he might not be Latino. He kept his attention on the road for the most part, but Milton caught him looking back in the mirror on occasion and saw that he had vivid blue eyes. The driver was smaller than the blond man, with a nervous tic that pulsed in his neck. His black hair was lank, greasy fronds falling over his collar, and dandruff was scattered across his shoulder. Neither man spoke and, after a while, the passenger reached over for the radio and turned the dial. Vapid pop music played.

They followed the narrow road up into the mountains. They passed through tiny villages and then, as the landscape opened up, they saw large plantations with *casas* that must have been worth decent money. The road split two grassy hills and, when they emerged on the other side, they arrived at a long gate that blocked the way. There was a guardhouse next to it and a man emerged. He was dressed in a T-shirt and slacks; the MP5 he wore on a sling was prominent and meant to be visible. He nodded at the driver and stepped back into the guardhouse, and the black iron gate slid to the right.

Milton looked out of the window as the car wound its way into the property. The acreage was impressive; it took them fifteen minutes to drive from the gates to the first buildings. It soon became evident that whoever lived on the *finca* was fond of horses. They approached a large barn on a flat stretch of land that was being used for pasture, then passed beyond a sand arena and a hay barn. They drove by a tennis court and pavilion and then another barn; a young woman led a powerful horse out of its stall, both rider and animal looking up as the car rumbled by.

They reached the compound. The main residence could have been in Santa Barbara rather than Antioquia. It was accessed through a graceful arch, and, beyond, the understated elegance of the home was framed by mature trees, a veranda that was draped with bougainvillea, and displays of flowers, shrubs and other plantings.

The car pulled up. Francisco got out and indicated that Milton should follow him. He did. The driveway was bisected down the middle by a long concrete trough that was filled with water. Two horses—both big and powerful and with neatly clipped coats—had their heads ducked down as they drank. The gravel on either side was immaculate, raked neatly, and the trees that bordered it had been planted with perfect order and trimmed so that they were of almost identical height. The *casa* at the end of the drive looked pristine, with whitewashed walls and tinted glass to mitigate the worst of the sun's glare.

"This way," Francisco said, leading him to the end of the drive and the veranda that offered access to the house.

Milton climbed the steps up to the wooden platform as the door opened and a man Milton had never seen before came out.

"Señor Smith," he said, "thank you for coming. My name is Hector del Pozo. I am pleased to meet you."

47

The man who had introduced himself as Hector del Pozo was wearing a white linen suit with a white shirt that had three buttons undone. He looked relaxed and tanned. He took Milton's hand and shook it, then indicated that he should follow him into a large reception room that adjoined the lobby of the property.

A maid in a black and white uniform had just deposited a tray of glasses and a pitcher of orange juice. Del Pozo went over to the pitcher.

"You must be thirsty." He poured two glasses of orange juice and handed one to Milton. "We grow these oranges ourselves. They were picked this morning."

Milton put the glass to his lips and drank. The juice was wonderfully fresh and had been chilled. He drank down half of the glass straight away and did not demur when del Pozo offered to top it up.

"I'm sorry," Milton said. "I don't know you. I was expecting Señor López."

"He had a change of plan," del Pozo said. "You'll be dealing with me while you are here."

"I'm sorry to have to ask—but who are you?"

"For your purposes, I am the man you have to persuade. I will decide whether we can work with you."

"And you've spoken to López about me?"

"Of course, Señor Smith. At length. I know who you are and what you want. We have a great deal to talk about. Come—I'll show you the horses."

Del Pozo led the way along the drive to the paddock that they had passed on their way to the house. Post and rail fencing marked the boundary of the field, with a separate space for a manège where the horses could be exercised. Milton watched as a young woman guided a big Appaloosa around the arena, the horse showing a little flightiness before she tightened the reins and brought it under closer control.

"Do you ride?" del Pozo said.

"Never been much of a fan," Milton said truthfully. "Seems like a long way to fall."

Del Pozo chuckled. "That is true, but only if the horse decides that it doesn't want you to ride it."

The young woman brought the Appaloosa up to the rail and gave it a little nudge with her heels, sending it into a brisk canter.

"How was your journey from Amsterdam?"

"Fine," Milton said.

"And the drive from the city?"

"Good. Your men were very efficient."

"I am pleased to hear that."

The hospitality was welcome, but Milton was experienced enough not to be beguiled by it. This was business, pure and simple, and he was being assessed.

"Can I ask you a question?" he said.

"Of course."

"Has Anthony Jackson been out here?"

Del Pozo paused for a moment. "The man you hope to replace? Yes, of course. We wouldn't do business with anyone on that scale without being very sure that they were the kind of man that we would be comfortable working with. Señor Jackson has been here twice." He indicated that he should follow him into the *casa*. "You are in the guest suite, Señor Smith. This way, please."

Milton trailed del Pozo into the house. It was a large building, with grand proportions. The windows offered views of the well-tended gardens on one side and, on the other, several acres of paddocks in which a number of horses were kept. It must have been worth millions, and the impression of wealth was maintained with the décor and choice of furniture. There were arches that led to quiet little alcoves, enormous vases filled with sunflowers and orchids, and pieces of furniture that included both obvious antiques and statements of modernity.

They continued along a corridor and passed two wide double doors. The room inside was vast—two thousand square feet, Milton estimated—and had been equipped with its own two-lane bowling alley, a variety of classic arcade cabinets and gaming tables, a separate caterer's kitchen and bar, and a gym.

"This is all very impressive," Milton said.

"Thank you. We like it."

"You live here with your family?"

"I do. My wife and my daughter."

"That was your daughter on the horse?"

He nodded. "Esmerelda lives for riding. It is a very expensive pastime."

"I'm sure you can afford it."

Del Pozo smiled. "Business has been good."

They continued on their way, working toward the rear of the property. Del Pozo opened a door and gestured for Milton to go inside.

"Here," he said. "I think you will be comfortable."

There was a large bed, a wardrobe and a plush two-seater sofa. The open bathroom door revealed a glimpse of marble.

"Thank you," Milton said.

"You must make yourself comfortable. Perhaps you are tired?"

"I'm fine."

"Then maybe a swim to freshen up? You have your own pool outside, and you'll find clothes that you can use in the wardrobe. Please, treat this as if it were your own home." Del Pozo backed toward the door. "We will speak about business this evening before dinner. I will send someone for you at seven and we can talk on the veranda. The sunsets here are spectacular. We can enjoy the view and see whether we might be able to work together—pursue the proposal that you have made. You should relax until then."

48

Milton found a pair of swimming shorts in the closet; he changed into them and went outside. There was a small pool surrounded by pale marble tiles that shone in the sun. Two mahogany sun loungers sheltered beneath a wide parasol, and an outdoor refrigerator contained bottles of drink and a plate of cut fruit. Milton lowered himself into the water and drifted out into the middle, enjoying the coolness against his hot and clammy skin. He breathed in and stretched out his arms, floating on his back and staring up into the powder-blue sky.

∽

Milton was reading on the bed when there came a knock on the door to his room. He looked at the clock on the wall: it was just before seven. He folded the corner of the page he had been reading, set the book down on the bedside table and crossed the room as the knock was repeated.

"I'm coming," Milton said.

He opened the door. Francisco was standing there. "Señor del Pozo is waiting for you," he said. "Follow me."

Milton paid attention again as they made their way through the house. He wanted to get a sense of the layout, the best ways to get outside, perhaps even the rooms where he might be able to equip himself—there had to be an armoury somewhere, for example—in the event that things took a turn for the worse. Francisco was silent, leading the way through the opulent corridors until they emerged onto a veranda that furnished views of the spectacular landscape that enveloped the *finca*.

Hector del Pozo was sitting on a low chair with a newspaper spread out on his lap. He heard the sound of their footsteps on the wooden slats of the terrace and stood.

"Señor Smith," he said, "how is your room?"

"Perfect. Thank you."

"Good." He dismissed Francisco with a wave of the hand and then indicated that Milton should sit. "I think we should get down to our business—yes?"

The chairs were arranged so that they were facing out onto the paddock. It was a beautiful vista, but the orientation meant that Milton would not have been able to see if anyone approached him from the *casa*. He guessed that the arrangement was deliberate. Del Pozo, for all his warmth, wanted him to be as uncomfortable as possible.

"As you probably know, the cocaine that you would like to buy is produced and distributed by the cartels in Colombia and Mexico. It is produced here, in the jungle, by El Centro. Distribution is taken care of north of the border. I am Mexican. I represent La Frontera."

"But you work closely with El Centro?"

"Very closely," he said. "And, for your purposes, the two are one and the same."

Milton nodded his understanding.

"Señor López also works for La Frontera. I've discussed your offer with him. I will be frank—it is a generous offer, and, under normal circumstances, it would be one that we would be very happy to recommend. However, as you know, there is a problem."

"Anthony Jackson," Milton said. "Yes, I know. We discussed it."

"Indeed. Señor Jackson has been a valued partner for several years. That comes with certain benefits."

"Exclusivity."

"Yes," he said. "Certainly at the scale you say you would like to do business."

"But you still brought me out here."

"Yes," del Pozo said. "Because I'm curious."

Milton spread his arms. "I'm an open book. What do you want to know?"

Del Pozo was watching Milton carefully. "How did you do it?"

Milton knew what he meant, but manufactured a puzzled frown. "How did I do what?"

"Oh," he said with a smile. "You know."

"I really don't."

"Señor Jackson's arrest. How did you arrange it?"

"I don't know what you're talking about."

Hector shook his head. "Come, now, Señor Smith. Honesty and openness are important. Please—how did you do it?"

"I wish I could help you, but…" He shrugged.

"Disappointing."

"I didn't even know that he had been arrested."

"He was involved in a car crash. From what we have been able to ascertain, a car drove into him and there was an altercation. We know that Señor Jackson has a temper. We know of his criminal history. But, on the other hand, he is not a fool, and I find it very difficult to believe that he would do something so rash in front of so many witnesses. It appears that he had a weapon, and the police found it."

"This is all news to me."

"That is not the extent of his legal difficulties. When the police arrived, they found cocaine in Señor Jackson's car. A kilogram. The police charged him for it—intent to supply. We've examined the evidence, and, as far as we can tell, there really is no possibility that he could be acquitted. There were witnesses to the argument with the other driver, there was the gun, and he can't explain how the cocaine happened to be in the back of his car."

Milton held del Pozo's gaze. "I'd like to say that I'm sorry to hear that," he said, "but that would be a lie. I'm not sorry at all. If he's having legal problems, that means he's not going to be able to continue to work with you. And perhaps that means the problem we had with exclusivity has gone away."

Del Pozo kept his eyes on him, his bottom lip caught between his teeth as he considered what Milton had just said. "No," he said at last. "You're lying. I don't believe you."

"What do you want me to say? I didn't know about his problem. It has nothing to do with me. You can either believe that or not. But my offer still stands. I want to do business with you on a bigger scale than López said was possible. Maybe this changes things. I don't know, but we're not going to get anywhere if you accuse me of something that I don't know anything about and didn't do."

"You can understand why I am sceptical. You can see how convenient this looks."

"Yes, of course. It *is*. But it's a lucky coincidence. You want me to say it again? It has nothing to do with me."

Del Pozo got up from his seat and walked across the veranda to the balustrade. He folded his arms and leaned against it, gazing out into the quickening gloom.

"You say your offer still stands?"

"It does."

"What is the maximum amount that you would be looking to buy?"

"A million dollars."

"And how much do you expect to receive in return for that?"

"Fifty keys."

Del Pozo turned around, leaned back against the balustrade and looked down at Milton, his arms crossed. "Twenty thousand per kilo?"

"That's right," Milton said. "Plus shipping."

Del Pozo shook his head. "No," he said. "Twenty-five."

"I just paid that for a key," Milton said. "Now I'm buying in bulk. I don't think it would be unreasonable to ask for a discount."

"We can go to twenty-three," del Pozo said. "But that is as far as we would be prepared to move. It's either acceptable to you or it isn't."

Milton drew in a deep breath. "No," he said. "Too much. What was Jackson's price?"

"That's none of your business."

"Of course it is. You've been doing business with someone indiscreet enough to get caught by the police with product—I'm assuming it's *your* product—in the back of his car. He's unreliable. He makes mistakes."

"What does this have to do with you?"

"I don't want to tell you your business, but can you afford

to take another chance? You need someone who can reliably move as much of your product as possible. But not *just* move it—move it in a way that is completely under the radar, in a way that won't lead to a situation like this happening again."

Del Pozo still looked unconvinced.

"You don't have a distributor in the UK. You're not in the same negotiating position as you were when I met López in Amsterdam. I'll move a little in your direction so we can get this done. One million for forty-five keys. Twenty-two per key. If you still don't trust me, even after the first deal, then I'll make a deposit of half a million tonight—you just need to give me back my phone so I can make a call. I'll need longer for the balance, but I'm good for it."

Del Pozo smiled. "How much longer would you need?"

"A week."

The Mexican steepled his fingers. "Let me think about it."

PART VI

SUNDAY

49

The rest of the evening passed pleasantly enough. Del Pozo employed a staff at the *casa*, and a uniformed waitress brought out a three-course meal that, del Pozo said, was a celebration of Colombian gastronomy. There was corn and tomato soup, scallops and heart of palm ceviche, yucca gnocchi with sweet plantain and pecorino foam, and freshly caught grouper with a tamal and criolla sauce. The chef brought out the chocolate dessert himself, and Milton complimented him on the food. They retired to the veranda again, where they were served *tinto*—freshly ground coffee served with sugar—and continued to talk as they watched the sun going down.

They did not discuss business again, although del Pozo asked him a series of questions about his past. He asked about conditions inside prison, comparing them to the institutions in Mexico that he said he had passed through as a younger man. Milton had expected there to be further references to Jackson, but del Pozo did not mention him again. Milton had no idea whether he had persuaded del Pozo that the cartel should do business with him.

"I hope you have a comfortable night," del Pozo said as he finished his coffee and stood.

"Thank you," Milton said.

"I will see you in the morning. We will talk more then."

Milton thanked him again and returned to the guest suite. He shut the door and locked it, then gazed around at the room. He knew that he was being watched, and that there was nothing that he could do about it. It was no matter. He sat down on the edge of the bed and levered off his boots. His thoughts turned to Ziggy's tracking device. He doubted that there was cellphone reception out here. He had noticed Hicks and Chase as they followed him from the hotel, but had known that there was no way that they would have been able to trail him all the way to the *finca*. There was no way that they could know where he was. He was alone.

He thought that the evening had gone about as well as it could have done, but it was difficult to say anything more than that. He had known, of course, that the subject of Jackson would be raised. He had detected nothing that would suggest that del Pozo knew he was lying. He had been careful in Manchester to ensure that he had not been seen by any witnesses, nor had his image been recorded on any of the cameras that they had identified near the junction. The only way that he could have betrayed his involvement was by a lack of credibility when the accusations were put to him this evening. He thought he had responded with the appropriate confusion and then indignation, but the matter was out of his hands now.

They either believed him, or they didn't.

And if they didn't?

Nothing he could do about that now.

Milton undressed and got into bed. He was tired. It had

been a long day, and the effort of maintaining his legend had been draining.

He closed his eyes and was quickly asleep.

50

Milton awoke. He didn't know what time it was, but, as he slowly came back to full consciousness, he realised that he had heard a noise. He held his breath and listened, lying still as he looked out into the gloom of the bedroom.

Had he heard something?

Perhaps not. Perhaps he had imagined—

He was blinded as a flashlight came on; the beam shone directly into his face from the foot of the bed. He looked away, but the damage was already done; his night vision was compromised, splashes of white pulsing across his retinas. He tried to scramble up the mattress, but he was too sleepy and too slow. Strong hands grabbed him by the shoulders and yanked him around, turning him so that he was flat on his chest. A heavy weight pressed down on his back; he realised that someone had straddled him, their hands on his shoulders as a second person pinned his flailing right hand and fed something around his wrist.

"Get off me," he grunted.

His left hand was pinned down and then yanked behind

his back. He felt something around that wrist, too, and then he gasped with pain as both wrists were forced together and the restraint—a zip tie, he thought—was pulled tight.

He was dragged off the bed and dumped onto the floor. His left shoulder hit first, taking all of his weight until his legs came over the bed and he crashed down onto his side. He looked up, blinking to clear his vision, and saw three shadows. He felt hands beneath his shoulders as he was hauled upright. The door that led out of the bedroom to the terrace was opened, and Milton was dragged out.

It was dark, and Milton couldn't see well enough to distinguish the three men who had assaulted him, save that one was much bigger than the other two. Neither could he prevent them from dragging him to the edge of the swimming pool. He felt a sharp pain as he was kicked behind the knees, his legs going from under him as he was shoved down once more. The hands stayed on his shoulders and pushed him down so that his face was inches above the surface of the water.

"I'm only going to ask you this once," the voice from before said. "You're lying about what happened to Anthony Jackson."

The man spoke in English with a distinct accent: Scandinavian. It was unmistakable.

"You're lying," the man repeated. "Admit it."

"No," Milton gasped out. "I'm not."

"Bullshit."

"I had no idea what happened to him."

"I don't believe you."

"I had no idea until I was told about it this evening."

Milton's head was thrust down beneath the surface of the water. He tried not to struggle so that he could conserve his oxygen, but it was impossible to overrule the impulse of his body to try to get back to the surface. His back arched, but the hands holding him down were too strong. The effort spent his last breath, and his mouth automatically came open. Water rushed down his throat.

He was yanked back to the surface of the pool.

"Fuck," he said, spluttering, retching out the water.

"How did you do it?"

"Do *what?*" Milton said, gasping for the air that he knew he was going to need.

He was plunged back down beneath the surface of the pool once more. He struggled again, but the man holding him down had the benefit of leverage. Milton was jackknifed over the side of the pool and had nowhere to go.

He was hauled out for a second time.

"What's your real name?"

"What the fuck does that mean?"

"Your name. Your name isn't John Smith. What's your real name?"

"That *is* my name," Milton said. "I—"

The man dunked him for the third time. They held him down for longer, and the thought crossed Milton's mind that, perhaps, he was going to die here. He tried to separate his mind from the involuntary thrashing of his body, but it was impossible. He couldn't do it.

He was dragged up again.

"We know you're lying."

Milton readied himself for a fourth dunking, but it didn't come. Instead, he was dragged up and muscled backwards until the backs of his knees touched against a chair. He was pressed down into it.

There was enough light now for Milton to see the men who were arrayed around him. He recognised them all from the drive to the *casa* yesterday. The man who had come into the lobby to get him and who had ridden in the back of the Escalade with him, the big man with blond hair who had been in the passenger seat, and the skinny driver. The big man was in charge now. Milton blinked the water from his eyes and looked at him. He was huge, a good four inches taller and fifty pounds heavier than Milton. His hair was blond, almost white, and razored close to his scalp.

"We know you're lying," he said again.

"You keep saying that. *Please*—lying about what?"

"About Jackson. About who you are. *Everything*. I doubt anything you've said since you've been here is true."

"No," Milton said.

"What's your name?"

"John Smith."

"Where were you born?"

"Islington."

"Date of birth?"

"Tenth of October."

"Year?"

"Nineteen-seventy."

"Bullshit."

"No," he protested. "It's not. It's—"

"You did time."

"Yes."

"Where?"

"HMP Woodhill. Full Sutton. Wakefield. Wormwood Scrubs."

"What'd you do?"

"What do you mean?"

"Why were you inside?"

"Robbery. Assault."

"We had someone look into your record. He says that it's a pack of lies. He says it was manufactured."

"It's not."

Milton had no alternative but to trust that Ziggy's work had been thorough. He had to stick to it; if he didn't, he was dead. On the other hand, of course, if Ziggy had made a mistake, he was dead anyway.

"What are you?" the man said. "You're not police. Security services? MI6? Am I getting warm?"

"MI6? Come on. That's ridiculous."

"I don't think it's ridiculous." The man reached around and pulled out a pistol from the waistband of his jeans. He aimed it at Milton, his finger resting on the trigger. He held it like he had held a weapon many times before; Milton was in absolutely no doubt that if the blond man did not believe him, he would be shot. "It's time to tell the truth."

"I am."

The man stepped closer and pressed the barrel of the pistol into the middle of Milton's forehead. "This whole thing is a fabrication. Where's your backup?"

"I don't have backup. It's just me."

"How are you going to move forty kilograms of coke if it's just you?"

"It's just me *here*," Milton said. "I have people waiting for me."

"Where?"

"In London."

The man pushed down; Milton felt the metal pressing between his eyes, just above the bridge of his nose. "What about Jackson?"

"What about him?"

"You set him up, didn't you?"

"No."

"You manufactured the accident; you distracted him; then you planted the coke in his car."

"No, I didn't."

"What do you think we'll find when the police analyse the coke? You know each batch can be traced back to its source, don't you? Like a fingerprint. I mean, *John*, you wouldn't be so dumb as to use the coke that you bought from López to set up López's biggest customer, would you?"

"I don't know," he said, very aware of the cold metal pressed hard against his forehead, "but it seems to me that Jackson got caught with cocaine he bought from the cartel. I bought cocaine from the cartel, too. They probably *will* match. What's that going to prove?"

The man pushed harder, forcing Milton's head back against the slats of the chair. Milton closed his eyes, wondering if he had pressed him too far, or whether his bluffs had not been persuasive enough, but instead of pulling the trigger, the man removed the pistol and stepped back.

"Hold him down."

The man backed away. The other two stepped up and put their hands on Milton's shoulders, securing him in place. The Scandinavian took a phone from his pocket and held it out in front of him; the flash popped as he took a picture and then another.

"Give me his hand."

Milton was bent forward so that they could get to his shackled wrists. The restraints were removed and one of the men grabbed Milton's right wrist and held it out. Milton wondered whether they were going to break a finger or pull out a nail, but, since there was no point in resisting, he didn't. The Scandinavian took a device from his pocket: a small plastic oblong, about the size of a credit card and a centimetre deep. It was matte black with a screen in the centre and an optical reader right at the top. The man took

Milton's index finger and pressed it against the reader. The machine bleeped, and the man repeated the process for the rest of his fingers and his thumb, then pressed a button on the display and put the machine back into his pocket.

"I'm going to be watching you," he said. "You give me even the *smallest* doubt, and I'm going to end you."

The men dragged Milton from the chair and onto his knees. They left him on the ground as they went back inside. His head and shoulders were soaked, and the water was bracing against his skin in the cool night air. He heard the sound of the door opening and closing and got to his feet, swiping the water from his face. Back in his suite, he dried himself with a towel in the bathroom and then stared at his reflection in the mirror. He had passed the first test. They would have killed him if they had any proof that he was not who he said he was, or if they could be sure that he had framed Jackson.

They had not.

He had one main advantage in his favour: the cartel had just lost their way into a lucrative market, and Milton was offering alternative access. He had purchased a kilo, had paid for it promptly, and had successfully smuggled it across the border. They needed a way to ensure that the flow of product continued unabated and, right now, Milton probably looked like he was their best shot.

Greed would be their downfall.

He would see to it.

Milton tossed the wet towel into the bath, switched off the light and went back to bed. It was difficult to predict what tomorrow might hold, but he knew that his odds of navigating it successfully would be improved if he was rested.

51

Milton awoke with the dawn. He got out of bed, opened the shutters and looked out at a spectacular sunrise. The horizon had exploded with colour, reds and oranges that poured above the peaks of the mountain range in the distance and dappled the saguaro cactus, prickly pear and yucca that had been planted to obscure the fence that divided the *casa* from the rest of the property. Milton's focus drew in closer, to the crystal-blue water of the pool and the chair that had been turned over during his interrogation last night. He remembered what had happened, and hoped that his story had stood up to the scrutiny that had been focused upon it.

The Scandinavian had taken his fingerprints. That had only happened twice in the years since he had left the Group: once in Texas when he had been arrested after a brawl, and then again in Michigan. Ziggy had told him that he had found those records and expunged them; once again, Milton found that he had no option but to trust that he had been as thorough as he had promised. He had used the name of John Smith during both of those arrests, but *this*

John Smith—the ambitious London drug dealer—would have been in prison when the *other* John Smith was in the States. Milton would not be able to bluff his way around the questions that would inevitably follow if the discrepancies were found.

He showered and dressed, took a moment to compose himself, and, finally ready, he opened the door and followed the corridor back to the front of the house.

~

HECTOR DEL POZO was having his breakfast on the veranda. Milton sat down opposite the Mexican.

"Did you sleep well?" del Pozo asked him.

"Seriously?"

Del Pozo looked at him quizzically.

"I had an unpleasant visit."

"Ah," del Pozo said. "Yes, of course. Apologies. But we have to be thorough. Some might think that your story might be a little too good to be true. The coincidence that you should appear just as Señor Jackson had his legal difficulties..."

"I told you—again and again and again—that has nothing to do with me."

"Of course. But we need to be sure."

"The big guy—who is he?"

"I'm sorry?"

"Big guy. Blond. Looks like Thor."

"Eidur? He concerns himself with security for the cartel."

"What is he? A mercenary?"

"You'd have to ask him."

Milton wondered whether del Pozo would expect his

indignation, but decided that there was no point in dragging it out. If they wanted to maintain the charade of civility, that was fine. He could do that.

"Next time you have a question, please, just ask me. There's no need to rough me up."

Milton looked out at the desert beyond the *casa* and the mountains that prickled the horizon. Del Pozo's daughter was cantering an Arabian horse around the paddock and, as Milton watched, she nudged it in line with a brush fence and held on as it cleared it with distance to spare.

A member of the household staff came over and asked what Milton would like for breakfast. Del Pozo had a bowl of fruit and a mug of coffee on the table, and Milton said that he would like the same. The woman gave a nod and went over to a serving area where a buffet had been set out.

"So," del Pozo said once the woman was gone, "shall we continue our discussion from dinner?"

"Have you thought about it?"

"I have."

"And?

"We might be open to a relationship."

"I'm pleased to hear it. And my terms?"

Del Pozo spread his hands on the table. "They are acceptable to us."

"Excellent," Milton said.

"The arrangement is agreed in principle."

"Meaning?"

"You have proposed a significant relationship. Señor Jackson was an important distributor for the cartel. Replacing him—replacing the *income* that he generated, and the presence in your market—will not be a simple matter." Milton started to protest, but del Pozo stalled him with a raised hand. "Perhaps you can do it. Perhaps. But before we are prepared to consider what a relationship with you might look like, there are certain formalities that must be taken care of."

"Like what?"

"You will travel into the jungle."

Milton paused. "What? Why?"

"I represent La Frontera, as you know. We are responsible for moving the product. It comes to us in Mexico and we prepare it for its onward journey. We have developed transit routes to take it around the world—to America, to Europe, to your country. But, as I explained yesterday, we are in a relationship with the cartel responsible for the production of the product."

"El Centro."

"Yes," del Pozo said. "El Centro. Our relationship is collaborative. We might be satisfied with you—but now they must be, too. For a market as important as yours, the Colombians will want to assure themselves that you are who you say you are, and that you can deliver on your promises. They do not leave the jungle, so you must go to them."

"Where?"

"Not very far from here."

"And if I don't want to go?"

"Then there will be no deal," del Pozo said. "And we would have to question your seriousness. You have told us how keen you are to work with us. If the prospect of a further trip is a reason for you to change your mind…" He paused and shrugged. "It would not be taken kindly. The woman whom you will meet is not a person whom you would want to offend. Snubbing her invitation would be unwise."

Milton leaned back in his chair and spread his hands. "Fine. When?"

"This morning," del Pozo said. "I see no reason to wait. We will leave after breakfast. This will all be sorted by the end of the day."

Milton nodded.

Del Pozo stared at him for a long moment. "One other thing," he said. "We know that whatever happened to Mr. Jackson was the result of something that you orchestrated. You can continue to deny it, of course, but you would be wasting your breath. I do not believe in coincidence. You would be unwise to think that you're fooling us."

"I'm not trying to fool anyone about anything."

Del Pozo smiled beatifically. "I admire your ruthlessness," he said. "Your resourcefulness, too. But—and although I do not want to spoil the atmosphere—if you ever do something like that again, we will cut your legs off, three inches at a time."

~

IT HAD JUST GONE eight when there was a knock at the door of Milton's room. He opened it and found that the big Scandinavian was waiting.

"Morning," Milton said, as if last night had never happened.

If Milton's sangfroid perturbed him, the big man did not show it. "The helicopter is waiting."

He stood there with his foot blocking the door from closing; they were evidently leaving immediately.

Milton followed the man through the house, exiting through a rear door and then taking a gravelled track between paddocks to a wide, flat field in which sat a helicopter. It was a Bell 505 Jet Ranger, a medium-range transport that Milton knew would have cost more than a million dollars. Hector del Pozo was leaning against the fuselage.

"Get in," he said.

Del Pozo opened the door at the side of the chopper and waited for Milton to embark. There were three seats in the back and then two for the pilot and a fourth passenger ahead of them. Milton took one of the seats in the rear, sliding his arms through the safety harness and clipping the straps into the receiver between his legs. Eidur took the seat next to the pilot. Del Pozo clambered in, slammed the door and secured it, and then got into the pilot's seat.

Milton settled in as del Pozo went through his preflight checks. The engine fired up and the rotors began to turn. Milton looked out of the window as the helicopter lifted into the air, turned through ninety degrees and, with a dip of its nose, started to accelerate away.

52

Hicks cleared away the empty pizza boxes from last night's meal and dumped them in the trash. He was restless. The three of them had been in the hotel room for hours and it had very quickly become tiresome. He had never been good at sitting around doing nothing. His career in the Regiment had included lots of it —waiting for hours for the right moment to take action— and he had hated it then, too.

The hotel room was starting to smell a little funky. They had a balcony, and Hicks went over and pulled the door back, allowing the morning heat to wash over him as he went outside. Medellín was laid out beneath him; he looked down on the chaotic grid of streets and wondered where Milton was.

The door slid open again. Hicks turned his head and glanced back; Chase had joined him on the balcony. He had two bottles of water and he offered one to Hicks.

"Thanks," Hicks said, taking a sip. His throat was already dusty.

Chase rested his elbows on the balustrade. "How long do you think we'll be waiting here?"

"As long as it takes," Hicks said.

They stared out onto the city in silence for a moment.

"Can I ask you a question?" Chase said.

"Sure."

"Who is he?"

Hicks shifted. "Who? Milton?"

Chase nodded. "He doesn't say much, does he? I can tell he's capable. You can see it—he's got plenty of notches on his gun."

Hicks shrugged. "He's capable."

"He's more than that. I mean, he's not a regular guy—right? A regular guy doesn't fly all of us to Amsterdam like that and start fixing to fool a drug cartel. A regular guy doesn't fly us to England just so we can ruin some other guy's life by doing a deal with the cartel." Chase shook his head. "So, no. No, sir. He ain't a regular guy."

"Why do you care?"

Chase stared out over the city. "He's military?"

Hicks took another pull on his water, unsure of how much Milton had told Chase about who he was and what he had done. "I know about as much as you."

"Come on," Chase said, glancing across at him. "You and him and Ziggy? I can see it. You're tight enough to raise a blister. Seems to me like y'all have done this kind of thing before."

"That doesn't mean that I know any more about him than you do. Don't waste your time worrying about who he is—he'll tell you what you need to know and that'll be that. You'd be better to focus on why we're here. On what the goal is. Don't worry about things you aren't going to get an answer to." Hicks shook his head. "It won't get you anywhere."

Chase chewed on his bottom lip for a minute. "What about you?"

"What about me?"

"Military?"

"Just a guy on a job."

Chase frowned. "Come on. Give me *something*."

"It's better you don't know."

"How'd you figure that?"

"The less we know about each other, the less we can say if we get into trouble with the police or the cartel. I'm serious. I know it's dull, but you've got to stay focused. Don't waste time and energy on things that don't matter."

"It does matter to me. It matters because I'm putting all my trust in some guy who says he knew my old man. I met him once; then the next thing I know, my dad's dead and he's saying he'll help me fix the mess he probably made in the first place. I'd like to have a better idea of just who he is."

"That works both ways. Milton didn't need your help to go after the cartel. He would've done it anyway. And he doesn't know *you*, either, yet here you are. He's brought you in. He's trusting you not to fuck up. A guy he barely knows."

Chase thought about that for a moment, then took another gulp of water. "You trust him?"

"Completely."

They heard an exclamation from the room and went back inside. Ziggy had stood up and, as he saw Hicks and Chase, he turned his laptop around so that they could both see the screen.

"What is it?" Hicks asked him.

"I got a hit," Ziggy exclaimed.

"Where?"

"South. The first one was from a tower at the edge of Medellín. Southeast."

"They took him out that way yesterday," Chase said.

"And then?" Hicks asked.

"The second and third pings came quickly after that, fast, like he was travelling."

"By road?"

"Too fast for that. There's rush-hour traffic. Looks like they're flying."

"To where?"

"I lost the signal again at San Antonio de Prado," Ziggy said.

"Which is where?"

"Western side of the city."

"So we don't know where he is?"

"No," Ziggy said. "But we can be pretty confident that he's still alive."

53

They flew for thirty minutes, eventually touching down in a clearing to the west of a small town. They disembarked and made their way across the clearing to an idling Mercedes. Eidur opened the rear door and indicated that Milton should get inside. He did and then shuffled across as the big Scandinavian slid in next to him. Del Pozo sat in the passenger seat next to the waiting driver.

They drove west for three hours, passing through the towns of El Morrillo and Heliconia. They eventually rolled to a stop in Santa Isabel, parking against a whitewashed building that had been identified with a blue-painted legend—ALMACEN EL DESVARE—and then, in red beneath it, 'Tuercas Y Tornillos.'

"This is it?" Milton asked.

"Not yet," del Pozo replied.

"So why are we stopping?"

"We need to change cars."

They didn't have to wait long. A dusty green Land Rover Defender pulled up. Milton guessed that it was ten years old, with a battered cargo rack on the roof and dents and scratches along the doors and the wing. A young man in his early twenties got out of the passenger seat. He was wearing a green golf shirt and tan shorts. His hair was cut short and a diamond sparkled in the lobe of his left ear. Eidur and del Pozo opened their doors and got out. They spoke with the younger man. Eidur turned to gesture to where Milton was sitting, and the kid looked, then gave a nod and went back to the Land Rover.

Eidur leaned into the cabin. "This way."

Milton got out; he was aware of locals staring at them as they crossed the street to the Defender. The big Scandinavian with his pale skin and platinum hair would have been an unusual sight in a place like this. Milton, too, with his bright blue eyes. Eidur opened the door and Milton got in, sliding into the seat behind the kid. Eidur climbed in and pulled the door shut. Del Pozo got into the front.

The driver reached down and then handed a piece of fabric back to Eidur.

It was a hood.

Eidur opened the bottom of the hood, pulled it over Milton's head and then tightened a drawstring to bring it closed.

"Go," the Scandinavian said to the driver.

The engine cranked into gear and the car pulled away.

54

Ellie was more nervous than she would have cared to admit. Yesterday had been a case of waiting for a signal that did not come, but today had been different. CHILD had sent a message that WITCH was in the jungle and that there would be a window tonight when she would be vulnerable. It was the green light. The operation was scheduled to begin at twenty-two hundred hours, but they would be transiting to the jungle sooner than that. The briefing had been called for midday, and the SEALs had gathered at one end of the garage in front of two large blown-up satellite images that had been stuck to the wall. Ellie went over to join them just as Commander McSweeney clapped his hands to bring them to attention.

"All right," he said. "Settle down." McSweeney took a small laser pointer and shone the light on the first image. "Here's your recap, so pay attention. There are two teams involved in this operation: Alpha Troop and Bravo Troop. Alpha is already in-country—I'll get to them in a moment." He nodded to the map, where the pinprick of red light danced around a tiny collection of buildings that was surrounded by the green of the jungle. "This is our target. CHILD suggests that it is a cocaine laboratory belonging to the El Centro cartel. CHILD also suggests that WITCH is at the laboratory right now."

A SEAL raised his hand. "We sure of that, sir?"

"She was seen here"—the commander moved the laser so that it shone on a settlement to the east of the laboratory site—"yesterday afternoon. CHILD suggests that she was last seen trekking into the jungle in the direction of the kitchen. She has been almost impossible to track down. The reason for that is she keeps a very, very low profile. She's not ostentatious. She doesn't show off her money like some of her predecessors. She moves every night or every other night, spending her time in jungle hideouts like this or houses and apartments in San Javier, Belen and Robledo— the places in Medellín where you wouldn't want to go. Getting a fix on her like this has been practically impossible until now."

The commander stepped across so that he could shine the laser onto the second map. This one was at closer scale, showing a collection of huts and other structures, most of which were shielded by the canopy of vegetation that stretched overhead.

"Alpha deployed two days ago to the area northwest and northeast of the cartel camp. *Here* and *here*. They've got close enough to suggest that you will encounter armed resistance, but nothing that you won't be able to handle. You will approach from the south." He moved the pointer and played the light over an area notable only for the emerald green of the jungle and the blue swipe of the river that ran through it. "You will drive out of Medellín in the chicken truck until you get to the swap point, *here*. The road gets more difficult at that point, so you'll transfer to three Land Rovers that

Alpha have secured. You'll drive on as far as you can and then go on foot through the jungle until you reach this staging point *here*"—he flashed the pointer—"where you will wait for the signal to attack. The narcos use emergency guidelines to get them out of the jungle at night. Your job is to push north and flush them out. Alpha will be waiting for them to the north of the camp, at the end of the guidelines. Their orders are to shoot anything that moves."

"Fish in a barrel," one of the soldiers observed.

"Fish might have a better chance."

"What about WITCH?"

"She'll be with her personal security detail. We don't know anything about them, but we can assume that they will be dangerous. The source suggests that she is followed by a Scandinavian ex–special forces operator."

"A merc?"

"That's what we think. He's supposed to be big and nasty —one to look out for. The goal is to capture and exfiltrate her, but, if that isn't possible, there is approval to use deadly force. She's coming out of the jungle tonight—I'd rather it was in cuffs, but I don't particularly care if it's in a box."

The men all nodded that they understood.

"Now," the commander said, "you've got guests coming along today. Special Agent Ellie Flowers has been running the FBI's investigation into the assassination of Ambassador Cochrane. Ellie—put your hand up, please."

Ellie did as she was asked, nodding to the men as they turned to check her out.

"And over there, behind Ellie—put your hands up, guys. That's Luis Miguel and David Fuentes. They're DEA agents and they've been on WITCH's trail for the last six months. You want to add anything, fellas?"

"Just to say that we'd love to get her alive if we can. I

know that's easier said than done, but if we get her, then there's a chance we can roll the whole organisation up. We're also looking for any documents or digital equipment that she might have with her. We'll be in charge of checking the camp once it's been cleared, but if you see anything that you think might be useful, then let either one of us know and we'll check it out."

McSweeney folded his arms. "You clear?"

The SEALs answered in the affirmative.

"Good luck. You got two hours to get ready. It's four hours to the jungle and it's not going to be comfortable."

55

The hood was made of a thick material that blocked all light. It also muffled the sound, and, even though Milton tried to listen out for something that might give him an idea about where he was being taken, it was impossible to distinguish anything recognisable. He usually had a good sense of the passage of time but, without sight or sound, even that felt unreliable.

He guessed it was an hour—although it could easily have been more—when the rough surface of the road on which they had been travelling changed to something more uneven. The Land Rover bounced through potholes and across rougher patches. The sound changed, too, with the occasional rumble of a passing car or truck gradually fading away to be replaced by a quiet that was punctuated only by the squeaking of the suspension and the calling of nearby birds.

Eventually the car rolled to a stop. Milton heard a brief conversation in Spanish and the sound of the door opening.

"Out," Eidur said, grabbing Milton's arm and pulling him across the seat.

Milton put his feet down, feeling loose dirt and stones beneath the soles of his boots.

"I don't think we need that anymore," del Pozo said.

The hood was yanked from his head.

Milton blinked against the blast of bright sunlight. He waited until his vision had adjusted and then looked around. They were in a settlement of some description, but there was nothing that he could use to identify it. The village comprised a series of raised huts. The land ran down to a wide river, the sunlight sparkling off the purplish surface. There were signs that the waters often overflowed, and a gaggle of dirty children played in the muddy fields on this side of the river.

"Where are we?"

Del Pozo shook his head. "No, Señor Smith. You don't need to know that."

"Is this it? We're meeting here?"

"No. We go deeper into the jungle. We're stopping here for a moment to take a drink."

It *was* hot. The position of the sun suggested that it was early afternoon, and Milton guessed the temperature was in the nineties. Del Pozo led the way into the nearest hut. It was made entirely from wood, from the walls to the roof and all of the furniture inside. A reservoir had been constructed from a sheet of tarpaulin suspended between four wooden posts that had been driven into the ground.

A set of wooden steps led up to a porch upon which an old woman was drying coca leaves. Milton nodded a greeting to her and continued through the door and into the hut. The accommodation was arranged as one large room with mattresses stacked up against the wall, and a hammock hung from two joists. Another room was hidden behind a closed door. The kitchen was part of the main space with an open fire. An elderly man with rheumy eyes and weather-beaten skin pointed in the direction of the door.

Milton opened it and went through. The toilet was primitive—no more than a hole in the floor—and he relieved himself into it, then took a moment to look through the narrow slit that served as a window. The jungle was on the other side of the hut, with stands of ceiba and myrtle and laurel then, a little further away, tall *emergentes* that pierced the canopy and reached up for twenty or thirty metres.

Milton opened the door and went back into the hut. The woman from the porch was in the kitchen now, attending to something on the stove. She prepared a flask of coffee, the metal blackened from being exposed to the heat, and ladled out a bowl of lentils. The man cut slices of bread from a crusty loaf and handed one, and a bowl, to Milton. He took it outside and ate it, using the bread to scoop out the lentils. Del Pozo was sitting on the lowered tailgate of the Defender with Eidur next to him. The Mexican slid down and came over to stand next to him.

"The owner of this hut is Geronimo," he said, gesturing to the building. "He runs the kitchen that we will be going to."

"The kitchen?"

"'Laboratory' is too grand a word, but that is what it is. It is where the coca paste is prepared."

Milton scooped out the last of the lentils.

The Mexican was relaxed and evidently in a loquacious mood. "This is a good opportunity to show you how efficient our operation is. I think you will benefit from understanding the process—you only see the cocaine when it arrives to you. It is ready for the market then. I'm sure you cut it—add your baby powder, your laxative, whatever—but you never see what it is like before, when it is new. When it is *pure*. It will be good for you to know. You will treat it with more respect when you see how much work is required to bring it to you." He chuckled. "From the jungles of Colombia to the noses of your gringo customers. You should be grateful, Señor Smith. This will be a useful education for you."

"That's what this is? You're showing me what I'm buying?"

"That is part of it."

"The other part?"

"I told you. The cartel wants to know more about the man who wishes to do business with it."

"*You're* the cartel," Milton said. "We really couldn't have done this in Medellín?"

"I have an opinion on your suitability. But others want to meet you, too." He paused. "I say others, but there is only one person whose voice really matters."

"And who is that?"

"The boss," he said.

56

Ellie watched as the men checked their weapons and equipment. Now that they were getting close to go-time, they were *all* business. She had watched them over the course of the afternoon, and they had been relaxed and carefree, sharing jokes at their own expense and speculating upon what they would find when they arrived at the target. They had become progressively less relaxed as midday became one o'clock and then two, and now, almost ready to go, they had their game faces on. They were a fearsome proposition. Ellie did not rate the odds of survival for any *traficantes* who might be foolish enough to put themselves between them and WITCH.

"Nervous?"

Ellie turned. It was Fuentes. Miguel was behind him.

"Of course."

"Same," Fuentes said.

"It's a good plan," Miguel said.

"I know that."

Fuentes nodded over at the SEALs. "And these guys don't fuck around."

She nodded. *Neither do I.*

Commander McSweeney joined them.

"You all ready to go?"

They all said that they were.

McSweeney nodded and turned back to his men. "Load up," he said, pointing to the large truck that had pulled into the yard at the back of the garage. "Go get that murdering bitch."

57

The rain came quickly and almost without warning. The skies had been clear when Milton had gone outside with his meal, but, as he returned from taking his empty bowl to the kitchen, clouds had started to gather. The locals looked up with knowing eyes, and, within moments, the clouds broke and a tumult of rain hammered down at them.

Milton retreated to the porch. "What do we do? Wait it out?"

"We cannot," del Pozo said. "You have an appointment."

Milton had no problem with trekking into the jungle in the rain—he had attended the Regiment's jungle warfare school in Borneo, after all, and this was nothing compared to some of the biblical deluges that he had been subjected to there—but John Smith did not share that experience. He knew that they would expect him to react in a certain way, and, as Milton swiped the rain from his eyes, he saw that Eidur was watching him.

"We'll get soaked," he protested.

The Scandinavian shook his head derisively.

Geronimo returned with two horses on lead ropes. A younger man followed with another two horses.

"Can you ride?" del Pozo asked him.

"Not really. I'll manage."

That, at least, was the truth. Milton *had* ridden before, but not for several years and, even then, he would not have said he was particularly comfortable in the saddle. Geronimo, del Pozo and Eidur all mounted their horses. The young man led the final horse over to Milton and offered to boost him up into the battered old saddle. Milton nodded his thanks, waited for the man to make a cradle with his hands, and raised his left boot so that the man could help him to clamber up. He swung his right leg up and over the horse's back and settled on the saddle. He took the reins and slid his feet into the stirrups.

Geronimo led the way and Eidur brought up the rear. There was just enough space on the trail for Milton and del Pozo to ride side by side.

"This part of the jungle," Milton said, gesturing. "It's all about coke?"

Del Pozo nodded. "Coca makes life possible for the people who live here. Geronimo is from Putumayo. He has worked with the leaves all his life. He worked for Pablo and, after Pablo was killed, he went south to work in Cali. The gringos dismantled that cartel, too, and Geronimo came north again, and, eventually, he worked for us. It is a difficult life. A hard life. Before all this, he was captured by ELN paramilitaries. He has been held by FARC. He has seen kitchens torched by soldiers guided to them by the American DEA."

"Maybe he should think about changing jobs."

Geronimo snorted. Milton had assumed he spoke no English, but now he wondered.

"It pays well," del Pozo said.

The old man turned in his saddle and rubbed his thumb and forefinger together. "*Dinero*," he called back. "*Mucho dinero*."

They rode deeper into the jungle. The track ran down to the river, and they followed along it, the horses struggling through patches of shallow mud and loose earth before they turned away from the water and started a gentle ascent to a plateau. The jungle was thick and there were stretches where the vegetation was so close that they had to go in single file; even then, the branches scraped against their legs and the horses snorted nervously. Milton had absolutely no idea where they were; they could have been in another country for all he knew.

58

They rode in the back of the truck from the safe house in Medellín to the changeover point. It was a big boxy vehicle that was painted a grubby white, with the name of the business and a cartoon chicken painted on the side. It looked—and smelled—as if it had been an authentic delivery truck in the not-too-distant past, and that verisimilitude, combined with its generous capacity, made it an ideal vehicle for their purposes. They could move the SEALs and their gear, plus Ellie and the two DEA agents, without arousing attention.

That didn't mean that the ride was comfortable; far from it. They had to sit on the floor of the truck, pressed tight against one another, feeling every bump and judder as the roads became progressively less and less smooth. Ellie closed her eyes and tried to take herself to a place where she could find peace and ignore the nerves that were already making her feel a little nauseated. She had seen action before, but this was something that was outside of her experience. McSweeney had told her and the DEA agents to stay back, behind the SEALs, but they were going to be assaulting a cartel stronghold that was surrounded by jungle, at night, and with only patchy intelligence from CHILD and Alpha Troop. It was impossible to be sure about what they might find and, in that uncertainty, in the greys between black and white, doubt was able to fester and spread.

Ellie heard the squeal of the brakes and felt the truck decelerate, eventually rolling to a stop. The engine was switched off.

Lieutenant Commander McCoy stood up. "We're at Checkpoint Yankee," he said. "Take a piss if you need to. We'll be moving out again in two minutes."

The roller door was unlatched and thrown up; bright late-afternoon sunlight streamed into the back of the truck. Ellie blinked into it, waiting for her eyes to adjust, and then followed the SEALs outside. She hopped down and looked around.

The truck was parked in a clearing at the side of a narrow track. The surface of the track was mud, a series of troughs and ridges between large waterlogged patches. A river ran across the track fifty yards ahead and, beyond that, the mud looked much deeper and less penetrable. The truck had done well to get this far; it wouldn't be able to proceed any farther. Instead, they would be travelling by way of three rugged Land Rovers. The vehicles had been hidden beneath the treeline, hidden by camouflage tarpaulins and guarded by two of the SEALs from Alpha Troop. They had prepared the vehicles for their onward journey, driving them out of cover so that Bravo Troop could transfer into them.

"Let's go, let's go," Lieutenant Commander McCoy called out.

Ellie hauled herself into the back of the Land Rover at the rear of the formation. It was going to be a tight squeeze again, and she was pressed up against the door as two brawny SEALs slid onto the bench seat next to her. They had already daubed their skin with camouflage paint, and they both had night-vision goggles on swivel mounts that were attached to their helmets.

"How long to the RV from here?" Ellie said to the driver.

"An hour in the Land Rover and then an hour on foot."

The lead vehicle started its engine and bumped ahead on the road, and each of the vehicles in line followed along. They splashed through the river, water spraying out on either side, and then settled into a steady pace as they headed deeper into the jungle.

59

Milton and the others rode on until they reached a clearing. Geronimo brought his horse to a stop and dismounted. Hector and Eidur slid from their horses, too, and waited for Milton to do the same. Geronimo tied the horses to a hitching post.

"Is this it?" Milton asked.

"Nearly," del Pozo said. "Just a short walk."

Milton turned to see Geronimo making his way deeper into the jungle. Del Pozo followed, gesturing for Milton to stay close. Eidur waited to bring up the rear. The path was hardly there at all, the kind of trail that might have been made by an animal, only just passable for a person. They descended into a shallow depression, forded the stream that wound its way along the bottom, and then climbed up the opposite bank until they were inside the jungle again.

"This is a dangerous life," del Pozo said. "The government is always looking. Thousands have been jailed. Others have been shot. And they fly planes overhead and dump gallons of poison onto the trees."

They pressed on, the rain hammering on the canopy of

leaves overhead, a deluge that shook the branches and flooded the ground whenever there was a gap in the cover. They squelched through mud and forded more streams that, despite seemingly being so far away from civilisation, smelled strongly of petrol.

At last Geronimo stopped and pointed. "We are here."

The kitchen was hidden in the centre of a stand of tall palm trees. Their fronds had reached out and knotted together over the years, providing a natural roof and a screen to prevent detection from the air. The trees were wrapped with vines, and, as Milton watched, he saw a man clamber up one of them with a machete to hack down the fruit so that it didn't fall and injure someone below. Vegetation had been stripped away from between the trunks of the trees, and the laboratory established among them. It was a simple wooden structure, the tarpaulin roof held up by joists and ropes that were wrapped around the trunks. A short distance away from the building was a stack of jerrycans that must have accounted for the pungent smell of gasoline that Milton had noticed as they made their way to the kitchen, and perhaps for the effluent that he had seen in the streams.

Milton saw a line of men and women making their way to the kitchen from the other side of the small clearing. They were each carrying burlap sacks, some balancing a single larger one on their shoulders, others hefting two, one in each hand. The men and women formed a queue in front of a man with a notebook and pen. The man addressed the peasant who was at the head of the line, weighed his sack on a large set of digital scales, handed over a sum of money and then scribbled down a note in his book.

"What's he doing?"

"This is a perfect supply line," del Pozo said. "The

farmers bring coca leaves to the kitchens. They sell it—five thousand pesos for twenty pounds."

"Five thousand? How much is that?"

"Two dollars." Del Pozo grinned. "But two dollars goes a long way here. They can make more money selling coca than coffee or coconuts."

Milton trailed behind del Pozo as they moved under a makeshift roof and then to a section covered by a plastic tarp. The floor was scattered with coca leaves, presumably poured out after being bought from the farmers. Two men ground the leaves into a mulch. This was then emptied into plastic basins, after which a woman added lime, retrieving it from a bag by her side. The blend was then transferred into a plastic drum. Gasoline was added, the resulting mixture churned with a lengthy wooden spoon.

The woman with the lime looked to be in her early to mid-forties. She was wearing a white vest that was cropped an inch or two above her waist, the fabric stained with grease and residue from the process of refining the coca leaves. She had long brown hair that was tied back in a ponytail; a few rogue tresses were plastered to her face by either her sweat or the rain. Her eyes were brown, too, and, as she turned her attention to Milton, he saw that they were deep and soulful.

"*Inglés?*" she said.

"Yes," Milton replied. "English."

She switched to English. "You want to know what happens here?"

He nodded.

She took Milton to a table that held a large container that looked as if it had been standing for a while. She nodded to the man who was tending to it, and he turned a tap, opening a valve that allowed the contents to flow out into a pot for collection. The man handed the can of liquid to the woman, and she proffered it to Milton so that he could look at it more closely. The process had produced a lime-green liquid.

"We strain this until we have the paste. Here." She walked over to the table and held up a tray that was filled with paste. "Then we heat the paste until we have a cream. That is turned into the powder that people like you are so keen to buy."

Milton stopped and wiped the sweat from his eyes. "Thank you," he said. He turned back to del Pozo. "It's as hot as hell here. Who am I supposed to be meeting?"

Del Pozo didn't answer; instead, he angled his head so that his gaze fell somewhere behind Milton's shoulder.

"You are here to meet me."

Milton turned back. The woman with the brown eyes was still standing there.

"I am La Bruja," she said. "You must be Señor Smith."

"That's right," she said. "Señor Jackson. I met him once. A *fanfarrón*—do you know this word?"

Milton shrugged. "I don't."

"A braggart," del Pozo said.

"Yes, a braggart." She made a motion with her thumb and fingers, suggesting someone talking. "His favourite subject was himself, and how much money he was going to make us. *Blah blah blah*. He was a very boring man."

"Was?" Milton said.

She looked at del Pozo. "You did not tell him?"

"No," he said.

"Señor Jackson was found dead in his cell this morning," she said. She clenched her fist, raised it to her throat and jerked it upwards. "The sheets. He made a *lazo*. How do you say?"

"A noose," Milton finished.

"Yes, a noose. The guards found him. They will say that he did it himself, but he didn't. We have friends everywhere. They can make problems like this go away." She clicked her fingers by way of emphasis.

Milton had no doubt that Jackson had been murdered. She had no reason to lie. He knew that she had told him this to underline the gravity of his proposed business, and what would happen in the event that they decided that he was a liability. The cartel had a long reach; eliminating someone in a prison cell on the other side of the world was clearly not a problem for them.

Del Pozo took another step into the hut and leaned back against the wall. He was ten feet away from Milton; close enough for him to get up and get over to him before he would be able to draw his weapon. Milton would fire out a right-hand punch to stun him, then reach down for the weapon with his left. How long would that take? Ten seconds? Less. He rearranged himself so that he was sitting on his crossed right leg, which would allow him to move quickly.

"Jackson was a *fanfarrón*, yet he *did* make us a lot of money. I can put up with irritation if a person is valuable, and he was. You can imagine how concerned we were to find out that he had found himself in trouble with the police."

"Of course," Milton said. "But, as I've explained to Señor del Pozo, I had nothing to do with that."

She smiled sweetly. "It was just a harmless coincidence?"

"I don't know," Milton said.

The atmosphere was beginning to concern him. He had hoped that the interrogation into his *bona fides* was over. Would they have brought him all the way out here—flown him from Medellín and driven him into the jungle—if they still harboured doubt that he wasn't who he said he was, or that his denials over Jackson's arrest were lies? Wouldn't they have killed him at the *casa*? They surely would. This was just another check, he told himself. Just a little added turbulence before he got to where he needed to be.

"I know that you have said that you had nothing to do with what happened to Jackson, but we know that's not true. Hector?"

Del Pozo reached into his pocket and took out a piece of paper. He unfolded it and held it out so that they could both see it. Milton looked and saw an image of himself at Manchester Airport. He was waiting in line for security, his carry-on luggage on the ground next to his feet and his jacket off, ready to be put through the scanner.

"What's this?" he said, tensing a little as he prepared to move.

"This is you on your way from Manchester to Amsterdam," she said. "We always check those who want to work with us. López found your story less than convincing, so he arranged for a little additional investigation. You were in the same city as Señor Jackson on the day that he was arrested —indeed, within hours of the incident. I suppose that might have been a coincidence, although I don't really believe in them. And then..."

She looked over at del Pozo and waited for him to hand down a second photograph. It was a piece of police evidence, complete with a stamp that denoted it as having originated with the Greater Manchester Police. The photograph showed the brick of cocaine that Milton had purchased from López. The end of the brown paper wrapping was sliced open, revealing the latex inner layer and the dense white substance beneath.

"This is how we pack our product," La Bruja said. "First we use the latex and then we wrap it in the paper."

"I told him this," Milton said, indicating del Pozo. "I bought my coke from you. He bought his coke from you. They're the same."

She ignored his protest. "I suppose it could have been a brick that Señor Jackson had bought from us himself, except that when the police tested it, the results indicated that the substance included a chemical—potassium permanganate—that we only started to use in the preparation of our product after his last shipment had been delivered."

"But before yours," del Pozo said.

La Bruja stood. "So we know, Señor Smith. We *know*. We know that you used the cocaine that you bought from us to frame Señor Jackson."

Del Pozo stepped back, out of range. Milton noticed that his hand had drifted to the butt of his pistol.

"So?" Milton said. "You brought me out here to tell me

that? Why didn't you just have one of your goons shoot me at the ranch?"

La Bruja smiled. "Because, John, I do not care."

"What?"

"Jackson was a liability. He did not take things as seriously as he should have. You demonstrated that. It was clever, yes, what you did, but he should not have put himself in a position where he was vulnerable, no matter how cunning you were. We have had reports for several months that he was... how you say?"

"Making too much noise," del Pozo finished.

"Showing how much money he had," she added. "Fast cars. Property. The police, they are not as stupid as he thought they were. They started an investigation into his business. They knew that there was no way that he could have been making the money that he said through legitimate means. It is the same in Colombia and Mexico. Escobar became a problem for the government because he was *bigger* than the government. El Patrón was the same in Mexico. He made too much noise—him and his son—and now they are dead because of it."

Milton nodded blandly as she mentioned El Patrón, thinking that she wouldn't believe him if he told her what had really happened to the old Mexican *narcotraficante* in the mountains.

"I do not make that mistake," she said. "Look around you." She swept a hand out to indicate the settlement and the dense trees that surrounded it. "This is where I live. In the jungle. No one knows where I am. I live quietly. Carefully. No noise."

"If you're worried about discretion," Milton said, "you don't need to be. I've never been interested in flaunting my success. I agree—it's stupid. The police notice. The competition notices. You might as well paint a target on your back and invite them to come and have a go at you. I don't need to judge my success by how many people know that I'm doing well."

Del Pozo grinned at him. "You would rather look at your bank balance?"

"Money has always been a good way of keeping score."

La Bruja nodded and got to her feet. "On that we can agree."

Milton rose, too. Del Pozo was close. Milton readied himself, feeling the adrenaline, anticipating sudden action. A right-handed jab to stun the Mexican, release the weapon with his left hand, swap it from left to right and then fire. One round into del Pozo, two rounds into La Bruja, then run.

The door opened. It was Eidur.

"What are we doing?" he asked.

"We will have dinner here," La Bruja said.

Del Pozo stepped away, out of range.

Milton bit down his frustration.

"And tonight?" Eidur said.

"We'll stay here," she said. "We'll eat and discuss how we can work together, and then Señor Smith can go home to find the money he says he has to pay us."

62

Milton stepped outside and noticed a man and a woman who had not been there before. He assumed that they had been inside one of the other huts. They were not Colombian. They were tanned and dirty with the grime of the jungle, but Milton could see that they were white. They were wearing jungle camouflage and carrying AR-15 rifles. Eidur crossed the clearing, intercepting the two newcomers.

Milton watched them for a moment. It was obvious that the three of them were familiar with one another: the woman said something and the two men laughed. They had an obvious ease, both with each other and with the surroundings within which they found themselves. They were far from home, deep within the jungle at an illegal drugs kitchen, surrounded by armed *traficantes*. The Scandinavian worked for La Bruja; the newcomers evidently did, too. He wondered what they were. Ex-military, certainly. Mercenaries. Personal security for the cartel leadership?

The woman noticed that Milton was watching them.

"What are you looking at?" she said.

Milton had to fight the urge to gape: the woman spoke with a broad Newcastle accent.

"Sorry?" Milton said.

"What's the matter? You deaf? I said what are you looking at?"

"I wasn't looking at anything."

The woman stared him out. Milton didn't want an altercation and looked down.

"I need a beer," the woman said. She turned to the man next to her. "Your turn. Chop-chop."

The man grumbled about something, but made his way across the camp to one of the huts and disappeared inside. The woman gave Milton a final hard stare and then went over to take a place by the fire. Eidur followed.

La Bruja had been watching from inside the hut. She wore a sly smile.

"Who are they?" Milton said, nodding to the departing mercenaries.

"My job has certain... challenges."

"I can imagine. They're security?"

"They are."

She offered nothing else and Milton got the message: she didn't want to discuss them. Instead, she told Milton to follow her to a small wooden structure that had been weatherproofed with a sheet of tarpaulin. She pulled the tarp back to reveal a course of wrapped oblong packages stacked along the wall. She went over to the bricks and took one down. She hefted it and then tossed it over to Milton. He caught it.

"This business," she began. "It offers incredible opportunities. Take the fields outside this village. The farmer plants one hectare of coca. He harvests a thousand kilos of leaves. We process them, add our ingredients, and we are left with a kilo or two of paste. It seems ridiculous, no? All those leaves and so little at the end of it. That paste will make a brick. We sell the bricks for thirty thousand dollars each, and our distributor—perhaps you, Señor Smith, perhaps someone else—can put them into the market for fifty."

Milton looked more closely at the course of bricks. There must have been thirty bricks along the bottom, and it was ten bricks high. The three hundred bricks were worth nine million to the cartel and fifteen million on the street. He replaced the brick he was holding in the same spot it had come from.

"I can do the maths," he said.

La Bruja cocked an eyebrow. "So—you are satisfied with our operation?"

"Of course. It's very impressive."

"Good," she said. "Are you hungry?"

"Very."

"We will eat. Come."

63

Night had fallen, and the darkness swallowed everything. Ellie relied upon her goggles to enable her to see the way ahead, following the spectral shapes of the SEALs as they made their way along the narrow track; it looked as if it had been laid down by larger animals as they made their way to the river to drink. Ellie took regular glances down at the ground to ensure that she did not stumble into the muddy patches where the water table had risen high enough to drench the earth. She clutched her pistol in her right hand, holding her left hand out ahead of her to brush aside dangling creepers and branches that scratched at her skin and caught in the fabric of her jacket.

The SEALs slowed right down as they advanced upon the camp. Their main concern was the possibility that their approach would be noticed and that word would then be passed to La Bruja. Their route to this point had been chosen to minimise that possibility. It was the best that they could do, but it was impossible to say with complete confidence that their arrival would be a surprise. The tactical assessment was that, if WITCH was warned that she was under attack, she would flee along the guidelines to the northeast or northwest, making her way to the river where an exfiltration attempt could be made. That would not be a wise move for her tonight; Alpha had radioed that they were in position, waiting for the attack to start. Bravo were the gun dogs, flushing the birds out of the undergrowth and right into the shooting party.

"Thirty seconds," McCoy hissed over the radio. "On my mark."

∼

Milton followed La Bruja outside and saw that Geronimo was preparing food for them all.

La Bruja went over to the pot that was being heated on a small stove. "You like *Bandeja Paisa*, Señor Smith?"

"What is it?"

"The most traditional dish from Antioquia. In English it is the 'Paisa Platter.' White rice, red beans, shredded meat. Peasant food. It fills the stomach and gives energy to those working in the fields."

The Scandinavian and the two mercenaries who had arrived from the jungle were on one side of the fire. They had found a crate of beer and had shared them out between them, relaxing in the warmth and talking amongst themselves. Milton would have loved to have been able to hear what they were saying, but they were too far away, and the crackle and hiss of the fire and the chirping of insects beyond the treeline made it difficult to discern.

Del Pozo was next to Milton. The Mexican had drawn his pistol and was checking the load. Milton gritted his teeth in frustration. The arrival of La Bruja's security made it much more dangerous to attack now. They had deposited their rifles inside one of the huts, but they still wore holstered pistols and knives in scabbards that were strapped around their legs or ankles. Milton knew that he was going to have to make a move sooner rather than later.

He knew, too, that might mean that he wouldn't leave the jungle alive, but he could accept that. He had done his best to live his life by the Steps that had saved him from his disease, and had tried to atone for the things that he had done before he had come to his senses. He knew that he would never be able to balance both sides of his ledger, that the debt of blood that he owed could never be repaid, but he had tried to do more good than bad, and, on balance, he allowed himself to believe that he had achieved that. If his life was to come to an end, he could think of no better way to mark his exit than by eliminating the leadership of the cartel that was responsible for so much pain and misery and suffering.

It would be a fitting consequence for Beau's murder.

And it would give Chase the revenge that he deserved.

Del Pozo slotted the magazine back into the butt of his pistol and clicked it home. He held the weapon in his right hand, his attention elsewhere.

Milton inched a little closer to him, then a little closer still.

He would assume the magazine was full.

La Bruja first.

Then del Pozo.

Then the mercenaries.

Milton gazed through the flames and saw that the woman and the Scandinavian were on their feet, and that they were coming around the fire to where he was sitting.

"I've heard about you," the woman said.

"That so?"

"It is. You served, right?"

"I did."

"What Regiment?"

"Three Para."

She turned and called back to the other man. "Come here."

He idled over to them. He was a big man, taller and heavier than Milton, although nowhere near as big as Eidur.

"He says he was Three Para," she said.

"That right?" the man replied. "Where were you based?"

"Colchester," Milton said, cleaving as closely as possible to the legend that Ziggy had created.

"Small world," the man said. "Same. When?"

There was nothing for it. Milton had to stick to the script. "Ten years ago."

The man was English, too. Milton thought he heard a West Country burr in his voice.

"You know Ian McKay?" he said.

"Can't say that I do."

"Really? Everyone knows him. QM at Colchester."

Milton shrugged. He felt the buzz of adrenaline. He knew that if they were testing him, and he failed the test, there was a good chance that he would end up with a bullet in his head. The legend was thorough, and Milton had memorised it, but that didn't make it any less fake. If this soldier had been in the same Regiment, he would easily be able to unravel Milton's lies. The squadron quartermaster sergeant was someone John Smith would certainly have known.

"Doesn't ring any bells," he said. "But I wasn't there for long."

"No? What happened?"

"Drug test. I was court-martialled and binned."

The man stared at him, his eyes cold and hard as flint. Milton couldn't read him, but he prepared himself for the worst.

"So we ought to be able to get your discharge papers?"

"I imagine so."

The woman was closest; if he moved quickly, he thought he might be able to separate her from her weapon. He would take it, then take as many shots at the men as he could before making a run for the jungle. He doubted he would be able to get very far, but that was the best he could do.

"You sure about all that?"

"What is this?" Milton protested.

"This is me doing my job, you lying piece of shit."

La Bruja looked over at them. "What is it?"

"He's lying. Ian McKay was killed in the Falklands. He got the VC. Any soldier who really served in 3 PARA knows his story. This guy?" She took out her pistol and waved it at Milton. "This guy doesn't."

Hector del Pozo rested his own pistol on his lap, lazily pointing it at Milton.

"Whoever checked you out really fucked up," the woman said.

La Bruja's expression changed; the wariness with which she had greeted Milton had never entirely gone away, but now it was underlaid with suspicion. "Ask him something else."

The woman stared at him. "What's the name of the Regiment's mascot?"

Milton's stomach fell. Ziggy's background research had been thorough, but it could only ever be superficial. Real depth—the depth of experience of a soldier who was actually in the Regiment—was impossible to manufacture, and Milton's bluffing could only ever go so far.

They had him.

"Señor Smith," La Bruja pressed, "answer the question, please."

He felt vulnerable and exposed. There was disappointment, too, and frustration that—despite being close enough to reach out and touch his ultimate targets—the chances of him being able to meet his objectives were now very small indeed.

"Señor Smith?"

64

Ellie found that her breathing came faster and faster, a combination of exertion and excitement, the anticipation of danger and the violence that they were about to mete out.

She heard a hissed command across the radio and saw the men ahead of her bringing their weapons to bear.

She heard Lieutenant Commander Mark's voice.

"Go, go, go."

∽

"Señor Smith," La Bruja said, "answer the question."

Milton heard something in the forest. Movement. The rustle of leaves.

Eidur heard it, too. "What was that?"

"What was what?" the woman replied.

The big man peered into the gloom. "Movement."

There was quiet now, just the crackle of the fire, the bubble of the stew in the pot. Del Pozo was standing with his back to Milton now so that he could look into the jungle. Milton edged closer.

There came a clatter of wingbeats as a large bird—it looked like a night heron—burst through the undergrowth and launched itself into the air.

"Go and check," Eidur said.

Milton took his chance. He closed the distance to del Pozo in a single stride, looped his left arm around del Pozo's neck and yanked him back so that their bodies were pressed close together. He reached down with his right hand and pulled the Springfield from its holster, his finger sliding through the trigger guard at the same time as he raised it and pressed the muzzle against the side of the Mexican's head. Eidur noticed, but Milton was too quick to be stopped.

"Guns down," Milton said.

"I don't think so," Eidur said.

Milton didn't care about their weapons; his attention was on La Bruja, to his right. He angled del Pozo a little so that he could see her more easily. He would shoot her and then use del Pozo as a shield, back up to the treeline and then run.

"What are you going to do?" Eidur said. "Look at where you are. Where are you going to go?"

"Put your weapons on the ground *now*."

The words had only just left his lips when Milton saw the shape of an object as it arced out of the trees. It landed on the ground a little way away from them, bounced once and then twice, and rolled closer. Two more objects followed.

"Grenade!"

Milton squeezed his eyes shut as the flash bangs detonated with the brightness of a million suns.

∼

Ellie and the two DEA agents stayed back as the flash bangs exploded in a shower of mercury and magnesium powder; she had been warned and had looked away at the moment of detonation so as not to compromise her vision in the sudden cascade of light.

The noise of the explosions echoed back at them from the trees, the last reverberation barely fading out before the SEALs opened fire.

65

Gunfire rang out, bullets winging through the air and thudding into the shacks and, beyond them, the trees at the other side of the clearing. Milton held del Pozo against his body as he backed up, then felt the impacts as three rounds thudded into the Mexican's chest. Milton heard his grunts of pain, then had to grapple hard to keep him upright as his legs gave way. Milton angled his body to the treeline and backed up quickly, reached the edge of a building and let go. Del Pozo collapsed onto the ground, his right leg jerking with involuntary spasms.

Milton pressed himself to the ground and crawled around the side of the building, trying to put something solid between himself and whoever was shooting at them from the treeline. He heard someone running, caught the sound of a thud and then a gasp of pain as someone crashed down atop him. The body twitched and lay still; Milton crawled out from underneath it and saw that it was one of the paste cookers he had seen earlier.

He slid around to the back of the hut, putting his shoulder to the boards. There was blood on his arm; he quickly checked it, found that he was unharmed, and concluded that the blood must have belonged to del Pozo. The gunfire continued to ring out, a clatter that was mixed with cries of pain and angry shouts of command. Milton tuned it out and took a moment to compose himself. He had no idea what was happening; whoever was attacking the camp was well armed, and that made it most likely that it was a government raid. On the other hand, there was a long history of cartels brawling for superiority in this part of the country, and it wasn't impossible that this might be another flaring of that internecine violence.

It didn't really matter. The bullets were the same no matter who was firing them.

He looked left and right. One of the camp guards had abandoned his post and was sprinting for the trees. The man's body jerked to the right as he was pegged in the shoulder, but, somehow, he managed to stay on his feet and kept going. Another round punched him in the back and, arms flung wide, the man crashed down to the ground and lay still.

He saw the Scandinavian and La Bruja. The big man and the woman were together and, as Milton watched, they kept low and ran for the trees.

Milton readied himself, breathing deeply in and out, and counted down.

Three.

Two.

One.

Go.

He ran after them.

∼

Björn grabbed La Bruja by the elbow and dragged her deeper into the trees.

"The government," she said between gasps.

"Maybe."

"What do we do?"

"Run. The guidelines—do you know where they are?"

"North of the camp. There's a stream. The first one is tied around a rock."

"We need to get to it," Björn said.

She swore colourfully. He knew that she wouldn't want to run. She was a fighter; she wanted to fight. But she was a pragmatist, too, and she knew that the prudent play was to take advantage of the escape route and get away from the soldiers. They were outgunned and outmanned, taken by surprise and with no idea of the strategic situation.

"This way," she said.

66

Milton crashed through the undergrowth and forced his way deeper into the mahogany and myrtle trees that populated the rainforest around the camp. The racket of the firefight—the rattle of automatic gunfire, the dull explosions of flash bangs, the yelled voices ordering people to surrender, the shrieks of pain—became more and more muffled as he pressed ahead. The jungle was dense here, with orchids and bromeliads filling the spaces between the laurel and acacia, and ferns and grasses carpeting the ground. He crashed through a collection of cycads, stumbling over their stout trunks and crowns of stiff leaves.

A startled tapir shot out into his path; Milton didn't see it until it was too late and collided with it, sending him sprawling to the ground. The pistol popped out of his hand and disappeared into the undergrowth. He cursed and reached for it, grunting with pain as he shoved his hand into the middle of a bush that was equipped with an array of sharp spikes.

He heard the sound of someone across to his right and

froze. The sound grew louder. Milton held his breath and waited for whoever it was to come into view. It was very dark, with just the faintest traces of silvery moonlight reaching down through a gap in the canopy. Milton stayed still, aware that he ought to be putting more distance between himself and the camp, yet unwilling to reveal himself to whoever was about to reach him. The attackers were wearing night-vision goggles. He would give himself away in an instant if he left his cover.

There came a crash, a curse—a male voice, in Spanish—and then the sound of someone scrabbling back to their feet. Milton counted down to allow the man to draw near.

It was one of the local guards from the camp.

Milton stood up, extended his arm and clotheslined the man, catching him between his throat and sternum with enough force that his legs flew forward as he was sent down onto his back. The man had been taken completely by surprise and had no defence as Milton dropped down onto him and knocked him out with a stiff short-armed right jab. His head jerked around and he lay still.

Milton moved with quick and practiced efficiency. He reached for the man's holster and found that it was empty. His hands were empty, too. Milton patted the ground in search of a weapon, with no luck. He would have preferred to arm himself with the Springfield or this man's pistol, but it was dark and the grasses were thick, and he didn't have the luxury of time to search.

He saw muzzle flash from the direction of the camp, and then heard the corresponding rattle of gunfire. It was the prompt he needed. He left the narco where he lay, put the camp to his back and pushed on to the north.

∾

BJÖRN FOUND the little creek that ran through the rainforest and, at La Bruja's instruction, followed it upstream.

"Who was that?" she said to him.

"Soldiers," Björn replied. "Cartels aren't equipped like that."

"How did they find us?"

"I'd like to know that, too."

They continued to follow the line of the creek until they came to a large rocky outcrop that reached up above their heads. It loomed as a shadow, too dark for Björn to make out any detail, too dark for him to see the thick carpet of moss that had grown over it as he probed with his hands for the start of the rope that would help guide them out. He patted and poked the damp lichen until his fingertips alighted on the cold metal hoop that had been fixed to the rock; he traced his way around the circle until he felt the rough fibres. He placed it in his palm and, with his other hand anchoring La Bruja's elbow, he started to follow it.

"This goes to the river?"

"Yes," she said. "It's half a mile from here."

"And then?"

"There's a boat."

Björn shook his head, although he didn't say anything. They weren't going to take a boat. It would be too noisy and if, as he suspected, the army had deployed from the air, they would be sitting ducks for any chopper that was in the area. It would make more sense to stay in the rainforest, to get north and then turn with the river. He pictured the terrain: it was dense jungle for hundreds of miles in all directions. If they could get away from the immediate vicinity, they would be impossible to find.

"You think it was Smith?" La Bruja said.

"It must have been. He comes to camp and then the camp gets hit—he's the only thing that changed."

"But how? You took his phone?"

"Of course I did."

"So how could they have followed him?"

"It could be the Americans," Björn said. "Maybe they have a drone."

The rope ran through a thicket of bamboo, and Björn powered through it.

He couldn't stop thinking about Smith. There were too many red flags: Anthony Jackson's sudden and convenient legal plight, and now this. One could be chalked up as a coincidence.

Two, though?

It was starting to look like a pattern.

He would get his charge to safety and then he would send a flare to Weaver. He was still waiting for the results on the biometrics he'd sent to be analysed. He didn't know who Smith was, but maybe that would help.

He wanted better intelligence in time for their next meeting.

Björn was sure—there would be a next meeting—and he was already looking forward to it.

67

The terrain descended at a shallow angle and the undergrowth thinned out a little. Milton suspected that he was approaching a watercourse and, as he stepped over a litter of rocks and through a loose patch of scree, he saw that he was right. The trees gave way to cacao and orchids, and beyond them was a narrow stream. The water glittered with the reflection of the moon overhead. There was a tinkle and splash as the stream negotiated a short descent through a band of rock that had been eroded into a channel.

Milton saw that there was a rope following the line of the stream. It was too random for it to have been left there, and, as he wondered what it might be, he saw it jerk up so that it was suspended a few inches above the ground. His guess that it was a guideline that had been left to assist the narcos in the event that they needed to flee the camp was confirmed when he heard the sound of voices.

He heard movement and ducked down so that he was hidden by the vegetation. The voices were also coming from his left. He couldn't see much further than a few feet, with everything beyond that cloaked in darkness. He strained his ears so that he could place the location of the noise more precisely.

They were coming toward him, no doubt following the guideline.

A man and a woman.

He recognised them: Eidur and La Bruja.

There was a thick branch on the ground next to Milton's feet. It ended in a knuckle of wood and would make a useful club. He clenched his hand around the end of the branch and picked it up.

Perhaps he would be able to meet his objectives after all.

Milton knew that he would have to proceed carefully. The Scandinavian was definitely armed, with, at the very least, a pistol. Milton thought it likely that he would also have something with a little more pop; the security detail had been toting shotguns and automatic rifles, too. La Bruja also had her pistol, meaning that he would be at a disadvantage if it was not for the fact that he knew where they were and they, as far as he could tell, did not know that he was there.

He stayed low, shuffling forward a step or two until there was just a single, thick bush between him and the clear margin of grass that ran down to the water's edge. The voices were nearer now and, as he waited with his hands wrapped around the branch, Milton thought he could see movement coming his way through the gloom.

He lowered the branch to just above waist height and waited another beat, and then another, until the shadowy figures were close enough for him to be able to see them in the moonlight. Eidur was leading the way, his left hand on the guideline and his right hand reached behind him so that his hand could grip La Bruja by the arm.

Milton surged upwards, taking two steps toward the big man and, as he did so, beginning his swing. Eidur was faster than Milton would have given him credit for, and as the thick end of the club came towards his head, he dropped the line and managed to raise his arm just enough to deflect the blow. Instead of landing flush against his chin, the end of the branch cracked against his scalp. The big man's knees buckled and he toppled to the side, falling into the stream with a splash.

La Bruja had her pistol in her right hand but had no time to raise it and take aim before Milton slammed the branch into her shoulder on the backswing. She grunted in pain, but did not drop the weapon; Milton closed the distance on her in two loping strides, grabbed her right wrist with his left hand, and forced the gun away from them both. He continued the movement, twisting the gun around him to the right as he faced away from the direction that she was facing. He levered her arm over his shoulder and yanked down, throwing her over his shoulder at the same time as he liberated the gun from her grip.

She slammed down into the water. Milton stepped back and pivoted, covering them both with her gun.

La Bruja looked up at him, her face twisted with anger and pain.

"You did this?" she said.

Milton had no interest in a discussion. The Colombian army were somewhere to the south, and if he had been able to find the guideline, then they would be able to find it, too.

Eidur put both hands down in the water and pressed himself up into a sitting position. Milton couldn't see a weapon, but he had to assume that he had one somewhere about his person.

He stepped back and covered him with the pistol. "Hands where I can see them."

La Bruja was staring hard at him. "Who are you?"

Eidur moved his hand a little, bringing it up to the scabbard that was strapped around the top of his thigh. Milton nudged his aim a little to the left and fired. The round blasted into the stream and sent up a little plume of spray and chipped rock. The sound of the shot echoed back at them from the trees.

"Don't do that," Milton said.

"Why are you here?" La Bruja said.

"One of my friends died because of you. One of your *sicarios* in Las Vegas. He killed a man I respected. A policewoman, too, and three civilians."

Milton saw puzzlement and then recognition in her face. "That was you?" she said. "In Italy? You killed him?"

"That was me getting started. I made a promise to my friend's son that there would be consequences for what you did. And here we are—these are the consequences."

Milton switched up his aim and drew a bead on Eidur. There was no more than ten feet between them; he wouldn't be able to miss.

"Money," La Bruja said, with a desperation that Milton had not heard in her voice before. "How much would it take?"

"For what?"

"To stop this. Ten million? Twenty?"

"This isn't a negotiation," Milton said. "I can't be bought."

He slipped his finger through the guard until he could feel the solid weight of the trigger between the joints.

"Stop!"

The shout came from behind Milton. He turned his head to see a soldier who had a shotgun aimed right at him.

"*Abaja. Las rodillas.*"

"I speak English," Milton said.

There was a splashing from the stream. Milton looked back and saw Eidur was halfway across it, disappearing into the darkness on the other side.

"Don't get any stupid ideas," the soldier said. His accent was American. "We're everywhere. He won't get far. Drop the weapon."

Milton gritted his teeth.

"Last chance. Put the gun down."

The man didn't look as if he was the type to bluff. He levelled his shotgun right into the centre of Milton's torso. Milton did as he was told, lowering his arm, withdrawing his finger from the trigger and letting the weapon fall to the ground.

"Get on your knees."

Milton dropped. The shotgun was a Mossberg 590. They would be picking bits of his body out of the jungle if the soldier decided to fire it from this range.

"Face down. Hands behind your back."

Milton lowered himself to his knees and then flattened himself to the damp grass. There came a crash through the vegetation as another man joined the first; Milton didn't know which one of them attended to him, but he felt the point of a knee in the small of his back and the nick of cable ties as they bit into the flesh of his wrists.

"Is that her?" the second man said to the first.

"That's her. I'd recognise her anywhere."

"Good work."

"What about the big guy? Went through the stream."

"Call it in."

Milton watched from the ground as La Bruja was secured. Their eyes met. She blazed hatred at him.

"We got her," the first man reported, presumably into a radio. "We got her and another guy. Third man went north into the jungle. We'll bring the ones we got back. Request backup."

68

The man removed his boot from Milton's back. "Get up."

It wasn't easy with his arms secured, but Milton rolled onto his side and jerked himself up into a sitting position.

"I said *up*, you sack of shit."

The soldier grabbed the restraint and tugged at it, hard. Milton winced in pain, using the show of discomfort to mask a quick check of his surroundings. The second soldier had secured La Bruja, her wrists fastened with similar plastic cuffs. Milton looked beyond the trees, but all he could see was darkness. Eidur was gone.

The soldiers were dressed in jungle multicam with wide brimmed boonies and jungle boots. They wore knee pads and netting scarves, with every square inch of exposed skin daubed in black camo paint. They wore recon kit bags and tactical gloves and were both well armed: the man on the right had a shotgun and the man on the left an HK416 carbine. Both were using night-vision goggles.

They were well armed and professional. American

special forces? DELTA or a SEAL team, he guessed. Getting away from them was going to be very difficult indeed.

The soldier shoved Milton in the back and he stumbled ahead.

"Move."

~

THEY WERE TAKEN south through the jungle. The two soldiers were joined by two more, and the team of four escorted them at gunpoint, one pair clearing the way ahead and the second pair bringing up the rear. It was difficult to negotiate the trail with his hands behind his back; the darkness made it hard to follow the way ahead, and there were creepers and vines to step over and around. They climbed up to an escarpment dominated by a huge kapok tree, and Milton tripped over a root and fell against the trunk. The tree bore spines and conical thorns and, unable to use his hands to protect his face, he felt the sharp scrape as they drew scores across his cheek and the side of his neck.

One of the soldiers grabbed him beneath the shoulder and dragged him up.

"Keep moving."

Milton heard the occasional clatter of automatic gunfire from behind them; there were others in the raiding party, hunting down those they had surprised at the kitchen. He wondered about the mercenaries again. What would they do? They must have been paid to protect La Bruja and they had failed. Would they come after them in an attempt to get her back? Or would they run? There was no way of knowing.

The soldier released Milton's shoulder and shoved him ahead.

"I'm English," Milton said.

"I don't care if you're the Prince of Wales."

"I'm not with them."

"With who?"

"The narcos."

"You can spill your story when we get you out of here. You don't need to worry about that, buddy. You're gonna have plenty of time."

PART VII

MONDAY

69

They continued for an hour until they reached a track that had been cleared through the jungle. It was wide enough for a truck, and Milton guessed it had been cut through the jungle to allow access for the loggers who cleared out the mahogany and teak. They followed the track for another hour, moving much more quickly now that they didn't have to contend with the undergrowth. The track turned left and right, tracing a route along the bottom of a shallow valley, before it straightened out and they came to a wider stretch where three vehicles were waiting with their engines on and their lights off. They drew closer and Milton saw more soldiers.

"Keep going," one of the soldiers said to Milton, shoving him between the shoulders and sending him towards the nearest vehicle.

They were Land Rovers. La Bruja was taken to the vehicle in the middle and Milton to the one at the rear. A soldier got out of the driver's side and, before Milton could protest, took a hood and draped it over his head. He pulled a drawstring to close the open end around his throat.

Milton was guided into the back of the vehicle, almost tripping over the sill. He shuffled around a little so that he could avoid leaning his weight against his arms. He heard the sound of the driver clambering aboard and then felt the suspension jolt as another man got into the back and sat alongside him. Milton felt something hard against his ribs.

"You do anything that makes me feel even a little bit jumpy," the man said, "and I'll put a bullet in you. You're coming with us. It doesn't matter whether it's dead or alive. I'll leave that up to you."

"I'll be honest," Milton said. "I'd prefer alive."

"So shut up and do as you're told."

He slapped his hand against the back of the driver's seat and the Land Rover grumbled as the engine turned over. The driver released the handbrake and touched the gas. The vehicle bounced over the rough ground as they started on their way.

The hood made it impossible to see anything. Just as he'd done during his earlier trip into the jungle, Milton tried to listen for anything that might give him an idea of where he was being taken, but again, it was difficult. The Land Rover's engine was loud and, behind that, he occasionally caught the sound of the nocturnal birds and animals that were disturbed by its passage: the screech of an owl, the cries of capybara and the howling of a distant jaguar.

"Where are we going?"

The man next to him elbowed him in the side. Milton gasped.

"Shut your mouth. I don't want to hear a word out of you, buddy. Not a single word."

∼

MILTON GUESSED it was an hour before the rough, uneven track was replaced by a smoother surface. They continued on the new road for another few minutes before Milton felt the Land Rover slow down. The suspension bounced a little as they crossed over another rougher patch of ground, and then the brakes squeaked as the vehicle came to a stop.

The door opened and Milton felt the man to his left getting out. He felt hands on his shoulder and he was pulled across the bench seat, getting his legs down just in time to prevent himself from toppling out. He could just see out from where the drawstring had loosened at the bottom, and he saw a dusty and stony surface that then changed to asphalt. He walked on until the hands held him back. He heard the sound of a roller door being opened, and then allowed himself to be pitched forward until he saw the opening of what he guessed to be the rear loading bay of a small truck. He felt hands on both sides of him—two people —and then he was both hauled up and thrown forward at the same time. He landed on his chest and was then pulled forward until he was inside the new vehicle.

He understood that they were transferring him and La Bruja into something that would melt into its environment more easily. Three Land Rovers would stand out in most places, especially if their destination was an urban area. That gave him a little more to go on. Medellín or Bogotá, he assumed. He had heard only American voices so far, with no one who could have been mistaken for a local. That made Bogotá less likely, especially when added to the distance that they would need to travel from Antioquia to there. So, most likely Medellín.

He thought of the transmitter in the sole of his boot. A city would mean that there was cellphone coverage, and that might mean that his location could be tracked. He wondered how much charge was left in the device. What had Ziggy said? Two days? Three days? It was difficult to remember how long ago it was that he had been picked up at the hotel.

"Get your filthy gringo hands off me!"

Milton turned in the direction of the voice. He couldn't see through the hood, but he recognised La Bruja's voice. She was indignant, her voice taut with anger. He heard grunts of exertion as others hoisted themselves into the back of the truck and then the thud of their rubber-soled boots as they made their way to empty spots along the wall where, Milton guessed, they would wait out whatever part of the journey came next.

"What's going on?" Milton said. "Where are we going?"

"We're halfway there," a male voice said. "You two need to shut your mouths and keep them shut. You don't, and I'll jab you so full of barbiturates that you'll be out for a week. You understand?"

"I'll be quiet," Milton said.

"¿Entiendes?"

"Yes," La Bruja said coldly, making a point of answering in English. "I understand."

The door rattled as it was pulled shut, and then there came a metallic *thunk* as the lock was engaged. The engine started and the truck rolled out.

Milton sat quietly and waited.

70

Milton had no idea of the time. It was impossible to say how long they had been driving, but it must have been hours. He couldn't see a thing through the hood, and, even if they had removed it, he doubted that there would be windows in the back of the truck.

The soldiers spoke amongst themselves, their voices low, but Milton caught enough of their conversations to confirm that they were definitely American and, most likely, a SEAL team. Two men to Milton's left made reference to Little Creek and Coronado. Those were the garrisons responsible for accommodating that component of the US Naval Special Warfare Command; Milton was familiar with the former, having trained there for a month during an exchange at the beginning of his career.

He wondered whether Eidur had managed to get clear. Milton did not hear mention of the mercenaries or any other foreigners who had been caught up in the assault on the camp. Perhaps they had been able to slip through the cordon that had been thrown up. There was no way of knowing.

Milton started to hear the sounds of an urban area outside the truck. There were other cars now, the rattle of a train passing nearby, the sound of a jet overhead. A city? He tried to picture the map of the region and concluded that it could only really be Medellín. It was difficult to be sure, but he doubted that they had been travelling for more than three hours, and there were no other cities that would have been near enough to reach in that time.

The truck slowed down and turned to the right, bumping over something—a kerb, perhaps—as it left the road. The sound of the engine changed in tone, adding an echo that suggested that they were now inside a building.

The truck stopped and the roller door rattled as it was opened.

"We're here," a voice said. "Out you get."

Hands grabbed Milton by the shoulders and yanked at him, dragging him along the floor to the edge of the truck. They gave him a chance to shuffle around so that he could get his feet over the edge. He was pulled out, his boots landing on a concrete floor; he saw through the gap in the hood that it was wet with puddles that glistened with little slicks of spilt oil.

"This way," the voice said, shoving Milton ahead.

He walked on.

71

Milton was guided through the building. They left the hood on and pushed and prodded him in the directions that they wanted him to go. He tried to work out where he was, but it was impossible. All he could see was directly beneath him, and then only when he pressed his chin against his chest and looked down through the opening in the hood. The floor was still concrete, with more puddles and smears of grease and oil. It looked industrial.

"Here," the voice behind him said, pushing him through a doorway.

Milton stumbled forward, was held in place and then pulled back. The backs of his knees bumped against the wooden seat of a chair and he sat down. Something was used to cut through the plastic restraints but, before Milton could even begin to massage his aching wrists, strong hands grabbed his forearms and fresh restraints were applied, fastening his wrists to the arms of the chair.

The hood was left on.

"All right, shitbird. I've got some questions and you'd better answer them."

"Please. I don't understand—"

"Who are you?"

"Can you take this off? I can't see—"

"Who are you?"

"John Smith."

"Really? John Smith?"

"Yes."

"Bullshit."

"Please—take the hood off."

"No."

"Where am I?"

"I ask the questions."

"I want to see someone from my embassy."

"I don't care what you want."

"You can't just hold me here."

"Really?"

"I want to speak to someone."

"You got a short memory, buddy? You forgotten where you were last night? No, no—don't answer. Let me tell you—you were in the rainforest at a cocaine laboratory run by a drug cartel. You remember that?"

"I want to speak to someone from the British embassy."

"And, get this, you were at the lab at the same time as the woman who runs the cartel. This woman—she's pretty much the most wanted woman in the world. Apart from running the cartel, which would put her at the top of the list all by herself, she's responsible for the murder of the US ambassador in Bogotá. So, all that being said, you can see why we're really fucking interested in why someone like *you* would be in a place like *that*. And—between you and me—

asking to speak to someone from your embassy just ain't gonna cut it. You need to start answering my questions or things are gonna get worse for you, and fast."

"Embassy."

The man chuckled with dry, bitter amusement. "Let me tell you what's going to happen, you smug shit. It doesn't matter whether you answer me now or later. I don't care. You and that bitch we picked you up with are going to be going on a little trip with us. We've got a jet coming to get you. We're going to fly you somewhere nice and quiet, the kind of place where you can be dropped into a deep, dark hole. The kind of place where no one will know you're there. Not your friends. Not your family. Not even your government. It will be as if you just fell off the edge of the world." The man clicked his fingers. "It might be somewhere in Eastern Europe. The Middle East. There's a place in Thailand that's real nasty. We get you to a place like that and the gloves come off. No rules there, buddy. We can do whatever the fuck we like."

"Embassy."

"Let's try this. The SEALs who hit that camp said they saw three mercenaries there. Two men, one woman. They said the three of them put up a fight before they retreated into the jungle. They also said that the two of them spoke with what they figured were British accents. You got an accent just like them. So—you want to tell us how you've been working with them?"

"I'm not working with anyone. I told—"

The hood was yanked off. Milton blinked in the sudden light, waiting for his eyes to adjust.

"There we are," the man said. "That's better. I can see you now."

He was in a medium-sized room, with brick walls and a concrete floor. There was a light overhead and another shining into his face from the front. His interrogator was sitting down opposite him, his features hidden in the shadows.

"The boys said you looked like you might have been military. They're right. You have that look about you."

"I was," he said. "A long time ago."

"And now? You're a merc?"

"No," Milton said. "I'm not."

He needed time to think, but the interrogator wasn't going to give him the space to do that. He didn't have much in the way of options. He could tell them the truth—that he was in the jungle to kill La Bruja and any other cartel leaders that he could find—but he knew that was going to sound fantastic without evidence to back it up. Another alternative was to fall back on the legend, but that would mean trying to persuade them that he was a drug dealer looking to score a new supply line. It sounded like a bad option, but, perversely, it might be the best of a bad lot. The Americans wouldn't prosecute him; it was more likely that he would be given to the Colombians. He preferred the odds of breaking out of a Colombian prison cell to an American supermax.

The man got up and came closer.

"You know what I think?" he said. "You're a liar."

"I want to speak to someone from my—"

The man drilled Milton in the gut. He hadn't expected it and the man had a decent right hand. Milton felt the flash of pain as it radiated out from his stomach and would have doubled over if it wasn't for the fact that his wrists were attached to the arms of the chair.

The man leaned in so that Milton could smell the

deodorant that he was wearing and feel the flecks of spittle that spattered against his ear and the side of his face.

"Who are you?" the man said.

"Santa Claus."

The man clenched his fist and drilled Milton again.

72

La Bruja was showing absolutely no sign that she was about to crack. They had put the narco in one room and the man who had been found with her in another, and Ellie had taken a place at the back to watch as she was questioned. She had insisted that her name was Esmerelda Dos Santos and that she was a *campesino*—a peasant farmer—who had been employed in the camp. She said that she was responsible for helping to prepare the paste that would eventually be turned into the cartel's powder. She appeared to be confused and frightened, nothing like what Ellie would have expected from the ruthless mass murderer who had spread her poison like a web across the world from her little nest in the jungle.

Denying her identity was a reasonable strategy. Proving that she was La Bruja might be difficult for them.

She caught Fuentes's eye and indicated that she was going to go and see what was happening in the other room. He nodded and turned his attention back to the woman on the chair.

The garage had three smaller rooms attached to the main space, and they had made their interrogation rooms in these spaces. They would not be here long enough that the rudimentary facilities would be a problem. The plan was for them to leave the city that evening and fly to New York.

She opened the door to the second interrogation room and went inside.

Miguel was leading the questioning of the man. Ellie had not seen him yet, and he hadn't been identified. He was secured in a chair and Miguel was in front of him, blocking her view. Miguel asked him who he was, the man replied that he was Santa Claus, and Miguel drove his fist into his gut.

"Hey!" Ellie said. "What are you doing?"

Miguel turned to her. "You want to get him to speak or don't you?"

"I do. But not like that."

The man in the chair looked up and Ellie nearly gasped in surprise.

Miguel was still looking back at her. "What?"

She swallowed, her throat suddenly dry. "Let me have a go."

Miguel collected his jacket from the back of the chair and made his way to the door. He gave a shrug as he passed her on the way out. "You want a crack at him, you go right ahead."

The door closed.

Ellie waited for a beat.

"What is this?" the man in the chair said, blinking into the light. "He's roughed me up, and now you're going to play nice? You're the good cop, right?"

She made her way forward, passing into the cone of light

cast down by the naked bulb that was suspended above the chair.

"Hello, John," she said.

Milton stared at her, dumbfounded.

"Shit," he said. "Hello, Ellie."

73

Ziggy Penn woke to the sound of his laptop's alarm: a pattern of three short bleeps and then a pause that repeated over and over. He sat up, scrubbed the sleep from his eyes and tried to remember where he was. He saw the bland hotel room and, out of the uncovered window, the light of the city beyond.

Medellín.

That's right.

Colombia. He was in Colombia.

The alarm bleeped again and it took Ziggy another ten seconds to remember its significance.

Oh shit, he thought.

Shit!

He swung his legs out of bed, and, in his haste to cross the room, got his feet snagged in the sheet and tripped. He thudded down onto the floor, kicking his legs in an attempt to unwind them from the bedclothes, and, finally free, he scrambled across the room to the desk.

The alarm sounded again.

He opened the screen, hit the return key and waited for

the computer to wake. The screen stayed dark; Ziggy hit the space bar, then stabbed it repeatedly until the screen lit up. He stared at it. The red dot was moving west, passing through San Bernardo and La Palma toward Belen.

Oh shit, oh shit, oh shit.

He picked up the laptop and made his way to the door before realising that he was just in his underwear. He went into the bathroom, rested the laptop on the edge of the sink, and pulled on the complimentary bathrobe. He collected the computer again and went outside, forgetting, in his haste, the key card to get back inside.

Never mind. He padded down the corridor to Hicks's room and banged on the door.

"Hicks!" he hissed. "Wake up!"

He heard Hicks's footsteps as he made his way to the door. It opened.

Hicks blinked the sleep from his eyes. "What is it?"

"It's Milton. I know where he is."

74

Ellie couldn't help herself: she slapped him, hard, her palm clapping off the side of his face.

"Ouch," he said.

"You deserved that."

"I know I did."

She looked down at him—at his scarred face, at the blue eyes that she remembered so well—and felt a mixture of anger and surprise.

"I'm sorry," he said.

"About what? Standing me up?"

"Yes."

"Why would you do something like that?"

"Because..." He paused and looked away. "Because I didn't think it was such a good idea."

"You thought it was a good idea by the lake," she said, unable to stop herself from recalling the night that they had spent together under the stars.

"I know," he said. "And it wasn't a good idea, then, either." He paused again, clearly finding the conversation awkward. "Jesus. I'm hopeless. I have no idea about this kind of thing."

"'This kind of thing'? What does that mean?"

He nodded at her, then at himself.

"Relationships, John?"

"Yes," he said. "Relationships."

"What are you? Ten years old?"

He shook his head, a wry and self-deprecating smile playing on his lips.

"It doesn't have to be so hard," she said, not quite ready to let him off the hook. "If you don't want to have dinner with someone, you just say it—'I'm sorry, I don't think I want to have dinner with you tonight.' And the good thing about doing that is that the other person—me, in this case—doesn't have to wait for an hour in a shitty bar in Green Bay while everyone—including the douchebags who hit on me while I got half drunk at the bar—looks at me as if I'm some sort of love-struck teenager who's just been stood up on her first date. That, *John*, is what you do when you don't want to have dinner with someone."

"I did want to have dinner with you. It's just..." His brow creased as he looked for the right words to say what he wanted to say. "Look. Okay. Shit. I would've been more trouble than I'm worth."

There was a boxcutter on the table. She picked it up and turned it so that the light from above caught on the tip of the blade.

"Easy," Milton said, although there was a smile in his eyes.

She slid the blade beneath the plastic tie that secured his right wrist and sliced through it, then repeated the process on the left-hand restraint. Milton massaged each wrist, one after the other. He smiled and shook his head in amusement.

"What?" she said.

He gestured around the room. "This doesn't strike you as funny? I don't even know where I am."

"We'll get to that," she said. She pointed to the reddened abrasions. "You okay?"

"They've had me in cuffs ever since they found me in the jungle," he said.

"The jungle," Ellie said. "I'm going to need to understand how you're mixed up in this."

He exhaled. "It's a long story."

She smirked. "You're not going anywhere until I say so."

"Fair enough."

"Why were you there? Are you working?"

"No," he said.

"I was just thinking—back in Michigan, all I know is that one minute my bosses were looking at investigating your role in what happened to that militia and then, next minute, they weren't. I was told that there were conversations between governments. High-level shit. That only happens for people with special status. I know people like that—we've got some of them down here now."

"The CIA, you mean?"

"That'd be one example. I would've asked you about all that if you hadn't run out on me."

"I'm not CIA."

"MI6?"

He smiled. "No," he said. "I used to have a security clearance. Can we leave it at that?"

"Not if you're working down here. I kind of have to know."

"I'm not working. I retired from that kind of work a long time ago—before Michigan."

"So you're here as a civilian? That's not going to go down well if that's the line you want to take."

Milton glanced to the right and frowned. Ellie could see that he was working out what he wanted to say.

"All right," he said.

"Everything," she told him.

He nodded. "Everything."

75

They had arranged the meet at Chadwick's, a bar and grill on K Street. Control had worked in the intelligence industry for two decades and, as such, was something of an aficionado of classic espionage. She was very well aware that it was in this Washington restaurant, back in 1985, that Aldrich Ames had handed over his dossier of information to his Russian handler in exchange for a bag of cash. She wondered whether the man she had come to meet was aware of that, or whether it was a coincidence. She suspected the former.

She gave her name to the host at the front of the house and followed him to a table in the back. The man she had travelled here to meet was seated in a booth, and he stood and came out to greet her as she approached.

"Mr. Lincoln," she said.

"Good afternoon," he said, taking her hand and then waiting as the host helped her with her coat and carried it away to the cloakroom.

There was a second man in the booth, hidden from view by the raised back of the banquette.

"I'm sorry," Control said. "I don't believe we've met."

"This is Edward Navarro," Lincoln said. "He's worked with me for years. How long, Eddie?"

"Forty? I don't know. I lose count."

Both men were old. Lincoln was overweight, with folds of skin that drooped over the collar of his black turtleneck. His nose was squashed against his face, and his cheeks bore the permanent scars of the acne that must have afflicted him when he was a youth. His hair was a thinning thatch of greys and whites, a coronet arranged around a bald spot that exposed blotchy skin. Navarro was slimmer than his colleague, with a wiry energy about him that contrasted with Lincoln's more indolent bearing. His ears and nose were too large for his head, and his skin was the colour of old leather; Control diagnosed a life spent outdoors and wondered whether he might have served the agency overseas. Control knew that Lincoln's career had started in Vietnam, and that he was in his mid-seventies today. Navarro looked to be of a similar vintage.

"Please," Lincoln said. "Sit."

This was not the first time that Control and Lincoln had met. The American had reached out to her within a month of her appointment as head of the revived Group Fifteen. He was a career spook who had been deputy director of the Special Operations Group for years and then, five years ago, had been promoted to full deputy director. He was a power broker, maintaining links to the SOG that he had run as a personal fiefdom for years. Control knew that he ran it in much the same way as she ran Group Fifteen; it comprised a roster of tightly vetted, intensely loyal operatives who could be deployed at short notice and with scant regard for the usual norms of international relations or national law.

A waitress approached with three menus.

"I'm not going to eat," Control said.

"Could I get you a drink, then?"

"Water," she said. "Thank you."

Lincoln and Navarro ordered water, too, and said that they would eat. The waitress left two menus and went to get the drinks.

"First of all," Lincoln began, "I want to say sorry."

"You couldn't have given me a warning?"

"We didn't know they were going to attack the camp."

"Seriously?"

"We were as surprised as you. The FBI and the DEA have been driving the operation, and they've somehow managed to quarantine it from the rest of the community. I only found out when they started crowing about the fact that they'd picked up La Bruja."

"I had three agents there when they hit it," Control said, his apology giving her the licence to gripe a little more. "Three—including my best man."

"They got clear?"

"They did. But next time, please…"

"I know," he said, flashing a little irritation.

"No sense crying over spilt milk," Navarro said. "It is what it is."

The waitress returned with a jug of water and three glasses. They paused the conversation while she poured; it was a useful reset. Lincoln was more composed when he spoke again.

"I'm pleased we could meet like this. I wanted to thank you in person for the assistance that you've provided. The whole matter is delicate, as you know. Having someone completely separate from Langley to run the ops on the ground was essential. I like to think that my operational security is solid, but you can never really be completely sure."

"I agree," she said. "A firewall is sensible."

"It really is. And there are few people I would have been confident in approaching. The reputation of your Group goes before it—not that we had any doubt, but it's pleasing to see that it is justified."

Agreeing to help Lincoln had not been an altruistic choice. Assisting with something as delicate as this had enabled Control to bank an enormous favour that she would be able to call in whenever she needed it. She was new in a job that had historically proven to be difficult, and one that had never before been filled by a woman. Having the patronage of one of Langley's most influential operators could prove to be a significant benefit. She chose not to mention that now, though; the debt was obvious, but good manners meant that it was best left unsaid.

"I'm afraid that I am going to have to ask you for something else," Lincoln said.

Control had anticipated that. "I thought you might. Do you know where she is?"

"I do. The operation to take her out was a four-way deal: the FBI, the DEA, the DoD and State. We've got a source within the DEA delegation in Colombia, and they're providing us with intel. The task force has taken her to a safe house in Medellín."

Control was surprised. "Really? I thought they would have taken her out of the country by now."

"They're keeping it on the down-low," Navarro said. "The Colombians don't know anything about it, much less that she's been taken. I understand that the FBI looked at sending a helicopter to fly her out, but they decided against it. It would've been a long flight over dangerous terrain, and then there's the question of where it would put down."

"They could have taken her to the coast."

"They looked at that, too. Too dicey."

"And so?"

"It's quite elaborate," Navarro said. "The Colombians think the Americans are in country to lead a joint investigation into the cartel. They have no idea that the operation has already happened. They took her out of the jungle, put her in the back of a truck and drove her to a safe house in Medellín. They're going to fly a jet to Olaya Herrera and rendition her from there."

"When?"

"The jet is scheduled to land tonight."

"So we need to move fast."

"You do," Lincoln said. "We don't want to waste the investment that we've made in the cartel by losing her. Her influence in Mexico and Colombia has already been useful, and there's a lot more potential there that we haven't tapped. We *cannot* have her leaving the country."

"Another thing," Navarro said. "We want to question the FBI agent who has her. If she's in the car when they transport her, you should bring her with you."

Control nodded. "I'll speak to my people."

"Thank you."

"What if we think she's been compromised? She knows a lot."

Lincoln sighed. "Too much to risk that she might talk. We're looking into it, but that might be a call for whoever gets to her."

"And I have operational freedom on that?"

"You do."

"Send me the details of the safe house," she said. "I'll have it scouted."

She shuffled around the booth and stood.

"You can't stay?"

"You said it was urgent."

"It is."

"Then I need to get started."

Lincoln slid out of the booth and stood. He put his hand on her shoulder. "Thank you, Control. We appreciate your help."

She found his touch repugnant, but was experienced enough to mask her distaste.

"Send me the intel," she said. "I'll let you know if I need anything else."

76

Milton told her the whole story. He started in Vegas, with how he had been fooled by the Russos into helping them get away from the cartel with the money that they had stolen from them. He explained how, during the double-cross, Beau Baxter had been shot and then, over the course of the next couple of days, how the cartel *sicario* who had been dispatched to find the missing money and punish the thieves had murdered Beau in cold blood. He explained how he had followed the Russos to their bolthole in Tuscany and, using them as bait, had lain in wait for the hitman to make his appearance.

"And he did?" she asked.

"He did."

"And?"

Milton shrugged, finding it difficult to admit to her what he had done to the man.

She didn't press. "It doesn't explain how you ended up in the jungle with La Bruja."

"The *sicario* pulled the trigger, but he didn't give the order. He caused chaos in Vegas—it wasn't just Beau who suffered. There was a police officer, her girlfriend, a security guard... I've had dealings with the cartels before. They think that they can do whatever they want. Who's going to come after *them?*"

"You?"

He continued as if he hadn't heard her. "I've done a lot of bad things, Ellie. I'll never be able to make up for them. I want to, but..." He thought of the ninth step, of making amends, and how, for him, it was impossible. "I can't atone for my past, but I can try to make a difference now. I travel around a lot. And I try to help the people I meet. They're usually the little guys—the ones who get pushed around by those with money or power or influence. This felt different. This isn't a bully. This isn't the drug dealer on the corner, threatening his neighbours. This is much more than that— this is where the drug dealer *gets* his drugs. I can help a lot of people, all at once, by shutting La Bruja down."

"And get revenge for your friend."

"Justice," Milton corrected.

"Right," she said. She paced. "How did you get to here?"

Milton explained how he had followed the cocaine's supply chain backwards: from Anthony Jackson's retail operation in Manchester, to López's wholesaling in Amsterdam, and eventually to distribution and production in South America.

"And you did all this on your own?"

"I put a little team together. A couple of friends I used to work with and the son of my friend."

"They weren't in the jungle, though. We would've picked them up."

"I don't know where they are. The cartel flew me out to a *finca* and I doubt they know. Actually, come to think of it, I don't even know where *we* are. Medellín?

"Yes," she said. "A safe house."

"La Bruja is here, too?"

"There's another room over the way. She's being questioned. She's going to get the justice you want—it might just be a different kind."

"Why'd you go after her?" Milton asked. "Because of the ambassador?"

She nodded. "FBI jurisdiction extends to crimes committed against US citizens and interests. His murder is squarely within our wheelhouse. We ran the Benghazi investigation on the same grounds. POTUS couldn't let this stand, so here we are."

"'We'?"

"State, DEA and FBI."

"And the men in the jungle?"

"SEALs."

"Do the Colombians know?"

She shook her head. "We can't be sure who to trust. We know that the cartel has bought senior politicians before, and we know they own the police here. We involve them and the whole thing goes south."

"So this is off the books?"

"Completely. We're going to take her back to the States. She'll be tried and she'll spend the rest of her life in prison."

Milton stretched out his legs.

"Thirsty?" she said.

"Very."

Ellie went to a cold box at the back of the room, pulled out a couple of bottles of water and offered one to Milton. He took it and unscrewed the cap, downed half, then set it down on the table. Milton watched her, remembering how attractive he had found her spikiness, her take-no-shit attitude, and her toughness. He had no doubt that she would have had to fight harder than a man to get to the position she was in, and recalled the nonsense that she had dealt with from her senior officer before they had met. But there was more to her than the toughness; she was smart and resourceful and sassy and... Milton tried not to think about what he liked about her for too long for fear that he would do something that he had promised himself he would never do. He didn't deserve a woman like her, and she didn't deserve a man like him. That was just how it had to be.

"When are you moving her?"

"Tonight. She'll be put into the back of a car and driven to the airport. From there, it's a one-way flight to Uncle Sam."

He took another slug of water. "What about me?"

Ellie folded her arms and grinned at him. "You stood me up, John. There'll have to be consequences for that."

77

Number One left a message on Weaver's phone. It was mundane—a suggestion that they meet for a drink to catch up—but the precise wording was predetermined and signified both the urgency of the request and the location. The meet was to take place in an hour at the safe house that the logisticians from Group Five had arranged in advance of the operation.

Weaver conducted a careful dry-cleaning run to ensure that he was not being tailed, driving out to the Parque Zoológico in Santa Fe, leaving his car and walking north until he came to the train station at Industriales. He took a train back south and disembarked at Aguacatala. He walked the rest of the way and, in an abundance of caution, he went by the entrance to the warehouse on Calle 89 before going around the block. Then, when he was finally confident that he was black, he knocked on the plain wooden door.

He heard the sound of approaching footsteps and saw a darkening of the peephole as whoever was inside the warehouse looked out. He heard the sound of the locks being turned and the door opened.

Björn Thorsson stood there, his huge frame blocking the way ahead.

"Can I come in?"

"You're clean?"

"*Please*, Number One," he said. "I've been doing this a while. Out of the way."

Thorsson stood aside so that Weaver could make his way into the building. He hadn't been here before, and, as he looked around, he saw that it was not much more than a couple of medium-sized rooms with a kitchen and a bathroom. There was no furniture inside, and the floors were dusty wooden planks without carpeting or any other covering. There was no natural light; the two small windows were covered with newspaper that had been stuck to the glass.

Jessie Hester and Craig Connor were seated on the floor. Number Eight was in the process of disassembling his sidearm so that it could be cleaned, his equipment laid out on a sheet of newspaper that was spread out in front of him. Number Six was leaning back against the wall, smoking a cigarette. She was wearing a vest top that exposed the tattoos that ran up and down her arms. Her face was bruised, with a nasty contusion around her right eye.

"What happened?" Weaver said, pointing at her face.

"I was hoping you could tell me that, sir," she said.

"We were *all* hoping you could," Connor said.

"Are you okay?"

She waved his concern away with a flick of her hand. "It's just a black eye. I got into a scuffle on my way out of the camp. Took an elbow to the face."

Number One locked the door and turned to face the room. "So?"

"It was the Americans," Weaver said.

"Why didn't we know about it?"

"Apparently, our CIA friends were sidelined. This was State, the DEA and the FBI. The soldiers who attacked the camp were SEALs. I know—it's frustrating."

"Frustrating?" Eight said. "You want to know what frustrating is? It's getting shot at and then trekking through the rainforest for hours until you're able to get clear."

Weaver let that pass; planning and preparation were hallmarks of Group Fifteen, and they had been blindsided here. He agreed with Connor; it didn't look good. It looked sloppy.

"I thought we were exclusive on this operation?" Thorsson said.

"We are," Weaver said. "Why?"

"Hector del Pozo brought an Englishman out to the *finca*. His name is John Smith. Del Pozo said Smith has been pushing them to sell him product that he can move into the UK."

Eight looked up. "Didn't they have a retailer there already?"

"They did. Anthony Jackson."

"'Did'?"

"Jackson was arrested. The cartel took the decision that he was too dangerous to leave alive and they asked us to help. Number Four paid him a visit." Weaver shrugged. They all knew what the visit would have entailed. "What about Smith?"

"I gave him a little shake to see if his story held up," Thorsson said. "I didn't believe him, but I couldn't prove anything, either. I warned del Pozo, but he ignored me. He took him to the jungle so La Bruja could meet him. Turns out I should've listened to my gut. They hit the camp a couple of hours after he arrived there."

"Want me to run a check on him?"

"I'd appreciate you seeing why the check I already filed has been stalled. I took his prints and his picture and sent them to Group One. I got a weird response. They said his details were on file, but that they were classified."

"I'll take care of it."

78

Ziggy tossed Hicks the keys for the second hand Nissan Altima that he had sourced. He got into the back, taking out his laptops and going through the rigmarole of tethering them to his phone so that he could get online. Hicks opened the driver's side door and dropped down into the seat. He put the key in the ignition and turned it, waking the engine after a couple of grumbles. The dash lit up.

"One hundred and forty thousand miles," he said. "I hope this was cheap."

"Five hundred bucks," Ziggy replied, "and, more to the point, he took cash. When I checked the police registry, the car was clean."

"Clean in one sense," Hicks said, running his finger along the dash and holding it up to show the grime.

"Look," Ziggy said, punctuating his sentences with rapid-fire taps of the keyboard, "if this isn't up to your usual standard, you can be in charge of finding the wheels next time."

"I'm pulling your leg," Hicks said. "It's inconspicuous. Well done."

Chase got in the front next to Hicks. "As long as you can find us somewhere to get a tetanus shot afterwards," he said, "we're all good. Let's go."

∼

THE INDUSTRIAL ZONE was on the western edge of Medellín, between the districts of Las Violetas and La Palma. There were apartment blocks dotted between the dilapidated warehouses and workshops, and a handful of pedestrians made their way along the crumbling sidewalks on the way to and from their homes. Hicks did not find it difficult to imagine what this area would have been like in Escobar's day; it was down at heel and poor, and, he guessed, would have been the sort of district the police would not willingly have entered. It was better now, but, as they made their way along Calle 30, they passed young men who eyed them with suspicion and women who stood, cigarettes clamped between their lips, in hope of business.

"Nice area," Chase observed from the passenger seat.

They reached a junction.

Hicks looked into the rear-view mirror. "Which way?"

Ziggy checked one of his laptops. "Turn right on Carrera 83. Should be on the left."

Hicks flicked the indicator and turned right, then dabbed the accelerator. The new road was just the same as the last: prefabricated apartment blocks on the left, warehouses on the right.

Chase stared out of the windshield. "Which one is it?"

Hicks watched in the mirror as Ziggy looked between the screen and the street outside.

"There," he said. "That one."

It was on the right: a business had been established on a patch of land that stretched back from the road. A vinyl sign stretched over a narrow passageway that cut between two whitewashed buildings: Parquedero Y Lavadero.

"It's a garage," Ziggy said.

"And car wash," Chase added.

There were cars parked up close to one another and a truck with a tarpaulin stretched over the back. It looked as if the cars were washed behind the buildings and then parked at the front to be collected. Hicks took his foot off the gas and the Altima slowed to a crawl. He paid extra attention to the two buildings on either side of the passageway. The building on the left was two storeys tall, with blue metal doors on the ground floor, a red-and-white striped awning above them and then two windows above that. The windows were uncovered and there was no light from within. The three-storey building to the right did show signs of occupation; there were lights in the windows on the first and second floors. It looked as if it might be residential, perhaps where the owner of the business might live.

"Can you be more precise?" Hicks asked Ziggy.

"The tracker only gives an approximate location. Ten metres or so."

"So which one is it? We need to know."

"That one," Ziggy said, pointing to the building with the lit windows. "The one on the right."

Hicks squeezed the gas and pulled away, taking the next right and sliding the Nissan against the kerb next to a café with cheap plastic tables laid out beneath the cover of a corrugated iron sheet. The café was too far away from the car wash to use as a place to watch, but it would serve as a staging post. He switched off the engine and killed the lights.

"What do we do?" Chase asked.

"We need to scout the area. We need to find a spot where we can keep an eye on the buildings. I don't want to do anything unless I'm one hundred per cent confident that he's in there."

"He's in there," Ziggy said defensively.

"The *tracker* is in there," Hicks corrected.

"He wouldn't have taken off his boots."

"Probably not. But I'm not in the business of taking chances. I'd like to be sure."

79

Weaver walked to the window, gently pulled back the edge of the newspaper that was covering it, and looked outside. A lorry rumbled along the road to one of the other warehouses, and cars trundled slowly in its wake.

"So?" Thorsson said. "What's next?"

"I spoke to Control. She's spoken to our friends from Langley. The FBI and the DEA have La Bruja in a safe house on the outskirts of the city. The plan is for her to be flown from Medellín to the United States."

"How do they know that?"

"They've managed to find a source inside the operation."

"I wish they'd done that sooner."

"It is what it is," Weaver said.

"What do you want us to do?"

"Make sure that doesn't happen," Weaver said. "Go get her and take her back to the jungle. Her and the FBI agent who she's likely to be with."

"Name and description?"

"A woman: Ellie Flowers. I'm expecting a file on her—I'll forward it when I get it."

"Do you have a location?"

"Yes," Weaver said. He pointed down to the laptop that was set up on the floor. "Open a map for me."

Six lowered herself down to the laptop, woke it and navigated to Google Maps. Weaver read out the address and she typed it in. The map that was displayed was of the west of the city, with the location pin a mile to the east of the university campus. Six switched to Street View and turned the screen around so that they could all see it.

"There's a garage there," Weaver said. "It's been a DEA safe house for years, since Escobar. That's where she is."

Thorsson knelt down and dragged the cursor around the screen, changing the angle so that he could see through three hundred and sixty degrees. "Mix of residential and commercial. We know anything else about it?"

"All I have is the address. You'll have to scout it."

"What about the Colombians?" Eight asked. "Are they involved?"

"No. The Americans don't trust them."

"Not unreasonable," Thorsson said. "El Centro owns the police. They wouldn't let them get her to the airport if they knew. This will have been kept very, very quiet."

Eight got up. "Do you know when they're planning on moving her?"

"An FBI Gulfstream is inbound now. Wheels down in two hours. They'll turn it around, fuel it up and get it ready to head back out again. We suspect that they'll transfer her to the airport once it's dark, get her onto the jet, and that'll be that. The next time she'll be seen will be in a courtroom in New York, and by then it'll be too late."

"We might need more than three of us," Thorsson suggested.

"Agreed. I sent for reinforcements. Ten and Eleven were already in theatre in Mexico. They're flying down now. Two got on a plane from Dallas at seven this morning. He'll be here mid-afternoon. You've got a team of six."

"Better," Thorsson said, and nodded.

Weaver looked at them, one after another, and saw that they were already considering how they could best achieve the objective that they had been set.

"Do you have the equipment that you need?"

Thorsson nodded in the direction of the second room. Weaver walked over and looked through the open doorway: the room held a small arsenal of weapons and other equipment. He saw M4 rifles and M9 pistols, three Mossberg 12-gauge shotguns, plate carriers with side plates, a crate of flash bangs and thermite grenades. In addition, there were flexicuffs, helmets, CamelBaks, helmet lights, dump pouches, and MBIT radio units. The Group Five quartermaster who had supplied this safe house had gone above and beyond. There was enough to equip a small army here.

"We're good," Number One said. "But we'll need to know how many we're going up against."

"They sent two troops of SEALs to get her. She's been handed over to the FBI and DEA agents. A small number of SEALs are staying behind to assist with security."

"We need to scout it," One said.

"I can help with that," Six said.

She went over to a large plastic case, flicked open the clasps and opened the lid. She took out two long pieces of curved plastic, each around eighty centimetres long, and a more bulbous component with a propeller at one end. It was a drone.

"I thought it might come in useful in the jungle, but it'll help here, too."

"Good," Weaver said.

"What about Smith?" Thorsson said. "You think he's involved?"

"I don't know," Weaver admitted.

"You don't think it's a coincidence that he was in the camp at the same time as the Americans hit it?"

"I do," Weaver said.

"What do we do with him?"

"Treat him the same as anyone else who gets in the way."

"Fine," Thorsson said. He signalled for Six to get up and pointed to the drone. "Let's go and take a look."

80

Björn parked their van a mile away from the target property. The white Renault Master had been sourced for them by the quartermaster. It was old and looked as if it must have rolled out of the factory in the early nineties. It had a two-litre engine, a couple of hundred thousand miles on the clock, and bodywork that had been nicked and dented by innumerable collisions throughout its working life. It was big, though, with a deep cargo space and a cabin that was separated by a panel with a viewing hatch. It fitted in with the other vehicles on the street and was perfect for what Björn had in mind.

There was an expanse of scrubby wasteland to the west of Las Violetas, on the other side of the road to what looked like an abandoned prison. It was surrounded by a fence with a pair of wire mesh gates fastened with a padlock; he picked the lock, opened the gates and drove through. Their vantage point was on a plateau that offered a broad vista of the city below. It was quiet, shielded from the road by a brick wall and mature trees, and there was no one else around. It was ideal for their purposes.

Björn and Six got out of the van. He wiped his cuff across his forehead to mop up the sweat.

"You need any help?" he asked her.

"I think I can manage."

It was a privilege of being Number One that he had a little input into the composition of the team that was deployed. Björn had flicked through Six's file and knew that she had been one of the first three female soldiers to be admitted into the SAS. Hester had served in Afghanistan with the Special Reconnaissance Regiment and had made a name for herself with a series of daring and successful covert operations. She had developed a specialism in reconnaissance and had honed it during her time at Hereford. She was confident and very competent; she had a temper on her, too, and Björn reminded himself not to get onto her bad side. He didn't think that would be a particularly pleasant place to be.

He watched as she went around to the rear of the Renault and opened the doors. She took out the plastic case, opened it and withdrew the parts that, when assembled, would constitute the small drone that had been part of their load-out for this assignment. It was a creation of the engineers in Group Six and was based on the design of the Wasp UAV that was used by the US military. She took the fuselage, the wings and the tail assembly, and clicked them all into place. She took out the avionics equipment and attached them to the underside of the fuselage.

"How long can it stay up?"

"Fifty minutes," Six said.

"We'll need it tonight, too."

"I've got a spare battery. It'll be fine."

Six busied herself with the drone. She adjusted the wings and started the propeller. The engine whined as it got up to speed. She took a step back, turned to face the field, and held the drone as high above her head as she could. She brought her arm forward and launched it, watching it race away and gently increase its altitude. It looped around in a gentle arc so that it could begin to follow its preprogrammed trajectory to the GPS location of the safe house.

Björn watched as it climbed to a thousand feet and settled onto a vector that would take it over the surrounding neighbourhood and into a sentry position, where it would provide a clear view of the house and its immediate environs. Six clicked on the small control unit, waited for the screen to flicker into life and for the radio connection to be established. The drone's downward-facing cameras passed back their feed, revealing a crystal-clear view as the vehicle passed over Parque Quimbaya en route to its destination.

81

Hicks had moved the Altima so that he had a clear view of the garage and the road that it abutted, with an unobstructed line of sight in both directions. Ziggy was in the back with his laptop, an open line to Chase's phone audible through the device's speaker. Hicks had decided against driving past the property again for fear of alerting anyone inside to their presence, and was not about to park in a spot where it would be obvious that they were watching. Instead, he had decided on oblique observation from this position, with Chase scouting on foot. The apartment buildings that faced the garage were screened first by a line of trees that had been planted by the municipal authorities, and then by a hedge that marked the boundary between the sidewalk and the ill-kempt lawns on the other side. The coverage would make it more difficult for anyone in the safe house to notice an observer, but, as Chase had noted, he would still look like a trespasser to anyone inside the apartments. He would take advantage of the cover, but wouldn't overstay.

"You see anything?"

"Property on the left looks empty," Chase said. *"No sign of anyone inside."*

"And on the right?"

"Movement on the top floor. One—check that—two people, possibly more." There was silence, save for the sound of Chase's breathing. *"You want me to take a closer look?"*

Hicks bit his lip. "You think you can get into the back without being seen?"

"I don't know."

"Cameras?"

"None that I can see from here."

Hicks decided against it. Chase was confident, but Hicks concluded that the close work would be something that he ought to do himself. He was about to tell Chase to walk around the block to see if he could get a look from the other side of the building when he spoke again.

"Eyes out, boys. There's a car coming your way. White van, two occupants—license plate—shit, hold on—license plate is MBW 801."

"What about it?"

"It's the second time I've seen it. I saw it from the car before I got out."

Hicks saw the van rolling toward them. It was an old Renault Master.

"Ziggy," he said.

"I got it."

Ziggy took a digital camera from his rucksack and held it between the seats. The van picked up a little speed as it approached them. Hicks pretended to be looking at his phone, but glanced up just as it went by. He got enough of a look to tell that the driver was a big white guy with blond hair and the passenger was female, late twenties to early thirties.

"Run the plates," Hicks said.

"Already doing it."

Hicks watched in the mirror as the Renault turned right and disappeared from view.

"You see it?" Chase said over the phone.

"We did. Watch to see if it comes around again."

Ziggy sucked his teeth. "All right," he said. "It's a private vehicle. Registered to a Miguel Reyes Domingas."

"The driver didn't look like a Miguel Reyes Domingas," Hicks said.

"No," Ziggy said. "Pale skin, blond hair. Looked European."

"Did you get a picture of him?"

"I did. The passenger, too."

"Can you check them?"

"Already on it."

Ziggy was never one to be shy about his achievements, and on more than one occasion he had mentioned that, during his employment at Group Two, he had arranged backdoor access to the databases maintained by police and intelligence services all around the world. He had maintained that access even after leaving the Group. Hicks was sure that he must have been in breach of all manner of laws, but that had never been something that had caused Ziggy any kind of visible concern. Indeed, he wore his illegality as a badge of honour.

"Anything?"

"Give me a chance. Do you have any idea how big these databases are? It could take hours."

"We don't have hours," Hicks muttered impatiently.

"I'll do my best."

82

The three additional Group Fifteen agents arrived over the course of the afternoon. Ten and Eleven had the shortest distance to cover, and arrived together at just after four. Number Two landed after them, knocking on the door of the safe house at six. Their involvement in the operation had not been planned, so Björn knew almost nothing about them. Two was in his mid-thirties, with a well-kept beard and a thick mop of black hair that had not received the same care and attention. Ten was in her late thirties, with porcelain skin and red hair that she wore in a ponytail. Eleven was black, around six three and built like a truck. He had evidently been involved in recent action, given that the side of his face was marked with a sickle-shaped cut that was only halfway toward healing.

The six agents and Weaver stood around the long table that had been left in the larger of the two rooms. Björn had considered the best course of action after his earlier reconnaissance. With a black Sharpie, he had sketched out the grid of streets on the table and the route he suspected the Americans would use to take La Bruja to the airport.

"It's not going to be easy to predict which way they might decide to go, so our best option is going to be to hit them soon after they leave the compound."

He took two empty cigarette packets and placed them at the location of the safe house. "Our intelligence suggests that they'll go in convoy. Two cars." He tapped a finger on one pack and then the other. "La Bruja will be in the lead car with backup behind. The airport is to the east of the city—a forty-minute drive, maybe less when it's quieter at night and they're pushing it." Björn moved the packets along the roughly drawn roads. "They'll come out of the compound here and head to Calle 32. My best guess is that they'll go left onto Avenida 80 and then right onto Avenida 33. It's a straight shot through the city and then out to the airport from there."

Ten tucked a loose frond of hair behind her ear. "So we hit them there?"

"No," Björn said. "The road is too wide and it'll be busy, even if they go late. The best place is here." He moved the packets to the point on the map where Calle 32 connected to Avenida 80. "This is a narrow two-lane road. One way only with poor visibility. There's a barrier to the left and buildings to the right, and here"—he laid his finger on a stretch of the map—"one lane has been closed while they dig it up. It's a pinch point. If we pen them in there, there'll be nowhere for them to go."

"That works," Eight said. "How do you want to do it?"

"Three vehicles," Björn said. "I'll have the van. Ten, Eleven—you'll ride with me."

The two agents nodded their agreement.

"Six—you take the Toyota. I want the drone in the air so we can track them without being too obvious about it. Close in and assist once we stop them."

"Right," Six said.

"Two, Eight—you've got the minivan."

The agents nodded.

"Six—you give the signal when they set off, and then I want you to get eyes on the cars from the ground."

"Yep," she said.

Björn pointed to the junction of Avenida 80 and Calle 32.

"We're going to split up the convoy," Björn said. He took a matchbox and a lighter and positioned them on the map. "The minivan waits here"—Björn placed the matchbox at the junction where Calle 32 met Carrera 82—"and you'll get in between the two vehicles." He moved the matchbox ahead, pushing it between the two cigarette packets. "You fake a problem so you can stop the trail car before they get to the next junction."

"Isolating the lead car," Two said.

Björn nodded. He took the lighter and placed it on the junction with Avenida 80. "I'll be waiting here." He moved the lighter forward so that it was blocking the road. "I'll close the trap, and then we get her out."

"Not just her," Weaver said. He took out his phone, laid it on the table and swiped the screen until a picture of a woman was visible. She was attractive, mid-thirties, with dark hair that seemed to have a natural wave to it. "Her, too."

"Who is she?"

"Her name is Ellie Flowers. She's the FBI lead in the operation against the cartel. The CIA want to know how much the bureau knows."

"Anyone else? What about the Americans?"

"No witnesses," Weaver said. "Take them out."

83

Ellie paced the floor of the office above the garage. It was just coming up to nine and that was the hour that they had decided to move. She went to the window, standing at the side so as not to present an obvious silhouette, and looked out. This part of Medellín was quiet, with just the occasional car and pedestrian. A chequerboard of lights shone in the apartment block on the other side of the road, and there was a little clutch of young men on the corner; she could see the red tips of their cigarettes and hear the sound of their raucous laughter. A lone prostitute leaned against the trunk of one of the trees that separated the road from the apartment building, her face lit by the glow of her phone as she waited in vain for business.

"Are you okay?"

She turned. Milton was standing in the doorway.

"I'm good," she said. "A little on edge."

"I'm not surprised. But nerves are good."

"I've done this before," she said.

"I know you have."

She turned back to the window again and gazed out. "This guy you say the cartel killed."

"What about him?"

"Was he a good friend?"

"I don't have many good friends," he said.

"But he was?"

"One of my better friends. He helped me out more than once. And he was murdered because he helped me."

"So, you're here for what? Revenge?"

"I told you—justice," Milton said.

Ellie turned to face him again. "Why do you feel *you* have to do this? You could've left it to the police. It was the same in Michigan. You didn't know those kids. Why would you do that? It's not as if you were going to get paid for it—not then, not now."

"I told you," he said.

"I know. You've done bad things. Shit, John—*I've* done bad things, but you wouldn't find me chasing narcos around a place like this."

"There's bad," he said, "and then there's *bad*. I decided, when I stopped doing what I used to do, that I was going to spend the rest of my life trying to make up for what I've done. To make amends."

"Even if it gets you killed?"

He shrugged. "If that's what it takes."

"You were lucky in the jungle," she said. "You could easily have been shot."

Milton smiled. "It'll happen one day," he said. "I'm at peace with it."

Ellie looked at him. She saw the hurt that he carried with him, the absence of self-esteem. She remembered it from before, too, from the time they'd spent trekking through the Upper Peninsula and the night they'd spent on the shore of Mirror Lake. She had drawn him to her then, and she found that she wanted to do it again now.

She started to step toward him, but, before she could, McCoy put his head around the door.

"Ready?" he said.

She turned to him. "Now?"

"We're good to go."

84

Ellie and Milton followed McCoy down the stairs to the hallway. McCoy and four of his SEALs—Rhames, Peterson, Wood and DuPlessis—were waiting. They were wearing civilian clothes, but all had pistols worn in shoulder holsters that were hidden by their jackets. Miguel and Fuentes were there, too.

"You know the plan," McCoy said. "We take both cars. I'll drive the lead car. Rhames brings La Bruja. Flowers, Smith—you're with us, too." He pointed to the other men. "You drive the trail car. Stay close. There's nothing to suggest that we've been made, but it couldn't be more unfriendly outside. We don't stop for anyone or anything. Time to the airport from here should be forty-five minutes max."

"Are they ready for us?"

"The jet landed an hour ago. We drive straight out onto the strip, load her up and away we go."

There was murmured assent. Ellie knew that the plan had been discussed and that the SEALs were content with what was being proposed.

McCoy turned to the two DEA agents. "You two okay to get out under your own steam?"

"We've been down here for months," Fuentes said. "We got it."

McCoy turned to Rhames. "All right, then. Go get her."

The SEAL made his way to the holding room where La Bruja was being kept.

Ellie held her hands together and drummed her fingers against one another. She knew that this had the potential to be dangerous. Very dangerous. They were proposing something that might charitably be called audacious.

She corrected herself.

Audacious?

No.

Risky.

Rash.

Foolhardy.

But what other choice did they have?

Milton was leaning against the wall, watching her. "It'll be fine."

She nodded. She knew that he was doing his best to give her confidence, but her mouth was still dry.

"There's one thing that would make me a lot more comfortable," he said.

"What's that?"

"Get me a weapon."

"No," McCoy said.

"I know what I'm doing," Milton protested.

"So you say," McCoy said. "But, with respect, I don't know you. And we don't need another shooter. There are five of us plus Agent Flowers. We have it covered."

Milton ignored McCoy and kept his eyes on Ellie.

She shrugged. "It's his call."

They heard the sound of feet as Rhames returned with La Bruja. She was ahead of him, her hands still secured behind her. The SEAL had his hand on her back, his fist knotted into the fabric of her shirt to help her as she ascended.

She stopped at the top and glared around at them. "Who is in charge?"

"For now?" McCoy said. "That'll be me, ma'am."

"This is your last chance."

"That right?"

"You think you can take me across Medellín? I *own* Medellín."

"That might be the case, but no one knows you're here. No one will see anything other than a couple of vehicles on their way to the airport. No one's coming for you."

"Let me explain something to you," she said. "To *all* of you. This won't be the last time we are in a room together. The next time? It will be different. I will find your wives." She turned to Ellie. "Your husband. Your children. Your parents. You think you understand pain? You do not. I will show you what pain means."

McCoy listened with his arms folded across his chest. "Listen, honey, you can make all the threats you want, but when you wake up, you know where you'll be? You'll be over the border. There's a nice Texas welcome waiting for you. You'll be in front of a grand jury before you know it."

"When I wake up?"

McCoy nodded, and Peterson took a plastic case out of his pocket. He opened the lid. There was a syringe inside. He withdrew it carefully, together with an ampoule that contained a clear liquid. He removed the plastic sheath that covered the tip of the needle, pushed the point through the seal and into the ampoule and then drew back the plunger, filling the barrel with the liquid.

La Bruja watched and, the blood draining from her face, started to struggle. It was a futile effort: her hands were secured and Rhames was there, pushing her against the wall with his left forearm as he secured her arms a little more forcefully with his right. Peterson approached, pressed the needle into the vein at the back of her wrist, and depressed the plunger. Ellie watched as the fight and tension drained out of her. Her head lolled down so that her chin was resting against her chest, her shoulders relaxed and her knees buckled and gave way. Rhames caught her, placing his left arm behind her back and then scooping her up.

"Thank the Lord for that," McCoy said. "She was beginning to get on my nerves."

"We ready?" Ellie said.

The SEAL nodded. "Let's do it."

85

Björn rolled around the corner, drove a little way up the road and then pulled over. He had used his phone to shoot video of the property's frontage as he drove past it five minutes ago, and now he scrubbed back through the footage so that he could examine it more carefully. The building on the left still showed no signs of habitation, but that was not the case with regards to its twin on the right. The windows on the top two floors were lit, and, as he slowly scanned through the film, he saw shadows moving through the exposed rooms beyond. He paused the video, laid his thumb and forefinger on the display and dragged them apart to zoom in as far as he could. The image degraded a little as he enlarged it, but it was still clear enough for him to be able to make out that there was a woman looking out.

He zoomed out and reviewed the footage again. The property did not look as if it was particularly well defended. That tallied with the intelligence that Weaver had been able to provide: four or five of the SEALs were remaining in close proximity, together with the agents from the FBI and DEA.

He thumbed his radio to open the channel they were using for the operation.

"One, channel. Comms check."

"Six, receiving."

"Eight, receiving."

"Two, receiving."

Ten and Eleven were in the back of the vehicle with him. They checked in, too, to confirm that their radios were good.

"Synchronise watches. I have twenty-one-zero-five."

The others confirmed that they had the same time.

"Six—is the drone ready?"

"It's on station. Feed is excellent."

Björn looked up into the night sky. The drone was invisible.

"Can you see anything?"

"Negative," she replied. *"It's clear."*

"Stand by. One, out."

86

Milton watched as McCoy pushed down on the handle and opened the door. It swung back, revealing a yard outside. It was concreted over, with six cars and two vans slotted into the available space. It was a tight squeeze, with a channel down the middle that had been left to allow the vehicles to be driven out. The exit was blocked by a solid wooden gate. McCoy paused, his pistol aimed out into the space, his stance low and compact and ready for movement.

"We're good," he said.

They moved quickly, with McCoy and Rhames leading the way to the Chevrolet Captiva that was parked with its nose pressed up close to the gate. It was a seven-seater SUV with manual transmission. It wasn't an impressive car and would not be particularly resilient or useful if they were to find themselves in a chase. It would not have been one that Milton would have chosen save for the fact that it was anonymous. There were a lot of them on the streets and it would not stand out once they were beyond the gate.

The second car was a Renault Duster, a compact SUV in

a five-door station wagon configuration. Two of the remaining three SEALs got into the Duster, with the third going to the gates.

The back door of the Chevrolet was opened and Rhames muscled La Bruja inside. He moved her to the rear seat, strapping her in and then sliding down next to her. She was still senseless, her head lolling against his shoulder. Ellie got in next, taking a seat in the middle row, and Milton climbed aboard to take the seat next to her. McCoy shut the door and went around to the other side, climbing up into the driver's seat.

McCoy took a walkie-talkie and pressed the button to transmit. "Ready?"

"Ready," came the reply from behind.

"Once we start, we don't stop. Foot down all the way to the airport."

"Copy that."

McCoy signalled to the man at the gate. He withdrew the metal bar that secured the two gates and pulled them open. McCoy started the engine and rolled out onto the street beyond.

Milton looked left and right. A car went by, cruising slowly, and he saw kids playing soccer in a patch of open land on the other side of the road. It was quiet, with nothing out of place, no overt cause for concern.

That didn't help.

Milton was still nervous.

87

Number Six was wearing TacPro concealable armour beneath her black shirt. It was equipped with lightweight panels that made it difficult to see, yet it offered decent stopping power. The edge was chafing under her arm and she loosened the strap a little and adjusted it.

The drone maintained its steady orbit above the safe house. She watched the footage, flicking between standard HD and infrared. Her attention flicked to the back of the property as the drone's IR camera picked up a new heat source. A figure came out of the building into the yard behind it. The drone's targeting computer helpfully overlaid a reticule over the figure, and then a further two reticules as two more people emerged from the house and followed.

"Channel, this is Six," she said into the microphone. "Movement at the rear of the property."

The figures got into two vehicles and the gate was opened.

Six pushed the button to transmit. "They're on the move."

ZIGGY WAS BUSY. The laptop to his right was displaying the location of the GPS transmitter in Milton's boot. The machine to his left was running the photograph of the man in the car through all of the databases to which Ziggy had illicit access. The laptop in front of him was tuned in to a local police scanner; since he didn't speak Spanish, he had set up a workaround that recorded each new piece of speech and then ran the recording through a piece of software that translated it into English. It wasn't the most elegant way to do it, but it was working, and he didn't have time to prepare an alternative.

He had just reached over the screen of the right-hand computer for his packet of cigarettes when he noticed that the flashing red dot that represented the tracker had started to move.

The dot moved again, going beyond the boundary of the property.

He reached for his phone. "Hicks, this is Ziggy. The tracker is moving."

"Where?"

"Looks like it's in a car." He refreshed the screen and saw the dot move again. "They're turning left onto Carrera 83 and heading north."

"Copy that. Chase?"

"Got it. I'm on my way."

"Me too," Hicks said. *"Chase—tell me if you can see him. Ziggy—keep watching. I need to know where that tracker is at all times."*

"Copy that."

"Hicks out."

MILTON SAT QUIETLY AS they made their way through the city. The cars had formed up in a convoy, with their car in the front and the trail car a length behind. They turned left out of the safe house and headed north. Milton watched through the window as they followed a bend in the road that took them onto a one-way road that was enclosed on the left by a wooden fence and on the right by a narrow sidewalk and then a metal fence that was itself topped with rolls of razor wire. The wooden fence fronted a series of trees, while the metal fence demarked the boundary of an apartment block. Milton felt an itch at the back of his head.

Nerves.

"Have you scouted the route?" he asked.

"This afternoon," McCoy said from behind the wheel. "It's fine."

"You'd be better avoiding stretches like this," he said.

"What?"

"We're boxed. If they come at us on a road like this, there isn't going to be anywhere to go."

McCoy glared at Milton in the mirror. "You think we haven't done this before?"

"I don't know," Milton said. "Maybe you have; maybe you haven't. Either way, it doesn't mean you're immune to making mistakes. And this isn't safe."

"Agent Flowers, will you please tell your English friend to shut the fuck up?"

Ellie reached over and laid a hand on Milton's leg. He turned to look at her and she gave him a smile and a slight shake of her head. Milton drew in a breath, trying to ignore the empty feeling in the pit of his stomach.

They reached a crossroads. They had right of way and

McCoy kept them moving. Milton saw a yellow hatchback approaching and held his breath until it stopped. He stared at it, the sodium yellow from a streetlamp directly overhead catching against the glass and rendering it opaque. He had a moment of concern that the car might accelerate and crash into them from the side, but it didn't; instead, the driver brought it to a stop and waited.

They negotiated the crossroads and continued to the east, following the same one-way road.

~

Hicks brought the hatchback to a halt at the junction and watched as the two cars rolled in front of him. A Chevrolet Captiva in the lead with a Renault Duster just behind it. It was dark, but he thought he could see Milton in the back of the Captiva.

He put the car into gear and turned right, following behind the Duster.

"They're in a Chevy Captiva and a Renault Duster," Hicks reported. "Registrations MXU 689 and GMO 140."

"Copy that," Ziggy said.

"What about Milton?" Chase asked.

"I got eyes on. He's in the lead car. There are at least three in the Chevy and another three in the Duster."

"Got it."

"We don't know who he's with. We don't know whether he needs us or not."

"He's with the cartel," Chase said. *"Gotta be—right?"*

"I don't know," Hicks said, biting his lip a little. "I saw the driver. He didn't look local."

He noticed the lights of a car coming up behind him in the outside lane.

"So we follow along until we know what's happening?" Chase said.

"Where are you?"

"Calle 32B."

"He's parallel with you," Ziggy clarified.

"Stay close. Hicks out."

He dabbed the brakes and drifted back a little. He didn't want to get too close and give himself away to whoever was in charge of that convoy. They didn't really have a plan. They didn't even know who Milton was with, save that it had to be something to do with the cartel. The exit from the safe house had taken them by surprise, and now they were just treading water until they could get it all figured out.

He settled in behind the Duster and watched.

88

Number Eight reached down into his lap and picked up the balaclava. He pulled it over his head and dragged it down so that only his eyes were showing. Number Two did the same. They were in a Dodge Journey at the junction of Calle 32 and Carrera 32. The minivan was sluggish and a struggle to drive, but that was of no concern. Eight wasn't intending on using the vehicle to chase the convoy; he had another part to play.

This was the spot that One had selected for them. It was a good choice: no space to run off on either side of the road and, whereas it had been two lanes up until this point, work to resurface the road had meant that the inside lane was sealed off. The asphalt had been scraped off by a bulldozer that had then been left to block the road. The result was that there was only one lane for twenty metres, with no way for a car to overtake anything that was in its way.

Eight waited. The engine rumbled and the vibration caused the crucifix on a chain that had been hooked around the stem of the rear-view mirror to swing to and fro.

He saw the first car—the Chevrolet—and released the brake.

The Dodge rumbled out of the turn. He wrestled the wheel around and pressed the gas pedal all the way down to the floor. The Duster was close by, but not so close that Eight couldn't turn in ahead of it. The driver of the SUV sounded his horn, and Eight held up his hand in apology.

"Eight, channel. In position. Get ready to close the door."

∽

McCoy swore. "Ah, *shit*."

Ellie looked ahead, saw that he was looking into the rear-view, and looked back herself. The Duster was no longer there. Its place had been taken by a red Dodge Journey minivan.

"Shit," McCoy said again. "He's got in between us."

Milton looked back, too. "You need to get off this road."

"We can't," McCoy said. "This is the fastest route."

"*Look*—you've been compromised."

"Could just be he's a bad driver," McCoy said.

They pulled up to a set of red lights.

"You need to get off the road," Milton said again.

"Please. Enough. Everything's fine."

The lights went to green and McCoy pulled away.

Ellie watched through the rear windshield. "The Dodge isn't moving."

The minivan was stuck at the junction. The roadworks meant that there was only one lane of traffic and the Dodge was obstructing it, with no way around on either side. She heard the honk of the Duster's horn, but it didn't generate any movement in the minivan. She could see the driver as he raised his hand out of the window in apology. Had it stalled?

∼

Number Six hit the gas and came out of the junction. The Dodge was on her left, blocking the road and trapping the Duster behind it. The Chevy was on her right, moving away from the junction. She accelerated until her Toyota had closed the distance.

She glanced down at the drone's control unit. She had placed it on the passenger seat so that she was able to see the screen. The drone was programmed to triangulate off the Chevrolet, and she was able to look down from a thousand feet and observe the procession as it made its way through the quiet streets. She could see all of the relevant vehicles: the Chevy, marked with a bright white reticule; the Duster, marked in orange; the Dodge Journey blocking the road.

"Channel, this is Six," she said into the radio. "Package is heading to the box."

∼

McCoy said something on the radio, but Ellie missed it. Her attention was drawn to the Toyota that had come out of the junction that they had just crossed and accelerated until it was behind them. A woman was driving.

"They're boxing you," Milton protested. "When's the next turn?"

"We're not turning off."

Milton had been following their route on the vehicle's satnav. "Up ahead on the right," he said, pointing. "Calle 32 goes east and west. Loop around in the direction we've come from and plot another route."

"I told you," McCoy snapped, "it's *fine*. Agent—tell your friend to sit still and shut up."

"They're *boxing* you."

McCoy slapped his hand against the wheel.

"Get off the road now," Milton urged.

"Shit!" McCoy swore.

Ellie turned to look forward.

She saw a flash of motion through the windshield.

"Look out!"

A large white van came out of the junction ahead of them. McCoy hit the brakes and the Chevy's wheels locked, the tyres squealing as the sudden deceleration left rubber on the asphalt. Ellie and Milton were pitched forward, caught by the snap of their seatbelts. McCoy grunted, his head thumping against the wheel before the momentum bounced him back in his seat.

Ellie heard the sound of an engine behind them. Milton reached out and put his arm across her chest just before the Chevrolet was struck from behind by the Toyota, bulldozing the vehicle down the road. They were jerked forward again, the belt cutting into Ellie's shoulder, Rhames bouncing into the back of her chair. She heard the jangle of shattering glass and metal as the car was twisted and crumpled and bent.

The Chevy came to a stop.

"You okay?" Milton asked her.

"I think so."

He looked around her and out of the window. "They're going to hit us now," he said calmly. "Do what they say. Do *exactly* what they say."

89

Björn yanked his balaclava down, pulled his pistol, opened the door and stepped outside. Ten and Eleven took their shotguns and did the same. The Chevrolet had been shoved forward and to the side by the impact from Six's Toyota. A horn—either the Chevrolet's or the Toyota's, it was hard to say—droned out.

The driver of the Chevrolet was stunned. Ten levelled her shotgun at the windshield, covering him.

Eleven went left.

Björn went right.

Six approached from the rear.

The Duster was two hundred yards behind them, boxed behind the minivan. Björn could see Two and Eight on either side of that vehicle, their weapons trained on the occupants, keeping them inside.

Björn reached the passenger-side door and looked inside. The driver had shaken off his grogginess and had seen Ten's shotgun. He had his hands up. Björn moved down the SUV and opened the rear door at the same time as Eleven opened its opposite. They both aimed their weapons inside. Björn scanned the interior quickly: the woman Weaver had identified as a possible federal agent was in the middle row, closest to Eleven; John Smith was beside her, closest to Björn; a man who looked like a soldier and an unconscious La Bruja were in the rearmost row.

"You," Björn said to Smith. "Out."

Eleven was busy on the other side. He pointed to the soldier. "Bring the woman out."

"No," the soldier said. "I'm not doing that."

They had expected resistance and had discussed how to get around it. Eleven reached into the cabin, grabbed the federal agent by the lapels and hauled her out of her seat. He dumped her onto the asphalt, took a step back and aimed the shotgun down.

"Bring her out now or I'll shoot her. And then I'll shoot you."

∼

HICKS WATCHED IT ALL. The minivan stopped abruptly and the Duster had slammed on the brakes to avoid rear-ending it. Hicks had been far enough behind to stop with plenty of space to spare, and the distance between him and the Duster ahead meant that he was able to look around it and the Dodge and see the Chevrolet. A white van had raced out of the junction and blocked it, and then the Toyota had accelerated into the back of it. Hicks had no idea what was happening, save that it was a classic ambush, well planned and perfectly executed.

"What's happening?" Ziggy said over the phone. *"You've stopped."*

"The convoy's being hit," Hicks reported.

"Hang on," Chase replied. *"On my way."*

The doors of the Dodge opened and two people stepped down to the asphalt. They were wearing black, with black balaclavas pulled down over their heads, and they were carrying submachine guns. The figures approached the Duster with their weapons cradled in two hands. They opened the doors on both sides of the SUV and took aim at those inside.

∼

MILTON SHUFFLED across the bench and stepped down onto the road. He recognised the big man's voice: it was the mercenary La Bruja had referred to as Eidur. The big man had kept the pistol on him, stepping back a couple of paces so that there was no possibility that Milton might think that he could disarm him before he could pull the trigger.

Milton put his hands up.

"Turn around."

"Take it easy," Milton said.

"Turn around now. Hands behind you."

Milton did as he was told. He had noticed that the man was wearing flexicuffs looped into his armour, and he felt the familiar sensation as the loops were secured around his wrists and then yanked tight. How many times had he been restrained since he had arrived in South America?

"Just take her," Milton said. "There's no need to hurt anyone. You've won."

"Tell your friend in the back to play ball," the man said, "or we'll shoot you all."

Milton faced into the car. Rhames was still on the back bench, his hand dangerously close to his weapon. Reaching for it would have been suicide; he was badly outgunned. The police would be using tweezers to pick bits of him out of the upholstery for weeks if he did something as foolish as pull it.

"Do what she said," Milton said. "Bring her out. There's no play for you here."

He heard the sound of raised voices from back up the street. The soldiers in the Duster had realised what was happening, and two people who had been in the Dodge minivan—both wearing balaclavas—were holding them in place with submachine guns. Milton knew that their ambushers didn't have long before the police arrived; he guessed, from the professionalism that they had displayed, that they would be aware of that, too. The horn was still blaring out of the Duster, and the authorities wouldn't be far away. Milton doubted that it would have made much practical difference if the police had intervened. El Centro owned the cops, but Milton guessed that these mercenaries would have had no interest in negotiating custody of an unconscious La Bruja when they would have wanted the credit for her rescue themselves. It would go some way to make up for the fact that she had been taken on their watch in the first place.

Rhames, having weighed up his options, apparently agreed with Milton's assessment. He pushed up the seat in front of him and manoeuvred his unconscious prisoner outside. He draped her arm over his shoulder, grabbed her wrist with his hand and locked it in place, and followed the woman's direction that he should bring her to the back of the van. The woman followed him, covering him with the rifle, and waited as he raised the door and lifted her into the back.

"You've got her," Milton said. "All right?"

"Who's your friend over there?" Eidur asked him, gesturing to Ellie. "DEA? FBI?"

"I've no idea," Milton replied.

"I don't believe you. You're both coming with us."

He reached forward, grabbed Milton's bound wrists and, aiming the pistol back at the two cars with one hand, he hauled Milton backwards to the waiting van.

90

Chase was on Avenida 33, four blocks to the north of Hicks's location. The roads in this part of the city were arranged so that some were eastbound and others were westbound, often on an alternating basis. Hicks had suggested that they needed at least one car in a floating role, able to respond quickly to changes of direction or the need to replace one trail car with another in the event that the first was made. That was Chase's responsibility.

"Head south," Ziggy directed over the phone. *"Two blocks."*

He hit the gas, pulling ahead and then swinging the wheel hard to the right. There was a bus ahead of him, blocking the road as it dropped off passengers. Chase swerved around it into the opposite lane, then turned hard right to miss the taxi that rushed by him with its horn blaring.

He reached the junction with Calle 32B and skidded into it, pumped the gas again and then turned the wheel hard left, accelerating along Carrera 81A. He raced over the junction with the westbound lane of Calle 32 and drove into the short connecting road that linked it with the eastbound lane. Chase saw a white Renault van and the blocked-in Chevrolet. He hit the brakes and rolled to a stop.

He saw a big man wearing a balaclava standing between the Renault and the Chevrolet. He had a pistol in one hand and was shoving a prisoner toward the open doors of the van.

The prisoner had his hands secured behind his back.

Chase recognised him.

Milton.

∼

"THEY'VE GOT MILTON," Chase said over the open line. *"What do we do?"*

"Hold your position," Hicks replied.

His attention snapped back to the two vehicles that were blocking his way. Hicks reached over to the passenger seat and slid his hand under the blanket that he had spread out there. He felt the hard edges of the pistol that Chase had procured, stretching his fingers out until he had the grip against his palm and his finger inside the trigger guard.

The man covering the left-hand side of the Duster shouted something to his partner on the right and then, without any warning, both men fired their weapons. The SMGs flashed as they were fired, automatic rounds puncturing the Duster's glass and riddling those inside.

It would have been a massacre. The car's occupants stood no chance.

And Hicks was a witness to their murders.

He knew that he would be next.

He let go of the pistol, crunched the gearbox into reverse and stamped on the gas.

He saw the flash of the submachine guns and lowered

himself so that he was shielded by the dashboard. Bullets chinged against the hood and flank of his car, and then one —followed by a second, third and fourth—cracked into the windshield. The safety glass holed, but did not shatter.

The phone fell off the dash and disappeared into the footwell.

"I'm under fire," Hicks shouted into it, unsure whether Ziggy and Chase could hear him.

He was reversing blind now. The car crashed into something and stopped. Hicks grabbed the pistol, opened the door and slid out, staying low, using the door for cover.

Another barrage thudded into the car, the door juddering as a bullet clipped the frame. Hicks took a breath, counted to three, and then popped up. The two men were both facing him, one on either side of the wrecked Duster. Hicks aimed at the man to the right, nearest to him, and pulled the trigger three times. The return fire was instantaneous, another volley that peppered the car and forced him back down behind the door.

The door panel was not substantial enough to offer reliable cover, so Hicks scurried around to the back of the car, his progress prompting yet another volley. The windshield took the brunt of it and, already weakened, chunks of glass broke loose and crashed into the cabin. Hicks's phone was still in there, but there was no way that he was going to be able to get to it.

He was penned in.

91

The gunfire was loud, the reports echoing off the buildings and sending a roosting bird up into the air in panic. Chase watched as the unconscious woman and then Milton were bundled into the back of the van. The second captive—Chase didn't recognise her—was struggling with the masked woman who was next to her. It looked as if she was being pushed toward the back of the van, too, and that she really didn't want to go.

Chase opened the door and got out of the car, then reached back inside for the Marlin. It was already prepared to fire: magazine tube loaded, .45-70 cartridge in the chamber, hammer cocked, safety off.

He raised it, pressed it against his shoulder, and squinted down the iron sight to aim.

He pulled the trigger, absorbed the recoil, and immediately cycled the lever to put another cartridge into the chamber.

ELLIE'S HANDS had been secured behind her back, and now the woman who had done it grabbed her, wrapping her arms around her and trying to manhandle her toward the van. Ellie struggled, trying to free herself. She was a fed. She knew what would happen if she was delivered to the cartel. They had already killed the US ambassador. An FBI agent would be small potatoes by comparison.

Milton and La Bruja were already in the back of the vehicle when the shot crashed into the side of the Chevrolet. The boom that followed was big and ominous, suggesting that someone was firing large-calibre rounds their way.

"Incoming!" the woman next to Ellie yelled.

Ellie turned her head in the direction of the junction and saw a man with a long gun aiming it in their direction. The man fired again and the windshield of the van was punctured in the middle, the corresponding deep boom following in short order, peeling off the buildings on either side of them.

Her captor was distracted. Ellie took her chance and shoved the back of her head in the direction of the woman's face. She made a solid connection, the impact rattling her jaw and her teeth clashing together. The woman behind her grunted with pain and loosened her grip. Ellie butted her again and, this time, the woman let her go.

Ellie ran. She pounded the asphalt, knowing she had to get as much distance between herself and La Bruja's people as she could. She stumbled east, crossing over the junction. She put her head down and sprinted for all that she was worth.

∼

HICKS HEARD the rifle shot and knew that it must be Chase.

He took a breath, held it, then exhaled, popping up from behind the trunk and bringing the pistol with him. The two shooters had been frozen by the boom of the rifle and, for a moment, their attention was elsewhere. He would make their neglect of him expensive. He sighted one of them, the man on the left of the car, and fired, pulling the trigger three times. The first two rounds missed, high and to the right, but the third smacked him in the leg. The impact unbalanced him and he fell, landing heavily on his side.

His partner turned and fired a barrage that smashed into the car, forcing Hicks down again. He was next to the passenger door. He was getting low on ammunition and he remembered that he had a magazine on the seat. He opened the door, reached in and found the spare. He saw his phone on the floor and grabbed that, too.

"*Hicks!*"

It was Ziggy over the speaker.

"I'm here," he said.

"*You need to move. The police are coming. There's a car on its way.*"

Hicks would have *loved* to be able to move, but that was easier said than done. He was penned in and outgunned.

He heard the sound of an engine, and the screech of rubber on asphalt.

"*Hicks?*"

He peeked around the side of the door and saw that the Dodge minivan was moving away from him. He shuffled forward to the front of the car, gripped his pistol tightly, and stood. He checked down the road and couldn't see either of the men who had been shooting at him. He took the chance to move forwards, reaching the back of the Duster. The vehicle had been shot to pieces, riddled at close range with automatic gunfire. There were three men inside, all of them unmoving, all of them struck multiple times, all of them already dead.

Hicks took a breath, readied himself to shoot, and stepped around the corner of the van. The Dodge was a hundred yards away, across the junction and already out of range. Next was the Toyota, with a woman in a balaclava sheltering behind it. Hicks looked across the junction and saw Chase; he was crouched behind his car, leaning against the hood with the big lever-action rifle aimed at the junction.

The van was still blocking the road, but, as Hicks watched, the big man got into the driver's seat and negotiated the space, bumping the wheels over the kerb and pointing the vehicle in the same direction as the fleeing minivan. The woman popped out of cover, loosed a wild volley in Chase's direction—enough to pin him down for a moment—and then hauled herself into the van as it rolled by.

He looked up again. The Dodge and the Renault were racing away.

Milton was inside.

"Chase," he said into the phone, "get in the car and pick me up!"

∼

Ellie ran. She approached a crossroads and stumbled around to the left, following the main road north to where she could see a store with its lights still shining. If she could get there, get inside, maybe she would be able to call for help.

She heard the sound of an engine from behind her and turned to look: the white Renault van screeched around the corner and followed her up the road. Distracted, she caught her foot against the kerb and, with her hands still secured behind her back, she toppled over. She came down heavily on her shoulder, gasping from the sudden jarring spur of pain. She pushed herself further onto the sidewalk, her boots scraping against the asphalt.

The van raced by and then the red Dodge followed. She expected them to stop, for someone to get out and grab her, but they didn't. Instead, they accelerated away along the road, passing the store and continuing to the north.

She heard a third vehicle approaching her from behind and turned to see a teal Nissan Altima.

The car braked heavily as it reached her.

There were two men inside.

The man in the back opened the door and got out.

"Stay away from me," Ellie said.

"We're on the same side."

The man spoke in what Ellie thought was a British accent, like Milton.

"Come on," he said. "They're getting away."

There was no reason for her to trust him, but, as she turned to look north, she saw that what he had said was true: the Renault and the Dodge were disappearing from sight. She wanted La Bruja, and, more than that, she wanted to help Milton.

The man reached down and hauled her up to her feet. She crossed the sidewalk to the car, ducking her head so that she could slide into the back. The man slid in next to her and closed the door. The driver buried the pedal and they raced north in pursuit.

92

Ellie sat with her hands pinned behind her and looked at the two men in the car. The driver was in his late thirties with a solid build. He had neatly clipped hair and was handsome. The man next to her was middle-aged with a hard-looking face.

"Who are you?" Ellie said.

"Hicks," the passenger said.

"And you?"

"Chase Baxter," the driver replied. He sounded American.

"Who are *you*?" Hicks asked her in return.

"Special Agent Ellie Flowers," she said.

"You're a federal agent?"

"That's right." Her shoulder bumped against the side of the door as Baxter aimed the car around a sharp bend in the road. She winced in pain and indicated her shackled wrists. "Could you get these off me?"

Hicks took a butterfly knife from his pocket and released the blade with a flick of his wrist. She swivelled around so that he could reach her hands, and he sliced through the plastic, freeing her hands.

"Thanks," she said as she rolled her stiff shoulders and massaged the sore skin. "You want to tell me how you two are wrapped up in this?"

"A friend of ours is in the back of that van," Hicks said.

"John Milton?"

He glanced over at her. "You know him?"

"A little."

"You want to tell me how?"

"You want to tell *me*?"

"I've known him for a couple of years. We've worked together."

"He knew my old man," Baxter said. "Look out—hold on."

They swung a hard left, coming off the main northbound drag and then crossing the Medellín River by way of the Puenta Madre Laura. The two vehicles they were following were half a mile ahead. They were driving fast.

"Milton," Ellie said. "You're working with him now?"

"Yes," Hicks said.

"How?"

"We're his backup."

"Right," she said.

She was going to add that they weren't backing him up all that well, given what had just happened, but she let it pass. Hicks, though, saw what she was thinking.

"We lost him when he first got here. They took him for a meeting outside the city and we couldn't follow."

"They took him into the jungle," she said. "That's where we picked him up." She was unwilling to go much further than that with two men she had never met before.

"The place you had him, before you drove out—what was that, a safe house?"

"That's right," she said, and then—realising that they knew more than they should—she added, "How did you know he was there?"

"Later," Hicks said. "Your turn first. What's the FBI doing here?"

"I'm sorry," Ellie said. "I can't talk about that."

"Look, lady," Baxter said. "This has to be a two-way thing. I can always pull over and ask you nicely to get out. We're doing *you* a favour here."

Ellie grimaced. She didn't know either of them. She didn't really know Milton, either, and, although she thought he had told her the truth, what if he was hiding something? On the other hand, if she didn't get their help now, she was going to lose La Bruja. The operation—what was left of it, anyway—would be a bust.

"The FBI and the DEA are involved in an operation against the cartel. You read the papers? The ambassador got killed. You might have heard about it. We captured the cartel's senior leadership and we were taking her across town to the airport. The idea was that we would be on our way back to the States around about now. And then—well, I guess you saw what happened next."

"I was right behind you when you got hit," Hicks said.

"I heard shooting," Ellie said.

"They shot up the other car. I'm not sure—maybe someone pulled a weapon—but the guys you had in there are all dead."

"Shit," she said. "Shit." She took a moment, staring ahead at the white van and the Dodge and wondering what she should do. "Look—do you have a phone? I need to call for backup."

Chase hit the brakes before Hicks could answer. "They're going right," he said. "It's going to be pretty easy to make us if we follow."

Ellie looked out of the windshield. They were in the hills of the city, heading north towards Santa Cruz and Villa Niza and Acevedo. The districts around here were poorer than their neighbours to the south, populated by the underclass in shanties that were similar to the favelas of Brazil. This was cartel territory. They were running back to El Centro's stronghold.

"Keep going straight," Hicks said.

"What?" Ellie said. "No! You've got to follow."

"They'll see us," Hicks said. "And, if that happens, there's a good chance we won't get to drive out again. We've got to be patient."

"Shit," she said. "We'll lose them."

"No, we won't. Chase—give me the phone."

Chase reached for a phone on the passenger seat and handed it back to Hicks.

"Ziggy? You there?"

A voice sounded from the speaker. *"I'm here."*

"You get all that?"

"Loud and clear."

"You still got him?"

"I do. He's on Calle 105. Near the—" he paused *"—the Parroquia La Transfiguración."*

"The Church of the Transfiguration," Chase said, translating. He reached back for the phone and Hicks handed it to him. "Can you drop a pin on it."

"Sure." Ziggy paused. *"Done."*

Chase glanced down at the screen. "I got it. You can still track this phone, right?"

"There's coverage where you are. Should be fine."

Ellie gestured to the phone. "You can follow Milton?"

"He has a tracker in his shoe," Hicks explained.

Chase pulled over at the side of the road. There was a series of tiered streets to their right as the favela ascended the steep hill all the way to the top. They were outside a store that offered SERVICIO ELECTRICO by way of a hand-painted black-on-yellow sign. The store was penned in on both sides by tall, narrow houses. Alleyways snaked between them, vertiginous passageways that wound their way up.

"What are you doing?" Hicks said.

"We can't drive in there after him," Chase said. "They'll make us right away."

"I agree. That's why we need to figure out what we're going to do."

Chase ignored him. He turned in his seat so that he could look back to Ellie. "What's your plan? You go back and call in the cavalry?"

"Maybe," she said. "If we can track him, like you say…"

"What about her?"

"Who?"

"La Bruja."

"Why do you care?" she asked.

"She murdered my father."

There was evidently a lot that she didn't know. "We'll do what we can. I want her, too."

"And then what? Prison?"

"Probably."

Chase shook his head firmly. "Too good for her." He opened the glovebox and took out the Sig Sauer P226 that he had taken from the arms dump, then unlatched the door. "I'll watch the house. Call me when you have a plan."

"Chase!" Hicks reached for him, but the American was already out of the car.

Ellie looked over and watched as Chase retraced his way along the road before turning onto a narrow set of steps that climbed up to the next tier of the favela. He disappeared from view.

"Shit," Hicks said.

"We can't stay here," Ellie said, aware that a man outside the store was eyeing the car. "We need to get off the street."

Hicks got out and went around to the front, taking Chase's place in the driver's seat. He took out his own phone. "Ziggy—do you have a fix on Chase?"

"Yes," he said. *"What's wrong?"*

"He's doing his own thing. Keep an eye on where he is."

He put the phone on mute, started the engine and put the car into drive. Ellie looked back at the narrow staircases that climbed up into the favelas. A big six-foot gringo like Chase was going to stand out in a place like this.

"How savvy is he?" she asked.

"Chase?" Hicks shrugged. "I haven't known him for long. Impatient. Other than that? I don't know."

"I hope he's smart. Unless he gets off the street, someone's going to deliver him to La Bruja."

Hicks knew that she was right. Chase wouldn't last long out here on his own.

"You mentioned the cavalry," Hicks said. "How do we go about arranging that?"

93

They might have been in cartel territory, but Björn was not prepared to relax. The operation to recover La Bruja had proceeded as well as could have been hoped for, but he would not be able to let his guard down until they were safely off the street. Weaver had provided them with the address of an El Centro stronghold, and he followed the Dodge around narrow, winding streets until they were halfway up the hill. The buildings on either side were pressed in close, shoulder to shoulder, looking down onto the more prosperous districts on the other side of the river. It was late and, while the streets were quieter than might have been the case a few hours earlier, it was still busy. Both of their vehicles were inconspicuous, but he had noticed the car that had raced after them after the heist and, although it was not behind them any longer, he wasn't ready to discount it just yet.

Björn dabbed the brakes and turned the wheel to bring the van around a right-handed hairpin. He straightened out and pressed down on the gas again.

Six was on the phone with the others in the Dodge. She ended the call.

"Well?"

"Two's been shot."

"Shit. How bad?"

"The leg," she said. "Looks like it went in and straight out, so there's that. But he's lost a lot of blood."

Björn was irritated. It had almost been a perfect operation. Now he was going to need to call for a pickup.

He followed the Dodge around another hairpin and saw the building that they needed. It was a squat, ugly, concrete construction over three storeys, sitting at the apex of the next turn in a spot that would offer an excellent view of approaching traffic. Weaver had provided the address with the suggestion that it was cartel property, deep in the territory that they controlled. They would be safe here. He was hopeful that they would be able to deliver the woman and then melt away. The evening's activity had been noisy, and taking out the convoy would call down even more attention from the Americans. He didn't know what Control would want them to do, but he hoped that their involvement might now be at an end. This operation had been his focus for months and he was ready for a break.

"There," Six said, pointing.

Björn saw the men, too. Three of them came out of the building and waited. They must have been watching out for them. There was a narrow road that branched off from the one that they were on now. It ran alongside the building, and the Dodge steered into it, coming to a halt against the kerb. Björn parked behind it and immediately got out.

He went to one of the cartel soldiers, a weaselly man he recognised from a previous trip to Medellín with La Bruja.

"She's in the back," he said in Spanish. "They drugged her."

"*Sí*," the man said.

Björn drew his pistol, led the way to the back of the van, unlatched the handle and rolled the door up. It was dark inside, but he could see the three people: La Bruja, slumped against the wall; Number Eight, his pistol in his hand; and John Smith, on his side with his hands bound.

"And him?" the narco said, pointing at Smith.

"Bring him inside, too," Björn said. "He's got some questions to answer."

Björn stood to the side as Eight hopped down, both men observing as first La Bruja and then Smith were brought out of the van and taken through a door into the building. He was about to follow when he heard the sound of an engine. He turned to see a BMW roll to a stop behind them.

Benjamin Weaver opened the door and got out.

"Sir?" Björn said.

"We need to talk."

"Now? What about?"

"John Smith," he said. "He's not who he says he is."

PART VIII
TUESDAY

94

Chase moved with care. It was late and the streets were quiet, but he knew that he would stand out here and that the area was likely one in which the cartel held sway. The neighbourhood had been built on the hillside, a steep climb from the road where he had stepped out of the car and where he was now. Chase paused in the shelter of a doorway and looked back down the alley that he had followed: it dropped precipitously, a series of steps and dizzy slopes. The lights of the city on the other side of the river shone in the darkness, a more prosperous neighbour to these slums.

He took out his phone and checked the location of Milton's tracker once more. The flashing red dot had stopped moving fifteen minutes earlier, and Chase had hurried upward until he had reached his present vantage. He put the phone away, aware that the lit screen would be visible to anyone who might be standing sentry, and watched the street again. He was on Carrera 50, one of the main arteries of this part of the district. It was a two-lane road that wound left and right as it clambered up the side of the hill, eventually reaching the top. The buildings had been constructed on levelled-off slabs, each one taller than its predecessor, with the effect that they looked as if they were an ascending series of steps. Chase was standing in the lee of the buildings that bent around to the right, following the turn of the road. They looked as if they were residential, with concrete stairs offering access to front doors. The windows were barred, and thick lattices of telephone and electricity cables stretched between wooden poles. He watched as a green and white municipal bus rolled around the corner and descended the slope.

The building over which the red dot had settled was on the outside of the right-hand turn, fifty feet away. It was a three-storey concrete structure that looked as if it had been dropped into the neighbourhood. Its neighbours looked insubstantial by comparison, their pitched wood and tin roofs flimsy when stood against the brutal grey box. It looked like it might have been chosen for its defensive qualities: its bulk, the miserly windows, its position on the apex of the corner allowing clear lines of sight both up and down the hill. It put Chase in mind of the castles in the stories that his father had read to him as a child.

The thought of his father restored his focus. He was here because of him.

The woman who was responsible for his murder was inside the building.

She was close.

Another bus rumbled up from behind him, hydraulics wheezing as the platform lowered to allow a passenger to disembark. Chase glanced up at it and stared into the curious faces of locals who were heading up the hill after, he presumed, finishing late shifts at work. They stared at him as the bus pulled away, and he was reminded of the fact that this was not the sort of place where one would find a gringo, especially not as late at night as this.

He needed to get off the street.

One of the buildings on the side of the hill was in the process of being renovated. It looked as if it had been damaged in a fire, with streaks of black soot reaching up the beige walls and half of the roof missing, presumably burned. A stack of bricks had been placed at the side of the road with a dumpster that was already full of debris from the construction work. Chase waited until the road was empty and then walked out from his hiding place, crossing the street with a stride that mixed briskness with a lack of concern, and passed around the dumpster. The property was set back a little from the sidewalk and was accessed by a concrete bridge that traversed the ten-foot drop to the first floor below.

The door was protected by a metal grille and, when he tugged at it, Chase found that it had been locked. He followed a short passage to the side of the building where the wall extended out to mark the boundary with the adjoining house. There was another low wall at the edge of the passage that was then topped by metal railings. Chase clambered onto the wall, then onto the top of the railings—rusty and treacherous—and then turned back to face the property. He reached over his head, felt the sloping edge of the roof, and heaved himself up. It was difficult. The camber of the tiles meant that it was difficult to get an even grip, and the material was sharp enough to cut into his fingers and fragile enough to threaten to break. After a moment hanging out above the drop to the ground below, he managed to swing his boot up and over and, hooking his toes, dragged himself over the edge.

He lay there for a moment, gathering his breath and

staring up at the stars overhead, before the sound of a dog's bark spurred him to move deeper onto the roof so that he was harder to see from the road below. He went back far enough so that the lip of the roof obscured him from the street, while still ensuring that he had a clear view of the property next to the road's hairpin turn.

He reached into his jacket and took out the P226. He would rather have had the rifle, but it would have been difficult to bring it with him without it being conspicuous. He knew that he would likely be outgunned should he manage to put himself into position to take a shot at La Bruja, but there was nothing to be done about that. He would just have to make do.

95

Hicks drove them to the hotel. He had asked whether there was somewhere that Ellie wanted to go, but, after considering it for a moment, she had shaken her head and said no. The safe house where they had taken La Bruja had lacked the security that might have been expected, and, in the circumstances, Ellie decided that it would be better to avoid the fallback location that had been proposed in the event that the operation had been compromised. She said that she would make a call once she was off the street, and work out how best to proceed from there.

Hicks pulled into the hotel's parking lot and slotted the car into a space between two larger vehicles. He took the rifle that Chase had been using and, after ensuring that he wouldn't be seen, he stowed it in the trunk. He found himself both annoyed and impressed by Chase's act of bravado. It was impetuous, certainly, but there was sense in what he had done. They had an idea where Milton was, but that might only be temporary. Ziggy had made it clear that the battery in the transmitter would only last for a day or two and, even if it still had a little juice, there was no guarantee that Milton's captors would not find it. If they moved Milton and Ziggy was unable to track him... well, that didn't really bear thinking about. At least Chase would be able to give them a heads-up, assuming that he had found somewhere suitable to surveil the place where Milton was being kept.

Ellie got out of the car.

"Come on," Hicks said, pointing up at the hotel. "We're in here."

∼

ZIGGY HAD all of his computers up and running and was buzzing between them. He looked up as Hicks and then Ellie came inside.

"What happened?" he said, and then, as he noticed that Hicks wasn't alone, added, "Who's this?"

"This is Special Agent Ellie Flowers," Hicks said.

"Special Agent... what?"

"FBI," Ellie said.

Ziggy shrank back a little with the hesitation born of a lifetime's wariness of authority. "Why do I feel as if I'm completely out of the loop?"

"Ellie knows Milton," Hicks explained.

"I was with him when we got hit," she said.

Hicks took off his jacket, tossed it over the back of the chair and made a cup of coffee as he brought Ziggy up to speed. Ziggy listened, his attention still flitting between the screens, his fingers occasionally dancing across the keyboards.

"So Chase—he followed?" he said when Hicks was finished.

"Yes," Hicks said. "Do you know where he is?"

"I do," Ziggy said. He turned to one of the computers, opened a window and spun the screen around. "Here."

Hicks and Ellie came closer so that they could both look at the map that was displayed. They could see a nest of streets to the east of the Medellín River and, on a sharp switchback bend, there were two dots in what appeared to be close proximity to one another.

"This," Ziggy said, pointing to the dot at the start of the sharp right-hand turn, "is the location of Chase's phone." He tapped the second dot, on the apex of the curve. "And this is the location of Milton's tracker."

"How much juice does it have left?"

"Three per cent," he said. "An hour or two, if he's lucky."

"What if they move him?" Ellie said.

"We've got Chase watching the building."

"You think he'll be able to follow?"

"He'd need transport." He shrugged. "I don't know."

"If he can't follow, and if the tracker dies…" Ziggy started.

"We won't know where he is," Hicks said.

Ellie paced the room.

"We have to do something," Ziggy said.

"I'm thinking," she said.

"You have backup here?" Hicks said.

"Two troops of SEALs," she said.

"So tell them where they are," Ziggy said.

She shook her head. "The Colombians don't even know we're here. We can't drop SEALs into a neighbourhood in the middle of Medellín. La Bruja isn't going to go quietly. There'll be a firefight. A massacre." She shook her head. "We might be able to get some surveillance in place, but we can't have boots on the ground."

"So what do we do?"

"I'm not leaving him there," Hicks said. He stood up and reached for his pistol. "Maybe I should go up there with Chase and we can wait for them to move him."

"What if they don't?" Ziggy said. "What if they figure out he isn't who he says he is? Maybe they make a connection between him going out to the jungle and the SEALs hitting the camp. Maybe they decide to put a bullet in his head."

"Enough," Ellie said, hushing him. "Enough. That's not going to work. We could go up there and wait, but as soon as it gets light, we'll get made and then they'll have us, too. No. We can't do that."

"We have to do something," Hicks said.

She pointed at his phone on the table. "Give me that," she said. "I need to make a call."

96

Björn waited until Smith had been marched into the building before he followed inside with Weaver. There was a large industrial space inside, with a group of narcos drinking and playing cards in one corner. They looked up at the two gringos with surly distrust. Björn led the way to a small empty room where they could speak in private.

"Sir?"

"The biometric data you took from Smith raised concerns in London."

"I saw—the report was classified."

"Yes," Weaver said. "I spoke to Control. She opened it and sent me the results. You were right to be suspicious. Smith isn't his name. It's Milton."

Björn shrugged. "Should I know who that is?"

Group Fifteen was deliberate in ensuring that information was siloed within the organisation. Agents typically worked alone—operations like this one, with multiple agents deployed, were unusual—and the knowledge that they had of one another was kept to a bare minimum. Björn and the others put themselves in positions where capture was possible, and, even with the best counter-intelligence training, resistance to torture was, at the end of it all, simply a matter of biology. It could be resisted for a time, but, eventually, a good interrogator would always prevail. Everyone cracked. The best defence was ignorance; one could not reveal what one did not know. Björn knew that dictum pertained to both current and historic Group activity.

"What I am about to tell you is classified," Weaver said.

Björn nodded his understanding.

"Milton—John Milton—was a Group Fifteen agent. He was Number One, like you, and he held that spot for years until he had some sort of breakdown and tried to quit. Control—the Control at the time—wasn't happy with his decision, and, after trying to persuade him that he should reconsider, felt that he had to suspend him. Milton went AWOL. Control sent an agent to terminate him, but Milton escaped. They lost him for months until he showed up in South America. A team was sent to bring him back, but he evaded them. They found him in Russia after that, and another team was dispatched. Milton took them out."

"Took them out?"

"Killed them, Number One. They lost him after that, and when Control died and was replaced, the decision was taken to close the file. He's popped onto the radar now and again in the intervening years, but it was always decided to let him be."

Björn frowned. "So why is he here?"

"We don't know. But Control is very interested in finding out."

"I can question him," Björn said.

"Be careful," Weaver warned. "He's extremely dangerous."

"I understand, sir."

"And the Americans can't know about this. An ex-agent getting involved and causing trouble... it'll just make things more complicated."

"Agreed."

"What about La Bruja?"

"She's fine," Björn said. "They drugged her for the transfer, but she was waking up when they got her down."

"Very good."

"Two has been shot in the leg," Björn said. "We'll need to get him seen to."

"I'll sort that out now," he said. "I'll take him, Ten and Eleven. You, Six and Eight stay here."

"With what orders?"

"See that La Bruja gets back to the jungle."

"And Milton?"

"Control is clear," Weaver said. "Find out what you can and then kill him."

97

Chase called to check in as they drove to El Poblado. Hicks put the call on speaker and Ellie listened in. Chase reported that there had been no additional activity at the cartel property, save that two sentries had taken up position outside it. Hicks told him to stay where he was and await instructions. Chase said that he would and ended the call.

"He won't do anything on his own?" Ellie asked.

"I don't know. He's impatient."

"But not stupid?"

Hicks shrugged. "I don't know him all that well."

Ellie checked the map. "There," she said, pointing.

Hicks pulled over to the side of the street. Ellie looked out of the windshield. It was a pleasant neighbourhood, clearly reserved for *Paisas* with a little more financial heft behind them than other areas that they had passed through. The houses were set back from the street by a margin of grass that was, in turn, punctuated by well-kept trees. Some of the properties were sheltered behind brick walls. The house that Ziggy's research had identified was a poor relation to some of the others on the street—it was a single-storey villa that wasn't walled, and the car in the drive was a Nissan Leaf rather than a more expensive imported sedan—but it was neat and tidy and had a larger than average garden enclosing it.

Ellie gazed at the windows. Most were dark save for the one at the corner of the property; a little golden light bled out through the slats of a Venetian blind.

Hicks was looking, too. "This guy," he said. "He'll help?"

"I don't know. He's going to be pretty pissed off with me."

"Why?"

"Because we've been lying to him ever since we got here. But I don't really have an alternative if he turns me down. It's him or nothing—and nothing probably means that Milton and maybe Baxter don't have much longer to live."

"You'd better be persuasive, then," he said. "I'll wait for you."

~

ELLIE CROSSED the sidewalk and made her way along the gravel path to the front door of the property. She knocked tentatively on the door and then, when there was no reply, she rapped her knuckles against it with a little more force. She heard the sound of footsteps and saw a shadow move across the stippled glass.

The door opened a crack, still held in place by a security chain. "Who is it?"

"Special Agent Ellie Flowers."

There was a moment of silence and then the door closed. Ellie wondered whether it would remain closed, but then heard the rattle as the chain was disengaged and saw that the handle was turned again.

Colonel Jaime Valencia stood in the doorway. He was wearing a pair of jogging pants and a sweatshirt; he looked older out of his uniform. Ellie's eye was drawn to the pistol that rested on a small telephone table to the colonel's left. He saw that she had seen it, and gave a shrug. "It wasn't that long ago that my predecessor was murdered," he said. "A knock at the door after midnight is rarely good news, especially so in a place like this. Agent Flowers—how did you know where I lived?"

She shuffled uncomfortably. "I'm sorry, sir," she said. "I'm afraid it's probably best if I don't tell you that."

He regarded her with suspicion. "Not an auspicious start to our conversation."

"No, it isn't. I'm afraid I have some other things to tell you that you might not like."

"Isn't *that* intriguing? It's late, Agent. What is it?"

"Do you mind if I come inside?"

Valencia thought about that, and, for a moment, Ellie wondered if he was going to suggest that she make an appointment tomorrow. But he didn't; instead, he stepped aside and gestured that she should come through.

"This way," he said, leading her through the house to a room that was evidently used as an office. He took a stack of papers from a chair and indicated that she should sit. He went around to the other side, wheeled his chair away from the desk, and sat down. "Now, then. What is so important that you need to bother me so late?"

98

The cellar was dark. Milton looked around for any sign that there might be a window or a door, but found nothing. The floor was damp and he could hear the repetitive ticking of a drip as water fell down from the ceiling somewhere to his right. His hands were still secured with the zip ties.

He was in trouble.

They had tossed him into the back of the van and driven him here. There had been no windows in that part of the vehicle. He estimated that they had been travelling for fifteen minutes, so he was sure that they were still in Medellín. The sounds outside the vehicle had given him no clue as to which part of the city they had taken him to, but the final part of the journey had been uphill. The road had climbed quite steeply for some time, with a number of sharp switchbacks to the right and left. Milton didn't know the geography of the city as well as he would have liked, but he knew that some of the rougher neighbourhoods were found on the flanks of the hills that reached up from the river. He suspected that the cartel would have a redoubt in an area like that, where its members could melt away into familiar crowds and where the locals would be either sympathetic to its cause or terrified of the consequences of opposing them.

The van had stopped and the roller door had been thrown up. The big Scandinavian had dragged Milton outside and, before he had been muscled into the building, Milton had been rewarded with a glimpse that had confirmed his suspicions. He was in a neighbourhood of cheap housing that had been built on the side of a hill. He had been able to look down over the roofs of the buildings further down the slope to the open space of a river, a demarcation point between the neighbourhoods on opposite banks.

He got up and shuffled forward, feeling his way carefully in the darkness until his outstretched hands touched a wall. He ran his palms along the damp concrete, stepping gingerly sideways until he found a door. He put his ear to it and listened, straining for anything that he could use to give him a better idea of what might happen to him. He could hear muffled laughter and the sound of a television, but nothing else. He rested his shoulder on the door and leaned his weight against it. The door creaked a little, but there was no give. There was no easy way out, not that it would have mattered in any event. What was he going to do with his hands tied, stuck deep in an area he didn't know, surrounded by people who were loyal to El Centro either through money or fear?

He had no card to play, other than to wait and hope that Hicks and the others might be able to get to him.

He sat down and tried to think if he had anything on him that he could use to remove the cuffs. His belt would have been useful, but they had removed that in the back of the van. He remembered the tracker in his boot. He doubted that it had any juice left and wondered whether he could break it open and find a sharp piece of metal or plastic to use.

He had nothing to lose.

He reached down, unlaced his boots and worked them off his feet. He took the right-hand boot and turned it in his hands until he could rub his finger against the sole. It was too dark to see it, but he remembered what it looked like and how it had been adapted from when Ziggy had given it to him. He felt for the almost imperceptible join where the heel had been split and then glued back together again and worked his thumbnail into it, loosening the two parts until he could fit the tips of his fingers inside. He pulled the heel all the way apart and felt both pieces; the device was nestled into a cavity that Ziggy must have cut out, snug enough that Milton had to pry it free. He felt it: it was a long, thin rectangle, about the size of a credit card and perhaps three centimetres thick. The edges were rounded and the plastic casing was smooth, offering no sharp edge that he might have been able to use against the cuffs. He worked his fingers against it, trying to find where the plastic pieces had been fitted together, but it felt solid, as if it was a single piece.

Milton heard the sound of footsteps coming down the stairs outside the room. He palmed the tracker, raised his hands to his face and rotated them so that the free end of the zip ties was pointing up. He bit down on the plastic and wriggled his wrists until the locking mechanism was between his hands. He kept the plastic between his teeth as he pulled down, tightening the ties until he couldn't close them any more. Tightening them was a gamble, but he was out of time and out of options. He had one card left to play; it would have to be enough.

99

The discussion was not an easy one to have. Ellie was completely honest, holding nothing back. She apologised that she hadn't mentioned the operation in the jungle to him, and did not think to insult his intelligence with anything other than the unvarnished truth: that her superiors in Washington did not trust the Colombian government, the military or the police. She explained how they had been developing their own leads for months and, in the immediate aftermath of the assassination of the ambassador, they had redoubled their efforts to find La Bruja. Valencia listened intently, a frown developing as he realised how thoroughly he had been kept in the dark.

"And that is it?" he said when she was finished.

"Yes, sir. It is."

"You and your colleagues come here, to my country—to my city—and you lie to me for weeks. You tell me that the hunt for La Bruja continues, when, all along, you know where she is?"

"We didn't know where she was," Ellie corrected him, then wished that she hadn't.

"But you had intelligence that you kept from us," the colonel snapped, banging his palm against the desk. "The briefings we had, the plans you said you were working on—those were all based on lies?"

Ellie looked down at her hands.

Valencia laughed, but it was a laugh that had no humour in it. "You Americans," he said. "You think you can do whatever you like."

"If it's any consolation," she began, and then, when he snorted derisively, she added, "and, of course, I know it *won't* be, but I've always been very uncomfortable with the decision to keep you out of the loop. I'm speaking entirely out of line here, but there should have been a Colombian component to the operation."

"A 'component'? This is my country, Ellie. She is a Colombian citizen, and she has killed hundreds of other Colombian citizens. This should have been a Colombian operation—exclusively—without any interference. She should be detained by the Colombian military and tried in a Colombian court. It is an insult—surely you can see that?"

"I can, Colonel. I can. And all I can do is apologise."

He let her stew for a moment, watching her shrewdly.

"But something happened, yes? You wouldn't be here if you didn't need my help."

"That's right, sir. There's been an incident."

He leaned back in his chair and laced his fingers behind his head. "You will give me the truth?"

"I will."

"*All* of it?"

"All of it."

"Please," he said, nodding that she should continue. "Go on."

She explained that the operation had been successful,

and that La Bruja had been brought to Medellín in anticipation of being flown out to the United States that night. She told him about the convoy and about how it had been hit by a professional crew.

"That was you?" he said, interrupting.

"Excuse me?"

"There was a shooting tonight. Three men were found dead in a car, shot to death—none of them had any identification."

"Yes, sir. They were SEALs. The cartel executed them."

Valencia's face took on a sombre cast, and all of the slightly sarcastic edge was smoothed away. "I see. Who knows that you have come to me now?"

"No one, sir," she said.

"Your boss?"

"No. I haven't spoken to him since the convoy was attacked. He doesn't know that I'm alive."

"And you are here because?"

"Because I need your help, sir. A friend of mine was in the convoy when it was hit. He is in very serious danger, and, unless you step up, I'm worried that he's going to be killed."

"The cartel has him?"

"Yes."

"Then he is already dead."

"Maybe not," she said. "He's resourceful."

Valencia smiled. "And why, after all of the lies that have been told to me, would I agree to 'step up.'"

"Because he's with La Bruja, Colonel. You help me get him out and you can have her."

Hicks reached over and opened the car door for Ellie to get back into the cabin. The light of the dash washed over his face. It made him look even more anxious than she knew he already was.

"What did he say?"

"He's going to make a phone call," she said.

"But he's in?"

"Oh yes," she said. "He's in."

100

Milton composed himself; he knew that what was likely to happen was going to be unpleasant. His captors would suspect that he was connected to the raid on the laboratory, and they would want to know exactly what that meant. They would suspect that he had been responsible for passing on the location of the camp to the SEALs and would want him to tell them what might come next. Milton anticipated all of that and steeled himself to it. He had been tortured before. There had been training in the Regiment to prepare himself for what might be expected, and that training had been augmented by deeper sessions when he had joined the Group. He had been locked in dark, soundproof rooms for days on end. He had been blasted with the same song on repeat, again and again and again. He had been beaten. He had been thrown into icy pools and left to hover on the brink of hypothermia. Dealing with it was simple enough, he reminded himself, at least in theory. He would distance himself from the experience, lock himself away in his mind, and do his best to ignore what they did to his body.

He had little choice; he could tell them that he wasn't John Smith, but he doubted that they would believe the truth any more than his fiction. They would suspect he was an intelligence asset. It was a reasonable suggestion in the circumstances. The truth of it, though? That he was a single man on a mission, going up against the vast evil of the cartel to right a single wrong? That was a fanciful suggestion. And so, suspecting that he was stringing them along, they would increase the discomfort until they killed him.

Milton could live with that. He might not have met his objective, but at least he had made the attempt. He had lived his life in accordance with the Steps, right up until the end.

The door was unlocked and opened. A shaft of light from the floor above shone through the doorway, silhouetting the figure of a large man. It was the Scandinavian.

He stepped deeper into the room. "Hello, John."

Milton didn't respond.

The man reached for a light switch and flicked it. A bulb above Milton filled the room with a sickly sodium glow.

"I know who you are," the Scandinavian said.

"Because I told you."

"Yes, you did. But you were lying."

"Again?" Milton said. "We're doing this again?"

"There's no point in pretending. I know the truth. It's Milton, isn't it—not Smith? John Milton."

Milton's heart caught. He tried to keep his expression neutral, but he was surprised and there was a moment when he knew it had betrayed him. It was possible that a well-resourced investigation might have been able to dig through the layers of subterfuge that Ziggy had assembled; the legend was only as strong as its weakest link, and a diligent search would have teased out inconsistencies that, when taken as a whole, might peel back the disguise. But Milton hadn't used his real name—not in Vegas, not in Italy, not in the Netherlands and not here. His identity was classified. Discovering that should have been impossible.

"Surprised?"

There was no point in trying to continue the charade. "A little."

"The cartel has influential friends," the man said.

"Apparently so. But you have me at a disadvantage. I don't know your name—it's not Eidur, is it?"

"No," the man said. "My name is Thorsson."

"What are you? Danish?"

"Icelandic."

"Special Forces?"

"Once. I was in the SAS. Just like you, Milton. Years ago."

"And then what? They binned you?"

"No," he said. "I left."

"To become a mercenary?"

"No. Not that. Our careers have followed very similar paths. We have much in common."

"What does that mean? You work for the government?"

"I work for the *Group*," Thorsson corrected him.

"No, you don't. The Group was disbanded."

"And then put back together again. You didn't know?"

"I've been keeping myself out of the way."

"Yes," Thorsson replied. "You have. And it would have been better if it had stayed that way." He spread his arms. "But here we are. It is what it is."

Milton felt the zip ties against his wrists. They were good and tight. He wondered whether he might be able to engineer one last chance to do what he had come here to do.

"Look, Milton," Thorsson said. "There's no point in pretending—you and I both know that there's no way that you can leave here alive. You know too much. And you've made a nuisance of yourself. The cartel wouldn't allow it. *She* wouldn't allow it. She's very angry."

"Killing me isn't going to make her any safer than she is already. The Americans are after her now. Those men who found you in the jungle? They're SEALs. They won't just stop, especially after what you did back on the road. I saw—you gunned down a carload of them. You add that to the ambassador and they'll keep coming and coming and coming until they have her. And you."

"You know that's not why she'll kill you. She'll kill you because you've made her life difficult."

"So let me talk to her."

"About what?"

"She's not interested in how the Americans found her?"

"You led them to the camp. You've been working with them."

"That's right," he lied. "And you think she wouldn't be interested in what I know? I've been involved in this for months. The meeting with López in Amsterdam. Getting Jackson out of the way so that he would take my proposal more seriously. Coming here, then getting them to take me into the jungle. Are you seriously saying that she wouldn't be interested in everything I know? Who I'm working for. What they'll do next. Everything."

The bluff was as convincing as he could make it. Thorsson narrowed his eyes a little, but, before he could answer, the door to the room opened for a second time. La Bruja stood in the doorway, silhouetted against the light. Milton straightened his back a little. He felt the itch of incipient violence that he remembered so well.

Thorsson stepped to the side so that she could see Milton without obstruction.

"Señor Milton," she said.

Milton did not reply.

She angled her head to Thorsson. "What has he said?"

"He says that he has been working for the Americans."

"And do we believe him?"

Thorsson shrugged. "I'd say it's likely."

"Our friends don't know anything about it, though?"

"No," Thorsson said. "Apparently not. But that's not necessarily surprising. The FBI and DEA have partitioned their operation very well. We had no warning of it."

La Bruja took another step into the room. She was alongside Thorsson now, close to where Milton was sat on the floor. He needed her to come a little closer.

"How did you lead the Americans to us?" she said.

"They were following me," he said.

"And how would they do that?"

"They were watching," he said, pointing his shackled hands up to the ceiling.

She turned to Thorsson. "Is it possible?"

"Of course. A drone or a satellite. That's why we need to get you away from here."

"We are fine," she said. "A cowardly attack in the jungle is one thing. In Medellín? When we know that they might come?" She scoffed. "No, I do not think so. They would have to involve the government, and, if they did that, we would know. They should have shot me in the jungle. They had their opportunity then." She took another step closer to Milton. "You could have done it, perhaps. I know your history now. You are an assassin." She gestured behind her to Thorsson. "Like him."

"I could have killed you," Milton bluffed. "In the jungle—it would've been easy enough. But they don't want that. They want you in chains in a New York courtroom."

"Of course they do. They want their show trial. They

want to show the world how they are winning the war on drugs." She laughed. "Pathetic."

Milton's legs were outstretched, and she was standing just a little way beyond his feet. He wondered whether he would be able to sweep her to the floor. If he could do that, perhaps he could get to her before Thorsson got to him.

He needed to bring her just a little closer.

"I could work for you," he said.

She snorted. "Do you think I am a fool?"

"You wouldn't want someone inside their operation? I could do that for you."

"A desperate man will say anything to save his life. I couldn't possibly trust you. You could lead them to me again."

"Not if you pay me enough," Milton said. "I can be bought."

Thorsson shook his head. "That would be a bad—"

"Be quiet," she snapped, cutting him off. "I do not need advice on what to do in a situation like this." She stabbed a finger down at Milton. "Because of *you*," she said, "I have lost one of our most productive kitchens. Because of *you*, I have lost more than a thousand keys of cocaine. Do you know how much that has cost me, Señor Milton? Millions of dollars. *Millions*. Because of *you*."

Milton inched forward just a little. "You pay me enough," he said, "and I'll do anything you need. You want a warning when the Americans come after you again? I can do that."

She ignored him. "I was dragged out of the jungle like a petty thief. They drugged me. They would have taken me to America and they would have convicted me. Maybe I would have spent the rest of my life in prison. Maybe they would have killed me." She shrugged. "All of it—it is *your* fault,

Señor Milton. There is nothing that you could offer me that would make up for the inconvenience that you have caused."

"You want me to take someone out? You want to make a point to them? I have access to them. They trust me. I can do that. Ask him." He nodded at Thorsson, using the motion as a blind to shuffle another inch closer to her. "He'll tell you. I've killed before. Many times."

She shook her head. "No. There will be no deal between us."

Milton's stomach plunged as she stepped back. She turned and made her way across the room to the door.

"What do you want me to do?" Thorsson asked her.

She stopped. "They need to know that there are consequences for their actions," she said. "We'll make an example out of him. Kill him and hang his body from a bridge. We will let him instruct them in the error of their ways."

101

Hicks drove them to the north of the city. Ellie had her phone in her hand and was looking at a map of the surrounding area. Ziggy had sent her a link that, he explained, would initiate a short program that would then pass the data that he was collecting on Milton's location to the phones of anyone else who opened the link. The blinking dot that denoted the most recent transmission from his tracking device placed him in the same Moscú neighbourhood that they had visited earlier.

Hicks's phone was on the dash. He tapped the screen to place a call and waited for it to connect.

"I'm here," Baxter said, his voice low.

"You need to get out," Hicks said.

"That's a negative. If I'm not here, she could leave and we wouldn't know."

"The Colombian army are going to seal the district," he said. "There won't be any way in or out once that happens."

"Appreciate the concern," he said, *"but I'm staying where I am until she's either dead or in chains."*

"It's not safe," Hicks protested. "And you don't need to be there. She's not going anywhere."

"I hear you, Hicks, but the answer is the same. Keep your phone close. I'll let you know if they make a run."

The line went dead.

Hicks slammed his hands against the wheel. "He's impossible," he said. "He's going to get himself shot."

"Maybe not," she said. "And it will be helpful to have someone on hand who can update us."

"You don't trust the Colombians?"

"No," she said. "Not at all."

∼

THEY TURNED off Avenida Carabobo and started to follow Carrera 50 as it commenced its steep climb up the hill. They switched back twice until the road reached the junctions with Calle 103 and 104 and saw that the way ahead had already been closed. A military vehicle had been parked across the road, and soldiers toting automatic rifles stood guard.

"Jesus," Hicks said. "They don't hang about."

He brought the car to a stop at the side of the road and they both stepped out. Ellie led the way to the nearest soldier.

"*¡Alto!*" the man said, holding up his hand.

She took out her badge and showed it to the soldier. "FBI," she said, and then, in awkward Spanish, *"Estoy trabajando con el coronel Valencia."*

The soldier told her to wait, and went to confer with his colleague. A radio was produced, and the man conversed with someone else before bringing the unit over to Ellie. He handed it to her.

"Hola?" she said.

"Special Agent Flowers, how can I help you?"

It was Valencia.

"I want to be there when this goes down," she said.

"I'm not sure that is wise."

"I told you where she was."

"After pretending that you did not know."

"You know I had no choice." She clenched the unit a little tighter. "This is your operation. I'm not trying to steal the limelight. But my friend is inside that building and you don't know what he looks like. I'd rather you didn't put a bullet in him when you storm it."

There was a pause, a burst of static crackling from the radio.

"Colonel?"

"Fine," he said. *"Hand the radio back to the soldier. I'll see that you're escorted up the hill."*

"I'm with a friend," she said, glancing over at Hicks.

"This is not a social occasion, Ellie."

"He's a soldier," she clarified.

"I have plenty of those. You can come—but only you."

Ellie gave the radio to the soldier and listened as Valencia briefed the man on his orders. She turned to Hicks.

"Sorry," she said. "I tried."

"It's all right," Hicks said. "I'll wait on the edge of the cordon. I'll be nearby if I'm needed."

"Agent?"

The soldier beckoned for her to follow him.

"Good luck," Hicks said.

"You too. See you on the other side."

Ellie followed the soldier around the end of the vehicle and began to climb the hill.

102

Hicks watched Ellie as she followed the soldier up the hill.

Stay on *this* side of the cordon?

That wasn't going to happen.

He got back into the car, threw it into reverse and turned it around. He found first gear and jerked away, heading back down the hill along the same road that he had taken to bring them up here. He remembered seeing an alleyway on their way up, and, seeing it almost too late now, he brought the car to a sudden stop next to the entrance. He got out, instinctively patted for the pistol that he was carrying in the back of his trousers, and made his way into the alley.

His phone buzzed in his pocket.

"Hicks?"

It was Ziggy.

"I'm here."

"We've got a problem. That footage you shot earlier? The man who went past in the car outside the safe house?"

"The big guy? What about him?"

"I got a hit. I ran him through the databases that Group Two

and Group Ten operate. That gets access to pretty much everywhere: DGSI, CSIS, ISI, CIA, FBI."

"And?"

"I'm not quite sure how to explain it, but the man you saw is Björn Thorsson. He's ex-SAS, like you. Like Milton. And he's a member of Group Fifteen."

Hicks stopped in his tracks. "I thought the Group had been disbanded?"

"It was—but they've revived it. There's a new Control in place, and she's rebuilt it with twelve new agents. Hicks— Thorsson isn't just any agent. He's Number One."

103

The colonel was sitting in a car that had been parked fifty feet away from the safe house. The soldier delivered Ellie to him and indicated that she should get into the back. She did as she was told.

"Thank you, Colonel," she said. "I appreciate it."

Valencia nodded. "We don't know how many are inside," he said. "They've got two guarding the door."

Ellie looked through the windshield and saw them: two young men wearing football shirts were ambling back and forth on the sidewalk in front of the house.

"What's your plan?" Ellie asked.

"Hit it hard and fast. Don't give them the chance to react."

"What about my friend?"

"Male, late middle age, gringo with a scar on his face, dark hair and blue eyes. I've given them his description. They'll do their best, but, you know, something like this? There's going to be a lot of noise and confusion. I can't promise."

Ellie didn't protest; that really was the best that she

could have asked for. Milton had put himself into this mess. She would do her best to get him out of it, but whether he made it or not was largely going to be up to him.

Valencia took a radio from the dash and thumbed the transmit button. He spoke quickly and in hushed tones, his Spanish too fast for Ellie to translate. She heard check-ins from the members of the team that had been deployed around the property, and then the soldiers manning the cordon that had put a stop to the cars, trucks and buses that would otherwise have continued up and down the road. It was early in the morning and traffic would only have been sparse, but the sentries would notice its absence eventually.

There was one pedestrian. The man ambled along the street, descending the hill and passing around the corner. He was dressed in shabby clothes and was shuffling along. He slowed his pace as he reached the corner, looked down at his foot with seeming annoyance, and then dropped out of sight behind a parked car as he made to fasten a lace.

She leaned forward. "Colonel?"

Valencia held up his hand to ask for silence, his posture rigid and a nervous tic pulsing in his cheek. He took the radio, pressed the button to transmit, and spoke with clear certainty.

"*Vamos, vamos, vamos.*"

104

Chase watched from across the street. A team of four soldiers scaled the walls of a building near to the property where Milton was being held. They used grappling hooks, tossing them onto the roof and then hauling themselves up after them. The four figures—all men, he thought—met in the centre of the roof and waited there, crouched down low.

The shabbily dressed man who had stopped to attend to a lace stood up. He was close to one of the two cartel sentries that Chase had identified and, his voice just about audible across the street, said something to the man. The sentry shook his head. The shabbily dressed man pointed down the street, and the sentry turned to look, presenting his back to the man. A knife was drawn and sliced across the sentry's throat; a hand clamped across his mouth as the body was dragged into the alley that ran along the north side of the safe house.

The second sentry was making his way up from Calle 49b, the road that formed the boundary on the south side of the building. The white van from the ambush had been parked at the junction, and it provided shelter for a second soldier. He waited for the sentry to turn left to head up the hill and then rushed out, intercepting him in ten quick paces, grabbing him from behind and opening the man's throat with an efficient slice of a knife. The sentry's body was dragged back down Calle 49b and dumped on the sidewalk.

Three teams of soldiers hurried forward. One team of five ran up the hill to the junction of the main road and Calle 49b. Another team of five emerged from a narrow alley opposite the building. A final team descended the hill. All fifteen men were dressed in black, moving with the slight stiffness of those wearing light body armour. They wore black helmets and were armed with submachine guns.

There was a short pause, no longer than ten seconds, and then the breaching team at the top of the building commenced the assault. Each man went to one of the four protruding skylights that Chase had noticed and, on the signal of a man at the front of the building, smashed the glass.

105

La Bruja left the room and made her way up the stairs to the floor above. Thorsson waited for her to go and then turned his attention back to Milton.

"You don't have to do this," Milton said.

"You know I do. It's not personal."

"It never is."

Thorsson reached down to his belt and the knife that he wore in a scabbard. He popped the restraining strap with his thumb and slid the handle into his palm, beginning to withdraw the blade.

Milton brought his hands above his head and then brought them down, quickly, into his stomach. He flared out his elbows and made as if to touch his shoulder blades together. The motion applied pressure against the ties, all of it directed against their weakest point: the mechanism. The locking bar jerked against the tracks of the tie and then slipped free, sliding all the way through it so that the ties loosened enough for Milton to jerk his right wrist through the widened loop.

The sudden movement stymied Thorsson for a moment,

and, when he stabbed out with the knife, Milton was able to swerve to the left while bringing his right arm up and around in a blocking motion. The point of the blade cut into the flesh of Milton's forearm, digging in for half an inch and then scoring a track up to the crook of his elbow.

Pain flared, but Milton welcomed it, a sudden buzz of adrenaline juicing his muscles and desperation adding its own edge. He planted his right foot and pivoted on it, driving a left-handed hook into Thorsson's ribcage. The bigger man was unbalanced by Milton's block, his arm still out ahead of him and his torso left unguarded. Milton put everything into the punch and was rewarded with a grunt of pain.

Thorsson staggered to his left. Milton caught his wrist in both hands so that he could control the knife, then stepped closer to Thorsson until he had pressed his hand and the knife against his body. With his body pressed up tight against the bigger man's, Milton forced his shoulder into Thorsson's to knock him off balance, then pivoted his body and swept his legs to take him down to the ground. Milton followed him down, pinning the knife hand and twisting it all the way back until the fingers loosened and the knife fell free. They struggled and, in the confusion, Milton thrust his hand down and jammed the tracker into the pocket of Thorsson's jacket.

Milton lunged for the knife; Thorsson, invigorated by his own desperation, struck Milton in the throat with the straightened fingers of his left hand. Milton gagged, suddenly choked. Thorsson got both hands beneath Milton's chest and, with a grunt of effort, shoved up. He was hugely strong, and Milton was thrown off him as if he were a child. He landed on his knees and crawled back.

Thorsson got to his feet.

Milton, blood running from the cut to his forearm, stood opposite him and fought for breath.

The knife was on the floor between them. They both saw it. Thorsson was much bigger, and faster than Milton would have given him credit for. If it was a straight-up brawl, Milton knew that he would lose.

"You're slow," Milton goaded, even though it wasn't true.

"Faster than you, old man," Thorsson said.

Milton lashed out with a right-footed kick, aiming down at Thorsson's knee. The Icelander swept his hand down and brushed the kick away, then drilled Milton in the side of the head with a right cross that flashed out with a speed that was almost impossible to credit in someone so large. Thorsson's knuckles crunched into Milton's cheekbone. Points of light sparked across his vision. He stumbled back, getting his guard up just in time to block the left-handed hook that would have scrambled his brains if it had landed. He fell back again, against the wall, separated from the knife by another four paces.

"You're out of your depth," Thorsson said.

"I've heard that before," Milton said.

Thorsson kept his eyes on Milton as he reached down for the knife.

"You should've stayed away."

He straightened up, passing the blade from hand to hand.

They heard the sound of small arms fire from somewhere above them. Milton stayed loose and balanced, ready to react if Thorsson lunged with the knife. Milton opened and closed his fists and put his weight onto the balls of his feet. Blood ran down his forearm; he ignored it.

It happened quickly: a cloud of dust fell down from the ceiling at the same time as a deep bass roar rumbled down to the basement. Milton braced himself, recognising the hollow rumble of explosives. The ceiling shuddered and another cloud of dust fell down onto them.

Thorsson's face flickered with doubt.

"Sounds like you've got something else to worry about," Milton said.

The Icelander glanced up and then backed away.

"I'll see you again," he said.

Thorsson reached the doorway, stepped through it, and then turned and took the stairs two at a time. Milton heard a shout and then a furious fusillade of gunfire.

106

Björn reached the top of the stairs just as the doors to the building were blown off their hinges by a breaching charge. The sudden pressure washed across the room, deafening him and forcing the air out of his lungs. The assaulters had tossed smoke grenades, and he ducked down low, covering his mouth with his left arm. He saw a man on the floor and recognised one of the locals who worked with the cartel. He had been shot in the chest and was trying to staunch the blood with his hands. Björn knelt down and relieved him of his pistol. He saw a man in dark clothes flit through the newly opened door; Björn aimed and fired, sending two rounds in his direction. It was too dark and murky to know whether his bullets had found their mark, and he didn't have the time to wait and find out.

He remembered the layout of the building. There were three ways in and out: the front door, which had now been breached, a door to the side and one at the back. He assessed that each access point would now have been compromised by the assaulters, leaving the roof as the only way out. The stairs were at the end of the hallway that ran along the left-hand side of the building, and he started toward it, staying as compact as his large frame allowed.

He saw a starburst of muzzle flash ahead of him, the noise of the shots lost amid the deafening cacophony. Björn zoned it all out, concentrating on getting to the hallway in one piece. There was another flash of automatic gunfire, but this time the rifle jerked up high and discharged into the ceiling, its bearer plugged by a round he would never have seen. The man's face appeared through the smoke; it was one of La Bruja's guards.

Björn flinched as a round pulverised the wall behind him, but kept moving. A figure appeared from out of the smoke. Björn aimed and fired, not caring whether it was a cartel gunman or one of the assaulters. The man's momentum was arrested; his legs went from under him and he disappeared into the smoke again. Björn knelt down next to the spasming body; it was a soldier, dressed all in black. He was wearing plate armour, but Björn's shot had blasted a hole in the man's eye. The soldier had been toting a Tavor X95 bullpup rifle. Björn dragged the strap over the man's head and saw that the rifle had been fitted with an underslung grenade launcher.

He saw another blur of motion to his right and, operating on muscle memory, he swivelled at the hips and discharged a burst on full-auto. The fusillade disappeared into the smoke and Björn heard the grunt of pain as whoever it was he had seen was stitched by at least one of the rounds.

Björn set off again, reaching the doorway and then hurrying through it. The smoke had yet to reach the corridor, and he saw Six and Eight at the foot of the stairs. La Bruja was between them.

"We need to leave," Björn said. He pointed to the stairs.

"They're on the roof, too," Six said. "They dropped grenades through the skylights."

"Doesn't matter," Björn said. "That's the only way we're getting out. Move."

107

Milton took the stairs. The large room above was full of smoke and it quickly had his eyes watering. They must have dropped tear gas, he thought, as he quickly retreated back down the stairs to where the smoke was thinner. He took off his shirt, tore it down the middle and bound one half of it around his nose and mouth. The gas was still going to cause his eyes to water, but he would have to manage that as best he could.

He climbed the stairs again, his naked feet cold against the bare concrete floor. He stayed low, crouching down, and assessed the room. The assaulters looked to have breached through a door to his right; there was a breeze blowing from that direction, the shifting smoke suggesting that a door was open. Milton looked up and saw moonlight from several skylights, with muzzle flash starbursting as soldiers stationed up there fired down into the room below. The cartel soldiers were caught in a vicious crossfire; they fired back, but the flashes were intermittent and less and less frequent.

He took a step and winced at a sudden surge of pain. He

looked down and saw the sparkling debris of glass that had fallen down from above. He had put a foot down right in the middle of it. He stepped back, gritting his teeth against the pain. That sealed it. He wanted to pursue Thorsson and La Bruja, but he didn't know where they had gone and he doubted he would last very long if he tried to make his way across the room with an injured foot. A noble death would be pointless unless there was a chance that he might also be able to bring La Bruja with him, and, right now, he knew that was unrealistic. Better to try to stay alive so that he could live to fight another day.

He limped back down the stairs, but only just reached the bottom when he heard the sound of footsteps following him. A soldier, dressed all in black and wearing night-vision goggles and a respirator, came into the cellar. He raised a submachine gun.

Milton raised his hands. "No Spanish."

"*Abajo!*" the man yelled.

"Okay," Milton said. "I'm not with them. No cartel."

"Down. On the floor."

Milton lowered himself to his knees, his hands still raised above his head. He didn't know whether or not the soldier would understand him, and prepared himself for the worst as the man edged forward, aiming the muzzle of the weapon at his head. The soldier came around behind him and booted Milton in the back. He fell face first onto the floor, looking up just as a second person descended the stairs.

It was Ellie Flowers, a Glock clasped in a two-handed grip.

"It's okay," she said to the soldier. "He's with me."

108

Björn reached the top floor. Six and Eight were behind him, with La Bruja behind them.

He turned to her. "Can we get down from the roof?"

"You can get from this one to the one behind it," she said. "And then the one behind that. There's a fire escape. We can use that."

Björn turned back to the door that opened out onto the roof. He readied the X95, holding the bullpup's foregrip in his left hand as he took his right hand away from the trigger and reached for the door handle. He tried it; it was locked.

He took a step back, braced his standing leg and then drove his boot at the spot on the door that was just below the handle. The lock fell apart, the door flew open, and Björn aimed out onto the roof, immediately sighting the four soldiers who were positioned around the skylights, their weapons pointed down into the room below.

Björn fired, four fully automatic three-round bursts, aiming first at the man who was nearest to him and then cycling to the second, third and fourth. Each volley found its mark; the first man toppled forward, plunging through the glass and disappearing into the space below; the second man tumbled over the edge towards the street, and the remaining two collapsed onto the roof.

He led the way, following the roof to the south to where the adjacent building abutted against it. The roof of that building was higher, with an additional storey to negotiate in order to reach it, but there was an air-conditioning unit that was close enough to act as a step. Björn climbed onto it and then hauled himself up, scanning to ensure that the roof was clear—it was—and then turning back to help hoist La Bruja up with him. She wasn't heavy and he was easily able to pull her after him.

Six and Eight hopped from the air conditioner to the roof. Björn assessed the way ahead. This roof was thirty feet from one side to the other, and then there was a drop to the roof of the building beyond it. Björn set off, the bullpup held in both hands as he crossed from one side to the other. The lights of the city were visible to the left, the slope of the hill ending in the dark slash of the river. He knew it was going to be challenging to get away from the neighbourhood. The assaulters had been well organised and generously armed and, if Björn had been asked to guess, he would have ventured that they belonged to the urban anti-terrorist force. He doubted whether a significant number of men could have been put into the field in the time between their location being compromised and now. A platoon, perhaps? Surely no more than that.

They would soon find out.

He reached the edge of the roof and jumped down to the one belonging to the next building along. There was a ladder at the edge of it, leading down to the street. He jogged over to it, looking over the edge and checking in both directions. The ladder ended just above an alleyway that ran along the side of the block. An ornamental metal gate blocked access to the main street, but, since that was the direction from which the assault had commenced, Björn was not concerned about that. The alley continued along the block and looked as if it might open out onto the road that hemmed in the buildings on the northern side. It didn't much matter. They couldn't very well stay where they were.

Six and Eight brought La Bruja to him.

"Come down behind me," Björn said to La Bruja. He nodded to Eight. "Cover us."

He let the submachine gun hang from its strap and then started to descend. Eight trained his weapon on the alley as Björn and La Bruja made their way down to it.

109

Chase watched the assault unfold. He was impressed; the soldiers were coordinated and effective, breaching first through the roof and then through the doors at the front and side of the building. They did not look as if they were particularly interested in taking prisoners, either, and the clatter of small-arms fire echoed around the neighbourhood. Lights flicked on in windows and bleary-eyed *Paisas* came out of the doorways to watch. Smoke drifted out of the open doors and up through the skylights, the moonlight catching it and painting it silver.

Shit.

He saw a door open on the roof and then, a moment later, saw the bright white muzzle flash of an automatic weapon. It fired four times, in four concentrated bursts, and Chase watched as the soldiers who had commenced the attack from above were all hit. One fell into the skylight and another toppled over the edge of the building, flipping through an untidy somersault, bouncing off the ground and then flopping onto the sidewalk. Chase looked back to the roof and saw a man emerge from the opened door, closely followed by two others who were suspending a fourth person between them.

He called Hicks.

"It's Chase—are you there?"

"I'm here."

They're on the move. I can see her. The woman."

"La Bruja?"

"Yes. There are three others with her. Two men and a woman. They just shot the soldiers on the roof."

"Where are they now?"

He watched. "They're on the roofs, headed north."

"Okay. Hold up. You hearing this, Ziggy?"

"I am," Ziggy said. *"Is Milton with them?"*

"No," Chase said. "I don't see him. Why?"

"Because his tracker just left the building."

The building that Chase was hiding atop was on the downward slope of the hill. He had scouted it earlier and saw that there was a rough track that clung to the side of the slope; it offered a way for him to approach the safe house without being seen from the street. He crawled to the lip of the roof and dangled over the edge, his feet probing for something to support him and finding the sill of a window below. He let go with his hands, ducking down and then reaching for a drainpipe that took run-off rainwater from the roof to the track below. The pipe was loose and, as Chase put his weight on it, the screws popped free and the pipe started to come away from the wall. The track beneath him was narrow and, if he overshot that, he faced a deep enough drop that he would be lucky if the only injuries he suffered were two broken legs. The pipe bent out, but, before it could fall away completely, Chase managed to snake out a hand and grab onto a ventilation outlet. He slithered down the rest of the pipe, dropped onto the track, and started to run.

"Where are they?" he said into the throat mic.

A clatter of automatic gunfire echoed around the houses.

"They're going north," Ziggy reported.

Chase sprinted.

110

The alley came out at the back of the block of three buildings that included the safe house. There was a wooden gate, but it was flimsy and Björn was able to kick it down. They emerged onto a side street. Björn looked right and then left, checking that the street was clear. Björn knew what the soldiers would have done: they would have thrown a cordon around the building, blocking the main ways in and out.

He turned to La Bruja. "How well do you know this area?"

"Very well," she said. "I was born here."

"We need to find our way out, but not on any of the main roads. Alleyways and passages only. Okay?"

"Yes," she said. She pointed over the road to the mouth of a narrow passage that sneaked between the flanks of two dwellings. "We can go through there. There is a park northeast of us. We have another property on the other side of it. No one knows about it. I will be safe."

"Good," he said.

It wasn't much of a plan, but it would have to do. There

were three of them and La Bruja, but at least they were well armed. On the other hand, they had no backup; Ten and Eleven were occupied with the medevac of the injured Number Two.

It wasn't going to be easy, but they had a shot. Bjorn just needed to get them through the cordon and maybe they'd stand a chance.

He went to the head of the alleyway and looked left and right for a second time.

Still clear.

Björn held up his finger and spun it in the air, giving the signal to move. He clutched his weapon, stepped out and crossed the street with the others close behind.

They didn't get far.

There came the crack of a pistol from somewhere down the street. Stucco exploded from the side of the house to Björn's right.

"Get back!"

Another shot rang out and Björn heard a grunt of pain. He backed right up, bumping against La Bruja and pulling her with him. They fell back to the passageway from which they had just emerged. A third shot chased them there, this one cracking into the wood of a telegraph pole.

"I'm hit."

Eight was slumped against the wall, clutching his stomach with both hands. Blood had already saturated his shirt, and now it was pouring over his fingers. A gut shot, in a place like this, under circumstances like this? He was as good as dead.

∽

CHASE POUNDED the hood of the car behind which he had taken cover. La Bruja was there. He had seen her, taken a shot, and *missed*. The woman had been at the back of the group, and she had been pushed back into the cover offered by the narrow alleyway.

"Hey."

Chase swivelled around, bringing the gun with him, but saw that he wouldn't need it. It was Hicks. The Englishman kept low, slipping into the cover offered by the car and putting his back against the wheel arch.

Chase glanced up over the hood.

"They're in there," he said. "The alleyway."

"How many?"

"Two men, two women."

"And her?"

"Yeah. I took a shot. Missed her. Think I got one of the others, though."

Hicks nodded. "Ziggy," he said, cupping the microphone closer to his mouth. "Where's Milton's tracker?"

"Just across the street from you," he said.

Hicks muted his microphone. "Milton wasn't there?"

"I didn't see him. You think he planted the tracker on them?"

Hicks nodded.

"What are we going to do?" Chase said.

Hicks sucked his teeth. "They can't go back," he said. "The soldiers are on the other side."

"So?"

"We wait. We stop them coming out this way. Flowers is on top of this. We wait for the soldiers to get here and leave it to them."

Chase felt a flash of anger. "No. Not good enough."

"She'll be arrested."

"And you think that'll stick?"

Hicks didn't reply.

"It won't," Chase said for him. "She'll be out on the street again in a week and you know it. That's not justice. I didn't come all the way here for that."

111

Eight was losing a lot of blood. Björn had thought it was a gut shot, but it was worse than that. The wheezing suggested that his lung had been punctured, and, if he was right about that, Eight didn't have long at all.

Björn calculated their odds again: stay here and wait to be arrested, or run. Control had been clear in her orders. If Björn felt that La Bruja was compromised, and that there was a risk that she might fall into the hands of the local authorities or the Americans, then he was to terminate her and get out. The Group was deeply implicated in the recent history of El Centro, and, even though the firewalls between Björn and the others meant that it would be difficult to *prove* a connection to British intelligence, there would be enough circumstantial evidence for the implication to be made. That would not be tolerated.

La Bruja knelt down and took Eight's pistol from him.

"You've failed," she said. "You failed in the jungle and now you've failed again."

Björn eyed her. She had not reached her present position by scrupulously honouring her alliances. They all knew how she would view the situation: the most valuable asset with which she would be able to bargain was information. She could offer the locals proof that the American ambassador to Colombia had been assassinated by four British ex-soldiers. The government would deny all knowledge of them, and nothing would be proven, but the damage would be done.

Control couldn't have been clearer.

Björn had his orders.

He slipped his finger through the trigger guard of the Tavor.

"We stay here and they find us," La Bruja said. "I'm not waiting for that to happen."

And, with that, she ran.

∼

HICKS LOOKED through the window of the car, through the cabin and out of the windshield. His gun was clutched in both hands, ready to bring up and fire. Chase was next to him.

"Don't do anything stupid," Hicks warned him. "It's a stalemate right now. They—"

They both saw movement from the alleyway. A woman sprinted out of cover, a pistol clasped in both hands. She turned and fired at them, a storm of bullets that she sprayed liberally, some of them chinking against the bodywork of the car and punching through the glass, others studding into the surrounding buildings. Hicks fired back, missing the woman, then ducked back into cover as a volley crashed through the windshield.

It was her.

Chase took a breath and gripped his pistol a little tighter. "Cover me."

He stood, stepped around the rear of the car and sprinted after her.

"Shit," Hicks breathed.

He shuffled a pace to the right, rested his forearms on the hood and squeezed off three rounds, aiming at the alleyway, giving those sheltering there a reason not to follow.

112

Chase ran as hard as he could. The passage had turned and headed up and then down the hill, and he had quickly lost his bearings. He saw La Bruja, though, and pounded after her as she sprinted across the cobbles and rough ground. There was a sharp right into an even narrower passage and then a left, and, when he emerged into a tiny square, she was gone.

He looked around. It was quiet. No one was outside.

He heard something—a squeak—and saw something move against the wall at the opposite end of the passage. A door. It had swung back on rusty hinges.

He held the pistol in both hands and crossed the square. He paused by the door and listened. Nothing. It was open a crack and he looked inside. It looked like a community café. He pushed the door open and stepped through.

It was a small space. There were four tables with chairs resting atop them. A dimly lit refrigerated cooler hummed in the back. There was a counter and a display cabinet.

Chase listened, but did not hear anything other than the buzzing of the cooler.

He crept deeper into the café. There was a door on the other side of the room. He moved to it and put his ear against it.

Nothing.

He put his palm against it and pushed, gently, opening it slowly and carefully.

There was a short hallway beyond. It was empty. It led into what appeared to be a kitchen at the other end. Chase continued slowly. His breathing sounded uncomfortably loud, and every squeak of the floorboards was amplified. He thought of his quarry. She was armed, but she had fired a lot of rounds at them as she had crossed the street. He wondered whether she would have spare ammunition. There was no way of knowing. He would have to assume so.

He reached the kitchen and peered inside. It was low-ceilinged, just like the hallway. There were two counters. A gas stove. A rack of plates and glassware. Saucepans were hung from the ceiling. Cutlery stood in glass jars.

He heard the creak of a floorboard, turned, saw her behind a metal cabinet as she raised the gun and fired. Muzzle flash lit the room. Chase felt sudden pain in his stomach as he dropped down behind the counter.

Fuck. He was hit.

"I got you, didn't I?"

He clasped his hand against his gut. "Ain't nothing."

"Stand up where I can see you. I'll try again."

He lifted his hand. His shirt had been torn just above his navel. Blood was flowing freely and, when he tried to move his arm, the blast of pain was sudden and debilitating. Gut shot. That wasn't good. He leaned back against the counter and tried to gather his strength.

"Who are you?" she called out across the room.

"Chase Baxter," he grunted.

"And am I supposed to know you?"

"You killed my old man."

"Did I?"

He held his gut tighter, not that it made much difference. "In Las Vegas."

He heard her chuckle. "This *again?* Who would have thought one old man would be worth so much aggravation?"

"Yeah, well, he was a cantankerous old bastard and he's gonna haunt you from beyond the grave."

He clenched his teeth against the pain, took a moment, and, with his back still pressed against the stainless-steel counter, he shuffled on his backside until he could look around the side of the unit. She saw him, brought the pistol around and fired.

A stack of plates exploded, china shards falling all around him.

She cursed.

"You're gonna pay for what you did," he said.

"No," she said. "I don't think so. You've been shot."

He gripped the pistol more tightly, but it slipped in his hand. His palm was slick with blood. He wiped it on his shirt. He started to feel woozy. He had seen gut shots before. He remembered a Marine with whom he had served in Kandahar. A sniper had picked him off and pinned them down, preventing medevac. The man had lasted an hour and then bled out.

He blinked hard, trying to clear his head. He had to do something. He had to figure out a way to—

"Don't move."

He turned his head and saw that the woman had come around the other side of the counter. The pain had distracted him. He hadn't noticed. And now she was pointing her pistol down at him.

113

Chase knew there was no point in struggling. The blood was still running through the fingers of his left hand and he was weak, with no strength in his right. He wouldn't have been able to bring his gun up to shoot before she pulled the trigger. She was ten feet away and evidently comfortable with the pistol in her hand; she wouldn't miss from there. The fatigue rolled over him in waves. He didn't even have the strength to try to shuffle away.

He heard the sound of footsteps approaching along the corridor. He looked up at La Bruja and saw the wariness on her face. She took a step back and a quarter turn to the right so that she could see both him and the doorway; the gun was still trained on him.

"Don't shoot," a voice said, in accented English.

The fear on her face was replaced by uncertainty. "Eidur?"

"Yes. Are you okay?"

"I'm fine. Come in."

The door opened and the big man Chase had seen at the safe house stepped inside. It looked as if he had been running; there was sweat on his skin and he was breathing quickly.

"Who's this?" he asked, looking down at Chase.

"He came after me," she said. "He thinks I killed his father." She turned away from the big man and focused on Chase again. "The thing is, I don't even know who he is talking about. Perhaps we did kill him. Perhaps he got in our way, like his son. The result will be the same."

Chase looked up at her. He was damned if he was going to go out with his eyes closed. He watched as the big man raised his arm and aimed his pistol at La Bruja. She noticed, and the easy confidence on her face changed to bewilderment.

"What are you doing?" she said.

"I'm sorry," he said. "We've come to the end of the road."

"What are you talking about? You work for *me*."

"I don't."

Her mouth opened and she started to protest, but the words never came. The pistol was loud in the confined space and the distance the bullet had to travel was short. The man aimed at her head, and the bullet crashed into her temple, jerking her body to the left. The strength left her legs in an instant; she collapsed onto the counter and then slid down it, blood streaking against the stainless steel. She came to rest next to Chase, her body warm against his.

"That wasn't yours to do," Chase said. "That was my responsibility."

"She's dead either way," the big man said. He turned the pistol onto Chase. "I'm sorry about this. I can't let you live."

Chase bit his lip. He knew there was no point in protesting. The man had the look of a stone-cold killer, and nothing he said would make any difference to the decision that he had made. And he was weak. He was sitting in a pool of his own blood. He was finished whatever happened.

The man aimed the pistol.

"Hands!"

Chase raised his head.

The big man glanced to the side.

"Get your hands up *now*."

It was a woman's voice. American accent. Chase recognised it.

The big man did as he was told, slowly bringing his hands up until they were level with the side of his head. He saw the woman in the doorway, a weapon in her hand. It was the woman from the car, the FBI agent. He couldn't remember her name.

"Chase."

Milton was beside him.

"John?"

"You've been shot."

"She did it," he said, angling his head in the direction of La Bruja. "Got lucky."

"Well," Milton said, "looks like it was the last thing she did."

"Big guy," Chase said, finding the words difficult to speak. "He did it."

Chase felt as if he were drifting down beneath the surface of the water, unable to make out what he had said. The big man asking about how Milton had found him, and Milton answering that he had dropped a little something into his pocket? It didn't make sense. Chase felt a firm grip on his shoulder and surfaced, heard the squelch of static from a radio, and noticed there were more people in the room—men in uniforms—and that red and white lights strobed through the dusty windows, and sirens were loud in the street outside.

"Hold on," Milton said. "We're going to get you to a hospital."

EPILOGUE

The warehouse was in Amsterdam's Westport industrial district. The area was near the docks and was dedicated to the storage of cargo unloaded from ships that had arrived from all around the world. A series of large prefabricated buildings had been constructed on either side of a tree-lined road. This particular warehouse was smaller than some of the other units, located in a small complex behind a metal gate. It was sandwiched between a business that imported kitchen goods and another that dealt in garden furniture.

A single man, dressed all in black, emerged from the entrance to the building and made his way to the gate. Smoke was pouring out from beneath the door now, and he could hear the sound of the flames inside. He dropped the empty jerrycan over the fence and climbed after it, picked it up again and then jogged over to the car that he had left on the main road.

Alex Hicks put the empty can in the trunk, opened the door and dropped into the driver's seat. He took off his balaclava and gloves and dumped them on the seat next to him.

It had gone as well as might have been hoped. Ziggy had directed him to the building that Chase had identified as the hiding place of Juan Pablo López's stock of cocaine. It was very conveniently located for the purpose it served. The drugs would be unloaded at the docks, hidden in the warehouse and then distributed around Europe. Hicks had not stayed inside the building for long enough to scope it out properly, save to confirm that the cartel's product was *in situ*. There was a lot of it; Hicks guessed that the value must have been in the tens of millions.

It was all on fire now.

He started the engine, put the car in gear and pulled away.

He called Ziggy. "It's done."

∽

ZIGGY PENN HAD SET up his gear in the living room of the water villa that he had rented on Airbnb. It was near Sloten, ten minutes from the airport and twenty-five minutes from the city centre. The host provided two spotlessly clean bedrooms, two bicycles and high-speed fibre internet. It was the last amenity that had sealed the deal for Ziggy.

He put his phone down and tapped the keyboard to wake his laptop. He made sure that he had scrubbed the footage from the warehouse's security cameras and, satisfied that all evidence of Hicks's activity had been erased, he chose a camera that would give him the best view of the interior of the property. There was one just inside the entrance, and it showed how quickly the fire had already spread. Hicks had not been interested in hiding the fact that this was arson, and had doused the room with petrol. The fire had taken hold eagerly, with separate blazes feeding on the wooden pallets that were used to move the freight and on the plastic packaging that disguised it. The flames were starting to climb the walls and, in one spot, the ceiling had already started to burn. The *Brandweer* would be here soon to try to tackle the fire. It wouldn't matter if they were successful; the contents of the warehouse would be discovered. Millions of dollars of Colombian cocaine would be lost and a criminal investigation would be launched. Ziggy had already left digital breadcrumbs that would lead the police back to López.

He got up to fix a drink, but had only filled the kettle when the laptop sounded a shrill alarm.

He hurried back to the table. It had nothing to do with the fire; the footage was still being transmitted, the conflagration growing larger by the second. The alarm had sounded because the tripwire that Ziggy had established to protect his own network security had been activated. He felt cold panic crawling up his back. He had dozens of tripwires set up, little pieces of code that would flag anything that needed his attention. This particular tripwire was set up with one purpose in mind: to detect any attempt to take over his machine.

He switched between open windows, trying to find the intrusion. He had used his backdoor into the network that served the Firm and had spent an hour or two nosing around in an attempt to find anything that might explain why Björn Thorsson had been in Colombia. Milton had asked him to dig up whatever he could. Thorsson's presence suggested that Group Fifteen had an interest in what had happened to La Bruja, and, quite understandably, Milton had wanted to know more. Ziggy had found several recent references to Medellín and El Centro and had arranged for those files—some of which were large—to be downloaded.

He had been careful, just as he always was, and had routed the download through multiple nodes on the Dark Web, using the layered encryption to anonymise his identity.

And yet...

He stared at the screen as it dawned on him.

The data he was trying to download had been left as a honeypot. It had been too convenient, left unguarded on the network that served the various Groups that comprised the Firm.

He saw it now and cursed his naivety.

It was a trap, laid to reveal malicious actors on the network and provide intelligence against them.

Ziggy tore the Ethernet cable from the laptop, then took his bag and upended it, scooping everything out until he found his screwdrivers. He removed the screws on the laptop's casing and opened its body, revealing the workings inside. He disconnected the hard drive, took it into the kitchen, put it into the microwave and set the timer for a five-minute program. The rotisserie plate turned and, after a minute, the drive popped and sparked.

He let the program continue and found his phone.

"It's me," he said.

Hicks answered. *"What is it? Everything okay?"*

"We need to leave," he said. "Don't come back here."

"Why?"

"Because it's not safe. Group Fifteen are looking for us."

∽

Chase Baxter's eyes flickered as he started to come around.

The Hospital Pablo Tobón Uribe was on Calle 78b in the Altamira district of Medellín. Chase had been taken there by ambulance in the aftermath of the shooting. Milton had stood ready to offer to pay for his treatment, but it had not been necessary. The nurse to whom he had spoken explained that the Colombian system offered universal access to citizens, irrespective of their ability to pay, and promised that Chase would receive excellent care.

The hospital was well equipped. Chase's bed was surrounded by an array of medical machinery, and his vitals were being monitored by way of the probes and sensors that had been attached to his body. Chase had been sleeping when Milton arrived an hour earlier. Milton had spoken to a doctor, and she had explained that he was making good progress. He had lost a lot of blood, and in addition, thanks to the bullet making a mess of his lower intestine, he had been suffering from septic shock. They had performed abdominal surgery to repair the damage and had given him a massive dose of antibiotics and a fluid replacement. Chase had been on the table for six hours and had been put into a brief coma to help kick-start his recovery. It was going to take time for him to get back on his feet.

Chase opened his eyes.

Milton pulled up a chair and sat at the edge of the bed. "Hey."

Chase blinked, looked around the room, and frowned. "John?" he mumbled.

"That's right."

"Where am I?"

"Hospital."

"Colombia?"

"Medellín," Milton said. "You were shot. Remember?"

Chase looked down at his stomach. "Shit," he groaned.

"How are you feeling?"

His voice was weak. "Shitty. How long was I out?"

"A day and a half," Milton said. "It was touch and go for a

while. You lost a lot of blood and then you had sepsis. The bullet made a mess of your guts."

"Probably why I feel as weak as a baby."

"They've done a good job of patching you up. You're over the worst of it."

Chase tried to reach for the glass of water by his bedside and grimaced with the effort. "You sure about that?"

Milton picked up the glass and handed it to him. "Here."

"Thanks," Chase said.

He took a sip of the water, just enough to moisten his lips. Milton took the glass back from him and replaced it on the table.

"How long you been here?"

"The whole time," Milton said. "There's a hotel over the street where I stayed, but, apart from that, I've been here."

"Now why would you do a fool thing like that?"

"Do you have anyone else out here to keep an eye on you?"

"Don't suppose I have."

"Ziggy found your mother's details somewhere—probably best not to ask how—and I called her to tell her what had happened. Don't worry. I downplayed it, and I told her the doctors were certain that you'd recover. She's fine."

Chase closed his eyes and exhaled. "What about... her?"

"La Bruja?"

He nodded. "She's dead?"

"She is," Milton said. "Her bodyguard put one into her head."

"Why would he do something like that?"

"He wasn't what she thought he was," he said, hoping he wouldn't press it any more.

"Where is she now?"

Milton shrugged. "My guess would be that the police

have the body. They'll autopsy her and then hand her back to her family. You don't need to worry about her anymore. She got what was coming to her."

"Not at my hand, though."

"Does it really matter? She's dead. It's justice—whoever pulled the trigger."

"I guess." He shuffled up the bed, wincing with the effort. Milton moved to help him, but Chase waved him off. "What about the bodyguard?"

"He's in custody," Milton said. "I imagine they'll be getting ready to charge him."

"You know anything else about him?"

"Not much. They're saying he was a mercenary."

"That's it?"

"That's it."

Milton knew more about Thorsson—much more—but he had decided that there was no reason to share it with Chase or anyone else. He doubted that there would be consequences for any of the others following their interference with what had been—clearly, yet perplexingly—a Group Fifteen operation. There would be consequences for *him*, though; of that, Milton was quite certain. He had poked the bear. They knew he was active, and that he had caused them difficulties. He knew what would be coming next.

Chase reached for the glass again, taking it without Milton's help this time.

"Where's Hicks?" he asked.

"He flew out with Ziggy two days ago. They're in Amsterdam."

"Why?"

"Unfinished business with López."

"Shit," he said. "I remember. You closing that operation down, too."

"I'm going to cause as much damage as I can."

Milton got up and stretched his shoulders. He went to the window and looked outside. It was late, and the evening was quickly drawing in.

"What's next?" Chase asked him.

"You're laying up here until they let you out."

"What about you?"

Milton shrugged. "I'll wait."

"They say how long that might take?"

"A couple of weeks."

"You don't have to do that," Chase said.

"Got anyone else in Colombia to look out for you?"

Chase smiled and shook his head. "No, but I'm a big boy. I don't need a babysitter."

"It's not up for negotiation," Milton said. "I've already had to tell your mother about your father. I don't want to have to tell her about you, too. Understand?"

"Yessir," Chase said with a weary smile.

∽

MILTON HAD BEEN unable to stop thinking about the involvement of Thorsson and the other agents. Ziggy had started an investigation, but, save for confirming that Björn Thorsson was from Iceland and that he had served in the SAS, there was not much else to discover. Milton knew that his position had become tenuous. He had been granted an unofficial amnesty when Pope had served as Control, but now... well, he doubted that state of affairs would be allowed to continue. He needed to know more and, if Ziggy continued to strike out, he was going to have to contact a man who he knew would have the contacts within the intelligence community to help. He would have to ask Ziggy to find him so that he could pay a visit.

"Penny for your thoughts?"

Ellie Flowers was sitting on a chair in the waiting area. Milton had been distracted by his ruminations and hadn't noticed her.

"Sorry," he said. "I was miles away."

"How is he?"

"He's been through the wringer."

"But he'll make it?"

"They think so. I doubt he'll be going home for a while, though."

"I've had a word with the embassy. They're going to send someone down here to see if there's anything we can do to help."

"Thanks," he said. "That'll be useful."

Milton sat down next to her. He was tired. He had been operating on adrenaline for the better part of a week, and it had taken it out of him.

"You look cooked."

He laughed. "I am."

"I was going to suggest something."

"What's that?"

"That dinner you bailed on. You still interested? There's a steakhouse in Laureles. I asked one of the DEA guys who's been living down here for years. He says it's good. I just thought, you know, maybe you'd like to?"

She was speaking quickly, as if worried that he would turn her down for a second time, but, this time, do it face to face.

"I'd love to," he said.

"And you won't stand me up again?"

"Are you serious?" he said with a smile. "After you slapped me?"

∼

THE STRUCTURE HAD BEEN BUILT in the sixties, a brick and concrete edifice to fill in the space in a part of London that had suffered grievously from the Luftwaffe's bombs. It was small and unprepossessing and drew little attention from the occasional pedestrians who passed outside it. A metal gate barred the way to an underground car park, and the sign on the wall next to it read Global Logistics. Control waited for the barrier to withdraw into the roof and then touched the pedal to coast her Tesla down the ramp. It levelled out, and she guided the car to her usual parking space. It had been a busy morning and she hadn't tested her glucose; she took the hand scanner and held it against the sensor that was attached to her right shoulder. Her levels were a little higher than she would have liked, so she took out her insulin pen, inserted a cartridge, and pulled up her shirt. She injected herself in the abdomen, wincing a little from the sharp prick, and then checked her makeup in the mirror. She tucked her shirt back into her trousers, switched off the car and got out.

She ran through the agenda for the day as she rode the secure elevator to the third floor. She had a lot on her plate and she was keen to start working through it. The first item of business was to speak with Weaver. He had returned from Colombia late last night, and she had told him to report to the office for a debrief.

The lift shuddered to a halt and the doors opened. The space beyond was busy with activity despite the fact that it was still early. The staff who worked the office at night were in the process of leaving, their replacements arriving and taking over. Analysts researched new intelligence and built profiles of the targets that the Group had been asked to investigate, their work soundtracked by the rattle of fingers on keyboards and hushed conversations with covert sources. Control crossed the floor, too wrapped up in her thoughts to notice the tentative nods of greeting from the men and women she passed.

Her secretary, Eve, looked up as she arrived at the waiting area next to the door to her office.

"Morning, ma'am."

"Morning. Is he here?"

"Waiting inside."

She opened the door and went through into her office. Weaver was sitting on the sofa that Control used when she wanted to talk to guests away from the formality of her desk. Weaver was her private secretary, although that title was misleading. He spent his time in theatre for the most part, working with the twelve men and women who comprised the active assets of the Group.

Weaver stood.

"Sergeant," she said as she took off her coat and hung it on her hat stand.

"Ma'am."

She crossed the room. Eve had prepared a pot of coffee, and she poured two cups, adding milk to both and taking them over to the sofa. She handed one to Weaver and sat down in the armchair.

"Let's have it," she said.

"There's good news and bad news."

She waved a hand. "Bad first."

"We've had confirmation that Eight didn't make it. The

Colombians got him to a hospital, but he died just after he was admitted."

"There's no way back to us?"

"No, ma'am. None at all."

"And the good news?"

"Two is going to be fine," Weaver said. "Eleven took him to a doctor we have on the payroll. They'll be leaving the country today."

That was something, she supposed. "What else?"

"I spoke with Number Six. They've located the facility where Number One is being held. Their assessment is that it would be possible to break him out, but that the odds favour a more patient approach. His first hearing is in two days. They'll need to transfer him across the city, and the intelligence is that it'll be a normal police van with two or three officers. If you agree, they propose to do it then."

"Of course I agree," she said. "We can't have Thorsson standing trial."

"There's no possibility that they could connect him to British intelligence."

"Are you sure, Sergeant? Are you *completely* sure? I know Thorsson is good, but having him out there, possibly in the papers, means there are too many variables that we can't control. I need him out of Colombian custody and back in this office so he can explain to me just how this whole situation went south as quickly as it did. I want you to take part in that conversation, too. I need to decide whether you are still able to discharge your duties to the standard that I expect."

"Yes, ma'am," he said, dipping his head. "Of course."

Control got up and crossed the room to her desk. She reached into her in-tray and took the file that had been prepared for her. A cardboard folder held a wedge of paper perhaps an inch thick. The bundle had been tied with a red ribbon; that meant that Control had been authorised to send one of her agents to attend to the man or woman who was the subject. She untied the ribbon, opened the folder and looked at the photograph that lay atop the stack. It was of a man in his late middle age. He had dark hair, crisp, alpine blue eyes and a horizontal scar that ran from his cheek to the start of his nose. She took the photograph across the room and laid it on the coffee table so that Weaver could see it.

She laid a finger on the photograph. "What about him? Is it done?"

Weaver winced a little. "I'm afraid that didn't go quite as smoothly as we were hoping."

She sighed and waved a hand for him to continue.

"He was staying near the hospital where his friend was being treated." Weaver looked down at his notes. "The Hotel Central Caribe. He had dinner with the FBI agent who was leading the operation down there, and then he went back to the hotel. Six and Ten were given the green light to take him out, but they lost him."

"What? What do you mean?"

Weaver shrugged apologetically. "They saw him go up to his room, and gave him an hour to get to sleep. When they entered the room, he wasn't there. The bed was not slept in, and none of his belongings were there. The window was open. The best they can suggest is that he left through it and climbed down the fire escape."

"He knew they were there?"

"I think we have to assume that, ma'am."

She closed her eyes and waited for the flash of temper to pass. There was no profit in a hasty, emotional response. She knew the history of the Group. The man who had established it—Harry Mackintosh—had been prone to flashes of rage. He had enjoyed a long tenure in post, but she knew that his irascibility had contributed to the bad decisions that had ended with his death. She did not intend to make the same mistakes.

"I don't understand why he was given an amnesty before. If we had taken care of things when we had the chance, none of this would have happened."

"What would you like me to do, ma'am?"

She put the photograph back in the file, closed the folder and tied the ribbon around it once more.

"Find Milton," she said. "Find him and kill him."

GET EXCLUSIVE JOHN MILTON MATERIAL

Building a relationship with my readers is the very best thing about writing. Join my Reader Club for information on new books and deals plus a free copy of Milton's battle with the Mafia and an assassin called Tarantula.

You can get your content **for free**, by signing up at my website.

Just visit www.markjdawson.com.

ALSO BY MARK DAWSON

IN THE JOHN MILTON SERIES

The Cleaner

Sharon Warriner is a single mother in the East End of London, fearful that she's lost her young son to a life in the gangs. After John Milton saves her life, he promises to help. But the gang, and the charismatic rapper who leads it, is not about to cooperate with him.

Buy The Cleaner

Saint Death

John Milton has been off the grid for six months. He surfaces in Ciudad Juárez, Mexico, and immediately finds himself drawn into a vicious battle with the narco-gangs that control the borderlands.

Buy Saint Death

The Driver

When a girl he drives to a party goes missing, John Milton is worried. Especially when two dead bodies are discovered and the police start treating him as their prime suspect.

Buy The Driver

Ghosts

John Milton is blackmailed into finding his predecessor as Number One. But she's a ghost, too, and just as dangerous as him. He finds himself in deep trouble, playing the Russians against the British in a desperate attempt to save the life of his oldest friend.

Buy Ghosts

The Sword of God

On the run from his own demons, John Milton treks through the Michigan wilderness into the town of Truth. He's not looking for trouble, but trouble's looking for him. He finds himself up against a small-town cop who has no idea with whom he is dealing, and no idea how dangerous he is.

Buy The Sword of God

Salvation Row

Milton finds himself in New Orleans, returning a favour that saved his life during Katrina. When a lethal adversary from his past takes an interest in his business, there's going to be hell to pay.

Buy Salvation Row

Headhunters

Milton barely escaped from Avi Bachman with his life. But when the Mossad's most dangerous renegade agent breaks out of a maximum security prison, their second fight will be to the finish.

Buy Headhunters

The Ninth Step

Milton's attempted good deed becomes a quest to unveil corruption at the highest levels of government and murder at the dark heart of the criminal underworld. Milton is pulled back into the game, and that's going to have serious consequences for everyone who crosses his path.

Buy The Ninth Step

The Jungle

John Milton is no stranger to the world's seedy underbelly. But when the former British Secret Service agent comes up against a ruthless human trafficking ring, he'll have to fight harder than ever to conquer the evil in his path.

Buy The Jungle

Blackout

A message from Milton's past leads him to Manila and a

confrontation with an adversary he thought he would never meet again. Milton finds himself accused of murder and imprisoned inside a brutal Filipino jail - can he escape, uncover the truth and gain vengeance for his friend?

Buy Blackout

The Alamo

A young boy witnesses a murder in a New York subway restroom. Milton finds him, and protects him from corrupt cops and the ruthless boss of a local gang.

Buy The Alamo

Redeemer

Milton is in Brazil, helping out an old friend with a close protection business. When a young girl is kidnapped, he finds himself battling a local crime lord to get her back.

Buy Redeemer

Sleepers

A sleepy English town. A murdered Russian spy. Milton and Michael Pope find themselves chasing the assassins to Moscow.

Buy Sleepers

Twelve Days

Milton checks back in with Elijah Warriner, but finds himself caught up in a fight to save him from a jealous - and dangerous - former friend.

Buy Twelve Days

Bright Lights

All Milton wants to do is take his classic GTO on a coast-to-coast road trip. But he can't ignore the woman on the side of the road in need of help. The decision to get involved leads to a tussle with a murderous cartel that he thought he had put behind him.

Buy Bright Lights

IN THE BEATRIX ROSE SERIES

In Cold Blood

Beatrix Rose was the most dangerous assassin in an off-the-books government kill squad until her former boss betrayed her. A decade later, she emerges from the Hong Kong underworld with payback on her mind. They gunned down her husband and kidnapped her daughter, and now the debt needs to be repaid. It's a blood feud she didn't start but she is going to finish.

Buy In Cold Blood

Blood Moon Rising

There were six names on Beatrix's Death List and now there are four. She's going to account for the others, one by one, even if it kills her. She has returned from Somalia with another target in her sights. Bryan Duffy is in Iraq, surrounded by mercenaries, with no easy way to get to him and no easy way to get out. And Beatrix has other issues that need to be addressed. Will Duffy prove to be one kill too far?

Buy Blood Moon Rising

Blood and Roses

Beatrix Rose has worked her way through her Kill List. Four are dead, just two are left. But now her foes know she has them in her sights and the hunter has become the hunted.

Buy Blood and Roses

The Dragon and the Ghost

Beatrix Rose flees to Hong Kong after the murder of her husband and the kidnapping of her child. She needs money. The local triads have it. What could possibly go wrong?

Buy The Dragon and the Ghost

Tempest

Two people adrift in a foreign land, Beatrix Rose and Danny Nakamura need all the help they can get. A storm is coming. Can they help each other survive it and find their children before time runs out for both of them?

Buy Tempest

Phoenix

She does Britain's dirty work, but this time she needs help. Beatrix Rose, meet John Milton…

[Buy Phoenix](#)

IN THE ISABELLA ROSE SERIES

The Angel

Isabella Rose is recruited by British intelligence after a terrorist attack on Westminster.

Buy The Angel

The Asset

Isabella Rose, the Angel, is used to surprises, but being abducted is an unwelcome novelty. She's relying on Michael Pope, the head of the top-secret Group Fifteen, to get her back.

Buy The Asset

The Agent

Isabella Rose is on the run, hunted by the very people she had been hired to work for. Trained killer Isabella and former handler Michael Pope are forced into hiding in India and, when a mysterious informer passes them clues on the whereabouts of Pope's family, the prey see an opportunity to become the predators.

Buy The Agent

The Assassin

Ciudad Juárez, Mexico, is the most dangerous city in the world. And when a mission to break the local cartel's grip goes wrong, Isabella Rose, the Angel, finds herself on the wrong side of prison bars. Fearing the worst, Isabella plays her only remaining card...

Buy The Assassin

ABOUT MARK DAWSON

Mark Dawson is the author of the breakout John Milton, Beatrix and Isabella Rose and Soho Noir series.

For more information:
www.markjdawson.com
mark@markjdawson.com

AN UNPUTDOWNABLE ebook.
First published in Great Britain in 2020 by UNPUTDOWNABLE LIMITED
Copyright © UNPUTDOWNABLE LIMITED 2020

The moral right of Mark Dawson to be identified as the author of this work has been asserted by him in accordance with the Copyright, Designs and Patents Act 1988.

All the characters in this book are fictitious, and any resemblance to actual persons living or dead is purely coincidental.

All rights reserved. No part of this publication may be reproduced, stored in a retrieval system or transmitted in any form or by any means, without the prior permission in writing of the publisher, nor to be otherwise circulated in any form of binding or cover other than that in which it is published without a similar condition, including this condition, being imposed on the subsequent purchaser.

Printed in Great Britain
by Amazon